MIRGOROD

INCLUDING

❧❧ *The Old-World Landowner.*

❧❧ *Taras Bulba*

❧❧ *Viy*

❧❧ *Ivan Ivanovich and Ivan Nikiforovich*

MIRGOROD

by NIKOLAI GOGOL

Translated with an Introduction by
DAVID MAGARSHACK

Farrar, Straus and Cudahy   New York

Contents

✯✯ *Introduction*

The collection of four stories published under the title of *Mirgorod* first appeared in print at the beginning of 1835, but most of them were thoroughly revised by Gogol several times, particularly in 1842 and one year before his death in 1852. These stories show Gogol as a mature writer of genius whose creations transcend the narrow compass of Ukrainian tales and assume the universal significance of works of art in which man is drawn with all his foibles as well as with his indomitable will and his sense of destiny. Their tragi-comic characters at once reveal Gogol as a great satirist and, at the same time, a true realist, a creative artist who knew how to make pity into a catalyst that deprives his satire of its sting and lends it the quality that he himself described as "laughter through tears."

Gogol began writing "The Old-World Landowners" at the end of 1832 after the publication of his first two volumes of short stories under the title of "Evenings on a Farm near Dikanka." He was twenty-three at the time (he was born in Sorochintsy, a township in the Ukraine, on March 19, 1809) and had lived in Petersburg for only five years, having gone there in search of fame and fortune immediately after completing his course of studies at the Nezhin high school. It was in the summer of 1832 that he paid a visit to his native village of Vasilevka and his impressions of this visit are reflected in "The Old-World Landowners." The prototypes of the hero and the heroine of this typically Gogolesque idyl of country life—Afanasy and Pulcheria—are generally believed to be his grandparents Afanasy and Tatyana Gogol-Janovsky. In this story Gogol shows for the first time his mastery over the art of a poetic recreation of ordinary, humdrum events of everyday life. This was first clearly realised by Gogol's great contemporary the critic Visarion Belinsky. "Take Gogol's story 'The Old-World Landowners,'" Belinsky wrote. "What is there in it? Two parodies of mankind eat and drink, drink and eat for several decades and then, as has been the case since time immemorial, die. Whence then this enchantment? You are made to see the utter vulgarity, the utter nastiness of that kind of ugly, animal-like caricature of a life, and yet you cannot help taking a keen interest in the characters of the story. You laugh at them, but without rancour, and then you cry with Philemon for his Baucis. You are sorry for his deep, unearthly sorrow and you are angry with his scoundrel of an heir for squandering the fortune of the two simpletons. You get so vivid an impression of the actors of this silly comedy, you see so clearly their whole life, you, who have never been to the Ukraine, never witnessed such scenes and never heard of such a life."

Gogol worked on *Taras Bulba* for the best part of his life. The first version, published in 1835, differs radically from the final version, finished ten years later, the narrative having been enlarged from nine to twelve chapters. In addition, Gogol introduced a number of new characters, new incidents and new dramatic situations. The novel (recently filmed in America) deals with the wars of independence of the Ukrainian people against Catholic

Poland from the fifteenth to the seventeenth centuries, that is, even before the Ukraine had been annexed by Poland in 1569. (Gogol seems to have telescoped the events in his novel regardless of any strict chronological sequence.) Apart from a thorough study of the most important historical works dealing with this period, Gogol made a special study of the Ukrainian folk-songs which he regarded as "living and vivid" expressions of national history and as "laying bare the entire life of a people."

Taras Bulba was, according to Gogol, one of his "lucky" stories "which people of all tastes and temperaments seem to like." It is, in fact, much more than that. What Taras fights against is the suppression of a people's right to freedom, the aping of the manners of a foreign conqueror, treachery to one's kinsfolk, and so on. What he stands for is loyalty, justice, love of one's country, self-sacrifice and death rather than surrender, all, according to Gogol's ideas, rungs of the ladder leading to salvation. Taras and his two sons, the doughty Ostap and the romantic Andrey, are carefully conceived and brilliantly executed characters, but Gogol certainly put into their mouths ideas that were characteristic of the later period of his life. It is indeed in this novel that Gogol who is more than anyone responsible for creating the myth of the "Russian soul" and the belief, later to be so passionately espoused by Dostoevsky, for the redemption of Europe and the rest of the world by the Greek Orthodox faith. "Let us drink," Taras addresses his comrades-at-arms before the final battle in which he was defeated, "first of all to the holy orthodox faith and to the time when it will at last spread all over the world and everywhere there will be only one faith." *Taras Bulba,* then, is one of those works of art which has passed into the flesh and blood of a nation. It is, in fact, impossible to underestimate its importance in unconsciously (and therefore all the more powerfully) shaping a nation's thoughts and actions in the national as well as in the international field in a context which, though radically different from Gogol's own beliefs, bears the same stamp of blind fanaticism.

"Viy" is the only fantastic story in *Mirgorod*. Gogol began writing it in 1833, but revised it thoroughly in 1842 for the second edition of his collected works. In a footnote to the story Gogol claims that it is based on a folk legend and that he wrote it just as he heard it. This claim, however, is difficult to substantiate, since so far no trace of a single folk-lore story which bears any resemblance to "Viy" has been discovered. It is the realistic touches in the story, such as the descriptions of the Kiev seminary, where Gogol's father and grandfather had received their education, and the vagabond life of the seminarists that help to make the fantastic elements in it so vivid and terrifying. It is, in fact, one of Gogol's most powerful stories and it is not surprising that Leo Tolstoy should speak of it (in a letter to a correspondent in 1891) as one of the few stories that made a "tremendous" impression on him.

"The Story of How Ivan Ivanovich Quarrelled with Ivan Niki-forovich" was written at the beginning of 1833 and published for the first time in an almanach in the following year. Gogol got the idea of the story from the interminable lawsuits brought by the landowners of his district (Mirgorod is a district town near Vasil-evka, the family estate of Gogol's parents) against each other and, particularly, from his grandfather's lawsuit against one of his neigh-bours. This story brought Gogol for the first time into conflict with the censorship as well as with a number of influential people in Petersburg who regarded it as "sordid" and "vulgar." To placate or perhaps even to ridicule his detractors Gogol wrote a brief intro-duction to the story before re-publishing it in *Mirgorod*. "I consider it my duty," he declared, "to make it clear that the events de-scribed in this story have happened a long time ago. Besides, they are entirely fictitious. Today Mirgorod is not at all like that. The buildings are different, the puddle in the centre of the town has dried up long ago, and the high dignitaries of the town, such as the judge, the clerk of the court and the mayor are highly respectable and loyal citizens." This note appeared only in a few copies of the book, Gogol having apparently decided at the last moment to delete it.

Belinsky's appreciation of the story is so apt that it is worth quoting in full. "Really," the critic wrote, "to make us take the liveliest interest in the quarrel between Ivan Ivanovich and Ivan Nikiforovich, to make us all shake with laughter at the stupidities, worthlessness and feeble-mindedness of these living travesties of humanity is an amazing feat, but to make us afterwards feel genuine pity for these idiots, to make us take leave of them with a kind of deeply melancholy feeling, to make us exclaim with him, 'It's a tedious world, gentlemen!'—that is real divine art which is rightly called creative, that is the true expression of artistic genius which finds poetry wherever there is life."

Belinsky, it is clear from the above quotation, is quite exceptionally hard on the two heroes of the story. Are they really "travesties of humanity?" Is there not an Ivan Ivanovich and an Ivan Nikiforovich in all of us? All the stories in this collection are, in fact, remarkable for their masterly recreation of human folly and human greatness: in them the quintessential Gogol comes to life.

D. M.

PART I

◥◤ *The Old-World Landowners*

I am very fond of the modest life led by those solitary owners of remote estates in the Ukraine who are usually known as old-world landowners and who are like picturesque tumbledown houses, charming in their patches of different colour and their complete contrast to the smooth new houses, whose walls have not yet been discoloured by the rain, whose roofs have not yet been covered by green mould, and whose front steps do not yet show their red bricks through the peeling stucco. I sometimes like to descend for a moment into that extraordinarily secluded life, in which not a single desire strays beyond the palisade surrounding the small courtyard, beyond the wattle fence of the orchard, full of plum and apple trees, beyond the lopsided peasant cottages spaced round it under the shade of the willows, elders and pear-trees. The life of their modest owners is so quiet that for a moment you are lost to the world of reality and you imagine that the passions, desires and restless inventions of the evil spirit that trouble the world do not exist at all and that you have only seen them in some dazzling, garish dream. I can see, as though I were there at this moment, the little low-pitched house with its gallery of little blackened wooden pillars running all round it, so that in a thunderstorm one can close the shutters without getting drenched by the rain. Behind it a sweet-scented bird-cherry, whole rows of low-growing fruit trees, drowned in the crimson of the cherries and the sapphire sea of the plums covered with a dark bluish bloom; a spreading maple in the shade of which a rug is laid to lie down on for a rest; in front of the house, a spacious courtyard covered with short fresh grass and with a little path running from the storehouse to the kitchen and from the kitchen to the manorhouse; a long-necked goose with young goslings, as soft as down, drinking water; a palisade hung with strings of dried pears and apples and rugs hung out to air; a cartful of melons standing near the storehouse; an unyoked ox lying lazily beside it—all this is full of inexplicable charm for me, perhaps because I no longer see them before me and because everything from which we are parted is dear to us. Be that as it may, even as my carriage used to drive up to the steps of such a little house I would feel in a wonderfully pleasant and peaceful mood; the horses would trot merrily up to the steps, the coachman would alight imperturbably from the box and fill his pipe, as though he had arrived at his own house; even the barking set up by the phlegmatic watchdogs of every breed and colour was pleasant to my ears. But most of all I liked the owners of those modest little nooks, old men and old ladies who came out solicitously to meet me. Even now amid the noisy crowds of fashionable dress-coats, I can sometimes see their faces, and then I suddenly fall into a reverie and catch a glimpse of my past life. There is so much kindness in these faces, so much cordiality and frankness, that you can't help passing imperceptibly with all your senses into their humble life and giving up, if only for a short time, all your ambitious dreams.

To this day I cannot forget two people of the last century who, alas, are no more, and my heart is still wrung with pity every time I imagine going back one day to their old, now deserted, dwelling, and seeing the heap of dilapidated cottages, the pond choked with weeds, and an overgrown ditch where their little low-pitched house once stood—and nothing more. I feel sad. I feel sad even before going there. But let me turn to my story.

Afanasy Ivanovich Tovstogub and his wife, Pulcheria Ivanovna Tovstogubikha, as she was known among the peasants of the neighbourhood, were the old people I was beginning to tell you about. If I were a painter and wanted to portray Philomen and Baucis on canvas, I should never have chosen any other models than those two. Afanasy Ivanovich was sixty and Pulcheria Ivanovna was fifty-five. Afanasy Ivanovich was tall and always wore a camlet covered sheepskin coat; he used to sit hunched up and was almost always smiling, even though he were telling you something or simply listening. Pulcheria Ivanovna was of a somewhat serious disposition and scarcely ever laughed; but there was so much kindness in her face and eyes, so much readiness to regale you with everything of the best they had, that, I believe, you would have found a smile a trifle too cloying for her kind face. The fine wrinkles on their faces were arranged so attractively that an artist, I am sure, would have stolen them. Their whole life could, it seemed, be read in them, their serene and tranquil life, the life led by the old, simplehearted, and yet rich Ukrainian families, who always present such a contrast to the lowborn Ukrainians, who, leaving their trades as tar-dealers and hucksters, swarm like locusts in the law-courts and government offices, fleece their own countrymen of their last penny, inundate Petersburg with pettifogging lawyers, make their pile at last and triumphantly disguise their origin by adding a "V" to their Ukrainian surnames ending in "O." No, like all the old and indigenous families of the Ukraine, they were nothing like those contemptible and miserable creatures.

It was impossible to look at them without feeling touched by their love for one another. They were never familiar but always formal in addressing each other.

"Was it you, Afanasy Ivanovich, who made the hole in that chair?"

"I am sorry, Pulcheria Ivanovna, it was I. Please don't be cross."

They had no children, and that was why all their affection was concentrated on each other. As a young man, Afanasy Ivanovich had served in the cavalry and had risen to the rank of captain, but that was a long time ago and Afanasy Ivanovich himself hardly ever recalled his past. Afanasy Ivanovich was married when he was thirty. At the time he was a strapping young fellow and wore an embroidered sleeveless jacket. He even devised a clever plan for eloping with Pulcheria Ivanovna when her relations objected to their marriage; but he hardly remembered that now, at least he never spoke of it.

All those far-away, extraordinary events had given place to a quiet life of complete seclusion, a life full of those drowsy yet harmonious dreams you indulge in sitting on a rustic balcony overlooking the garden, when a lovely rain comes streaming down with a glorious sound, pattering on the leaves and flowing in bubbling rivulets, inducing a numbness in all your limbs, and meanwhile a rainbow comes stealing from behind the trees in the shape of a half-ruined arch, shedding its band of seven soft colours across the sky. Or when you are lulled to sleep in a carriage, driving between green bushes while the quail of the steppes call loudly and the fragrant grass, mingled with ears of corn and wild flowers, thrusts itself in at the carriage door, flicking you delightfully across the hands and face.

Afanasy Ivanovich always listened with a pleasant smile to the people who came to see him; occasionally, he talked himself, but mostly he asked questions. He was not one of those old men who bore you with their everlasting praises of the good old days and denunciations of the new. On the contrary, in questioning you he showed great concern and curiosity about the circumstances of your life, your successes and failures, in which all kind-hearted old people usually show an interest, though it is somewhat like the interest of a child who examines the seal of your watch while talking to you. Then his face, one may say, was imbued with kindliness.

The rooms of the house in which our old people lived were small and low, the sort of rooms old-world people usually live in. Each room had an enormous stove, occupying almost a third of it. These little rooms were terribly hot, for both Afanasy Ivanovich and Pulcheria Ivanovna liked warmth very much. The stoves were all heated from the entrance hall, which was always filled almost to the ceiling with straw, commonly used in the Ukraine instead of firewood. The crackle of the burning straw and the light it shed in the hall made it a very pleasant place in the evening when ardent youth, chilled with chasing after some dark-faced girl, rushed in, clapping their hands. The walls of the rooms were adorned with a few pictures in old-fashioned narrow frames. I am convinced that their owners themselves had long forgotten what they were about and if some of them had been taken away I doubt if they would have noticed. Two of the portraits were large and painted in oils. One was of some bishop and the other of Peter III. A fly-blown Duchess de La Valliere looked out from the narrow frame of a third. There were a large number of small pictures round the windows and over the door, which for some reason you get so used to regarding as stains on the walls that you never bothered to examine them. The floor in almost all the rooms was of clay, but so cleanly polished and so neatly kept as, I dare swear, no parquet floor in a rich house, lazily swept by some sleepy gentleman in a livery, has ever been kept.

Pulcheria Ivanovna's room was cluttered up with chests and boxes of every conceivable size. Lots of little bags and sacks of flower-seeds, vegetable-seeds and melon-seeds hung on the walls. Lots of balls of wool of different colours, rags of old dresses, made half a century ago, were stored in and between the little chests in the corners of the room. Pulcheria Ivanovna was a great housewife and collected everything, though sometimes she could not tell herself what she was going to do with the things afterwards.

But the most remarkable thing in the house was its singing doors. As soon as morning came the singing of the doors could be heard all over the house. I cannot say why they sang; whether it was the fault of the rusty hinges or whether the mechanic who made them had concealed some secret in the doors, but what was so remarkable was that each door had its own special voice: the door leading to the bedroom sang in the thinnest treble; the dining-room door sang in a hoarse bass; while the door into the entrance hall emitted a kind of strangely jarring and also moaning sound so that as you listened to it carefully you could hear very distinctly the words: "Lord, I'm freezing cold!" I know that many people dislike this sound very much, but I am very fond of it, and if I sometimes hear a door creak here, I immediately get a whiff of the countryside— the little low room lit by a candle in an antique candlestick, the supper already on the table, the dark May night peeping in from the garden through the open window at the laid table, the nightingale filling the garden, the house and the far-away river with the peals of its song, the mysterious rustle of branches and . . . Good Lord, what a long train of memories came rushing into my head just then!

The chairs in the room were wooden and massive, as was usual in the old days; they all had high carved backs, in natural grain, unvarnished and unpainted; they were not even upholstered and were a little like the chairs on which bishops sit to this day. Little three-cornered tables between the walls, a mirror in a thin gold frame carved with leaves, which flies had covered with black spots, a rug before the sofa with birds which looked like flowers and flowers which looked like birds—that was practically all the furnishing of the unpretentious little house in which my old people lived.

The serf-maids' room was crowded with young and not-so-young girls in striped petticoats; Pulcheria Ivanovna sometimes gave them some knick-knacks to sew or made them prepare the fruit, but for the most part, they ran off to the kitchen and slept. Pulcheria Ivanovna considered it necessary to keep them in the house and she was very strict about their morals. But to her great amazement hardly a few months passed without the waist of some girl or other growing larger than usual; this was all the more surprising as there was hardly a bachelor in the house, except the houseboy who used to walk about barefoot in a grey tail coat and, when not eating, was sure to be asleep. Pulcheria Ivanovna usually scolded the erring maid and made it quite clear to her that it must not happen again. Hundreds of flies kept up a terrible buzzing on the window-pane, drowned by the deep bass of the bumble bee and occasionally accompanied by the shrill wail of the wasps; but as soon as candles were brought in the entire gang went to bed, covering the whole ceiling with a black cloud.

Afanasy Ivanovich was not very active on his farm, though he did drive out sometimes to the mowers and reapers and kept a rather sharp eye on their work. The whole burden of administration lay upon Pulcheria Ivanovna's shoulders. Pulcheria Ivanovna's housekeeping consisted of continually locking up and unlocking the storehouse, and salting, drying, and preserving countless quantities of fruit and vegetables. Her house resembled nothing so much as a chemical laboratory. There was always a fire burning under the apple tree, and a cauldron or copper pan of jam, jelly or fruit cheese made with honey, sugar, and I don't remember what else, was hardly ever taken off the iron tripod on which it stood. Under another tree the coachman was everlastingly distilling peach-leaf, bird-cherry-flower, centaury or cherry-stone liqueur in a copper alembic, and at the end of the process was quite unable to control his tongue and talked such nonsense that Pulcheria Ivanovna could make nothing of it and sent him off to the kitchen for a snooze. Such a great quantity of all this stuff was boiled, salted and dried that the whole courtyard would most certainly have been submerged in it—for Pulcheria Ivanovna always liked to keep a store over and above what was necessary for use— had not more than half of it been eaten up by the serf-girls who, getting into the store-room, would overeat themselves so horribly that they kept moaning and complaining of stomach-ache all day.

Pulcheria Ivanovna had little opportunity of keeping an eye on the work in the fields or any other work on the farm. The steward and the village elder combined in robbing them mercilessly. They had made it their custom to deal with their master's woods as if they were their own; they made a large number of sledges and sold them at the nearest fair; moreover, all the thick oak-trees they sold to the neighbouring Cossacks to be cut down for building flour mills. Only once did Pulcheria Ivanovna express a desire to inspect her woods. For this purpose a four-wheeler with enormous leather aprons was harnessed; as soon as the coachman shook the reins and the horses, who had served in the militia, set off, the leather apron filled the air with strange sounds, and all of a sudden, a flute, a tambourine, and a drum could all be heard clearly; every nail and iron bolt made such a din that they could hear the lady of the manor driving out of the courtyard even as far as the mill, though the distance was almost two miles. Pulcheria Ivanovna could not help noticing the terrible devastation in the woods and the loss of the oak-trees which even as a child she had known to be over a hundred years old.

"Why is it, Nichipor," she said, addressing herself to the steward who was there at the time, "why is it that there are so few oaks about? Take care you are not left with as few hairs on your head."

"Why so few?" the steward, as usual, replied. "Because they got lost! Yes, ma'am, got lost: struck by lightning, eaten away by worms,—got lost, ma'am! Got lost."

Pulcheria Ivanovna was completely satisfied with this answer and, on her return home, merely gave orders to double the watch in the orchard near the Spanish cherry-trees and the big winter pears.

These worthy administrators, the steward and the village elder, found it quite unnecessary to take all the flour to their master's barns, thinking that half would be quite sufficient; in the end, they took to the barns the half which had gone mouldy or got wet and been rejected at the fair. But however much the steward and the village elder stole; however much all of them in the house gorged themselves, from the housekeeper to the pigs, who destroyed an immense number of plums and apples, and often pushed the trees with their snouts to bring a veritable rain of fruit down from them; however many presents the servants carried to their relations and friends in other villages, even dragging off old linen and yarn from the storerooms, all of which found its own way to the universal source, that is, the pothouse; however much was stolen by visitors, phlegmatic coachmen and footmen—the blessed earth produced everything in such abundance and Afanasy Ivanovich and Pulcheria Ivanovna wanted so little, that all these terrible robberies were scarcely noticed in their household.

Both the old people, as was the long-standing custom among old-world landowners, were very fond of a good meal. As soon as day dawned (they always got up early) and as soon as the doors set up their discordant concert, they would be sitting down at a little table and drinking coffee. Having finished his coffee, Afanasy Ivanovich would go into the entrance hall and, shaking his handkerchief, exclaim: "Shoo, shoo! Come on, geese, get off the front steps!" In the courtyard he usually came across the steward. As usual he entered into conversation with him, questioned him closely about the work in the fields, and gave orders which would have impressed anyone with his extraordinary knowledge of farming; indeed, it would never have occurred to anyone new to farming that one could steal from so sharp-eyed a master. But the steward was a man of great experience; he knew what answers to give and, what's more, how best to feather his own nest.

After this Afanasy Ivanovich would go back into the house and, going up to Pulcheria Ivanovna, say:

"Well, my dear, don't you think it's time we had a bite of something?"

"What could we have now, Afanasy Ivanovich? Lard cakes, or poppy-seed patties, or, perhaps, salted mushrooms?"

"Oh, I don't mind mushrooms or patties," replied Afanasy Ivanovich, and in a twinkling patties and red-brown mushrooms appeared on the table.

An hour before dinner, Afanasy Ivanovich had another snack, drinking an old silver goblet of vodka, and eating mushrooms, all sorts of dried fruit and other delicacies. They sat down to dinner at twelve o'clock. In addition to the dishes and sauce-boats, there were lots of little pots on the table, their lids most carefully sealed so that no concoction of old Ukrainian cuisine should lose its flavour. The conversation at dinner usually concerned subjects most closely related to the meal.

"I'm afraid," Afanasy Ivanovich would say, "this porridge is a little bit burnt. What do you think, Pulcheria Ivanovna?"

"I don't think so, Afanasy Ivanovich. Put in a little more dripping and then it won't taste burnt, or pour some of this mushroom sauce over it."

"Oh, well," Afanasy Ivanovich would say, passing his plate, "let's try it."

After dinner Afanasy Ivanovich would go to lie down for an hour, after which Pulcheria Ivanovna would bring him a sliced watermelon and say:

"Have a piece of this delicious melon, Afanasy Ivanovich."

"Don't be deceived by its appearance, Pulcheria Ivanovna," said Afanasy Ivanovich, taking a large slice. "Even if it is red in the middle, it may not be nice at all."

But the melon would disappear in no time. After that Afanasy Ivanovich would eat a few pears and then go for a walk in the garden with Pulcheria Ivanovna. On returning home, Pulcheria Ivanovna went about her business, while her husband sat under a lean-to facing the yard and watched the storehouse constantly displaying and concealing its interior, and the serf-girls pushing one another, bringing in or taking out various kinds of comestibles in wooden boxes, sieves, small troughs, and other receptacles for fruit storage. A little later, he would send for Pulcheria Ivanovna, or go to see her himself.

"Can you suggest anything for me to eat, Pulcheria Ivanovna?" he would say.

"Well, what will you have?" Pulcheria Ivanovna asked. "Would you like me to go and tell them to bring you the fruit dumplings I ordered to be kept especially for you?"

"Yes, I think that will do nicely," replied Afanasy Ivanovich.

"You wouldn't rather have some fruit jelly, would you?"

"I don't mind if I do," replied Afanasy Ivanovich, after which both were brought and, as usual consumed at once.

Before supper Afanasy Ivanovich would have another bite of something. At half-past nine they sat down to supper. After supper they went to bed at once and a dead silence fell upon this active, though quiet, little homestead.

The room in which Afanasy Ivanovich and Pulcheria Ivanovna slept was so hot that very few people indeed would have been able to stay there for several hours. But, to be even warmer, Afanasy Ivanovich would sleep on the stove-couch, though the intense heat often made him get up a few times in the middle of the night and take a turn round the room. Sometimes as he paced the room Afanasy Ivanovich would moan.

Then Pulcheria Ivanovna would ask:

"Why do you moan, Afanasy Ivanovich?"

"Goodness only knows, Pulcheria Ivanovna," replied Afanasy Ivanovich. "I seem to have a little stomach upset."

"Don't you think you'd better have a bite of something, Afanasy Ivanovich?"

"I'm sure I don't know, Pulcheria Ivanovna. But tell me what is there?"

"Some sour milk or some compote of stewed pears."

"Oh, well, I might as well try it," said Afanasy Ivanovich.

A sleepy serf-girl went off to rummage in the cupboards and Afanasy Ivanovich would have a plateful, after which he usually said,

"I seem to be feeling a little better now."

Sometimes, if the sun was shining and it was comfortably warm indoors, Afanasy Ivanovich, being in a merry mood, liked to pull Pulcheria Ivanovna's leg by talking of something else.

"Now," he would say, "what if our house suddenly caught fire, Pulcheria Ivanovna? Where should we go?"

"Goodness gracious, the things you say, Afanasy Ivanovich! How could our house burn down? God would never permit it."

"Well, but what if it did?"

"Well, we'd move into the kitchen then. You'd take over the housekeeper's room for a time."

"But what if the kitchen burnt down too?"

"What will you be thinking next? The Lord will preserve us from such a calamity. House and kitchen to be burnt down all at once! Why, if that should happen, we'd move into the storehouse and live there until a new house was built."

"And what if the storehouse burnt down too?"

"Goodness, what are you saying? I don't want to listen to you. It's a sin to talk like that and God will punish you for saying such things."

Satisfied with having pulled Pulcheria Ivanovna's leg, Afanasy Ivanovich just smiled as he sat down on his chair.

But I found the old couple interesting when they had visitors. Then everything in their house looked different. These kindly people could be said to have lived for visitors. The best they had of everything was all brought out. They vied with each other in trying to treat you to everything their farm produced. But what appealed to me most of all was that there was not a trace of gush in the way they entreated you to eat. This hospitality, this readiness to please you, was gently expressed in their faces and was so characteristic of them that you could not help giving in to their entreaties. For this was indeed what you would have expected from the pure and serene simplicity of their kindly, artless souls. This hospitality was not at all like that dispensed to you by some clerk in a provincial office, whom you have helped in his career and who calls you his benefactor and crawls at your feet. The visitor was never allowed to depart on the same day: he simply had to stay the night.

"You can't possibly set off on such a long journey at so late an hour!" Pulcheria Ivanovna always said (their visitor usually lived two or three miles away).

"Why, of course not," Afanasy Ivanovich said. "You never know what might happen: you may be attacked by a highwayman or some other evil person."

"God preserve us from highwaymen," Pulcheria Ivanovna exclaimed. "One shouldn't talk of such things at night. It isn't a question of highwayman at all. It's dark and it isn't the right time for travelling. Besides your coachman—and I know your coachman—is so frail, and he's such a little man too—why, an old mare could get the better of him! Anyway, I expect he must be dead drunk by now and fast asleep somewhere."

And the visitor had to stay the night there. Still, an evening spent in the low, warm room, friendly, warming, soporific conversation, steam rising from the served meal on the table, a meal always nourishing and prepared in quite a masterly fashion, was sufficient compensation for him. I can see, just as though I were there now, Afanasy Ivanovich listening to his guest with attention and even delight. The talk often turned on politics. The visitor, who also very rarely left his village, would often make all sorts of conjectures with an important air and a mysterious expression about a secret agreement between the French and the English to let Bonaparte loose in Russia again, or would simply speak of a war that was bound to break out shortly, and then Afanasy Ivanovich would say, pretending not to look at Pulcheria Ivanovna:

"I think I shall go to the war myself. Indeed, why shouldn't I go to the war?"

"Off to the war, are you?" Pulcheria Ivanovna would interrupt. "Don't you believe him," she would say, turning to the visitor. "An old man like him go to the war! Why, the first soldier he met would shoot him dead. Indeed, he would. He'd just take aim and shoot him."

"Well," Afanasy Ivanovich would say, "and what about me shooting him?"

"Just listen to him!" Pulcheria Ivanovna would exclaim. "Can you imagine him going to the war? Why, his pistols have been lying rusty and unloaded for years. You should see them: they'd explode with the gunpowder before they'd fire a shot. He'd blow off his hands and injure his face and remain a cripple for the rest of his life."

"Well," Afanasy Ivanovich would say, "I'd buy myself new weapons. Get myself a sabre or a Cossack lance."

"He's just romancing! Gets an idea into his head and starts spinning a yarn," Pulcheria Ivanovna would declare with vexation. "I know he's only joking, but I don't like hearing it all the same. He always talks like that. Sometimes you keep listening to him till you get frightened."

But Afanasy Ivanovich, pleased at having frightened Pulcheria Ivanovna a little, would laugh as he sat back in his chair.

I found Pulcheria Ivanovna most entertaining when she was inviting a visitor to help himself to some snacks before a meal.

"This," she usually said, taking a stopper out of a decanter, "this is a milfoil-and-sage brandy. It's an excellent remedy for a pain between the shoulder-blades or the small of the back. This one here is centaury brandy, an excellent remedy for ringing in the ears or a rash on the face. And this one here is distilled with peach-stones. Have a glass. It smells lovely, doesn't it? If you knock your head against the corner of the cupboard or table when getting up in the morning and a lump comes up on your forehead, all you have to do is drink one glass of this before dinner and it will go away, pass off in a minute, just as though it had never been there at all."

After which similar accounts followed about the contents of the other decanters, which all seemed to have some medicinal properties. Having loaded her visitor with all that pharmacopaea, she next led him to a table laid with countless plates full of all sorts of comestibles.

"These are mushrooms with wild thyme! These are mushrooms with cloves and hazelnuts. A Turkish woman taught me to pickle them when we still had Turkish prisoners of war here. She was ever such a kind woman, you wouldn't believe she was of the Turkish religion. She was just like any of us, except that she wouldn't eat pork. She told me that in her country there was some law against it. Now, these are mushrooms pickled with black-currant leaves and nutmeg. And these are large dace. It's the first time I have boiled them in vinegar. I'm afraid I don't know what they're like. I learnt the secret from Father Ivan. First of all you spread a few oak-leaves in a small tub and then sprinkle them with pepper and saltpetre, then put in the flowers of mouse-eared hawk-weed, which must be laid with stalks uppermost. And here are the pasties: These are stuffed with cheese, these with poppy-seeds, and those are the ones Afanasy Ivanovich likes so much—they're stuffed with cabbage and buckwheat."

"Yes, indeed," Afanasy Ivanovich used to add, "I like them very much. They're soft and sourish."

Pulcheria Ivanovna was, as a rule, in the best of spirits when entertaining visitors. Such a kindly old woman! She was simply devoted to her guests. I liked visiting them and though I gorged myself terribly, as anyone else who stayed with them did, and though it was very bad for me, I was always glad to go see them. As a matter of fact, I am inclined to believe that the very air of the Ukraine possesses a special kind of property which aids digestion, for if anyone took it into his head to eat like that here, he'd without a doubt find himself lying in his coffin instead of in his bed.

Dear old people! But I've now come to a very melancholy event in my story, an event that changed forever the life of this peaceful little corner of the world. This event is all the more striking since it was caused by a most unimportant incident. But such is the strange order of things that insignificant causes give rise to great events while, on the other hand, the consequences of great enterprises are often quite insignificant.

Some conqueror rallies all his country's forces, wages war for several years, his generals cover themselves with glory, and it all ends with the acquisition of a patch of land on which there is barely room to plant potatoes; while sometimes two sausage-makers have a fight over some trifle and in the end their quarrel spreads over cities, big and small villages and finally, the whole kingdom. But let us leave aside these reflections; they are out of place here. Besides, I am not fond of reflections when they merely remain reflections.

Pulcheria Ivanovna had a pretty little grey cat which almost always lay curled up at her feet. Pulcheria Ivanovna sometimes used to stroke her or scratch her neck with a finger while the pampered cat stretched as high as she could. I don't think Pulcheria Ivanovna was excessively fond of her cat; she was simply attached to her, being used to seeing her about. Afanasy Ivanovich, though, often teased her about her affection for the cat.

"I can't imagine what you can see in that cat, Pulcheria Ivanovna. What use is she? Now, if you had a dog, it would be different: a dog can be taken out shooting, but what's the use of a cat?"

"Oh, do be quiet, Afanasy Ivanovich," Pulcheria Ivanovna would say in reply. "You just like to talk and nothing else. A dog is not clean, a dog will make a mess, a dog will break everything, while a cat is a quiet creature, she does no harm to anyone."

Not that Afanasy Ivanovich cared more for dogs than for cats; he only said it to tease Pulcheria Ivanovna a little.

Behind their orchard was a large wood which had been completely spared by their enterprising steward, perhaps because the sound of the axe would have reached the ears of Pulcheria Ivanovna. It was overgrown and neglected: the old tree-trunks were covered with dense nut bushes and looked like the feathered legs of pigeons. In this wood lived wild cats. Now wild woodland cats must not be confused with those daredevils who run about on roofs of houses which living in towns are, in spite of their violent tempers, far more civilized than the inhabitants of the forest. The woodland cats are for the most part wild and gloomy creatures; they are gaunt and lean and they miaow in coarse uncultivated voices. They sometimes tunnel their way under storehouses and steal lard. They even appear in the kitchen, jumping suddenly through an open window, when they see that the cook has gone off into the tall weeds. As a rule, they have no trace of honourable feelings; they live a predatory life and smother little sparrows in their nests. These tomcats and Pulcheria Ivanovna's gentle little cat had for a long time been sniffing at each other through a hole under the storehouse and at last they enticed her away as a company of soldiers entice a silly country girl. Pulcheria Ivanovna noticed the disappearance of her cat and went to look for her, but she was nowhere to be found. Three days passed; Pulcheria Ivanovna was very sorry for her cat, but at last forgot about her. One day she had been inspecting her vegetable garden, and as she was returning with fresh green cucumbers picked by her own hand for Afanasy Ivanovich, she was struck by the sound of pitiful miaowing. As though by instinct she called: "Puss, puss!"—and suddenly her little grey cat, lean, skinny, came out of the thicket of tall weeds; it was clear that she had not tasted food for several days. Pulcheria Ivanovna went on calling her, but the cat stood miaowing and dared not come near her; it was clear that she had grown wild since her disappearance. Pulcheria Ivanovna walked on, still calling the cat, who followed her timidly as far as the fence. At last, catching sight of the old familiar places, she went indoors. Pulcheria Ivanovna at once ordered milk and meat to be brought for her. Sitting down before her cat, she enjoyed the avidity with which her poor little favourite swallowed bit after bit all the food and lapped up the milk. The grey little runaway was growing fat almost before Pulcheria Ivanovna's very eyes and was no longer eating so greedily. Pulcheria Ivanovna stretched out her hand to stroke her, but the ungrateful creature, who had evidently grown too used to the ways of the predatory cats or had adopted the romantic rule that poverty with love is better than life in a palace (for the wild tomcats were as poor as churchmice), jumped out of the window and none of the house-serfs could catch her.

The old lady sank into thought. "It was my death who came for me," she said to herself, and she could not get the idea out of her head. All day she was sad. In vain did Afanasy Ivanovich crack jokes and try to find out what made her so sad all at once: Pulcheria Ivanovna refused to say anything or said something that could not possibly satisfy Afanasy Ivanovich. Next day she grew perceptibly thinner.

"What's the matter, Pulcheria Ivanovna? You are not ill, are you?"

"No I'm not ill, Afanasy Ivanovich. I'd like to tell you something extraordinary that happened to me: I know that I shall die this summer: my death has already come for me."

Afanasy Ivanovich's lips twisted in a rather painful fashion. He tried, however, to banish the feeling of sadness from his heart and said with a smile: "Goodness me, what are you saying, Pulcheria Ivanovna? I expect you must have drunk some peach brandy instead of your usual decoction."

"No, Afanasy Ivanovich," said Pulcheria Ivanovna, "I have not drunk any peach brandy."

Afanasy Ivanovich felt sorry that he had made fun of her like that, and he looked at her and a tear hung on his eyelash.

"I beg you, Afanasy Ivanovich," said Pulcheria Ivanovna, "to carry out my last wish. When I die, bury me by the church fence. Put my grey dress on me, the one with the little flowers on a brown ground. Don't put on me my satin dress with the raspberry coloured stripes: a dead woman needs no dress. What use is it to her? It will be of use to you: have a fine dressing-gown made of it so that if visitors come to see you, you can look decent when you come out to welcome them."

"What are you saying, Pulcheria Ivanovna?" asked Afanasy Ivanovich. "One day we shall all die, but you are frightening me already by talking like this."

"No, no, Afanasy Ivanovich. I know very well when my death will come. You should not grieve for me though: I am an old woman and have lived long enough. And you're old, too. We shall soon meet in the other world."

But Afanasy Ivanovich was sobbing like a child.

"It's a sin to weep, Afanasy Ivanovich. Do not sin and anger God by your sorrow. I am not sorry to be dying. There's only one thing I'm sorry about" (a heavy sigh interrupted her speech): "I am sorry I do not know in whose care to leave you, who is going to look after you when I am dead. You're like a little child: you need someone who loves you to take care of you."

As she said this there was an expression of such deep, such shattering heartfelt pity on her face that I don't know anyone who could have looked at her that moment unmoved.

"Mind, Yavdokha," she said, turning to the housekeeper whom she had purposely sent for, "when I die you take good care of your master. Look after him as if he were the apple of your eye, like your own child. Make sure that what he likes is cooked for him in the kitchen, that you always give him clean clothes and clean linen, that when visitors come you put decent clothes on him, otherwise he may sometimes come out in his old dressing-gown, for even now he often forgets when it's a holiday and when it's not. Don't take your eyes off him, Yavdokha. I'll pray for you in the next world and God will reward you. See you don't forget, Yavdokha. You, too, are old and have not long to live, do not take a sin upon your soul. If you don't look after him properly, you will have no happiness in this world. I shall beseech God myself not to give you a peaceful death. And you'll be unhappy yourself and your children will be unhappy and all your family will have God's blessing in nothing."

Poor old woman! Just then she was not thinking of the great moment awaiting her, nor of her soul, nor of her own future life; she was thinking only of her poor companion with whom she had spent her life and whom she was leaving helpless and forsaken. With quite extraordinary efficiency she took all the necessary steps to make sure that Afanasy Ivanovich did not notice her absence when she was gone. Her conviction that her death was near at hand was so strong and her mind was so attuned to it that a few days later she really took to her bed and was not able to eat anything. Afanasy Ivanovich was all solicitude and did not leave her bedside for a moment. "Won't you have a little something, Pulcheria Ivanovna?" he asked, looking anxiously into her eyes. But Pulcheria Ivanovna said nothing. At last, after a long silence, she seemed to wish to say something, her lips stirred and—her breathing stopped.

Afanasy Ivanovich was struck all of a heap. What had happened seemed to him so absolutely outrageous that he did not even burst into tears. He looked at her with dull eyes, as though not grasping the significance of the corpse.

The dead woman was laid on the table, wearing the dress she had herself chosen to be buried in, her arms crossed and a wax candle put in her hand—he gazed at all this without betraying any feeling. A great number of people of every station in life filled the courtyard; a great number of guests came to the funeral; long tables were laid out in the courtyard; groaning under the weight of home-made brandies, pies and barley and rice puddings with honey and raisins; the guests talked, wept, gazed at the dead woman, discussed her qualities, looked at him—but he himself regarded it all strangely. The coffin with the dead woman was carried out at last, the people thronged after it, and he followed it;

the priests wore their full vestments, the sun was shining, babies were crying in their mothers' arms, larks were singing, half naked children were running about and playing in the road. At last the coffin was put down over the grave, he was told to walk up to it and kiss his dead wife for the last time; he walked up, kissed her, and tears started to his eyes—but unfeeling tears they somehow seemed. The coffin was lowered, the priest took the spade and was the first to throw in a handful of earth, the deacon and the two sacristans intoned the last prayer for the dead in deep, drawn-out voices, under a clear, cloudless sky. The sextons took up their spades and in no time the earth covered the grave and made it level.

At that moment he struggled forward, the crowd stepped aside and made way for him, curious to know what he was going to do. He raised his eyes, looked round him vaguely and said: "So you've already buried her, have you? Why?" He stopped short and did not finish what he was going to say.

But when he returned home, when he saw that his room was empty, that even the chair Pulcheria Ivanovna used to sit on had been taken away, he burst into sobs and he sobbed violently, he sobbed disconsolately, and tears, like a flood, flowed from his lack-lustre eyes.

Five years have passed since then. What grief does not time carry away? What passion can remain inviolate in the unequal struggle with it? I knew a man in the prime of his life, full of true nobility of character. I knew him in love, tenderly, passionately, madly, boldly, modestly, and almost in my presence, before my very eyes, the woman he loved so passionately—adorable and beautiful as an angel—was struck down by insatiable death. I have never seen such terrible outbursts of deep suffering, such frenzied, fierce anguish, such devouring despair as overwhelmed the unhappy lover. I had never imagined that a man could create for himself such a hell with no shadow, no shape of hope—nothing that remotely resembled hope. . . . He was not let out of sight, all weapons with which he might have killed himself were hidden from him. Two weeks later he suddenly mastered himself: he began laughing and jesting; he was given his freedom and the first thing he did was to buy himself a pistol. One day his family was terrified by the sudden sound of a shot. They ran into his room and found him stretched out on the floor with a shattered skull. A doctor, who happened to be there at the time and who was famous throughout the land for his skill, saw signs of life in him, discovered that his wound was not altogether fatal and, to everyone's surprise, he recovered. He was placed under even stricter supervision. Even at table a knife was not laid for him and they tried to remove everything with which he could have hurt himself; but in a short time he found another opportunity and threw himself under the wheels of a passing carriage. His arms and leg were broken, but he again recovered. A year later I saw him at a crowded party; he was sitting at a table, saying gaily *"petite ouverte"* as he covered a card, and behind him, leaning on the back of his chair, his young wife was turning over his counters.

At the end of the five years after Pulcheria Ivanovna's death I happened to be in those parts again and I drove to Afanasy Ivanovich's little farm to visit my old neighbour at whose house I used to spend a pleasant day and invariably to overeat myself on the most wonderful dishes of its hospitable mistress. When I drove up to the courtyard the house seemed to me twice as old as it had been, the peasant's cottage were lying completely on one side, as their owners no doubt were too; the palisade and the wattle fence round the courtyard were completely broken down, and I myself saw the cook pull stakes out of the fence to heat the stove when she had only to take a couple of steps to reach the pile of firewood. Sadly I drove up to the front steps; the same old watchdogs, by now blind or lame, started barking, raising their wavy tails covered with burdock. An old man came out to greet me. So it was he! I recognized him at once, but he was bent twice as much as before. He recognized me and welcomed me with the smile I knew so well. I followed him into the house. Everything seemed to be unchanged; but I noticed a strange disorder in everything, a sort of palpable absence of something; in short, I experienced the strange feelings which overwhelm us when we enter for the first time the house of a widower whom we have known before inseparable from the wife who had been at his side all his life. The feelings are like those we experience when we meet a cripple whom we have always known to be in good health. The absence of solicitous Pulcheria Ivanovna could be detected in everything; at table a knife was laid without a handle, the dishes were no longer prepared with the same skill. I did not want to ask about the farm, I was afraid even to look at the farm buildings.

When we sat down to dinner, a maid tied a napkin round Afanasy Ivanovich, and it was a good thing she did so, for without it he would have spilt sauce all over his coat. I tried to interest him in something and told him various bits of news; he listened with the same smile, but at times his eyes were completely vacant and his thoughts did not wander, but vanished. He often raised a spoonful of porridge and instead of putting it to his mouth put it to his nose; instead of sticking his fork into a piece of chicken, he poked it at the decanter, and then the maid took his hand and directed it towards the chicken. We sometimes had to wait for several minutes for the next course. Afanasy Ivanovich became aware of it himself and kept saying: "Why does it take them so long to bring the food?" But I could see through the crack of the door that the boy who was serving us was not thinking of it at all, but was asleep with his head drooping on a bench.

"This," said Afanasy Ivanovich, when we were served cheese pancakes with sour cream, "this," he repeated, and I noticed that his voice began to tremble and a tear was about to start in his leaden eyes, but he did his utmost not to let it, "this is the dish my dear de—depart—" and suddenly the tears gushed from his eyes. His hand fell on the plate, the plate tipped over, flew into the air and was smashed, and the sauce was spilt all over him; he sat there

dead to everything around him, not realising that he was still holding the spoon in his hand, and tears, like a stream, like a cease-
lessly flowing fountain, poured, poured uncontrollably, on the
napkin that covered him.

"Good Lord," I thought to myself, looking at him, "five years of
all destroying time, an old man who seems to be incapable of any
feeling, an old man who had apparently never been troubled by
any strong emotions, whose whole life seemed to consist of sitting
in a high chair, of eating dried fish and pears, of telling goodna-
tured tales—and such long, such consuming grief! What exercises
a stronger hold over us—passion or habit? Or are all the violent
impulses, the whole vortex of our desires and burning passions
merely the result of our bright-eyed youth and do they seem so
deep and shattering only because of that alone." Be that as it may,
at that moment all our passions seemed childish to me compared
with this long, and slow—almost insensible habit. Several times he
tried to utter his late wife's name, but, half way through it, his quiet
and ordinary face twitched convulsively, and his child-like weeping cut me to the very heart. No, those were not the tears dodder-
ing old men are so lavish with, when they complain about their
miserable position and troubles to you, nor the kind of tears they
drop over a glass of punch: No! They were tears which flowed by
themselves, uninvited, accumulated from the searing pain of a
heart already turning cold.

He did not live long after that. I heard of his death a few days
ago. The strange thing about it is that the circumstances of his end
had a certain resemblance to those of Pulcheria Ivanovna's death.
One day Afanasy Ivanovich decided to go for a little walk in the
garden. As he was walking slowly along a path without showing, as
was his wont, any interest in anything, without a thought of any
kind, a strange thing happened to him. He suddenly heard someone behind him say in a rather distinct voice: "Afanasy Ivanovich!" He turned round, but no one at all was there; he looked in
all directions, glanced into the bushes—there was no one any-

where. It was a calm day and the sun was shining. He pondered for a moment, then seemed to grow animated and, at last, murmured: "It's Pulcheria Ivanovna calling me!"

I have no doubt that some time or other you, too, happen to hear a voice calling you by your name, which the common people believe to indicate that a soul is pining for a human being and calling him, after which death follows inevitably. I confess I was always terrified by that mysterious call. I remember hearing it often as a child: sometimes someone suddenly distinctly uttered my name. The day, as a rule, was bright and sunny at the time; not a leaf stirred on the trees in the garden; there was a dead hush all around, even the grass-hoppers ceased churring just then; there was not a soul in the garden; but, to be quite frank, even if the wildest and stormiest night with all the fury of the elements had overtaken me alone in the middle of an impenetrable forest, I should not have been so frightened as by that awful stillness amid a cloudless day. Whenever this happened, I usually ran panting in a great panic out of the garden and only calmed down when I came across some person, the sight of whom dispelled this terrible feeling of emptiness in my heart.

Afanasy Ivanovich gave in entirely to his profound conviction that Pulcheria Ivanovna was calling him; he gave in with the willingness of an obedient child, wasted away, coughed, melted like a candle and, at last, snuffed out as it does when there is nothing left to feed its feeble flame. "Lay me beside Pulcheria Ivanovna," was all he said before he died.

His wish was carried out and he was buried near the church beside Pulcheria Ivanovna's grave. There were fewer guests at his funeral than at hers, but there were just as many peasants and beggars. The little manor house was now completely empty. The enterprising steward and the village elder dragged over to their cottages all that was left of the ancient furniture and the other things the housekeeper had not been able to carry off. Soon some distant relative arrived from goodness only knows where, the heir to the estate, who had been a lieutenant of I don't remember what regiment and who was a terrible reformer. He immediately noticed the awful disorder and neglect into which the estate had fallen and he decided to put a stop to it, to get it right and to bring order into everything. He bought six excellent English sickles, nailed a special number to each cottage, and arranged everything so beautifully that within six months the estate was taken over by a board of trustees. The wise trustees (consisting of a ex-assessor and a first lieutenant in a faded uniform) had within a very short time made short shrift of all the hens and eggs. The cottages, which were almost lying on the ground, fell to pieces completely; the peasants took to drink and most of them were soon registered as runaway serfs. The real owner himself, who was on the most amiable terms with the trustees and used to drink punch with them, visited his estate very rarely and did not stay there long. He still drives about to all the fairs in the Ukraine, carefully inquires the prices of all sorts of goods sold wholesale, such as flour, hemp, honey and so on, but only buys small trifles, such as flints, a nail to clean his pipe with and generally everything which at most does not exceed one rouble in price.

⚑⚑ *Taras Bulba*

⚑ I

ome on, son, turn round! Lord, what a sight you are! What sort of clerical frocks are you wearing? Do they all go about dressed like that at the Academy?"

With these words old Bulba welcomed his two sons on their return from Kiev where they had completed their course at the religious academy.

His sons had only just dismounted from their horses. They were two stalwart fellows, who wore a sullen look, like two seminarists who had recently been let out of school. Their strong, healthy faces, covered with the first down of youth, were yet untouched by the razor. They looked greatly embarrassed by such a welcome from their father and stood motionless, with downcast eyes.

"Wait! Wait! Let me have a good look at you!" Taras went on, turning them round. "Just look at their long coats! What coats! I'm sure you won't find such coats anywhere in the world! Now then, one of you, run across the yard, will you? I bet you get all tangled up in your skirts and fall sprawling to the ground!"

"Don't laugh at me, Dad! Don't laugh at me!" the elder of them said at last.

"A big man, aren't you? Why shouldn't I laugh at you?"

"I wouldn't if I were you. You may be my father, but, by God, if you laugh at me I'll thrash you!"

"Oho! So that's the kind of son you are, eh? Thrash your own father, will you?" said Taras Bulba, retreating a few steps in surprise.

"Well, what if you are my father? I won't take an insult lying down from anyone, no matter who he is!"

"So you want to have a fight with me, do you? All right. How shall we fight? With our fists?"

"I don't care how we fight, Dad."

"Very well, let it be with our fists then!" said Taras Bulba, rolling up a sleeve. "Let's see how good you are with your fists!"

And instead of exchanging greetings after so long a separation, father and son began pommelling each other in the ribs, and the back and chest, now breaking away and watching out for an opportunity of getting in a blow, now advancing again.

"Look at him! Look at the old fool! Gone clean off his head, he has!" said their pale, thin, tender-hearted mother, who stood in the doorway and had not yet had a chance of embracing her darling boys. "The children have only just come home, we've not seen them for over a year, and all he can think of is fighting with fists!"

"Damn it, the boy fights well!" said Bulba, stopping. "He certainly fights well," he went on, recovering a little. "So well that a man had better think twice before trying it on with him! Make a fine Cossack, he will! Well, welcome home, son! Come, let's embrace!" And father and son exchanged kisses. "That's right, son. Well done. Hit everyone as hard as you hit me: don't let anyone off! But all the same, your clothes do look funny, you know. What's this rope doing here? And you, what are you standing there like a dummy for?" he said, turning to the younger son. "Why don't you thrash your old dad, you son of a dog?"

"What will he be thinking of next, I wonder," said the mother, who was meanwhile embracing her younger son. "Have you ever heard of such a thing? A child beating his own father! The poor child is so young, he has come such a long way, he is tired out (the poor child was over twenty years old and exactly seven foot tall), he should have a good rest now and something to eat, and he wants him to fight!"

"Well, I can see you're a mother's darling, son!" said Bulba. "Now listen to me. Don't pay any attention to what your mother says: she's only a woman! She knows nothing. You don't want to be pampered, do you? All the pampering you want is to be out on an open plain on a good horse! See this sabre? That's a mother for you! All that damned rubbish they've been stuffing your heads with: academies, all those books, grammars, philosophies—pshaw! I wouldn't give a brass farthing for it!" Here Bulba imparted still greater force to his argument by using a word which never appears in print. "You know what I'm going to do? I'm going to send you this very week to the Cossack headquarters on the Dnieper, to the *Syech*. There they'll teach you something worth knowing. That's the proper school for you. It's only there you'll learn wisdom!"

"You don't mean they're going to be only one week at home?" said the frail mother in a plaintive voice, her eyes brimming with tears. "Why, the poor boys won't have time to enjoy themselves; they won't have time to get to know their own home; and I shan't see enough of them, either!"

"Stop your howling, woman. A Cossack can't afford to waste his time with women. I dare say you'd like to hide them under your petticoat, wouldn't you? And sit on them like a brooding hen on her eggs! Go on, go on, put everything you have on the table for us. We don't want your tarts, or honey-cakes, or poppy-seed cakes, or any other of your delicacies. Fetch me a whole sheep, or a goat, and some forty-year-old mead! And, mind, let's have plenty of vodka. Real vodka, I mean. None of your fancy stuff with raisins and what not. Pure vodka that foams and bubbles and hisses like mad!"

Bulba led his sons into the large room of the cottage. Two pretty maidservants with red necklaces, who were tidying the room, rushed out of it as soon as Bulba and his sons came in. They were apparently alarmed at the arrival of the young masters who were not in the habit of leaving a pretty girl alone, or they might have simply wished to observe the female custom of uttering a scream and rushing away headlong at the sight of a man and then keeping their faces covered a long time with their sleeves to hide their shame. The room was furnished after the fashion of that time, a fashion of which hints have been preserved in songs and popular ballads which used to be sung in the Ukraine by blind, bearded old men to the gentle tinkling of a bandore while a large crowd gathered round to listen; for that was the custom of those hard, turbulent days when bitter battles were just beginning to be fought in the Ukraine against the Poles who tried to impose the Uniate faith upon the people. Everything in the room was spotlessly clean, the walls and floor coated with coloured clay. On the walls were sabres, horse-whips, bird-nets, fishing tackle, muskets, a cunningly wrought powder-horn, a gold bridle, and hobbles with silver plates. The windows in the room were small, with opaque, round glass, such as can only be found nowadays in old churches, through which it was impossible to see anything without lifting a sliding pane. The window-sills and the door-lintels were painted red. On the shelves round the corners of the room stood jugs, large bottles and flasks of green and dark-blue glass, chased silver goblets, and gilt cups of various makes: Venetian, Turkish and Circassian, that had come into Bulba's parlour by various routes after passing through three or four hands, as was common enough in those adventurous times. All round the room were birch-wood benches; an enormous table stood in the corner under the icons; a wide stove, covered with brightly coloured tiles, with little nooks and all kinds of shelves and protrusions. All this was very familiar to our two young men, who used to walk home for their summer holidays every year; they walked because at that time they had no horses, for it was not customary for students to ride on horseback. All they had were their long tufts of hair over their foreheads, which every Cossack bearing arms had a right to pull. It was only now that they had finished their course at the Academy that Bulba had sent them a pair of young stallions from his own drove of horses.

In honour of his sons' arrival Bulba had invited to his house all the officers who were available at the time; and when two of them arrived, together with the Cossack Captain Dmitro Tovkatch, an old friend of his, he at once introduced his sons to them, saying, "See what fine fellows they are? I'll be sending them to the *Syech* soon!" The guests congratulated Bulba, declaring in one voice that nothing could be better and that there was no finer school for a young man than the famous Cossack settlement below the Dnieper Falls.

"Well, my friends, sit down at the table! Please sit down any-where you like!" Bulba said. "Now, sons, first of all let's have a drink of vodka," Bulba went on. "May God bless you, my sons. To your health, Sons! To you, Ostap, and to you, Andrey! God grant you should always be lucky in war. May you rout the in-fidels, the Turks and the Tartars, and the Poles, too, if they should attempt anything against our faith. Come, let me fill your cup again! How do you like the vodka, son? Good, eh? And what's vodka in Latin? Ah, there you are, son! They were a lot of fools, those Romans: they didn't even know there was such a thing as vodka in the world. Now what's the name of the fellow who wrote Latin verses? I'm afraid I'm not a very good scholar. Damned if I can remember his name. Horace was it?"

"What a cunning devil Dad is!" the elder son, Ostap, thought to himself. "Knows everything, the old hound does, and just pretends to know nothing!"

"I expect your abbot did not let you have a sniff of vodka, did he?" Taras went on. "And I suppose they gave you many a good scourging at the Academy with the birch and cherry twigs on the back and on everything else that a Cossack has, didn't they? And perhaps as you seem to have grown a bit too clever, they gave you a lashing with a leather thong, too? Come on, confess! I daresay you caught it not only on Saturdays, but every Wednesday and Thursday, too!"

"Never mind that, Dad," replied Ostap. "What's gone is gone. It's all over now, isn't it?"

"Let them try now," said Andrey. "Let anybody just try to touch me now; let some Tartar rabble only get in my way! They'll soon learn what a Cossack sabre is like!"

"Well said, son, well said! And, damn it, if it comes to that, why shouldn't I come with you? Upon my soul, I will, too! What the devil is the sense of my staying here? What am I supposed to do here? Grow buckwheat, look after the house, tend the sheep and feed the swine, or keep my wife company? Away with it all! I'm a Cossack! I won't do it! What if there is no war? I'll go with you to the *Syech* just to have a good time. Damned if I won't!" And old Bulba got more and more worked up and then he lost his temper altogether, got up from the table, drew himself up to his full height, and stamped his foot. "We'll go tomorrow! Why put it off? What kind of an enemy will we hatch out here? What do we want this cottage for? What do we want these pots for?"

Saying this, he began smashing the pots and the bottles on the table and throwing them about all over the room.

His poor wife, who was accustomed to such outbursts from her husband, sat on a bench and looked on disconsolately. She dared not say anything. Bulba's decision was a great blow to her and, on hearing it, she could not refrain from tears. She looked at her children, from whom she was to be parted so soon, and—but who could describe how great her mute anguish was? It seemed to tremble in her eyes and made her convulsively compressed lips quiver.

Bulba was as stubborn as a mule. He was one of those characters who could only have sprung into existence in the turbulent days of the fifteenth century in that semi-nomadic corner of Europe. At that time the whole of southern Russia, which was still in a primitive state, had been abandoned by its princes and laid waste and burnt to ashes by the ruthless Mongol freebooters. Deprived of home and shelter, man grew dauntless. He settled on the ashes of burnt villages, in spite of the perpetual danger and in the sight of his predatory neighbours, having grown used to looking them straight in the face and forgetting that there was such a thing as fear in the world. It was then that the traditionally pacific Slav spirit became tempered in the flames of war and the Cossack brotherhood arose—an expression of the boundless, reckless exuberance of the Russian character. All the country along the Dnieper, all the fording places, all the hills and dales suitable for cultivation, were settled by the Cossacks, whose numbers no one ever knew and whose bold comrades in arms were fully justified in replying to the Sultan who wanted to know how many of them there were, "Who can tell? They are scattered all over the steppe: where there's a hillock, there's a Cossack!" It was indeed quite an extraordinary manifestation of Russian strength: it was struck out of the heart of the Russian people, like a spark out of a flint, by one national calamity after another. Instead of the former feudal dukedoms, instead of small towns filled with huntsmen, instead of petty princes who were always fighting and selling their towns, warlike settlements arose, army units of regular troops and volunteers, united by common danger and a common hatred of the non-Christian robber bands. Everyone knows from history how their incessant struggles and their restless, rough and tempestuous life saved Europe from the ruthless raids which threatened to destroy it. The Polish kings, who had replaced the hereditary princes as rulers of these vast lands, were too far

away and too weak to defend them, but they realised the importance of the Cossacks and their great value as frontier troops.
They therefore encouraged the Cossacks and set great store on
their warlike disposition. Under their remote authority, the het-
mans, elected from the ranks of the Cossacks themselves, transformed the armed settlements and districts into regiments and
divisions. It was not a standing army; there were no troops to be
seen anywhere; but in the event of a war and a general uprising
every man appeared on his horse, fully armed, within eight days
and no more, receiving only one gold rouble of pay from the king,
and within a fortnight an army assembled such as no recruiting
levies could have raised. When the campaign was over, each man
went back to his meadows and ploughlands, to the Dnieper
ferries, and caught fish, traded, brewed beer, and was a free
Cossack. Foreigners in those days quite rightly marvelled at his
unusual qualities. There was no craft that a Cossack did not know:
distilling vodka, constructing a cart, grinding gunpowder, doing
the work of blacksmiths and locksmiths, and, in addition, indulg-
ing in reckless debauchery—drinking and carousing as only a
Russian can—he was equal to anything. Besides the registered
Cossacks who considered it their duty to appear in war-time, it was
possible at any time in an emergency to raise large detachments
of volunteer cavalry; the Cossack captains had only to go about
the fairs and markets of all townships and villages and, standing on a cart, shout at the top of their voices: "Hey, you beer-
brewers and distillers! leave your brewing and sprawling behind
the stove, feeding the flies on your fat carcasses! Come, win
for yourself knightly honour and glory! You ploughmen, buckwheat sowers, shepherds, whoremongers, leave your ploughs,
stop dirtying your yellow boots in the earth, stop running after
wenches and wasting your knightly strength! It is time you be-
thought yourselves of winning Cossack glory!" And those words
were like sparks falling upon dry wood. The ploughman broke
his plough, the distillers and brewers left their tubs and smashed

their barrels, the craftsmen and tradesmen sent their crafts and shops to the devil, smashed up the pots in the house, and everyone—whatever his trade or occupation—mounted his horse. In fact it was here that the Russian character acquired its amplitude, its strength and breadth, its firm exterior.

Taras was one of the old regular army colonels: he was created for the alarms of war and was distinguished by the coarse directness of his character. In those days the influence of Poland was beginning to be felt among the Russian nobility. Many of them were already adopting Polish manners, living in luxury, keeping resplendent retinues of servants, hawks and hounds, giving banquets, building country mansions. Taras loathed it all. He liked the simple life of the Cossacks and quarrelled with those of his friends who were disposed to adopt the Warsaw fashions, calling them the flunkeys of the Polish gentlemen. Always active, always on his feet, he looked upon himself as the rightful defender of the Orthodox faith. Taking the law into his own hands, he would go to a village whose inhabitants complained of oppression by Government licence holders and monopolists or of an increase in the tax on chimneys. Assisted by his Cossacks, he sat in judgment over the oppressors of the people and dealt with them according to the dictates of his conscience. He had made it an invariable rule to have recourse to the sword in three cases, namely, when the Government commissars showed the slightest lack of respect for the Cossack elders and did not take off their hats in their presence; when the Orthodox religion was held up to scorn and ancient customs were flouted; and, lastly, when the enemies were Tartars or Turks, against whom he always thought it right to take up arms for the greater glory of Christendom.

Now he was already thinking with pleasure how he would arrive with his two sons at the *Syech*, the Cossack military settlement below the Dnieper Falls, and say, "Look, what fine fellows I have brought you!" He saw himself introducing them to all his old battle-scarred friends or watching their first feats of arms or admiring their prowess in drinking, which he looked upon as one of the chief distinctions of a true knight. He had meant first to send them off alone, but, seeing what fine fellows they were, how strong and tall and handsome, his warlike spirit was aroused and he resolved to go with them himself next day, though the only necessity for doing so was his own stubborn will. He lost no time in making all the necessary arrangements for the journey, he issued orders, selected the horses and the harness for his young sons, looked into the stables and barns, and picked out the servants who were to go with them the next day. He handed over his authority to the Cossack Captain Tovkatch, together with a strict order to come at once with his whole regiment when he received a summons from the *Syech*. He forgot nothing, drunk though he was and his head dizzy from the fumes of strong liquor. He even ordered the horses to be watered and the best wheat to be put in their mangers, and he came back tired from his exertions.

"Well, children, to bed," he said. "Tomorrow we'll do as God pleases. No, no, don't make up a bed for us! We don't want a bed. We shall sleep in the open air!"

Night had only just enfolded the sky in her embrace, but Bulba always retired early. He stretched himself on a rug, covered himself with a sheepskin, for the night air was rather fresh and, besides, he liked to wrap himself up warmly when at home. He was soon snoring, and the whole household followed his example. Every man in his different corner of the yard was whistling and snoring in his sleep, the night-watchman being the first to fall asleep, for he had drunk more than any in celebration of the homecoming of the young masters. The poor mother alone did not sleep. She bent over the pillow of her beloved sons who were lying side by side; she combed out their young curls, hanging in careless disarray from their heads, and bedewed them with her tears. She gazed at them not only with her eyes, but with the whole of her being; all her feelings seemed to be concentrated in that gaze, and she could not gaze enough on them. She had suckled them at her breast, she had reared them, she had cherished them, and now she was seeing them only for a moment. "Oh, my sons, my dear, dear sons, what's going to happen to you? What awaits you?" she murmured, and tears lingered in the wrinkles which disfigured her once lovely face. She was indeed pitiful, like every woman of that adventurous age. Too brief, all too brief was her experience of love; it lasted only one moment and it was gone, only one moment of great rapture, only one moment of the fever of youth, and her harsh lover forsook her for his sabre, his comrades, his drinking bouts. She would see her husband for two or three days in a year, and for several years she would have no news of him at all. But even when she did see him, when they did live together, it was not much of a life for her. She had to put up with insults, even with blows; the only caresses she knew were given as a favour; she was a pathetic kind of human being among this crowd of wifeless adventurers, on whom the wild life of the Cossacks in the military settlement below the Dnieper Falls had left its harsh imprint. Her youth was gone in a flash without joy or pleasure, and the bloom on her cheeks had faded without kisses, and her lovely breasts had withered, and the beautiful girl became a wrinkled old woman in the space of only a few years. All love, every emotion, all that is tender and passionate in woman, had turned in her into one feeling of maternal love. She fluttered over her children like a gull of the steppes, passionately, ardently. Her dear, dear sons were being taken from her; they were taking them away, and never would she see them again. Who knows, perhaps in their first battle a Tartar would cut off their heads, and she would not know even where lay their abandoned bodies which some wayside bird of prey would pick clean; and for each drop of their blood she would gladly give her life. Sobbing, she looked into their eyes, heavy with sleep and on the point of closing, and thought to herself, "Maybe when Bulba wakes he will put off their going for a day or two; maybe he thought of going so soon because he had drunk so much."

High up in the sky the moon shed its bright light for hour after hour on the courtyard filled with sleeping men, on the thick clump of willows and on the tall weeds which smothered the palisade surrounding the yard. But she still sat by the pillow of her dear sons, never for a moment taking her eyes off them, and not thinking of sleep. Already the horses, scenting the dawn, left off grazing and lay down in the grass. The leaves on the topmost branches of the willows began rustling, and little by little a faint ripple ran down the trees till it reached the lowest branches. But she stayed there till daylight, not a bit tired and inwardly praying for the night to go on forever. From the steppe came the loud neighing of a colt; the sky was overspread with gleaming red bars of light. Bulba suddenly awoke and leapt to his feet. He remembered very well the order he had given the day before.

"Wake up, lads! It's time, it's time! Water the horses! And where's the old woman?" This was his usual name for his wife. "Hurry up, old woman. We want something to eat. We have a long journey before us!"

The poor lady, deprived of her last hope, dragged herself wearily into the cottage. While she was preparing breakfast and weeping quietly all the time, Bulba was giving his last orders and busying himself in the stables, picking out the best trappings for his sons himself.

The students were suddenly transformed. Instead of their muddy boots, they had boots of red morocco leather with silver-shod heels; breeches as wide as the Black Sea itself, with thousands of folds and pleats drawn in with a golden cord; long straps with tassels and various appurtenances for the pipe were attached to the cord. A Cossack coat of scarlet cloth, bright as fire, was girt at the waist with a gay-coloured sash; a pair of chased Turkish pistols were stuck into the sash, and a sabre rattled at their sides. Their faces, still scarcely sunburnt, looked handsomer and whiter; their young black moustaches seemed to bring out more lustrously the whiteness of their skin and their healthy bloom of youth; they looked very dashing under their black lambskin caps with gold tops.

When she saw them in their resplendent dress, their poor mother could not utter a word; her eyes became misted over with tears.

"Well, sons, everything's ready! No use wasting our time!" Bulba said at last. "Let's all sit down before the journey, according to the Christian custom."

All sat down, including the servants who had been standing respectfully at the door.

"Now bless your children, mother," said Bulba. "Pray to God that they may fight bravely, that they may always defend the honour of knighthood, that they may always champion the Christian faith, and, if they don't, that they may perish utterly and nothing be left of them in the world. Go up to your mother, children! A mother's prayer brings succour on land or sea."

The mother, weak as a mother, embraced them sobbing, and, bringing out two small icons, put them round their necks.

"May the Blessed Virgin keep and preserve you. . . . Don't forget your mother, my dear sons. . . . Don't forget to write to me. . . . Just a few words . . ." She could say no more.

"Well, come along, children!" said Bulba.

Saddled horses were standing at the front steps. Bulba leapt on to his Devil, which shied wildly, feeling Bulba's sixteen stone on his back, for the old Cossack colonel was very stout and heavy.

When the mother saw her sons already in the saddle, she rushed up to the younger one, in whose features there was more of tenderness, grasped his stirrup, clung to his saddle, and, with despair in her eyes, would not let him go. Two sturdy Cossacks took hold of her carefully and carried her off into the cottage. But when they rode out of the gate, she ran out with the nimbleness of a wild goat, which was so unusual in a woman of her age, and with a force that was hardly credible she stopped the horse and embraced one of her sons with a kind of blind, frenzied fervour. She was again carried away.

The young Cossacks rode on, feeling sad, and restraining their tears for fear of their father, who, for his part, was also feeling a little upset, though he tried not to show it.

It was a dull day; the green foliage glistened brightly; the birds seemed to twitter discordantly. Having ridden some distance, they looked back. Their farmstead seemed to have sunk into the earth and nothing could be seen above it but the two chimneys of their little cottage and the tops of the trees, which they used to climb like squirrels. Before them there still stretched the same meadow that could have recalled to them the whole story of their lives, from the time when they used to roll about in its dewy grass to the time when they used to wait in it for the black-browed Cossack girls who fled timidly across it on their swift, sturdy legs. Now all they could see was the pole over the well with the cart-wheel fastened to the top and sticking out forlornly against the sky, and now the plain they had just ridden across looked in the distance like a high hill and hid everything behind it.

Farewell, O happy, happy days of childhood! Farewell to play! Farewell to everything! . . .

❧ I I

All three horsemen rode in silence. Old Taras was thinking of his past, of his youth that was gone forever, of the years that would never, never return, the years a Cossack always mourns, for he would like his whole life to be one long protracted youth. He was wondering which of his old comrades he would meet at the *Syech*. He tried to remember which were dead and which were still living. A tear, a big, round tear, gathered slowly in his eye, and his grey old head drooped mournfully.

His sons were occupied with other thoughts. But we must say

more about those sons of his. They had been sent to the Kiev Academy in their twelfth year, for all people of quality in those days thought it necessary to give their children an education, though it was done with the intention that they should forget it completely afterwards. When they first came to school, they were, like the other new scholars, wild creatures who had been allowed to grow up in freedom, and it was at school that the boys received a certain polish and acquired some common characteristics which made them resemble one another. The elder boy, Ostap, began his academic career by running away in his first year. He was brought back, given a dreadful flogging, and set down to his books. Four times he buried his reading book in the ground, and four times, after being mercilessly whipped, he was bought a new one. He would quite certainly have done it a fifth time, had not his father given him his solemn word that, unless he finished his course at the Academy, he would be kept in a monastery as a lay brother for twenty years, adding the further threat, fortified by a solemn oath, that Ostap would never see the famous Cossack military headquarters below the Dnieper Falls. It is interesting that this was said by the same Taras who abused learning and, as we have seen, advised his sons to have nothing to do with it. From that time Ostap began to apply himself diligently to his tedious studies and was soon among the best scholars at the Academy. The kind of education in vogue at that time was entirely divorced from life. Those scholastic, grammatical, rhetorical and logical niceties had no relation whatever to the times in which they lived and were never of any practical use to them in life. Indeed, the learning they acquired at school could not be applied to anything afterwards, and that was true even of those subjects which were less scholastic. The most learned men in those days were also the most ignorant, for they altogether lacked experience of life. Moreover, the republican organisation of the school and the presence of such a large number of big and healthy young fellows was bound to arouse in them an interest in activities that had no connexion whatever with their studies. Their poor fare, the frequent punishments by starvation, the many cravings that are born in a young, strong, healthy lad, awakened in them that spirit of adventure which afterwards found its proper outlet at the Cossack military settlement below the Dnieper Falls. The hungry students prowled about the streets of Kiev and compelled every one to be on his guard. Immediately they caught sight of a student, the women stall-holders in the market put their hands on their pies, their bread rings, and their pumpkin seeds, guarding them as eagles do their fledglings. The prefect, whose duty it was to keep an eye on the school-fellows under his charge, had such enormous pockets in his breeches that he could easily have put the entire stall of a bemused market woman in them. The students of the Academy formed a world of their own: they were not admitted to the higher circles of society which consisted of Polish and Russian noblemen. Adam Kissel, the governor of the city, in spite of his patronage of the Academy, never introduced them into society, and he gave orders that they should be kept under the strictest possible control. This injunction, however, was quite superfluous, for the rector and the monk-professors did not believe in sparing the rod or the lash, and often the lictors by their orders flogged their prefects so unmercifully that the poor fellows rubbed their breeches for weeks afterwards. Many of them did not seem to mind it very much. The flogging to some of them seemed hardly more stinging than vodka spiced with pepper; others on the other hand were sick and tired of the incessant scourgings and they ran away to the Cossack military headquarters below the Dnieper Falls, if they could find the way there or were not themselves intercepted on the road. Ostap, though he now began applying himself very diligently to his studies of logic and even theology, did not escape the pitiless birch. It was natural that this should in a way harden the character and lend it that firmness that has always characterised the Cossacks. Ostap was always looked upon as one of the best comrades. He did not often take the lead in daring enterprises, such as the plundering of an orchard or a kitchen garden, but he was always one of the first to follow the lead of an adventurous student, and never under any circumstances did he betray his comrades. No rod or leather thong could make him do that. He set his face sternly against any allurements other than fighting and wild carousing; at least he scarcely ever thought of anything else. He was frank with his equals. He was kind-hearted so far as that was compatible with such a character and in those days. He was genuinely touched by the tears of his poor mother, and it was that alone that troubled him and made his head droop pensively.

His brother Andrey was of a much livelier disposition and his feelings were in some ways also more developed. He applied himself to his studies more willingly and with less effort than a stronger and sterner character usually devotes to them. He had more initiative than his brother and he took the lead more frequently in some dangerous enterprise, and, thanks to his resourceful wit, he sometimes managed to escape punishment, while his brother Ostap slipped off his coat without thinking twice about it and lay down on the floor, never dreaming of asking for mercy. He, too, was burning with the desire to distinguish himself in battle, but his soul was at the same time accessible to other feelings. He was overcome by a strong yearning for love after he had reached his eighteenth year and woman figured more and more frequently in his ardent dreams. As he listened to some debate on philosophy, he saw her before him every minute in his mind's eye, fresh, black-eyed, sweet; her dazzling, firm breasts, her lovely, delicate bare arms haunted him incessantly; the very dress that clung about her virginal yet strong limbs was invested in his dreams with some inexpressibly exciting voluptuousness. He carefully concealed from his friends these passionate stirrings of his youthful soul, for in those days it was considered dishonourable and shameful for a Cossack to think of woman and love before he had seen any fighting. Of late years he had generally taken part less frequently as leader of some student gang; more often he had prowled about alone in some secluded Kiev lane smothered in cherry orchards, between little houses that peeped out alluringly into the street. Sometimes he would even wander into the quarter of the aristocrats, into what is now old Kiev, where the Ukrainian and Polish nobles lived and where the houses were all built in a certain fanciful style.

One day as he walked along one of these streets lost in dreams, a nobleman's coach nearly knocked him down and the coachman, a man with an enormous moustache, caught him a terrific blow across the back with his whip. The young student flew into a rage. Without a moment's thought he recklessly seized one of the back wheels in his powerful hands and stopped the coach. But the coachman, afraid of a severe chastisement, whipped up the horses, which dashed forward, while Andrey, who luckily had just time to snatch away his hand, fell face downward in the mud. A loud peal of melodious laughter resounded above him. He raised his eyes and saw standing at a window one of the loveliest creatures he had ever seen in his life, with a pair of sparkling black eyes and a skin white as snow tinted by the rosy hues of the morning sun. She was laughing heartily and her laughter lent an added brillance to her dazzling beauty. He was struck dumb. He looked at her completely disconcerted, absent-mindedly rubbing the dirt off his face, but only succeeding in smearing it more and more over it. Who could this beautiful girl be? He tried to find out from the servants, a crowd of whom, all dressed in handsome liveries, were standing at the gate listening to a young bandore-player. But seeing his dirty appearance, the servants laughed at him and did not vouchsafe an answer. At last he found out that she was the daughter of the governor of Kovno who was on a visit to Kiev. The very next night, with an impudence characteristic of an Academy student, he got through the palisade into the garden, climbed up a tree whose branches spread over the roof of the house, clambered on to the roof and through the chimney of the open fireplace and made his way straight into the bedroom of the beautiful girl who was at the time sitting in front of a candle and taking the costly ear-rings out of her ears. The young Polish girl was so frightened to see an unknown man suddenly confronting her that she could not utter a sound; but when she saw that the student was standing with downcast eyes, too shy to move a hand, and when she recognised him as the same student who had fallen in the mud before her eyes, she was overcome with laughter again. Besides, it was not as if there were anything the matter with Andrey's looks; on the contrary, he was a very handsome fellow indeed. The girl went on laughing merrily and for some time amused herself at his expense. She was frivolous as all Polish girls are, but her eyes, those wonderful, piercingly bright eyes of hers, looked at him with a gaze that was as steady as constancy itself. The student could not stir a limb, and when the governor's daughter went up boldly to him, he felt as though he were tied up in a sack. She put her glittering diadem on his head, hung ear-rings on his lips, and threw over him her transparent muslin blouse with frills embroidered with gold thread. She dressed him up and played all sorts of silly pranks with him, with the careless abandon of a child, so characteristic of frivolous Polish women, and this threw the poor student into even greater confusion. He certainly cut a most ridiculous figure as he stood staring into her dazzling eyes with an open mouth. A sudden noise behind the door of her bedroom alarmed the girl. She told him to hide under the bed, and when all was quiet again she called her maid, a captive Tartar woman, and ordered her to take him out into the garden and see that he got safely over the fence. But this time the student was not so lucky: the awakened watchman caught him fair and square across the legs with his truncheon, and the governor's servants, who came running at the watchman's cries, gave him a good trouncing in the street, but he eventually got away, saved by his swift legs. It was very dangerous for him to go near the governor's house after this, for the Kovno governor had brought with him a large retinue of servants. But Andrey met the girl once again in the Catholic cathedral; she saw him, too, and smiled very charmingly at him, as though at an old friend. He caught one more glimpse of her on another occasion, but soon afterwards the Kovno governor left Kiev, and instead of the beautiful black-eyed Polish girl an unknown fat face stared at him out of the window. . . .

This was what Andrey was thinking of as he rode along with lowered head and eyes fixed on the mane of his horse.

Meanwhile the steppe had long since received them in its green embrace, and the high grass, hemming them in on all sides, hid them from view, only their black Cossack caps showing among its spikes.

"Cheer up, lads! Why are you so silent and woebegone?" Bulba said at last, rousing himself from his reverie. "You're not monks, are you? Now then, to the devil with your melancholy thoughts! Let's light our pipes, clap spurs to our horses and gallop faster than any bird!"

The Cossacks, bending low over their horses, disappeared in the grass. Now even their black caps could not be seen; only the waving grass, as they crushed it under their horses' hoofs, showed the track of their swift career.

The sun had for some time been shining from a clear sky, flooding the steppe with its bright, warm light. In a trice the Cossacks shook off their gloomy thoughts and their hearts fluttered like birds.

The further they rode, the more beautiful did the steppe become. In those days all the south, all that vast territory known today as New Russia, up to the shores of the Black Sea, was one green, virgin wilderness. No plough ever passed across its measureless waves of wild plants. Only the horses, which were lost in them as in a wood, trampled them. Nothing in nature could be more beautiful; the whole surface of the earth was like a vast ocean of green and gold sprinkled with millions of different flowers. Between the high slender stalks of grass light-blue, dark-blue and purple cornflowers stirred; the yellow broom raised aloft its pyramid-shaped head; white yarrow speckled the surface with its parasol-like plumes; an ear of wheat carried from heavens knows where ripened in the dense thicket of grass. Beneath their slender stems partridges darted about, craning their necks. The air was filled with a thousand different bird calls. Hawks hovered motionless in the sky with outspread wings, their eyes fixed immovably on the sea of grass. The cries of a large flock of wild geese moving aslant the sky re-echoed from heaven knows what far-away lake. A gull rose from the grass, flapping her wings slowly, and bathed luxuriously in the blue waves of the air, now melting away in the blue sky and becoming only a black spot, now turning over, her wings flashing in the sun. . . . Oh, how beautiful they are, the steppes, the devil take them! . . .

Our travellers only halted for a few minutes for dinner. The troop of ten Cossacks who accompanied them dismounted and untied the wooden kegs of vodka and the pumpkin rinds they used instead of bowls. All they ate was bread and dripping or flat cakes, and they only drank one cupful of vodka to keep up their strength—for Taras Bulba never permitted drinking on the road—and they continued their journey until nightfall.

In the evening the whole steppe was completely transformed. Its entire variegated expanse blazed up with the last bright gleam of sunshine and gradually darkened, so that a shadow could be seen creeping over it, and the steppe grew dark-green. The exhalations rose more thickly from it; every flower, every blade of grass exhaled a fragrance, and the whole steppe exuded a sweet perfume. Broad bars of rose-tinted gold stretched across the dark-blue sky, as if daubed on it with a gigantic brush; light, transparent wisps of white cloud drifted across it from time to time, and the freshest imaginable breeze, as enchanting as the waves of the sea, scarcely stirred the tops of the grass and brushed faintly against the cheek. All the music which had resounded during the day was hushed and replaced by another. Striped pouched marmots crept out of their holes, sat on their hind paws and filled the steppe with their whistling. The chirring of the grasshoppers became louder. Sometimes the cry of a swan came floating from afar and rang like silver in the air.

The travellers, halting for the night in the middle of the steppe, selected a camping place, built a fire and, putting a cauldron on it, cooked a stew; the steam from the cauldron rose slantingly in the air. Having supped, the Cossacks lay down to sleep, leaving their horses hobbled in the grass. They stretched themselves on their coats. The bright stars shone down upon them. They heard the countless myriads of insects that filled the grass, their whistling, buzzing and chirring resounding clearly in the stillness of the night, growing clearer in the fresh air and lulling the drowsy ear. If one of them rose and stood up for a short time, he saw the whole steppe dotted with the gleaming sparks of glow-worms. Sometimes the sky was lighted up here and there with the glow from dry reeds—which were being burnt in the meadows and along the banks of the streams, and a dark string of swans, flying northwards, would suddenly gleam with a silvery-pink light, and it looked as if red kerchiefs were flying across the dark sky.

The travellers rode on without any adventures. Nowhere did they come across any trees; before them stretched the boundless, free and beautiful steppe. Only from time to time did they catch a glimpse of the blue ridge of the distant woods which stretched along the bank of the Dnieper. Only once did Taras point out to his sons a little black speck far away in the grass. "Look, boys," he said, "that's a Tartar galloping there!" A little head with a moustache fixed its narrow eyes straight on them in the distance, sniffed the air like a bloodhound, and, seing thirteen Cossacks, vanished like a mountain goat.

"Well, boys, why don't you try to overtake the Tartar? Oh dear, no. It's no use trying, for you'll never catch him: his horse is swifter than my Devil."

Still, Bulba thought it wiser to take precautions now, fearing that an ambush might be concealed somewhere. They galloped up to the Tatarka, a small tributary of the Dnieper, plunged with their horses into the water and for a long time swam along with the current to conceal their tracks, then scrambled out on to the bank and continued their journey.

Three days later they were not far from their destination. There was a sudden chill in the air; they felt the proximity of the Dnieper. Then they saw it sparkling in the distance, separated from the horizon by a dark line. A chill wind blew from its cold waves, and it stretched nearer and nearer till at last it covered half the surface of the land. They had reached that part of the Dnieper where the river, no longer hemmed in by the rapids, at last asserts itself and, roaring like the sea, flows freely on its course. It is there that the islands in midstream force it still farther out of its banks and its waters spread far and wide over the earth, meeting neither rocks nor hills to impede their flow. The Cossacks dismounted, embarked on a ferry, and after three hours' sailing reached the shores of the island of Hortiga, where the Cossack military camp was situated at the time, the *Syech,* which so often changed its quarters.

A crowd of people on the shore were engaged in a heated argument with the ferrymen. The Cossacks got their horses ready. Taras drew himself up with dignity, threw out his chest, tightened his belt, and passed a hand proudly across his moustache. His young sons, too, spruced themselves up, feeling strangely alarmed, but at the same time also experiencing a vague sensation of pleasure. They rode together into the suburb of the Cossack settlement which was about half a mile from the *Syech* proper. As they rode in, they were deafened by the clatter of fifty blacksmiths' hammers striking in twenty-five smithies, dug into the ground and covered with turf. Strong tanners were sitting under the awnings on the front steps of their cottages and were kneading the hides of oxen with their huge hands; traders were sitting in their tents beside heaps of flints, tinder and gunpowder; an Armenian had hung out costly kerchiefs; a Tartar was roasting a sheep's head dipped in batter on a spit; a Jew, craning his neck, was drawing vodka out of a barrel. But the first man they came across was a Dnieper Cossack who lay asleep in the middle of the road with outstretched arms and legs. Taras Bulba could not help stopping and admiring him.

"Look at him! How grandly he lies in the middle of the road!" he said, stopping his horse. "Damn it, what a figure of a man!"

It was indeed an extremely picturesque scene: the Cossack was stretched out in the road like a lion, his long tuft of hair tossed proudly back and covering almost half a yard of ground; his wide breeches of costly scarlet cloth were smeared with tar to show the utter indifference with which their owner regarded them. Having admired him, Bulba made his way farther along the narrow street, which was jammed with artisans of every description, who carried on their trades in the street itself, and men of all nations who filled this suburb of *Syech* to overflowing; the suburb indeed was like a fair which fed and clothed the Cossacks of the military settlement who were only concerned with making merry and letting off their guns.

At last they passed the suburb and saw a few scattered Cossack barracks, covered with turf, or, Tartar-fashion, with felt. Some of them had a row of cannons in front. There were no fences, nor any of the little low houses with awnings on small wooden posts which were to be seen in the suburb. A small rampart and a barricade of felled trees, left entirely unguarded, revealed a terrible want of the most elementary precautions. A few stalwart Cossacks, lying right in the road with their pipes between their teeth, looked at them unconcernedly and did not dream of making way for them. Taras rode between them carefully with his sons. "Good day to you, gentlemen," he said,

"Good day to you, sir," they replied. Picturesque groups of people were dotted all over the plain. From their tanned faces it could be seen that they had all been hardened in battle and had suffered all sorts of hardships.

So this was the *Syech!* This was the nest from which so many lion-hearted and proud fighters came! This was the source whence freedom and Cossack chivalry flowed all over the Ukraine!

The travellers came out into a large square where the assemblies of the Cossacks were usually held. On a big upturned tub sat a Cossack. He had taken off his shirt and was mending it. Their way was barred again by a crowd of musicians, in the middle of which a young Cossack was cutting capers, his cap tilted jauntily on one side and his hands raised over his head. "Faster! Faster! Play faster! And you, Foma, don't grudge vodka to orthodox Christians!" And Foma, a Cossack with a black eye, dispensed a huge mugful of vodka to every man who approached him. Beside the young Cossack, four old warriors set their feet working at a tremendous pace, spun round sideways like a whirlwind almost at the head of the musicians and then, dropping to the ground all of a sudden, flung their feet out quickly and stamped the firmly beaten ground vigorously and sharply with their silver-shod heels. All over the vast space the earth resounded dully to the thud of flying feet, and the rhythmic beat of the silver-shod heels filled the air with a noise that could be heard for miles. One Cossack let out loud, ear-splitting yells as he flew after the others in the dance. His long tuft of hair waved in the wind, his powerful chest was exposed and, as he was wearing a warm winter sheepskin, sweat poured from him as from a bucket.

"Take off your sheepskin, man!" Taras said at last. "Why, you're all steaming hot!"

"Can't!" shouted the Cossack in reply.

"Why not?"

"Can't do it! Shall lose it if I do. Lose everything I take off.

That's the kind of man I am. If I take a thing off, I spend it on drink!"

The young fellow had neither cap, not belt round his coat, nor embroidered kerchief: all had gone long ago to pay for drinks. The crowd grew larger; other Cossacks joined the dancers. It was impossible to watch the dance without being thrilled by the wild abandon with which they all flung themselves into this most free and most furious dance the world has ever seen, a dance called *Kazachok* from its mighty originators.

"Oh," cried Taras, "if it weren't for my horse I'd join in the dance myself!"

Meanwhile old Cossacks with grey tufts of hair on their shaven heads appeared in the crowd, men who had been elders more than once and whose great services had won them general recognition in the *Syech*. Taras soon met a large number of old acquaintances. Ostap and Andrey heard nothing but greetings: "Hullo, Petcheritza!" "Good day, Kosolup!" "Where have you sprung from, Taras?" "How did you get here, Doloto?" "How are you, Kirdyaga?" "Glad to see you, Goosty!" "Never thought of meeting you again, Remen!" And the old warriors, who had met here from all over the turbulent world of eastern Russia, embraced and kissed each other and overwhelmed each other with questions: "What's happened to Kassyan?" "What's Borodavka doing?" "What about Kolopyor?" "Any news from Pidsyshok?" And all Taras Bulba heard in reply was that Borodavka had been hanged in Tolopan, that Kolopyor had been flayed alive at Kizirmen, and that Pidsyshok's head had been pickled in a barrel and sent to Constantinople.

Old Bulba bowed his head and murmured thoughtfully, "Ah, they were good Cossacks, every one of 'em!"

⚡ I I I

Taras and his two sons had been living for about a week at the *Syech*. Ostap and Andrey did little military schooling. The *Syech* scorned military exercises which it considered a waste of time. The young Cossacks were trained and instructed in the art of warfare by experience alone, experience gained in the heat of battles, which for that reason were almost continuous. The intervals between the fighting the Cossacks considered too precious to be spent on learning the discipline of war, with the exception perhaps of an occasional target shoot and, less frequently, horse racing and hunting wild game in the meadows and the steppes; the rest of the time was given up completely to junketing—a sign of a high exuberance of spirits. The whole military settlement presented an extraordinary spectacle: it was a kind of never-ending feast, a ball that began noisily and somehow forgot to end. There were some Cossacks who were occupied in a craft, and a few more who kept shops and engaged in trade; but the majority drank and danced and made merry from morning till evening, while there was still a pleasant jingle in the pocket and while the gold and valuables they had won in battle had not yet passed into the hands of hucksters and inn-keepers. This general banqueting had something spellbinding about it. It was not a gathering of drunkards who spent their last penny on drink to drown their sorrows; it was just one wild riot of high spirits. Every one who came here cast himself adrift from his old life and forgot all his former troubles and joys. He, as it were, bade a lasting farewell to his past life and threw himself gaily into the free-and-easy life of his comrades, carefree revellers like himself, for, like his comrades, he had neither kindred, nor a roof over his head, nor a family, nothing in fact but the open sky and the everlasting banquet of his soul. It was this that produced that wild gaiety which could not have arisen from any other source. The tales and idle talk heard among the crowds that gathered in the square and sat about lazily on the ground were often so amusing and revealed so natural a gift for vivid story-telling that you had to possess the imperturbable, placid exterior of a Dnieper Cossack to keep a straight face without even a twitch of the moustache—a characteristic feature that even today distinguishes the southern Russian from the rest of his countrymen. The gaiety was drunken and clamorous, but for all that this was not a grim drinking den where men seek oblivion in a brutish kind of gaiety. It was an intimate circle of schoolfellows, the only difference being that instead of sitting at a desk and listening to the dreary rambling of the schoolmaster they went out on a raid of five thousand horse, and, instead of a field to play ball in, they had vast, unguarded frontiers which no enemy could cross with impunity, in the sight of which the Tartar never dared to show his quick head, and beyond which the Turk in his green turban gazed, stern and motionless. The difference was that instead of being kept at school against their will, they had of their own free will forsaken their fathers and their mothers and run away from their homes; that there were men there who had had the noose round their necks and who, instead of pale death, saw life again, and life in all its riotous gaiety; that there were men there who regarded it as a point of honour never to keep a penny in their pockets; that there were men there to whom a gold rouble had always been a fortune and whose pockets, thanks to the Jewish tax-farmers and innkeepers, could be turned inside out without any fear of losing anything. There, too, were all the students of the Kiev Academy who had found the academic birch too much of a good thing and who did not bring a single letter of the alphabet with them from school; but among them were also those who knew something of Horace, Cicero and the Roman Republic. There were many of the officers there who afterwards distinguished themselves in the royal armies; there were hundreds of experienced partisans there who cherished the honourable conviction that it did not matter where a man fought so long as he fought and that it was dishonourable for a gentleman not to engage in warfare. There were also many there who had come to the *Syech* in order to be able to say afterwards that they had been to the *Syech* and were therefore veteran fighters. But who was not there? This strange republic was one of the necessities of the age. Lovers of military life, lovers of gold goblets, rich brocades, ducats and reals could find employment here at any time; only the lovers of women could find nothing here, for no woman dared show herself even in the suburb of the *Syech*.

It seemed exceedingly strange to Ostap and Andrey that hundreds of people arrived at the *Syech* almost daily and it never occurred to anyone to ask them where they came from, who they were, or what were their names. They came there as though returning to their own homes which they had only left an hour before. The newcomer merely went to see the general, who usually said:

"Hullo! Do you believe in Christ?"

"I do," the man replied.

"Do you believe in the Holy Trinity?"

"I do."

"Do you go to church?"

"Yes, sir."

"Well then, cross yourself!"

The man crossed himself.

"All right," the general said, "now you can go to any detachment you like."

And that was the end of the ceremony.

All the *Syech* prayed in one church and they were ready to defend it to the last drop of blood, though they would not hear of fasting or abstinence. Only Jews, Armenians, and Tartars, greedy of gain, ventured to live and trade in the suburb, for the Cossacks never liked bargaining and paid as much money as their hand happened to pull out of their pockets. However, the fate of these avaricious hucksters was most pitiable: they were like the people who live at the foot of Vesuvius, for as soon as the Cossacks ran out of money they smashed their stalls and helped themselves to everything they fancied without payment.

The *Syech* was composed of sixty separate military units or "houses," each very much like an independent republic, but still more like a boarding school where the children are provided with all the necessities. No one owned anything, or kept anything to himself; everything was in the hands of the commander of the detachment who for that reason was usually referred to as "the old man." He kept their money, their clothes, all their provisions, the flour and fats for their thin broth, their porridge, and their fuel; the Cossacks even entrusted him with their money for safe-keeping. Very often disputes arose between different "houses," and this invariably led to a free-for-all. The detachments swarmed all over the square and fought each other with their fists until one or the other party gained the upper hand, and then both indulged in an orgy of drinking. Such was the *Syech,* which provided so many attractions to young men.

Ostap and Andrey threw themselves into this sea of wild gaiety with all the ardour of youth, and instantly forgot their father's house, their school, and all that had interested them before; they gave themselves up entirely to their new life. Everything fascinated them: the riotous customs of the *Syech* and its uncomplicated justice and its laws which seemed to them rather severe in so freedom-loving a republic. If a Cossack was caught stealing from another Cossack, even if the thing he had stolen was of no value, it was regarded as a slur on the good name of all the Cossacks: he was bound to the whipping-post as a common thief and a cudgel was laid beside him, and every passer-by was obliged to deal him a blow with it until he was in this way beaten to death. If a man did not pay his debts, he was chained to a cannon where he had to remain until one of his friends took pity on him and set him free by paying his debt for him. But what impressed Andrey most was the terrible punishment meted out for murder. A pit was dug in his presence, the murderer lowered alive into it and the coffin with the body of the murdered man placed on top of him, and then both were covered with earth. Andrey was for weeks haunted by this terrible form of capital punishment and for a long time he could not get out of his mind the awful picture of the man buried alive in the same grave with the dreadful coffin of the man he had murdered.

It did not take the two young men very long to become popular with the Cossacks. They frequently went hunting with men of their own detachments and occasionally with the whole of their detachment and some of the neighbouring detachments as well, and shot large numbers of steppe birds, stags and wild goats, or went on the lakes, rivers and streams, each stretch of water assigned by lot to a different detachment, and cast nets and sweep-seines and drew out large hauls of fish to provide food for their entire "house." Although there was nothing there to test a Cossack's fitness for battle, they had already made a mark among the other young men by their initiative and daring and the luck that seemed to attend all their efforts. They were excellent shots, rarely missing their target, and they could swim across the Dnieper against the current, a feat for which a Cossack was accorded a triumphant reception in Cossack circles.

But Taras was preparing a different kind of activity for them. Such an idle life was not to his taste: what he wanted was real action. He was always trying to think of some way to rouse the *Syech* to some bold enterprise where a Cossack knight would have plenty of scope to show his mettle. At last one day he went to see the general and, without beating about the bush, said to him:

"Well, General, it's about time the Cossacks had some real work to do."

"There isn't any work for them at present," replied the commanding officer, removing his small pipe from his mouth and spitting.

"What do you mean? Couldn't they go on an expedition against the Turks or the Tartars?"

"No, sir. They can make war neither on the Turk nor on the Tartar," the general replied coolly, replacing the pipe in his mouth.

"Why not?"

"Because they can't. We promised the Sultan peace."

"But he's an infidel. Both God and the Holy Scripture command us to draw the sword against the infidel."

"We have not the right to do it. If we had not sworn by our faith, then perhaps we might have done it, but I'm afraid it's quite out of the question now."

"Out of the question, is it? What do you mean, we have not the right to do it? I have two sons, young men both of them. Neither has ever been in battle, and all you say is we haven't the right. Do you mean the Cossacks mustn't go to war?"

"What I mean is that they can't go to war now."

"Then according to you it is right that the Cossacks should waste their strength, that a man should perish like a dog without fighting for the good cause, without being of any use to his country or to Christendom in general? If that is so, then what the devil are we living for? What's the use of our life? Tell me that. You're a clever man; you weren't chosen commander-in-chief for nothing, were you? Well then, tell me what we are living for?"

The general made no reply to this. He was an obstinate Cossack, and after a short pause he just said, "There won't be any war all the same."

"So there won't be any war?" asked Taras.

"No, sir."

"And it's no use even thinking about it, is it?"

"No use at all."

"You wait, you stubborn old devil," thought Bulba to himself. "I'll show you!" and he made up his mind then and there to revenge himself on the commanding officer.

Having talked the matter over with a few of his friends, Taras invited all the Cossacks to a drink and it was not long before several drunken Cossacks went straight to the square and made for the post to which the kettle-drums, used to summon the Cossacks to a general assembly, were fastened. Not finding the drumsticks, which were always kept by the drummer, they each seized a log and began beating the drums. The first to come running at the noise was the drummer, a tall man with only one eye, and that one, too, very sleepy.

"Who dares beat the drums?" he shouted.

"Hold your tongue! Take your drumsticks and get on with it when you are told!" replied the tipsy elders.

The drummer immediately took the drumsticks out of his pocket, for he had taken the precaution of bringing them with him, knowing too well how such incidents ended. The kettle-drums rolled, and soon dark groups of Cossacks began to swarm, like bees, on the square. They all gathered into a ring, and after the third drum-roll the elders at last put in an appearance: the commander-in-chief with his mace, the badge of his office, in his hand; the judge with the official army seal; the clerk with his ink-horn; and the captain with his rod. The commanders and the elders took off their caps and bowed in all directions to the Cossacks, who stood proudly with arms akimbo.

"What's the meaning of this assembly, gentlemen? What do you want?" asked the general, but the shouts and the imprecations hurled at him made it impossible for him to continue with his speech.

"Put down your mace! Put down your mace, you son of Satan!" Cossacks shouted from the crowd.

Some of the detachments that remained sober were, it seemed, ready to resist the demand, and a fight immediately broke out between the sober and the drunken Cossacks. The shouting and the uproar became general.

The commander tried to speak, but knowing very well that the infuriated, undisciplined crowd might beat him to death, which almost always happened on such occasions, he bowed very low to the Cossacks, put down his mace, and disappeared into the crowd.

"Is it your wish, gentlemen, that we, too, put down our badges of office?" said the judge, the clerk and the captain, making ready at once to put down the ink-horn, the army seal and the rod.

"No, no! You can remain!" the crowd shouted. "The general is an old woman. That's why it was necessary to turn him out. We want a man for our general!"

"Whom will you choose for your general now?" asked the elders.

"Kukúbenko! We want Kukúbenko!" shouted some.

"We don't want Kukúbenko!" shouted others. "Too soon for him. The milk isn't dry on his lips."

"Let Shilo be our chief!" still others shouted. "Let's make Shilo our general!"

"To hell with Shilo!" the crowd began to curse. "The son of a bitch is a worse thief than a Tartar! Tie him up in a sack, the drunken devil!"

"Borodáty! Let Borodáty be our general!"

"We don't want Borodáty! To the devil with Borodáty!"

"Shout Kirdyaga," whispered Taras to several Cossacks.

"Kirdyaga! Kirdyaga!" shouted the crowd. "Borodáty! Borodáty! Kirdyaga! Kirdyaga! Shilo! To hell with Shilo! Kirdyaga!"

All the candidates, hearing their names called, at once left the crowd, so as to give no excuse to anyone for saying afterwards that they had taken a personal part in their election.

"Kirdyaga! Kirdyaga!" The shouts became stronger. "Borodáty!"

The supporters of each candidate came to blows, and the supporters of Kirdyaga triumphed in the end.

"Go and fetch Kirdyaga!" the crowd shouted.

About a dozen Cossacks, some of them hardly able to stand on their feet, so befuddled were they, went at once to tell Kirdyaga about his election.

Kirdyaga, a rather elderly but clever Cossack, had been sitting for some time in his "house" and pretended not to know what was taking place.

"Well, gentlemen," he said, "what can I do for you?"

"Come along; you've been elected general!"

"Really, gentlemen, I'm sure I don't deserve such an honour," said Kirdyaga. "What sort of general will I make? Why, I'm not clever enough for such a responsible post! Couldn't you have found a better man in the whole army?"

"Come along! Come along!" shouted the Cossacks.

Two of them took him by the arms and, in spite of his resistance, he was at last dragged to the square, the Cossacks who had been sent to fetch him swearing at him, punching him on the back and kicking him.

"Don't you try running back, damn you!" they exhorted him. "Accept the honour, you cur, when it's been offered to you!"

In this way Kirdyaga was at length led into the circle of the Cossacks.

"Well, men," those who brought him shouted at the top of their voices, "are you agreed that this Cossack should be our general?"

"Agreed! Agreed!" the crowd roared, and all the plain resounded with their cry.

One of the elders then picked up the mace and offered it to the newly elected commander. Kirdyaga, as was the custom, at once refused it. The elder offered it to him a second time, and again Kirdyaga refused; but when it was offered to him a third time, he accepted it immediately. A roar of approval rang through the crowd, and again the plain resounded far and wide with the Cossacks' cry. Then four of the oldest Cossacks with grey moustaches and grey tufts of hair (there were not any really old men in the *Syech,* for no Dnieper Cossack died a natural death) stepped forth out of the crowd, and, each taking up a handful of earth, which had been turned to mud by the recent rain, placed it on Kirdyaga's head. The wet earth ran down his head and trickled over his cheeks and moustache, and his whole face was covered with mud. But Kirdyaga never stirred, and thanked the Cossacks for the honour shown him.

It was in this way that the noisy assembly came to an end to the great gratification of Bulba, whatever the feelings of the rest of the Cossacks might have been, for that was how he had revenged himself on the former commander. Besides, Kirdyaga was an old friend of his and had been with him on many campaigns on land and sea, sharing the toils and hardships of war.

The crowd began dispersing at once and the Cossacks were soon celebrating the elections of a new general by an orgy such as Ostap and Andrey had not yet seen. The inns in the suburb were smashed, and the Cossacks helped themselves to mead, vodka and beer without payment, the innkeepers being too glad to escape with their lives. The whole night was spent in shouting and the singing of songs extolling Cossack feats of arms, and for many hours the rising moon gazed upon the crowds of musicians, marching through the streets with bandores, drums and round balalaikas, and upon the choristers kept in the *Syech* to sing in the church and to glorify the heroic deeds of the Dnieper Cossacks. At last drink and exhaustion laid low even the strongest heads, and here and there a Cossack could be seen sinking to the ground, and while friend was embracing friend and shedding sentimental tears over him, he would roll over and both would tumble down to the ground together. In one place a whole crowd of drunken Cossacks were lying in a heap; in another a Cossack reeled drunkenly for some time, trying to choose a more comfortable place to lie down and ending up by sprawling over a block of wood. The last and strongest of them all went on babbling incoherently for some time, but at last he, too, was felled by the power of drink, and all the *Syech* was asleep.

🎵 I V

Next day Taras was already conferring with the new general about how to rouse the Dnieper Cossacks to some warlike action. Kird-yaga was a clever and crafty Cossack who knew his men inside out, and at first he said: "It's quite impossible to break our oath! Quite impossible!" But, after a short pause, he added, "Well, I suppose it could be done without breaking our oath. We'll have to think of something. Some way could be found, I'm sure. Let's first get the people together, not at my command, you understand, but of their own accord. I expect you could manage that, couldn't you?

As soon as you get them out on the square, the elders and I will come along, too, just as if we knew nothing about it."

Scarcely an hour after their talk, the kettle-drums began beating a tattoo. There were plenty of drunken and reckless Cossacks about. Thousands of Cossack caps covered the square. A hubbub of voices arose. "What's up? What's the matter? What's the meaning of this meeting?" Nobody knew. At last, first in one corner, then in another, people were heard saying, "There's no war! Our Cossack strength is being wasted! Our commanders don't seem to care a damn! Grown too fat, the swine! There's no justice in the world!" The other Cossacks listened at first, and then they, too, began saying, "There's no justice in the world! Indeed, there isn't!" The elders seemed to be astonished at such speeches. At last the general stepped forward and said, "My friends, may I say a few words to you?"

"Speak! Speak!"

"What I wanted to talk to you about, my friends, and I daresay you know it as well as I do, is that many Cossacks have run up big debts with the Jewish innkeepers and with their own friends, too, so that they couldn't raise a penny from the devil himself at present. Then there is of course the further consideration that there are many young men among us who have never been to war and don't know what war is like, and I need hardly tell you that a young man cannot exist without war. What kind of a Dnieper Cossack will he make, I ask you, if he has not even once beaten the infidel?"

"He speaks well," thought Bulba.

"Now, friends, please do not think that I'm saying this because I want to break the peace. God forbid! I am saying this because, after all, it's true, isn't it? Then there is our church. . . . Yes, my friends, we have a church all right, and I hope I'm not committing any sin by telling you frankly that our church is a disgrace. A disgrace to *us,* I mean. Here, by the grace of God, our *Syech* has been in existence for many years, and to this very day not only the out-

side of our church but even the icons are without ornaments. Someone might at least have thought of providing silver frames for them!
But all that our church has ever received by way of adornments
is what some Cossack left it in his will, and what he left, my friends,
isn't very much, either, for the poor devil had squandered everything on drink in his lifetime. So, you see, I'm saying all this not
because I want to start a war against the Moslems. No! We have
promised peace to the Sultan and it would be a great sin if we
broke our promise, for we have taken an oath in accordance with
our laws."

"What the devil is he driving at?" thought Bulba.

"So you see, my friends, we just can't start a war; our knightly
honour forbids such a thing. But we might, in my humble opinion,
do this: let us send our young men on a trip across the Black Sea
and let them pick up a few baubles on the coasts of Anatolia. What
do you say, friends?"

"Let's all go! Take us all!" the crowd shouted. "We're ready to
lay down our lives for our faith!"

The general was alarmed. The last thing he wanted was to raise
the entire Dnieper Cossack force; to break the peace seemed in the
present circumstances to be utterly wrong to him.

"Will you allow me to say a few more words, my friends?" he
said.

"No! No!" the Cossacks shouted. "You'll not improve on what
you've said already!"

"Well, friends, if that is how you want it, I can't do anything to
stop you. I'm only your servant. It's well known, and we have it
also from the Scripture, that the voice of the people is the voice of
God. There can't be anything wiser than what the whole people
decides to do. But I'd like to tell you this. As you know, the Sultan
will hardly allow our young men's little escapade to go unpunished.
So in the meantime we'll get ready. Our forces will be fresh and we
need fear no one. Moreover, if we all went now, the Tartars might
fall upon the *Syech!* Those Turkish curs will not dare show them-

selves, let alone pay a visit to the house while the master is at home, but directly our backs are turned they'll fall upon us from behind and bite us hard! And as I am now speaking quite frankly to you, I may as well add that we have not enough boats in reserve, nor enough powder ground for us all to go. As for me, my friends, I'd be only too glad to do as you like, for I'm your servant and am ready to do whatever you decide."

The crafty chieftain fell silent. The Cossacks began discussing the matter in groups, while the detachment commanders consulted together. Fortunately few of them were drunk, and so they decided to listen to wiser counsel.

A number of people set off at once to the other side of the Dnieper where the army treasury and some of the weapons taken from the enemy were hidden in inaccessible places under the water and in the reeds. The rest immediately rushed to overhaul the boats and get them ready for the expedition. In a twinkling the bank of the river was covered with men. Several carpenters arrived with axes in their hands. Old, sunburnt, broad-shouldered, strong-legged Cossacks, some with grizzled and some with black moustaches, rolled up their trousers and stood knee-deep in the water, hauling the boats from the bank with stout ropes. Others dragged ready-made dry timber and trees of all sorts. In one place men were nailing boards to the boats; in another they had turned a boat upside down and were caulking and tarring it; in a third they were binding long bundles of reeds to the sides of the boats, as was the custom among the Cossacks, to prevent them from being sunk by the waves of the sea. Further up all along the shore campfires had been built and tar was being boiled in huge copper cauldrons for tarring the vessels. Old and experienced Cossacks were instructing the young. The tapping of hammers and the shouts of the workmen resounded all over the neighbourhood; the whole of the riverside sprang to life and began throbbing with activity.

Just at that time a large ferry-boat was approaching the bank. A group of people on board waved their hands frantically while still at a distance. They were Cossacks in torn coats. Their tattered clothes (many had nothing but the shirt on their backs and the pipe between their teeth) showed that they had either escaped from some disaster or had been drinking so well they had squandered all they had on them. A thick-set, broad-shouldered Cossack of about fifty left the group and stood in front. He shouted louder and waved his arms about more vigorously than the rest; but the hammering and the shouts of the workmen drowned his words.

"What's your news?" asked the general when the ferry-boat reached the bank.

All the workmen stopped their work, and, raising their axes and chisels, looked on expectantly.

"Bad news, sir!" the thick-set Cossack shouted from the ferry.

"What's wrong?"

"Will you give me leave to speak, gentlemen?"

"Speak!"

"Or would you rather call an assembly?"

"Speak, we're all here!"

They all pressed together, forming one huge crowd.

"Have you heard nothing of what's going on in the hetman's land?"

"Well, what is going on there?" asked one of the detachment commanders.

"What indeed! Has the Tartar stopped up your ears with wads of hemp that you've heard nothing?"

"Well, tell us what is happening there."

"What's happening there no man born and baptised has ever seen in his life."

"Tell us what's happening there, you son of a bitch!" someone shouted from the crowd, having evidently lost all patience.

"We're now living in such times, friends, that even our holy churches aren't ours any longer."

"Not ours? What do you mean?"

"What I mean is that they've all been leased out to the Jews. If you don't pay the Jew beforehand, no mass can be celebrated."

"What are you talking about?"

"And if the mean scoundrel of a Jew does not put a mark on the Holy Easter Cake with his unclean hand, it cannot be consecrated."

"He's lying, friends! Who ever heard of such a thing? An unclean Jew putting a mark on the Holy Easter Cake!"

"Listen, gentlemen, listen to me. I have something worse to tell you. Catholic priests are now driving all over the Ukraine in their two-wheeled carriages. But it isn't the carriages that matter; what matters is that they are not putting horses to their carriages, but orthodox Christians. Listen! There's something worse still I have to tell you. I have heard people say that Jewish women are making themselves petticoats out of our priests' chasubles. These are the things going on in the Ukraine, gentlemen. And you sit here and enjoy yourselves! The Tartar, it seems, has given you such a fright that you have neither ears nor eyes and you don't hear or see what's going on in the world."

"Wait a minute," said the general, who had been standing with his eyes fixed upon the ground, as is the habit of Dnieper Cossacks who, when important matters are at stake, never give way to their first impulse, but keep quiet and let the terrible force of their indignation accumulate in silence. "Wait a minute; let me say something, too. What were you doing while all this was going on? What were you—may the devil beat your father black and blue—what were you doing, I say? Where were your sabres? Or didn't you have any? How came you to permit such lawlessness to go untamed?"

"So you want to know how we came to allow such lawlessness, do you? What did you expect us to do with fifty thousand Poles about? And—why deny it?—there were many traitors among our people, too, who preferred to adopt their religion."

"And what about your hetman? What about your colonels? What were they doing?"

"What were our colonels doing? God grant we may never have to do the same!"

"What do you mean?"

"What I mean is, sir, that our hetman is now lying in Warsaw, roasted in a copper bull, and the arms and heads of our colonels are being carried about from fair to fair and displayed to the people. That's what our colonels have done!"

The crowd was deeply stirred. At first a dead silence fell upon the riverside like the stillness before a violent storm, then all at once people burst into speech and the whole bank of the river seemed to be talking.

"What's that? Jews letting out Christian churches? Catholic priests putting orthodox Christians between shafts? Are we going to tolerate such indignities on Russian soil at the hands of cursed infidels? Let them treat the hetman and the colonels like that? Never! Such things shall never be!"

Such words flew from mouth to mouth. The Dnieper Cossacks were in an uproar and they became conscious of their strength. This was not an outburst by a fickle mob. Grave and strong-minded people who were not easily roused, but who, once roused, kept up their indignation at white heat stubbornly and for a long time, were also deeply stirred.

"Hang all the Jews!" someone in the crowd shouted. "Don't let them make petticoats for their Jewesses out of our priests' vestments! Don't let them make marks upon the Holy Easter Cake! Let's drown the rascals in the Dnieper!"

These words were like a spark in a powder magazine, and the crowd rushed to the suburb with the intention of cutting the throats of all the Jews.

The poor sons of Israel, losing what little courage they had, hid in empty vodka barrels and ovens and even crept under the skirts of their wives, but the Cossacks fished them out from everywhere.

"Gracious lords," cried one Jew, tall and thin as a rake, thrusting his wretched face, contorted with panic, from a group of his companions, "gracious lords, a word, I pray you; let me say only one word to you! We've something very important to tell you, something of very great importance, something you've never heard before!"

"All right, let him say it," said Bulba, who always liked to hear what an accused had to say for himself.

"Noble lords," said the Jew, "such noble lords the world has never seen! Such good, kind, brave gentlemen!" His voice faltered and shook with terror. "How could we think evil of the Dnieper Cossacks? Those leaseholders in the Ukraine do not belong to our people at all! I swear to you they're not our people; they're not Jews at all! The devil knows what they are. Something to spit on and throw away. They'll tell you the same. Isn't that so, Solomon, or you, Samuel?"

"It's true! It's true!" Solomon and Samuel replied from the crowd, both in torn skull-caps and pale as death.

"We have never had any dealings with your enemies," the lanky Jew went on, "and we certainly don't want to have anything to do with the Catholics; may they dream of nothing but the devil! Why, we're like brothers to the Cossacks . . ."

"What's that? You want the Cossacks to be your brothers?" someone in the crowd of Cossacks shouted. "You won't live long enough for that to happen, you damned Jews! Into the Dnieper with them, friends! Let's drown the dirty rascals!"

These words were the signal. The Cossacks seized the Jews by the arms and began flinging them into the river. Their pitiful cries rang out on all sides, but the Cossacks merely laughed at the sight of a pair of Jewish legs in shoes and stockings kicking in the air. The poor orator, who had brought the trouble upon his own head, slipped out of his long coat by which he had been seized and in his close-fitting striped vest flung himself at Bulba's feet, clutching at his knees and beseeching him in a piteous voice, "My lord, my lord, my noble lord, I knew your late brother Dorosho! Oh, what a fine soldier he was, sir! A real ornament to all the Cossack knight-hood! I gave him eight hundred sequins that he might be ransomed from the Turks!"

"You knew my brother?" asked Bulba.

"Yes, sir. I knew him, sir. Oh, he was such a generous gentle-man!"

"And what's your name?"

"Yankel, sir."

"All right," said Bulba, and after a moment's reflection he turned to the Cossacks and said, "There'll always be time to hang the Jew, if need be, but give him to me today."

Having said this, Taras led the Jew to his own carts, beside which his Cossacks were standing. "Crawl under a cart, lie there and don't move! And you, lads, don't let the Jew go."

He then set off to the square, for the Cossacks had been flocking there for some time. Everyone had immediately left the bank of the river and the equipment of the boats, for now that they were going on a campaign by land and not by sea they did not want ships and Cossack canoes, but carts and horses. Now they all wanted to go, old and young, all of them, on the advice of their elders, their detachment commanders and their general and by the will of the entire Cossack army they resolved to march straight against Po-land to avenge all the wrongs and indignities against their faith and the Cossack good name, collect booty from the cities, set fire to the villages and the crops, and spread the glory of Cossack arms from one end of the steppe to the other. All of them were making ready on the square, putting on their belts and arming. The gen-eral seemed to have grown several feet taller. He was no longer the humble slave of every whim of a free people; he was a dictator, a despot, whose word was law. The headstrong and unruly war-riors stood shoulder to shoulder in their ranks, their heads low-ered respectfully, not daring to raise their eyes when the general was giving his orders: he issued them quietly, unhurriedly, and without raising his voice, pausing now and again, like an old and experienced Cossack, who was not for the first time putting his carefully thought out plans into execution.

"Inspect everything," he said. "See that you leave nothing undone. Make sure your carts are in good order, and your pails full of tar. Test your weapons thoroughly. Don't take too much clothing with you: one shirt and two pairs of breeches for each Cossack, one pot of broth and one of crushed millet—no one is to take more than that. We shall have all the provisions we need in our carts. Every Cossack is to take two horses with him. And we shall have to take about four hundred oxen, for we shall want them at the fords and in the marshes. And remember, gentlemen, discipline must be maintained above everything. I know there are some among you who, if God should put anything in their way that rouses their greed, will not hesitate to tear up a piece of nankeen cloth or expensive velvet to wrap round his legs. Give up that damnable habit of yours! Don't touch petticoats or dresses; take weapons only, if good, and gold pieces, or silver, for these won't take up much room and may come in useful in any eventuality. And I'm afraid there's one thing more I must warn you about: anyone getting drunk on the campaign can expect no mercy. I shall order him to be tied like a dog by the neck to a cart, whoever he may be, even though he be the most valiant Cossack of the whole army; he will be shot like a dog on the spot and his body left without burial for the birds to pick clean, for a man drunk on a campaign does not deserve a Christian burial. Young men, obey your elders in everything! If you get grazed by a bullet, or scratched by a sabre on the head or anywhere else, do not pay much attention to such a trifle: mix a charge of powder in a tankard of weak vodka, drink it off at a gulp, and all will be well, there will be no fever even; and on the wound, if it is not too big, simply put a little earth, first mixing it with spittle in the palm of your hand, and the wound will dry up. Now then, lads, to work, to work, and do everything without haste and thoroughly and well!"

So spoke the general, and as soon as he had finished all the

Cossacks set to work. The whole *Syech* was sober, and not a single drunken man could be found anywhere, as though there had never been any drunkards among the Cossacks. Some were mending the felloes of the wheels and changing the axles in the carts; others were carrying sacks with provisions to the carts or piling weapons on them; others still were rounding up the horses and oxen. From every side came the tramp of horses' hoofs, the firing of guns that were being tested, the rattle of sabres, the bellowing of oxen, the creaking of carts that were being placed in position, loud cries and urging on of horses and oxen—and soon the Cossack army stretched for miles over the plain, and if you wanted to run from the head to the tail of it you would have had to run a very long way. In the little wooden church the priest conducted a service and sprinkled all with holy water; and everyone kissed the cross. When the Cossack army set off, moving out of the *Syech* in a long line, all the Cossacks looked back, saying almost in the same words, "Farewell, our mother! May the Lord keep and preserve you from all misfortune!"

As he was riding through the suburb, Taras Bulba saw his Jew Yankel who had already pitched some kind of a tent with an awning and was selling flints, powder, and various kinds of medicaments and provisions which the troops might need on the road, including even white and black loaves of bread. "How do you like this damned Jew?" thought Taras to himself.

"You fool," he said, riding up to him, "what are you doing here? Do you want to be shot like a sparrow?"

In reply, Yankel went up closer to him and made a sign with both hands, as though he wished to confide some secret.

"Don't breathe a word about it to anyone, sir," he said, "but among the Cossack carts there is one that belongs to me. I'm carrying all sorts of stores for the Cossacks, and on the way I shall let them have provisions at a cheaper price than any Jew has ever sold. So help me, sir!"

Taras Bulba shrugged his shoulders, marvelling at the irrepressible nature of the Jews, and rode off to join the Cossack troops.

✶ V

Soon all the south-west of Poland became a prey to panic. Everywhere rumours spread: "The Dnieper Cossacks! The Dnieper Cossacks are on the march!" All who could save themselves saved themselves; all who could leave their homes fled and ran in different directions after the manner of that unsettled, happy-go-lucky age when neither fortresses nor castles were built and man put up his thatched hut anyhow and only for a short time. "Why waste money and labour on a cottage," he thought to himself, "when in his next raid the Tartar will raze it anyway to the ground?" All the countryside was in confusion. Some exchanged their oxen and plough for a horse and a gun and went to join the regiments; others fled to a place of safety, driving away their cattle and carrying away with them whatever could be carried away. There were also those on the roads who met the invader with arms in their hands; but mostly people preferred to flee while there was still time. Everyone knew how hard it was to deal with that violent and warlike crowd known under the name of the Dnieper Cossack army, whose external unruly disorderliness was merely a cloak for the disciplined orderliness that was best adapted for times of war. The horsemen rode without overstraining or overheating their horses; those on foot marched soberly behind the carts; and the whole army moved only by night, resting by day and choosing for their camp wastelands, uninhabited places and woods which in those days were still plentiful. Spies and scouts were sent on ahead to spy out the land and bring news of the whereabouts of the enemy forces, their disposition and strength. Very often they appeared suddenly in places where they were least expected—and then everything took leave of life: the villages went up in flames, the cattle and horses that were not driven off with the army were slaughtered on the spot, and it really looked as though the Cossacks were feasting rather than conducting a military operation. Today the evidence of brutality which the Cossacks left behind them everywhere in that semi-savage age would make people's hair stand on end: slaughtered babes, women with breasts cut off, men set free with their skin torn from their feet and legs to their knees—in short, the Cossacks paid off old scores with interest. The prelate of one monastery, hearing of their approach, sent two monks to tell the Cossacks from him that they were not behaving as they should, that there was an agreement between the Polish Government and the Cossacks, that they were violating their oath of fealty to the king and that by doing so they were also violating every national law. "Tell the bishop from me and from all the Dnieper Cossacks not to worry," replied the Cossack general. "The Cossacks have so far only been lighting their pipes." And soon the majestic abbey was a blazing heap of ruins and its huge Gothic windows were gaping caverns amid the leaping flames. The fleeing crowds of monks, Jews, and women soon filled to overflowing the cities which offered the slightest hope of safety because of their garrisons and the citizens' defence forces. The belated help sent occasionally by the Government and consisting mostly of cavalry battalions either could not find the Cossacks or were afraid to attack them, and, at the first encounter, turned tail and fled on their swift horses. Now and then it also happened that a number of Polish commanding officers who had been victorious in many battles in the past decided to join forces and offer joint resistance to the Dnieper Cossacks.

It was in those engagements that our two young Cossacks showed their mettle, for they shunned plunder, easy gain and a helpless enemy and were anxious to win their spurs before the eyes of their older comrades by engaging in single combat with the high-spirited and boastful Pole, flaunting on his mettlesome steed with his rich cloak flying in the breeze. That sort of training had its lighter moments; they had picked up a great many rich trappings, costly sabres and guns. In one month the callow fledglings had grown up and were completely transformed; they were men now, and their features in which till now a certain softness could be perceived looked strong and stern now. Old Taras was glad to see his two sons among the foremost. Ostap seemed to have been born for battle and the hard discipline of war. Never at a loss and never flustered by any unforeseen development, he could, with a coolness that was almost unnatural in a young man of twenty-two, instantly gauge the whole danger of any given situation and find a way of evading it, but only with the intention of overcoming it the more surely afterwards. All his movements were already beginning to be distinguished by a confidence that was born of experience, and it was impossible not to perceive in them the qualities of a future leader of men. His whole body conveyed the impression of great strength, and there was something of the tremendous power of a lion in the way in which he displayed his knightly prowess in the field. "He'll make a fine colonel one day," old Taras used to say. "A damned fine colonel! Shouldn't be at all surprised if he proved himself to be a better man than his father!"

Andrey fell completely under the spell of the enchanting music of the bullets and the swords. He did not know what it meant to stop and consider or calculate and gauge beforehand his own and his enemy's strength. A battle filled him with rapture and delight: it was a festival to him, a gay carnival, especially in those minutes when his head was aflame and everything danced and capered before his eyes, when heads were flying and horses crashing thunderously to the ground, while he dashed along, like one intoxicated, amid the whistling bullets and flashing swords, dealing out blows right and left and hardly feeling those he received himself. Many a time his father could not help admiring Andrey, too, seeing how, urged on by his fiery enthusiasm alone, he hurled himself into the thick of the battle where no cool-headed and prudent fighter would ever venture and merely by the fury of his onslaught achieved wonders that left veteran warriors gaping with surprise. Old Taras marvelled and murmured, "He's a good soldier, too. I only hope the enemy does not capture him one day. He's not Ostap, but he's a good soldier, a very good soldier!"

The Cossack army decided to march straight on the city of Dubno, which, according to rumours, had many wealthy inhabitants and much of the Polish king's treasure. In a day and a half the march was accomplished and the Cossacks appeared before the city. The inhabitants decided to defend themselves to the last and to put up with every hardship a long siege might entail. They preferred to die in the squares and streets of their city, on the thresholds of their own homes, rather than admit the enemy into them. The city was surrounded by a high mound of earth, and where the rampart was lower a stone wall jutted out, or a house, converted into a battery, or an oak palisade. The garrison was strong and was fully conscious of the importance of its task. At first the Dnieper Cossacks attempted to take the city by storm and tried to scale the rampart, but they were met with volley after volley of grape-shot. It seemed that the tradesmen and inhabitants of the city had no intention of remaining idle, either, and a crowd of them could be seen standing on the rampart. In their eyes could be read a desperate determination to resist the enemy at all costs. The women, too, decided to take part in the fighting, and they hurled stones, barrels and pots on the heads of the Cossacks, following it up with boiling water and, finally, with sacks of sand, which blinded the attackers.

The Dnieper Cossacks did not like to have anything to do with fortresses: laying siege to a city was not their way of conducting war. The general ordered a retreat. "Don't worry, men," he said; "let us withdraw. But may I be an accursed Tartar and not a Christian if we let a single one of them out of the city! Let the dogs die of hunger!" The troops withdrew and surrounded the whole

city, and having nothing better to do began laying waste the surrounding countryside, burning the neighbouring villages, setting
fire to the shocks of corn in the fields, turning their droves of horses
into the cornfields which had not been touched by the reaping
hook and where, as luck would have it, heavy ears of corn swayed
in the wind, the result of an exceptionally good harvest which that
year had generously rewarded the husbandman. The inhabitants
of the beleaguered city watched with horror the destruction of
their means of subsistence. Meanwhile the Dnieper Cossacks, having formed a double ring round the city with their carts, settled
down, as though they were in the *Syech,* in detachments, smoked
their pipes, exchanged captured weapons, played leap-frog and
odd-and-even, and every now and then looked with cold indifference at the starving city. At night they lighted camp-fires; the
cooks in each detachment cooked porridge in huge copper cauldrons; wakeful sentries mounted guard by the fires which burnt all
night. But very soon the Dnieper Cossacks began to weary of
their life of inactivity and prolonged abstinence, unattended as it
was by any fighting. The general even ordered the issue of a
double ration of vodka, a concession occasionally made to the
troops when no hard fighting was in progress or any difficult
marches ahead. The young men, and Ostap and Andrey in particular, disliked such a life. Andrey was quite plainly bored.

"What a silly fellow you are," said Taras to him. "Remember the proverb, 'Be patient, Cossack, and you'll be a chieftain one
day!' It is not enough that a man's spirits should never fail him in
a tight corner. That doesn't make him a good soldier. For a good
soldier is a man who in times of inaction never allows weariness to
get the better of him, but puts up cheerfully with everything and,
whatever you do to him, will have his own way in the end."

But a fiery youth will never agree with an old man: their characters are different and they look with different eyes on the same
thing.

Meanwhile Taras Bulba's regiment arrived, led by Tovkatch;

with him were two other captains, a clerk and other officers; there were over four thousand Cossacks in it, including not a few volunteers who had joined of their own free will and without any special summons as soon as they heard what was afoot. The captains brought Bulba's sons a blessing from their mother, who sent them each an icon of cypress wood from the Mezhigorsky Monastery in Kiev. The two brothers put the two holy icons round their necks and fell into thought as they remembered their old mother. What did that blessing portend? What did it tell them? Was it a blessing for victory over the enemy, followed by a merry homecoming with booty and glory, immortalised in the songs of bandore-players, or. . . . But the future remains for ever unknown and it stands before a man like the autumn mist that rises from the marshes: the birds fly about in it wildly, with a flutter of wings, not seeing or recognising one another, the dove not seeing the hawk, and the hawk not seeing the dove, and none knowing how far he is from his doom . . .

Ostap was attending to his duties and had long since gone off to the detachments; but Andrey felt (he hardly knew why) something weighing heavily on his heart. The Cossacks had long finished their evening meal. The last gleam of sunset had long died in the sky, and the air was full of the loveliness of a July night; but he had not gone back to the detachments, nor did he go to sleep, but seemed to have become unconsciously absorbed in the contemplation of the scene before him. Myriads of stars twinkled with a bright and sharp gleam in the sky. The plain was covered for miles around with carts, scattered all over it, each cart with its pail of tar hanging from it, each cart loaded with provisions and possessions of all sorts taken from the enemy. Beside the carts, under the carts, and at a little distance from the carts—everywhere in fact—Cossacks could be seen stretched on the grass. They were all sleeping in picturesque attitudes: one with a large sack under his head, another with a cap, a third simply using his comrade's side for a pillow. A sabre, a matchlock, a short pipe with copper mountings, a metal pipe cleaner, and a bag of flints and tinder were always within reach of every Cossack. The heavy oxen lay with their legs bent under them and their huge, whitish bulks might from a distance have been mistaken for grey boulders scattered on the slopes of the plain. From every side there rose from the grass the heavy snoring of the sleeping fighting men, answered from the fields by the resounding neighing of the horses, protesting against their hobbled feet. Meanwhile something grand and awe-inspiring was added to the beauty of the July night. This was the glow from the still smouldering fires of the burnt-down villages and buildings in the neighbourhood. In one place the flames still spread calmly and majestically across the sky; in another, meeting something inflammable, they suddenly blazed up, hissing and leaping like a whirlwind to the very stars, and torn, ragged balls of fire flickered out far, far away at the very edge of the horizon. There the black mass of a gutted monastery towered menacingly, like a grim Carthusian monk, revealing its gloomy grandeur every time its ruins reflected the flames. Yonder the monastery garden was burning, and the trees, it seemed, could be heard hissing amid the spirals of smoke, and every time a flame leapt out it threw a phosphorescent purplish-red light on the clusters of ripe plums or transformed the pears, which were here and there turning yellow, into red gold, and right in the midst of them there loomed the dark outline of the body of a poor Jew or monk, hanging from the wall of the building or the branch of a tree, and being consumed with the rest of the building in the flames. In the distance birds could be seen soaring over the fire, and they looked like a heap of dark tiny crosses upon a fiery field. The beleaguered city seemed to have fallen asleep; its spires, roofs, palisade, and walls fitfully reflected the faint glow of the distant conflagrations.

Andrey walked round the Cossack lines. The camp-fires, by which the guards were sitting, were on the point of going out any minute, and the guards themselves were asleep, having consumed their stew and the dumplings with true Cossack appetite. He was surprised at such carelessness, thinking, "It's a good thing there is no powerful enemy near and there's nothing to fear." At last he, too, went up to one of the carts, clambered into it and lay down on his back with his hands clasped under his head. But he could not go to sleep and he lay a long time gazing at the sky: it all lay open before him, the air was clear and transparent, the conglomeration of stars that compose the Milky Way and lie in a wide belt athwart the sky shone with unusual brightness. At times Andrey seemed to doze off, a light mist of drowsiness shutting out the sky from him for a moment, and then it grew clear again and everything was once more visible.

It was during one of those moments of forgetfulness that he seemed to have caught a glimpse of some strange human face. Thinking that he must be dreaming, he opened his eyes and saw a real human face, a wan, emaciated face, bending over him and looking straight into his eyes. Long coal-black hair, unkempt and dishevelled, crept from under the dark veil flung over the head; the strangely glittering eyes and the deathly pallor of the dark face, each feature of it standing out sharply, might well have made him think that it was an apparition rather than a human being. He put his hand on his musket instinctively and said in a strangled voice, "Who are you? If you're a spirit from hell, then vanish out of sight; but if you're a human being, you've chosen a bad time for a joke: I'll shoot you dead on the spot!"

In reply the apparition put its finger to its lips and seemed to implore him to keep silent. He dropped his hand and began to peer closer. From the long hair, the neck and the half-bared bosom, he saw that it was a woman. But she was not a native of those parts. Her face was swarthy and wasted with illness; her broad cheekbones protruded above her sunken cheeks; her narrow slits of eyes slanted upwards. The more he scrutinised her features, the more they seemed somehow familiar to him. At last he could not restrain himself and asked, "Tell me who you are. I seem to know you. Have I seen you somewhere?"

"Two years ago in Kiev."

"Two years ago in Kiev?" Andrey repeated, racking his brains for some surviving memory from his old student life. He looked at her intently once more and suddenly cried at the top of his voice, "You're the Tartar woman! The maid of the Polish young lady! The governor's daughter!"

"Hush! . . ." said the Tartar woman, putting her hands together imploringly. She trembled all over and turned her head round quickly to see whether anyone had been wakened by Andrey's loud cry.

"Please tell me how you got here and why you are here," Andrey said in a whisper, breathlessly, his voice breaking at every word with pent-up emotion. "Where's your mistress? She's still alive, isn't she?"

"She's here, sir. In the city."

"In the city?" he almost cried again at the top of his voice, feeling a sudden rush of blood to his heart. "Why is she in the city?"

"Because my master himself is in the city. He's been governor of Dubno for the past sixteen months."

"Well, is she married? Tell me, tell me how she is! Why do you look so strangely at me?"

"She has had nothing to eat for two days. . . ."

"What?"

"None of the inhabitants of the city has had a bite of bread for a long time, sir. They've been eating nothing but earth for days."

Andrey was dumbfounded.

"My mistress saw you with the other Cossacks from the city rampart, sir. She said to me, 'Go and tell the knight to come to me if he still remembers me, but if he doesn't, let him give you a piece of bread for my old mother, for I don't want to see my mother die before my eyes. Let me die first and her after me! Go and ask him, fall at his feet, clutch him by the hands! He, too, has an old mother—let him give you some bread for her sake!' "

Many different emotions awoke and blazed up in the youthful heart of the Cossack.

"How did you get here? Which way did you come?"

"By an underground passage."

"Is there such an underground passage?"

"Yes, sir."

"Where?"

"You won't betray us, sir?"

"I swear by the Holy Cross!"

"You have to go down into the ravine, sir, and then cross the stream. It's just where the reeds are . . ."

"And does it come out in the city?"

"Yes, sir. Straight by the city monastery."

"Let's go. Let's go at once!"

"But, sir, what about the bread? Just a piece of bread, sir, in the name of Christ and the Blessed Virgin!"

"All right, you shall have your bread. Stay here by the cart, or, better still, lie down in it. Nobody will see you; they're all asleep. I shan't be long."

He went off to the carts where the stores of provisions belonging to his detachment were kept. His heart was pounding. All his past, everything that had been submerged by his present Cossack bivouack existence and the stern realities of war, floated to the surface again, drowning, in turn, the present. Again the proud girl rose up before his mind's eye, as though from the fathomless depths of the ocean: her lovely hands, her eyes, her laughing lips, her thick nut-brown hair that fell in curls over her bosom; all the supple, harmonious lines of her girlish figure flashed through his memory. They had never really died, they had never vanished from his heart, they had merely made way for other powerful emotions which had for a time overwhelmed him; but often, very often, had the young Cossack's deep sleep been troubled by them, and often had he lain awake for hours unable to understand the cause of his sleeplessness.

He walked on while his heart was beating more and more violently at the mere thought that he would see her again. His knees trembled. When he reached the carts he seemed to forget what he had come for: he put his hand to his forehead and stood rubbing it a long time, trying to remember what he had to do. At last he gave a start and was all filled with dread: he suddenly remembered that she was dying of hunger. He rushed to a cart and put under his arm a number of large loaves of black bread; but immediately it occurred to him that that kind of food which was good enough for a stalwart and far from fastidious Cossack was too coarse and entirely unsuitable for her delicate constitution. Then he remembered that only the day before the general had reprimanded the cooks for having used up the whole of the buckwheat flour for their broth when there was enough of it for three whole meals. Fully confident of finding enough thin porridge in the cauldrons, he pulled out his father's small army kettle and went with it to the cook of his own detachment who was asleep by the two ten-gallon cauldrons under which the embers were still glowing. Looking into them, he was amazed to see that both were empty. It required superhuman powers to eat it all, especially as there were fewer men in his detachment than in the others. He looked into the cauldrons of the other detachments, but there was nothing anywhere. He could not help recalling the saying, "The Dnieper Cossacks are like children: if they haven't enough, they'll eat it all; and if they have too much, they won't leave anything, either." What was he to do? Then he remembered that on one of the carts of his father's regiment there was a sack with loaves of white bread which they had found when plundering the bakery of a monastery. He went straight to his father's cart, but the sack was not there: Ostap had taken it for a pillow and, stretched on the ground, was snoring for the whole plain to hear. Andrey seized the sack with one hand and pulled it away so violently that Ostap's head fell on the ground and he sat up in his sleep and, with his eyes closed, shouted at the top of his voice, "Hold him! Hold the damned Pole! Get his horse! Get his horse!"

"Shut up or I'll kill you!" Andrey cried in alarm, swinging the sack at him.

But Ostap stopped talking anyway. He lay down quietly and was soon snoring away with such vigour that his breath set the grass quivering. Andrey looked round apprehensively to see whether Ostap's outcry in his sleep had wakened any Cossack. One shaven head with a long tuft of hair was raised in the nearest detachment, but after looking round it fell back on the ground again. After waiting a minute or two, Andrey at last retraced his steps with the sack slung over his shoulder. The Tartar woman was lying in the cart, scarcely daring to breathe.

"Get up," said Andrey. "Let's go! Don't be afraid. They're all asleep. Can you take just one of these loaves, if I can't carry them all?"

Without waiting for a reply, he slung the sacks over his back, pulled another sack of millet off a cart, as he passed it, took under his arms even the loaves he had meant to give the Tartar woman to carry and, stooping a little under the weight, walked boldly between the rows of sleeping Cossacks.

"Andrey!" said old Bulba as his younger son passed him.

Andrey's heart sank. He stopped and, trembling all over, asked softly, "What?"

"Andrey, there's a woman with you! Take care, sir! I'll thrash you within an inch of your life when I get up! Mark my words, women will be the ruin of you!"

Saying this, Taras propped up his head on his hand and began scrutinising intently the Tartar woman, who was muffled in her veil.

Andrey stood more dead than alive, and did not have the courage to look his father in the face. But when he raised his eyes at last and glanced at his father, he saw that old Bulba was asleep, his head resting on the open palm of his hand.

He crossed himself. The panic which had gripped his heart disappeared even more quickly than it came. When he turned round to glance at the Tartar woman, he saw her standing motionless like a statue of black granite, all muffled up in her veil, and the glow from a distant fire which suddenly blazed up was reflected only in her eyes, which were glazed like the eyes of a corpse. He pulled her by the sleeve and they set off together, continually looking back, until at last they went down the slope to a low-lying dell, almost a ravine, in some places called a creek, at the bottom of which a stream overgrown with sedge and covered with small mounds trickled lazily. Having reached the bottom of the dell, they were completely hidden from the view of the whole plain on which the Cossacks had pitched their camp. At any rate, when Andrey looked round, he saw the slope rising up behind him like a steep wall above the height of a man. A few blades of grass waved on the crest of the slope and above them the moon was rising in the sky in the shape of an inverted sickle of brightly shining gold. The fresh breeze that blew from the steppe showed that dawn was not far off: but no distant crowing of cocks could be heard, for neither in the sacked villages nor in the city itself was there a single cock left. They crossed the stream over a small tree-trunk; the opposite bank looked much higher than the bank behind them and was much more precipitous. This place was apparently considered one of the most impregnable and safest natural strongholds in the city fortifications; at all events the rampart was much lower here and no sentries could be seen behind it. At the same time, a little farther away, there rose up the thick wall of the monastery. The steep bank was all overgrown with wild plants and grasses and the little dell between it and the streams was covered with reeds, almost as high as a man. At the top of the steep bank the remains of a wattle fence could be discerned, showing that at one time there had been a kitchen garden there; in front of it grew broad burdock leaves and behind it rose goosefoot, wild orach and prickly thistle, and a sunflower raised its head above them all. Here the Tartar woman took off her shoes and walked barefoot, pulling up her skirt a little, for the place was soggy and muddy. Making their way through the reeds, they stopped in front of a heap of brushwood and faggots, and, moving aside the brushwood, they found a vaulted entrance to a sort of cave, an opening not bigger than the opening of a bread oven. The Tartar woman, stooping, went in first; Andrey followed her, bending down as low as he could to be able to get through with his sacks, and soon they found themselves in complete darkness.

✠ VI

Andrey moved very slowly in the dark and narrow underground passage, following the Tartar woman and carrying the sacks of bread. "We shall soon be able to see," said his guide. "We're getting near the place where I left a candlestick." And, sure enough, the dark earthen walls soon became dimly visible. They reached a small subterranean chamber which seemed to have been used as a kind of chapel, at least there was a little narrow table, in the shape of a communion table, placed against one wall, and an almost completely faded and discoloured picture of a Catholic Madonna could be descried above it. A little silver lamp hung before the Madonna, throwing a faint glimmer on it. The Tartar woman bent down and picked up from the floor a copper candlestick she had left there, a candlestick with a small, slender stem and a pair of snuffers, a long pin for trimming the light and an extinguisher, all hanging on little chains round it. She picked it up and lighted it from the little lamp. The light grew brighter, and as they walked on together, now in the full glare of the light thrown by the candle, now hidden in the coal-black shadows, they looked like a painting by Gherardo della Notte. The fresh, handsome face of the young Cossack knight, brimming over with health and youth, contrasted strikingly with the pale, wan face of his companion. The passage grew a little wider and Andrey found that he could now walk upright. He examined these earthen walls with interest for they reminded him of the Kiev catacombs. Just as in the Kiev catacombs, there were recesses in the walls, in which here and there coffins stood; occasionally they even came across human bones which had grown so soft that they had disintegrated into white powder. It was plain that here, too, there had been holy men who had sought refuge from the storms of life, from human sorrows and temptations. In places the passage was very damp, and sometimes they had to walk through puddles of water. Andrey had to stop frequently to let his companion rest, for she was continually overcome by weariness. The small morsel of bread she had swallowed gave her a pain in the stomach, unaccustomed to food and unable to digest it, and she had to stop frequently and stand still for several minutes in one place.

At last they came to a little iron door. "Thank God we have arrived," said the Tartar woman in a faint voice, and she raised her hand to knock at the door, but she had not the strength to do it. Andrey struck a violent blow on the door instead of her, and the sound reverberated behind the door, showing that there was a big space there, and changed in tone, apparently on meeting a high vaulted roof. After a few minutes there was a rattle of keys and someone could be heard coming down a staircase. At length the door was unlocked and they saw a monk, standing on a narrow staircase with a bundle of keys and a candle in his hands. Andrey involuntarily stopped dead at the sight of the Catholic monk, for the monks aroused hatred and contempt in the Cossacks, who treated them more inhumanly than Jews. The monk, too, stepped back a little, but a word uttered softly by the Tartar woman reassured him. He held up the candle for them, locked the door, and led them up the stairs. Andrey found himself beneath the lofty, dark arches of the monastery church. A priest was kneeling at one of the altars on which stood tall candlesticks and candles, and was praying in a low voice. On each side of him two young clerics in purple vestments and white lace stoles knelt with censers in their hands. The priest prayed that a miracle might be wrought: that the city should be saved; that the failing spirit of the people should be fortified and patience vouchsafed to them; that the tempter, who incited the people to murmur and provoked them to give way to mean-spirited, cowardly lamentations over their earthly misfortunes, should be utterly confounded. A few women, looking like ghosts, knelt in different corners of the church, their weary heads resting or lying lifelessly on the backs of the chairs and the dark wooden benches in front of them; a few men knelt mournfully, propped up against the columns and pilasters on which the vaulted roof of the aisles rested. The stained-glass window above the altar gleamed with the rosy tints of morning, and large circular blobs of light, blue, yellow, and of different other colours, fell from it on the floor and in a trice illumined the whole church. The entire altar and the deep recess in which it was placed seemed suddenly bathed in radiance; the smoke from the censers hung in the air in a bright, iridescent cloud. From his dark corner Andrey gazed, not without amazement, at this miracle wrought by the light. At that moment the majestic strains of the organ suddenly filled the church and, growing richer and richer, swelled and turned into peals of thunder; then, as suddenly, they were transformed into heavenly music, and their sweet sounds, soaring higher and higher under the arched roof, resembled the thin clear voices of young girls, and finally they changed once more into a deep roar and peals of thunder, and then died away. But for a long time the peals of thunder reverberated through the church, quivering beneath the vaults of the roof, and Andrey, with a gaping mouth, marvelled at the majestic music.

At that moment he felt someone give him a pull by the skirt of his coat. "Come, sir," said the Tartar woman. They crossed

the church, unperceived by a soul, and went out into the square
in front of it. The sky had for some time been red with the dawn;
everything proclaimed the rising sun. The square was completely
deserted; in its centre there were still some little wooden tables
which showed that perhaps a week before there had been a food
market there. The road which in those days was never paved, was
just a heap of dry mud. The square was built round with little
stone and clay houses of one story, with wooden beams and
pillars all the way up their walls and with crossed timber ties, in
the manner in which the inhabitants usually built their houses in
those days, as may still be seen in some parts of Poland and Lith-
uania. All of them had high gables, with large numbers of dormer
windows and flues. On one side of the square, almost next door to
the church, rose a higher building constructed in quite a different
style from the rest, probably the town hall or some government
office. It was of two stories and on top of it was a belvedere,
built in two arches, and a sentry was standing inside it; a huge
clockface was let into the roof.

The square seemed dead, but Andrey thought he heard a faint
moan. Looking more closely, he noticed on the other side of the
square a group of two or three people, lying almost motionless on
the ground. He gazed at them more intently, wondering whether
they were asleep or dead, and at that moment he stumbled over
something lying at his feet. It was the dead body of a woman, apparently a Jewess. She seemed to have been quite young, though
from her contorted and emaciated features it was impossible to
tell her age. Her head was covered by a red silk kerchief; the
lappets over her ears were adorned with two rows of pearls or
beads; two or three long strands of hair, all in curls, fell from
under them on her withered neck with its rigid veins. Beside her
lay a baby, convulsively clutching her wasted breast with its
fingers and twisting it in an access of blind fury, having found no
milk in it. The child did not scream or cry, and it was only from its
faintly rising and falling stomach that it could be seen that it was

not yet dead, or at any rate that it had not yet breathed its last. They turned into the streets and were suddenly stopped by a raving lunatic who, seeing Andrey's precious load, sprang at him like a tiger and caught hold of him, shouting, "Bread!" But his strength was not equal to his frenzy; one push from Andrey and he toppled to the ground. Moved by pity, Andrey flung him a loaf, and he fell upon it like a mad dog, gnawing and biting it, and a moment later he died there in the street in terrible convulsions, no longer able to digest his food. Almost at every step they came across the terrible victims of famine. It seemed as if many of them, unable to bear their tortures within doors, had rushed out on purpose into the street in the vain hope of obtaining some nourishing balm from the air. At the gate of a house sat an old woman and it was impossible to say whether she was alseep or dead or simply lost in thought; at any rate she heard nothing and saw nothing and sat motionless in one and the same place with her head sunk on her breast. A stiffened, wasted body was hanging in a noose from the roof of another house. The poor wretch had not been able to endure the pangs of hunger any more and had preferred to hasten his death by suicide.

At the sight of these gruesome signs of starvation, Andrey could not help asking the Tartar woman, "Couldn't they really find some way of keeping body and soul together? Surely a man in his last extremity ought to eat anything, even what he had been too fastidious to touch before; he should even eat the animals forbidden by law; everything eatable ought to be eaten at such a time."

"Everything has been eaten, sir," replied the Tartar woman. "All the cattle, every horse and dog. You won't even find a mouse in the whole city. You see, sir, we used to get everything here from the villages."

"But how can you go on defending the city when you're dying so horrible a death?"

"The governor, sir, had already made up his mind to surrender the city, but yesterday the colonel in Buzhany sent a hawk into the city with a message not to surrender as he was setting out with his regiment to relieve the city and was only waiting for another colonel so that they might come together. Now they're expected to arrive any minute. . . . But here we are, sir. This is our house."

Andrey had noticed already from a distance a house which was quite different from the other houses and seemed to have been designed by an Italian architect: it was a two-storied house built of fine, thin bricks. The windows of the first floor were set in high, jutting granite cornices; the top story consisted entirely of small arches, forming a gallery; between the arches were tablets with armorial bearings, and at the corners of the house were more tablets. A wide outer staircase of coloured brick descended into the square. At the foot of the staircase were two sentries, one on each side, who picturesquely and symmetrically leant with one hand on a halberd standing beside them and with the other propped up their drooping heads, and in this pose looked more like carved figures than living men. They were neither asleep nor dozing, but they seemed to be utterly unconscious of everything, and did not even notice who went up the steps. At the top of the staircase they came upon a richly attired officer, armed from head to foot, who held a prayer book in his hand. He was about to raise his weary eyes to look at them, but the Tartar woman said something to him and he dropped them again on the open pages of his prayer book. They went into the first room, rather a spacious one, which was either a waiting room or just a vestibule; it was crowded with people sitting in different attitudes round the walls: soldiers, servants, huntsmen, cup-bearers and other members of the retinue regarded as indispensable for a Polish nobleman of high rank, who was both a soldier and a landowner. A candle went out and a wisp of pungent smoke rose with a faint sputter to the ceiling; two other candles were still burning in two enormous candlesticks which stood in the middle of the room, though the morning light had for some time been pouring through the large latticed window. Andrey was about to go straight through a wide oak door decorated with a coat of arms and many other carved ornaments, but the Tartar woman pulled him by the sleeve and pointed to a little door in the side wall. They went through the door into a corridor and then into a room, which he examined closely. The light, coming through a crack in the shutter, fell upon a few things: a crimson curtain, a gilt cornice, and a painting on the wall. The Tartar woman asked him to wait there, opened the door into another room, from which there came the gleam of a candle. He heard a whisper and a soft voice which shook him to the core. Through the open door he caught a glimpse of the graceful figure of a woman with long, beautiful hair which fell on her raised arm. The Tartar woman came back and told him to go in.

He hardly remembered how he went in or how the door closed behind him. Two candles were burning in the room and a little lamp glimmered before a holy image; under it, according to Catholic custom, there stood a high table with steps to kneel on during prayer. But this was not what his eyes were seeking. He turned round and saw a woman who seemed to have become frozen into immobility or turned to stone as she was about to make some quick movement. It seemed as though her whole figure had yearned to rush to meet him and had suddenly stopped dead. And he, too, stood before her in the same startled pose. He had never dreamt that she would look like that; this woman before him had nothing in common with the girl he had known before; there was nothing in her that was even remotely like that girl, but she was twice as beautiful and twice as lovely as she had been before; at that time there was something unfinished, something incomplete about her, but now she was like a work of art to which the artist has given the last finishing touch. That girl was a charming, frivolous creature; this one was a great beauty, a woman in all the perfection of her loveliness. In her raised eyes, he could read real feeling, not fragments or hints of feelings, but feeling in all its depth and amplitude. Tears still glistened in them, and that made them shine with an added brilliance that seemed to go through his heart. The lines of her bosom, neck and shoulders were now perfectly formed; the hair, which before fell in light curls over her face, was now a heavy, luxuriant mass, part of which was done up, while the rest fell over the full length of her arm in long, delicate, beautifully curling strands, and over her bosom. Every one of her features seemed to have been completely transformed. In vain did he try to find in them one of those he had preserved in his memory: there was none. However great her pallor was, it did not dim her exquisite beauty; on the contrary, it endowed it with something overpoweringly impetuous, something irresistibly triumphant. And Andrey was suddenly overcome by a feeling of reverent awe, and stood motionless before her.

The Polish girl, too, seemed to have been greatly struck by the looks of the Cossack, who appeared before her in all the beauty and strength of his youthful manliness, and who by the very immobility of his limbs revealed the ease and freedom of his movements. His eyes flashed with bright resolution; his velvety eyebrows rose in a bold arch; his sunburnt cheeks glowed with all the brilliance of a chaste flame; and his youthful black moustache shone like silk.

"No, there is nothing I can do that would repay you for your generosity, sir," she said, the silvery notes of her voice trembling. "God alone can reward you, not I, a weak woman. . . ."

She dropped her eyes, and her sweet, delicately-hued eyelids, fringed with lashes long as arrows, hid them, and her beautiful face was bowed and a faint flush spread over it.

Andrey did not know what to say to this; he wanted to open up his heart to her, to tell her all he felt for her and with all the passion with which he felt it, but he could not. Something seemed to seal his lips; his words were robbed of sound; he felt that it was not for him who was bred in the Academy and the rough life of the camp, to answer such speeches, and he felt furious with his Cossack nature.

At that moment the Tartar woman came into the room. She had had time to cut the loaf brought by the young Cossack knight into slices, and she brought them on a golden dish which she set before her mistress. The beautiful girl glanced at her and at the bread, and then raised her eyes to Andrey—and oh, how eloquently her eyes spoke! The tender look which showed how helpless, how utterly powerless she was to express the feelings that overwhelmed her was easier for Andrey to understand than words. His heart grew suddenly light; everything within him relaxed, and he felt so buoyant! His feelings, hitherto violently restrained, as though someone was pulling them in by a harsh bridle, were now set free, unrestrained, and he was about to pour them out in a torrent of words. But suddenly the beautiful girl turned to the Tartar woman and asked her anxiously, "What about mother? Have you taken her some food?"

"She's asleep, ma'am."

"And father?"

"I did take him some. He said he'd come himself to thank the knight."

She took the bread and raised it to her lips. With a feeling of intense delight Andrey watched her breaking it with her lovely fingers and eating; but suddenly he remembered the man who, frenzied with hunger, had died before his eyes after swallowing a piece of bread. He turned pale and, seizing her by the arm, cried, "That's enough! Please don't eat any more! You've had nothing to eat for so long that the bread will be poison to you now!" And she dropped her hand, put the bread on the dish and, like an obedient child, looked into his eyes. Oh, if it were possible to convey the meaning of that look in words! But no sculptor's chisel, nor painter's brush, nor the all-powerful word, can express what is sometimes seen in the eyes of a fair maid, nor the feeling of tenderness that overwhelms a man who gazes into them.

"My queen!" cried Andrey, his heart and soul overflowing with emotion. "Tell me what you want and I shall do it! Set me any task, however hazardous or impossible, and I shall fly to perform it! Command me to do what no man can do, and I will do it even if I die in the attempt! Yes, even if I should die, for to die for you—I swear it by the Holy Cross!—would make me so happy that . . . but I can't tell you how happy it would make me, for no words can describe it. I have three farms; half of my father's droves are mine; all that my mother brought my father, what she even conceals from him—all that is mine! No Cossack has such weapons as I have: for the handle of my sabre alone I could get the best droves of horses and three thousand sheep. And I shall renounce it all, I shall give it all up, throw it all away, burn it, drown it all, if you say only one word, or just raise that sweet, black eyebrow of yours! But perhaps I shouldn't be speaking like this to you. I know that I'm talking foolishly and also inopportunely and out of place, that it is not for me who have spent my life at the Kiev Academy and at the Cossack settlement below the Dnieper Falls to talk as men talk who are accustomed to move in the company of kings, princes and the noblest knights in the kingdom. I know all that. . . . And I know you're different from all of us and that all the other noblemen's wives and daughters are far beneath you. We're not even worthy to be your slaves; only the heavenly angels can serve you!"

The sweet maid listened to his frank and sincere words with ever growing amazement; she did not miss a single word of his speech, for in his words, as in a mirror, his young, strong spirit was reflected; and every simple word of that speech, spoken in a voice that came straight from the heart, was invested with great power. Her lovely face bent forward, she tossed back her unruly hair, and gazed at him with parted lips. Then she was about to say something, but suddenly stopped short, for she remembered that the Cossack knight was moved by different considerations, that his father, his brother and all his countrymen stood behind him like relentless avengers; that the Cossacks who were besieging the city were merciless and that all in the city were doomed to a terrible death . . . and her eyes suddenly filled with tears. She quickly snatched up a silk embroidered handkerchief and buried her face in it, and in a trice it was all wet with her tears; and for a long time she sat with her lovely head thrown back, biting her sweet lower lip with her dazzlingly white teeth, as though she had suddenly felt the sting of a poisonous snake; and she did not remove her handkerchief from her face that he might not see her great sorrow.

"Please say something to me! Just one word!" Andrey entreated her, taking her by the hand, which was as smooth as satin. His blood went racing through his veins at this touch, and he pressed the hand that lay lifelessly in his, but she made no reply, remaining motionless and without removing the handkerchief from her face. "Why are you so sad? Tell me, why are you so sad?"

She flung away the handkerchief, tossed back the long hair that kept falling over her eyes, and overwhelmed him with pitiful words, speaking in a soft voice, in a voice that was like the light breeze that, rising on a beautiful evening, suddenly goes rustling through the dense thicket of reeds on the bank of a stream—they murmur and they stir and, all of a sudden, a thousand mournful sounds are heard, and the wayfarer stops to listen to them, overcome by a strange sadness and paying no heed to the glory of the sunset or to the jocund songs of the labourers returning from their work in the cornfields, nor to the distant rumble of some passing cart.

"Tell me, don't you think I deserve to be pitied as long as I live? Don't you think my mother is one of the unhappiest women in the world to have given birth to a luckless creature like me? Think how cruel my destiny has been! How pitiless my fate! The common hangman is not as pitiless as that! The foremost noblemen, the wealthiest gentlemen of the land, men belonging to the most illustrious families of my country, counts and foreign barons—they were all at my feet, and every one of them would have thought himself the happiest man on earth if I had loved him. I had only to lift a finger and the handsomest man of them all, the most accomplished and the noblest, would have been my husband. But my cruel fate has not given my heart to any of them. Not to the fairest and bravest of my country, but to a stranger, to an enemy of my people, does my heart belong! Why, O Blessed Mother of God, do you persecute me so? For what sins, for what terrible crimes do you persecute me so heartlessly, so mercilessly? My whole life has been spent in luxury and riches.. The costliest dishes and the best wines were my daily food and drink. And what was it all for? To what purpose? So that my end should be more cruel than that of the poorest beggar in the kingdom? But it seems that it is not enough that I should be condemned to so horrible an end! It is not enough that before my end I must watch my father and my mother, for whom I'd gladly have suffered a thousand deaths, die in terrible agonies—all this is not enough: it seems that before I die I must experience love such as I have never experienced, and hear words such as I have never heard. It seems that my heart must be torn to pieces by his words, so that my bitter fate should be a hundred times more bitter, so that I should be a hundred times sorrier for myself, so that my death should appear a hundred times more dreadful to me, and so that with my last breath I should reproach you, O cruel fate, and you, too—forgive my transgression!—O Holy Mother of God!"

And when she fell silent a feeling of utter hopelessness was reflected in her face, each feature of which told of gnawing pain, and everything—from her mournfully drooping brow and downcast eyes to the tears which lingered and dried on her flushed cheeks—seemed to say, "There is no happiness on this face!"

"It is unheard of," cried Andrey; "it cannot be; it shall not be that the fairest and the best of women should suffer so bitter a fate when she was born to be adored by all that is best in the whole world. No, no. You shall not die. No, it is not you who will die. I swear to you by my birth and by all that is dear to me in the world —you shall not die! But should it so fall out that neither force, nor prayer, nor courage can turn aside your bitter fate, we will die together, and I will die first, I will die before you, at your lovely feet, and never will they part me from you, never while there's still breath in my body!"

"Do not deceive yourself and me, sir," she said, gently shaking her beautiful head. "I know and, to my great sorrow, I know it too well, that you must not love me. I know where your sacred duty lies: your father, your comrades, your country are calling you. And we are your enemies."

"What do I care for my father, my comrades, and my country?" said Andrey with a toss of his head and drawing himself up to his full height, his erect figure looking like a black poplar beside a stream. "If that is what is worrying you, then let me tell you this: I have no one, no one, no one!" he repeated in that voice and with that gesture with which an impetuous and indomitable Cossack expresses his determination to perform something which no man in the world has ever performed. "Who says that my country is the Ukraine? Who gave it to me for my country? A man's country is what his soul most desires, what is most dear to it. Yes, here is my country! And I shall carry this country of mine in my heart; I shall carry it there while I live—and let any Cossack try to tear it out! I shall sell, give away and destroy everything, everything there is, for such a country!"

Petrified for an instant, she gazed into his eyes like a beautiful statue; then suddenly she burst into tears, and with the glorious impetuosity of which only an extravagantly generous woman created for noble impulses of the heart is capable, she threw herself on his neck, flung her lovely, snow-white arms about him, and broke into sobs. At that moment there came from the street confused cries accompanied by the blowing of trumpets and the beating of drums, but he heard nothing. All he heard was the fragrant breath of her sweet lips on his face; all he saw was the tears that rolled down her cheeks in a flood; and all he felt was the touch of her perfumed hair that fell from her head, entangling him as with dark and glittering silken threads.

At that moment the Tartar woman ran in with a joyful cry. "Saved! Saved!" she cried, beside herself. "Ours have entered the city! They've brought bread, millet, flour and Cossack prisoners!" But neither of them heard who the "ours" were who had entered the city, what they had brought with them, or what Cossacks were taken prisoner. Full of feelings such as it is not given to man to taste on earth, Andrey kissed the fragrant lips that had clung to his cheek, and those fragrant lips did not remain unresponsive; they replied in the same manner, and in that moment of ecstasy when their lips had met and joined in one long, passionate kiss, they experienced what it is given to man to experience only once in a lifetime.

So did the Cossack perish! So was he lost to all the Cossack knighthood! Never will he see the Cossack camp below the Dnieper Falls again, nor his father's farms, nor the church of God. Neither will the Ukraine ever see one of her bravest sons who undertook to defend her! Old Taras will tear the grey hair from his head and curse the day when he begot such a son to his eternal shame and dishonour.

VII

The Cossack camp was in an uproar. At first no one seemed able to explain how the Polish troops had succeeded in entering the city. It was only after some time that it became known that the men of the Pereyaslav detachment, stationed in front of the side gates of the city, had been dead drunk; it was small wonder then that half of them were killed and the other half taken prisoner before they knew what was happening. While the next detachments, awakened by the noise, were snatching up their arms, the Polish troops were already entering the gates and their rear-guard had opened fire upon the sleepy and half-drunken Cossacks who rushed pell-mell after them.

The general gave the order for them all to assemble, and when they had all drawn up in a circle and, taking off their caps, fallen silent, he said:

"So that's what happened last night, my friends. That is what drunkenness has brought us to. That is how the enemy has snapped his fingers at us. It seems it is your way, if given a double portion of vodka, to get so blind drunk that the enemy of Christ's army will not only take the breeches off you, but sneeze in your face, and you won't know anything about it."

The Cossacks stood with bowed heads, realising too well that it was their own fault; only Kubúbenko, commander of the Nezamay-kov detachment, raised his voice in protest.

"Just a moment, sir," he said. "It may not be seemly to protest when the general is addressing the whole army, but if the facts warrant it one must say it. Your reprimand, sir, is not altogether just. The Cossacks would have been guilty, and indeed deserved to die, if they had been drunk on the march or in the field or while engaged on some hard task. But we had nothing at all to do; we were just wasting our time before this city. There was no fast, nor any other Christian reason for abstinence, so is it any wonder, sir, that, being idle, a man should take to drink? There is no sin in that. What we had better do now, sir, is to show them what it means to fall upon people who through no fault of their own are taken by surprise and are unable to defend themselves. Before we beat them hard, but now let us beat them so that there won't be any of them left to run away."

The speech of the detachment commander pleased the Cossacks. They raised their heads, which they had hardly hoped to be able to do, and many nodded approval, saying, "Well said, Kukúbenko! Good old Kukúbenko!" And Taras Bulba, who stood not far from the general, said, "Well, General, it seems that Kukúbenko has spoken the truth! What have you to say to this?"

"What have I to say to this? Why, I say, blessed is the father who begot such a son! It does not require great wisdom to utter a word of reprimand, but it does require a great deal of wisdom to utter a word which, while not offending a man who is in trouble, will cheer him up and raise his spirits, as the spur gives courage to a horse, refreshed by a drink of water. I myself meant to say a word of comfort to you afterwards, but Kukúbenko forestalled me."

"Well said, General! Good old General!" A murmur passed through the ranks of the Cossacks. "Aye, aye," others caught up the cry, "he spoke well!" And the oldest of them all, who stood there like grey-headed pigeons, nodded and, twitching their grey moustaches, muttered softly, "A well-spoken word!"

"Now listen, friends; listen carefully," said the general. "To take a fortress by storm, to scale walls, and to tunnel under them as foreign engineers from Germany do, is—the devil take it!—neither decent nor worthy of a Cossack. But to judge by what has happened, the enemy has certainly not entered the city with large stores of provisions; they do not seem to have had many carts with them. Now the people in the city are very hungry and it is ten to one that they will eat everything up at once, and there's the hay for the horses. . . . Well, I don't know, maybe one of their saints will drop it to them from heaven, though I doubt it, somehow, for all their priests are good at words, not miracles. Anyway, for one reason or another, they're quite sure to come out of the city. You will therefore divide your forces into three parts, each occupying the three roads before the three gates. Before the main gates five detachments, before each of the other gates three detachments. The Dyadykév and the Korsun detachments into ambush! The Tytarev and the Timoshev detachments in reserve on the right flank, and the Shcherbínov and the Styeblikív detachments on the left flank! And those of you who have sharp tongues in your heads step out of the ranks to taunt the enemy. The Poles are a feather-brained lot and they can't stand abuse, so that they may even come out of the gates this very day. Detachment commanders! Each of you carry out a careful inspection of your detachment! If you are short of men, fill up your ranks from what remains of the Pereya-slav detachment. Check everything again! Every Cossack to be given a cupful of vodka and a loaf of bread to take off the effects of last night's debauch, though I expect all of them had enough yesterday to last them for some time, for to be quite frank you've all gorged yourselves so much that I'm surprised no one burst from overeating in the night. And one last warning: if any Jewish inn-keeper sells a Cossack even one tankard of weak vodka I'll nail a sow's ear to the dog's forehead and hang him up by the legs! Now to work, men, to work!"

Such were the orders given by the general, and all the Cossacks bowed low to him and went bareheaded to their carts and encamp-ments, and it was only when they were a long way off that they put on their caps. All began getting ready for battle. They tested their sabres and broadswords, filled their powder flasks with gunpowder from sacks, rolled the carts back and put them in position, and picked out their horses.

On his way back to his regiment Taras could not help wondering what had become of Andrey: was he bound while asleep and taken prisoner with the rest? That seemed hardly likely, for An-drey was not one of those who would let himself be taken alive. But he was not to be found among the slain Cossacks, either. Sunk in thought, Taras was walking in front of his regiment, which was waiting to be led into ambush, and he did not hear that someone had been calling him by name for some time.

"Who wants me?" he said at last, coming to himself.

The Jew Yankel stood before him.

"Sir, sir!" the Jew was saying in a hurried voice, as though he had a matter of the utmost importance to impart to him. "I've been in the city, sir!"

Taras looked at the Jew and wondered how he had managed to get into the city.

"How the devil did you get there?" he asked.

"I'll tell you at once, sir," said Yankel. "As soon as I heard the uproar at dawn and the Cossacks began firing, I seized my coat and ran there without putting it on, getting my arms in my sleeves on the way, for I wanted to find out as quickly as I possibly could what was the reason for the uproar and why the Cossacks should be firing at daybreak. I reached the gates just when the last Polish troops were entering the city. And who do you think, sir, did I see riding in front of a detachment of horse? Why, standard-bearer Galyandóvich, an old acquaintance of mine: he has owed me a hundred gold pieces for the last three years. I went after him as though intending to get my money back and entered the city together with them."

"You mean you entered the city and wanted to get your money back as well?" asked Bulba. "Didn't he have you hanged on the spot like a dog?"

"Well, sir," replied the Jew, "it is quite true he wanted to hang me, and his servants had already got hold of me and were about to put the rope round my neck, but I implored the Polish gentleman to spare my life, telling him that I didn't mind waiting for the money he owed me as long as he liked and promising to lend him more if he'd help me to collect my debts from the other gentlemen. For you see, sir, standard-bearer Galyandóvich never has a single gold piece in his pocket, though he has farms and estates and four castles and steppeland right up to Shklov; but like a Cossack he has no money at all, not a penny. And even now he would have had nothing to go to the war in if the Breslau Jews had not equipped him. He did not attend the last meeting of the Seym because . . ."

"What did you do in the city? Seen any of us?"

"Of us, sir? Why, of course, I saw lots of us: Isaac, Rakhum, Samuel, Khayvalokh, the Jewish contractor . . ."

"Confound them, the rascals!" Taras exclaimed, flying into a rage. "What are you thrusting those scurvy knaves of your kindred into my face for? I'm asking you about our Dnieper Cossacks."

"No, sir, I didn't see our Dnieper Cossacks. I only saw your son Andrey, sir."

"You saw Andrey?" cried Bulba. "Well, where did you see him? In a dungeon? A pit? Dishonoured? Bound?"

"Good gracious, sir, who would dare to bind such a fine gentleman as Andrey? Oh, he's such a great knight, sir! Upon my soul, I hardly recognised him. Wears gold shoulder-pieces, and his armguards are of gold, too, and his cuirass is of gold, and his helmet is of gold, and there's gold on his belt—everything he wears is of gold, sir; there's gold everywhere. Just like the sun in the spring, sir, when every little bird chirps and sings in the garden and every wild flower smells sweet, so he is all shining in gold! And the governor, sir, has given him one of the best horses to ride: I should think the horse alone must have cost two hundred gold pieces."

Bulba was dumbfounded. "Why has he put on someone else's accoutrements?"

"Why, sir? Because it is better! He rides about, and the others ride about; he's intructing them, and they're instructing him. Like the richest Polish gentleman, sir!"

"But who has forced him to do it?"

"Forced him to do it, sir? I never said that anyone had forced him. Don't you know, sir, that he's gone over to them of his own free will?"

"Who's gone over?"

"Why, your son Andrey, sir."

"Gone over? Where?"

"Gone over to their side, sir. To the Poles. He's one of them now."

"You're lying, you scoundrel!"

"Why should I be lying, sir? Am I such a fool as to tell you a lie?

Don't I know that a Jew will be hanged like a dog if he tells a lie to a gentleman?"

"So according to you he has sold his country and his faith, has he?"

"I never said he had sold anything, sir. I only said he had gone over to them."

"You lie, you damned Jew! Such a thing has never happened in a Christian country! You must be mistaken, you cur!"

"May the grass grow on the threshold of my house, sir, if I'm lying. May everyone spit on the tomb of my father, and my mother, and my father-in-law, and my father's father, and my mother's father, if I am mistaken. If you wish, sir, I can even tell you why he went over to them."

"Why?"

"Because the governor of the city, sir, has a beautiful daughter. My goodness, what a beauty! What a beauty!" Here the Jew tried his best to show how beautiful the governor's daughter was by spreading out his arms, screwing up his eyes, and twisting his mouth, as though tasting some titbit.

"Well, what's that got to do with it?"

"Why, sir, it is for her sake that he's done it all. You see, sir, if a man falls in love he's like the sole of a shoe that's been soaked in water: you can bend it any way you like."

Bulba pondered deeply. He remembered how great is the power of a weak woman, how many strong men she has ruined, and how highly susceptible Andrey's nature was where women were concerned, and he stood there rooted to the ground for a long time.

"Listen, sir, I'll tell you everything," said the Jew. "As soon as I heard the uproar and saw the Polish troops going through the gates of the city, I snatched up a string of pearls, just in case . . . For you see, sir, there are many noble and beautiful ladies in the city, and I said to myself, 'They're sure to want to buy pearls even if they have nothing to eat.' So when the standard-bearer's servants let me go, I ran to the governor's courtyard to sell the pearls. I found everything out from their Tartar maid. 'There'll be a wedding soon,' she said. 'As soon as they drive off the Cossacks.' Your son Andrey, sir, seems to have promised them to drive off the Cossacks."

"And didn't you kill him on the spot, the damned traitor?"

"Why should I have killed him? He's gone over of his own free will, hasn't he, sir? How can you blame him? He's better off there, so he's gone over there!"

"And you saw him face to face?"

"Why, of course I did, sir. Face to face! What a splendid soldier he is, sir! The most splendid soldier of them all! Bless my soul, he recognised me at once, and when I went up to him he said to me . . ."

"What did he say?"

"He said . . . But as a matter of fact, sir, he first of all beckoned to me with his finger and then he said, 'Yankel,' he said, and I said, 'Sir,' I said. 'Yankel,' he said, 'tell my father, tell my brother, tell the Cossacks, tell 'em all, that my father is no father to me, my brother no brother, and my comrades no comrades, and that I will fight them all, I will fight with all of them!' "

"You're lying, you damned Judas!" Taras shouted, losing control of himself. "You're lying, you cur! Didn't you crucify Christ, too, you man accursed of God? I'll kill you, you Satan, you! Run, run as fast as you can, or I'll kill you on the spot!"

With these words Taras drew his sabre, and the terrified Jew took to his heels and ran as fast as his thin, spare legs would carry him. He ran for a long time without looking back through the Cossack camp and for miles over the open plain, though Taras never thought of pursuing him, reflecting that it was unfair to vent his anger on the first man who happened to cross his path.

He now remembered that on the previous night he had seen Andrey walking through the camp with some woman, and he bowed his grey head; but he still refused to believe that such a disgraceful thing could have happened to him and that his own son should have sold his faith and soul.

At last he led his regiment into ambush and disappeared with it behind a wood, the only wood that had not been burnt by the Cossacks. Meanwhile the Dnieper Cossacks, foot and horse, were taking up their positions across the three roads before the three gates. One after another the different detachments marched by: the Uman, the Popovich, the Kanev, the Styeblikiv, the Nezamáy-kov, the Gurguziv, the Týtarev and the Timoshev. The Pereyaslav detachment alone was missing: its Cossacks had drunk deep and drunk away their lives and freedom. Some of them awoke bound in the hands of their enemies; some of them without waking passed in their sleep into the damp earth; and Khlib, their commander, found himself in the Polish camp without his breeches and his coat of mail.

The movement of the Cossack troops was heard in the city. Everybody hastened to the rampart, and the Cossacks beheld a picturesque scene: the Polish knights, one more handsome than the other, stood on the rampart. Their copper helmets shone like suns, plumed with feathers white as swans. Others wore light blue and pink caps, with the tops bent on one side. Their doublets had wide, loose-hanging sleeves and were embroidered with gold or adorned with rows upon rows of little cords. Some wore swords and weapons in sumptuous settings, which must have cost the Polish gentlemen a great deal of money, and there were many more accoutrements of all sorts. Foremost stood the Buzhany colonel, looking haughtily about him, in his red cap trimmed with gold. The colonel was a corpulent man, taller and stouter than any other Polish officer, and his wide, costly coat barely met round him. On the other side of the rampart, almost at the side gates, stood the other colonel, a small, dried-up man; but his keen little eyes looked out sharply from under his beetling eyebrows, and he turned quickly in all directions, pointing smartly with his thin, sinewy hand and giving orders; it was plain that, in spite of his frail body, he was well versed in the art of war. Not far from him stood the standard-bearer, a tall, lanky man with a thick moustache, and his face did not seem to lack colour: the Polish gentleman, it was evident, dearly loved strong mead and a merry feast. And behind them were hundreds of Polish nobles of every description, some of them equipped at their own expense, others at the expense of the king's treasury, others again on money borrowed from the Jews, having pledged all that was left in their ancestral castles. There were also quite a few senatorial darlings there, men who, invited to banquets because their illustrious names shed a certain lustre upon their hosts, did not hesitate to help themselves to silver goblets from the tables and sideboards, and who, after being thus honoured one day, found themselves sitting on the box of some grandee's carriage the next in the humble role of his lordship's coachman. There were all sorts and conditions of men there. Some of them could not afford a drink, but they had all put on their best attire for the war.

The Cossack ranks stood quietly before the walls. There was no gold on any of them; only here and there did it gleam on the hilt of a sabre or the mountings of a musket. The Cossacks did not like to dress up in costly coats for battle: they wore plain coats of mail and long garments of plain cloth, and their black, red-topped sheep-skin caps stretched for miles over the plain.

Two men rode out in front of the ranks of the Dnieper Cossacks. One quite young, the other older; both were renowned for their rich vocabulary of taunts, and both not such bad Cossacks in action, either. Okhrim Nash and Mikita Golokopýtenko were their names. After them rode out Nemid Popovich, a thick-set Cos-sack, who had been in and out of the *Syech* for many years. He had been at the siege of Adrianople, and had suffered many hardships in his day; was nearly burnt alive and escaped to the *Syech* with his head singed and his moustache burnt off. But Popovich had put on fat, grown a new tuft of hair on top of his shaven head of so prodigious a length that it went round his ear, grown large and bushy moustaches, black as pitch—and a biting, caustic tongue had Popovich.

"Look at their red coats," he cried. "They look fine in them, don't they? The whole damned army in red coats! But what I'd like to know is whether there's any red blood under those red coats of theirs!"

"I'll show you!" the stout colonel shouted from above. "I'll have you all trussed up! Hand over your horses and your muskets, you villains! Have you seen how I've trussed up those friends of yours? Bring the Cossacks out on the rampart! Let them have a look at their friends!"

And they led the captured Cossacks out on the rampart, with their hands tied tightly behind their back. Ahead of all walked detachment commander Khlib, without his breeches and coat of mail, just as they had captured him drunk. The Cossack commander hung his head, ashamed of his nakedness before his comrades and even more ashamed of having allowed himself to be caught in his sleep, like a dog. His head had turned grey in a single night.

"Don't worry, Khlib! We'll get you out of this!" the Cossacks shouted to him from below. "It isn't your fault they took you naked; accidents will happen to anyone. It is they who ought to be ashamed of themselves for having brought you out without decently covering up your nakedness, to humiliate you!"

"Seems to me you're a brave enough army when it comes to fighting men who're asleep," Golokopýtenko said, looking up at the rampart.

"You wait, we'll shave off your long locks!" the Poles shouted from above.

"I'd like to see you shave off our long locks!" said Popovich, turning round on his horse to show them the long tuft of hair behind his ear, and then, glancing at his own comrades, he said, "Who knows? Maybe these damned Poles are right; if that big-bellied one brings them out, they won't have anything to worry about!"

"Why won't they have anything to worry about?" asked the

Cossacks, knowing that Popovich had some scathing answer on the tip of his tongue.

"Why, because their whole damned army can hide behind that belly of his and you'll never be able to reach any of them with a spear!"

All the Cossacks burst out laughing, and long afterwards many of them kept shaking their heads and saying, "What a fellow that Popovich is, to be sure! Only let him start poking fun at a man and well . . ." But what they meant by "well" the Cossacks did not say.

"Fall back from the walls! Quick!" the general shouted, for the Poles seemed to have been cut to the quick by Popovich's last sally, and the colonel waved his hand.

No sooner had the Cossacks moved aside than there came a volley of grapeshot from the rampart. A commotion arose on the wall. The grey-haired governor himself appeared on his horse. The gates were opened and the Polish army marched out. In front, in straight lines, rode the hussars in their embroidered coats, behind them came men in coats of mail, then cuirassiers with lances, then soldiers in copper helmets, then the Polish nobles, each accoutred in his own fashion and each riding apart from the rest. The proud gentlemen did not wish to mingle with the others in the ranks, and those of them who were not in command of the regular troops rode apart with their retinues of servants. After the nobles came more lines of soldiers, followed by the standard-bearer; then still more lines of soldiers, followed by the stout colonel; and in the rear of the whole army rode the short colonel.

"Attack them! Attack them at once! Don't let them form into ranks!" the general shouted. "All detachments press upon them at once! Leave all the other gates! Týtarev detachment attack on the flank! Dyadikiv detachment attack on the other flank! Kukúbenko and Palývoda attack them in the rear! Harass them, harass them! Keep them apart!"

And the Cossacks attacked on all sides, broke up their lines and threw them into confusion and were themselves thrown into confusion. They did not give the enemy time to fire; the battle developed into a fight of sword against sword and lance against lance. Their ranks got all mixed up, and every man had a chance to show his mettle.

Demid Popovich speared three common soldiers and unseated two of the finest Polish nobles, saying, "Oh, what lovely horses! I've wanted such horses for myself a long time!" And he drove the horses far out into the plain, shouting to the Cossacks who were standing there to catch them. Then he forced his way again into the thick of the fray, once more attacked the two Polish nobles he had thrown from their horses, killed one and threw his lasso round the neck of the other, fastened the rope to the saddle and dragged him across the whole plain, having first taken off his sword with its costly handle and untied from his belt a purse full of gold pieces.

Kobíta, a stout Cossack and quite a young man still, engaged in combat with one of the bravest warriors of the Polish army. They fought a long time. Both were unseated and both went on fighting on foot, hand to hand, and the Cossack was almost on the point of winning, having knocked his enemy down and driven a sharp Turkish dagger into his chest, but he did not escape himself: he fell on top of his dead enemy, struck on the temple by a hot bullet. The man who killed him was one of the most illustrious of Polish knights, the handsomest gentleman of them all, the scion of an ancient princely family. Like a slender poplar, he dashed along on his dun-coloured steed. And many acts of great bravery had he accomplished already. Two Cossacks had he cut in pieces; he had thrown Fyodor Korzh, a gallant Cossack, to the ground, together with his horse, fired at the horse and killed the Cossack with his lance from behind the horse; many a head and many an arm had he severed; and now it was the turn of Kobíta, whom he felled with a bullet in the head.

"That's the man I'd be glad to try my strength with!" shouted

Kukúbenko, commander of the Nezamaykov detachment.

Spurring on his horse, he fell straight upon him from the rear with so loud and piercing a whoop that all who were near shuddered at the unnatural sound. The Pole wanted to turn his horse around and meet his enemy face to face, but the horse refused to obey. Frightened by the terrible shout, it shied to one side, and Kukúbenko hit the Pole with a bullet from his musket. The hot bullet struck him between the shoulder blades, and he fell from his horse. But even then the Pole would not yield, and he tried to deal a blow at his foe with his sword, but hand and sword sank powerlessly to the ground. Taking his heavy broadsword in both his hands, Kukúbenko drove it straight into his pale lips. The sword knocked out two teeth, white as sugar, cleft the tongue in twain, smashed the neck-bone and penetrated deep into the earth: so he pinned him there to the damp earth forever. The noble blood welled out of his body, deep-red as the guelder-rose over the bank of the stream, staining his gold-embroidered coat all red. Kukúbenko left him at once, rushing into the midst of another large enemy force with his Nezamaykov Cossacks.

"Fancy leaving such rich trappings!" said Borodáty, commander of the Uman detachment, and he left his followers and rode up to the place where the Polish nobleman slain by Kukúbenko lay. "I've killed seven Polish squires with my own hand, but such trappings I have not yet seen on any!"

And overcome by greed, Borodáty bent down to take the costly armour off the dead man. Already he had taken off a Turkish dagger set with precious stones, untied a purse of gold pieces from the belt, taken off his chest a knapsack containing fine linen, costly silver and a maid's curl, carefully treasured in remembrance. Borodáty did not hear the red-nosed standard-bearer, whom he had once thrown from the saddle and given him a good knock for luck, rush at him full tilt from the rear. The standard-bearer swung his sword and smote the stooping Cossack across the back of the neck. The Cossack's greed had been his undoing: the mighty head flew off and the headless body fell to the ground, bedewing the earth with blood far and wide. The Cossack's stern soul flew up into the high heavens, frowning and indignant and also marvelling that it had so soon flown from so mighty a body. The standard-bearer had scarcely time to seize the commander's head by its long forelock to tie it to his saddle before a grim avenger was upon him.

As a hawk, soaring in the sky and circling round and round on powerful wings, suddenly hovers motionless in the air over one spot and then drops like an arrow upon the quail calling for its mate at the edge of some country road, so did Ostap, Taras Bulba's son, suddenly swoop down on the standard-bearer and fling a noose about his neck. The standard-bearer's red face grew purple as the cruel rope tightened about his throat. He grasped his pistol, but his hand clawed the air convulsively, and the shot went wide of the mark. Swiftly Ostap untied from the standard-bearer's saddle the silken cord, which the Pole carried for binding prisoners, bound him hand and foot with his own cord, fastened one end of it to the saddle and dragged him across the plain, calling to the Cossacks of the Uman detachment in a loud voice to come and pay their last honours to their slain commander.

When the men of the Uman detachment heard that their commander Borodáty was dead, they left the battlefield and hurried to take up his body, and they began discussing there and then whom they should choose to succeed him. At last they said, "Why discuss it at all? We could not find a better commander than Ostap Bulba. It's true he's younger than any of us, but he has the understanding of an old man."

Taking off his cap, Ostap thanked all his Cossack comrades for the honour done him. He did not plead either his youth or his inexperience, knowing that in war-time there were more important

things to think of, but at once led them against a large force of the
enemy and showed them that they had not done amiss in choosing
him for their commander.

The Poles soon realised that things were getting too hot for
them and they retreated, racing across the plain to rally at the
other end of it. The short colonel waved to the four companies of
fresh troops, each a hundred strong, who were standing apart at
the very gates of the city, and a volley of grapeshot was immediately fired from there at the Cossacks; the bullets struck the Cossack
oxen that were staring wildly at the battle. The panic-stricken
oxen bellowed and raced off towards the Cossack encampments,
smashing the carts and trampling many underfoot. But Taras, who
rushed out of the ambush with his regiment at that very moment,
galloped off with a loud shout to head them off. The whole mad-
dened herd, frightened by his shout, turned back and stampeded
the Polish regiments, scattering the cavalry and trampling and dispersing them all.

"Oh, thank you, thank you, oxen!" the Dnieper Cossacks
shouted. "In the past you've served us faithfully on the march, and
now you've done your bit of active service, too!" And they attacked
the enemy with renewed force. Many enemies did they slay in
that attack and many Cossacks showed their mettle: Metélitza,
Shilo, the two Pisarénkos, Vovtúzenko and not a few others.
The Poles saw that things were going badly with them, so they
raised a banner and began shouting for the city gates to be opened.
The iron-studded gates opened with a creak, and, like sheep
returning to their fold, the spent and dust-covered horsemen
crowded through the gates. Many Cossacks wanted to pursue
them, but Ostap stopped his Uman men, saying, "Keep back!
Keep back, friends! Don't go too close to the gates!" And he was
right, for they opened up a murderous fire on the Cossacks from
the walls with everything they could lay their hands on, and
many were struck. At that moment the general rode up and com-
manded Ostap, saying, "Here's a new commander, but he leads

his troops like an old one!" Old Bulba turned around to have a look who the new commander might be, and he saw Ostap on his horse at the head of the Uman detachment, with his cap tilted rakishly on one side and the commander's staff in his hand. "Well, I'll be damned!" the old man said, looking at Ostap, and he was overjoyed and he thanked the men of the Uman detachment for the honour shown his son.

The Cossacks withdrew once more, in readiness to go back to their encampments, while the Poles appeared on the city ramparts again, this time in tattered cloaks. Many costly coats were stained with gore, and the fine copper helmets were thick with dust.

"Well, did you bind us?" the Dnieper Cossacks shouted to them from below.

"See this?" the fat colonel shouted from above, showing them a rope. "I've got it all ready for you!" and the dusty, exhausted warriors went on uttering threats, and the more defiant on both sides hurled taunts at one another.

At last all dispersed. Some went to rest, worn out with the fighting; others were scattering some earth on their wounds and tearing into bandages kerchiefs and costly garments taken from the slain enemy; and those who were not so tired went to collect their dead and pay them the last honours: they dug graves with their broadswords and spears, scooped the earth out with their caps and the skirts of their coats, laid out the Cossack bodies honourably and covered them up with fresh earth, so that no crow or eagle or other bird of prey might claw out their eyes. But the bodies of the Poles, gathered anyhow in bundles of ten or more, they bound to the tails of wild horses and, setting them loose on the plain, they kept chasing them for hours, lashing them across the flanks with their whips. The frenzied horses galloped over fields and hillocks, across ditches and streams, and the dead bodies of the Poles were battered against the earth, covered with blood and dust.

Then all the Cossack detachments sat down in rings to supper, and for hours they went on recounting the share each of them had taken in the day's battle and the acts of heroism that had fallen to the lot of each, a tale to be told and retold a hundred times to strangers and posterity. They did not lie down to sleep for a long time, but old Taras was awake longer, for he was wondering all the time why Andrey had not been seen among the enemy. Had the Judas been ashamed to take up arms against his own comrades, or had the Jew deceived him and had Andrey simply been taken prisoner by the enemy? But then he recalled that Andrey's heart had always been exceedingly susceptible to women's speeches, and he was overcome with grief and vowed vengeance against the Polish girl who had bewitched his son. And he would have carried out his vow. He would have paid no heed to her beauty; he would have dragged her out by her thick, luxuriant hair; he would have pulled her along all over the plain among the Cossacks. Her lovely breasts and shoulders, gleaming like the never-melting snow on the summits of high mountains, would have been crushed on the earth and covered with blood and dust. He would have torn to pieces her lovely, sweet body. But Bulba knew not what God had in store for man on the morrow, and slumber began to assert his sway over him, and at last he fell asleep. But the Cossacks still talked among themselves, and all through the night the sentries, wide awake and sober, stood watch by the campfires, peering keenly in all directions.

✦ V I I I

The sun had not yet travelled half across the sky when all the Dnieper Cossacks gathered in circles. News had come that in the absence of the Cossacks the Tartars had plundered everything in the *Syech,* dug up the treasures the Cossacks had secretly buried in the earth, slain or taken prisoner all who were left behind, and with all the captured herds of cattle and droves of horses set off straight for Perekop. Only one Cossack, Maxim Golodúkha, had succeeded in escaping from the Tartars on the way. He had stabbed the *Mirza,* taken off his bag of sequins and ridden away from his pursuers on a Tartar horse and in Tartar dress for a day and a half and two full nights. He had ridden the horse to death, mounted another on the road, ridden that one to death, too, and arrived at the Cossack camp on a third, having learnt on the way that the Cossacks were laying sieze to Dunbo. He could only tell them the bare facts of the disaster, but how it had happened—whether the Cossacks had drunk too deep according to their custom and had let themselves be carried off into captivity while drunk, or how the Tartars had found out where the army treasury had been buried—of that he could say nothing. The Cossack was too worn out, he was all swollen, his face scorched by the sun and weather-beaten; he sank down and immediately fell fast asleep.

In such a case it was the accepted rule among the Dnieper Cossacks to set off at once in pursuit of the raiders, with the idea of overtaking them on the road; for otherwise the prisoners might find themselves in the bazaars of Asia Minor, Smyrna, or the island of Crete, and indeed no one could tell in what places their Cossack heads with the long tufts of hair might not be seen. This was why the Cossacks had assembled. They all had their caps on, for they had not come to receive the orders of their officers, but to consult together as equals.

"Let the old men speak first! We want to hear their advice!" some shouted.

"The general! Let the general speak! We want to hear his advice!" others shouted.

The general took off his cap and thanked all the Cossacks for the honour, not as their commanding officer, but as their comrade.

"There are many among us," he said, "who are old and wise in counsel, but since you've done me the honour, my advice is not to lose time, friends, but to go in pursuit of the Tartars. For you all know what a Tartar is: he will not wait for us to overtake him with his plunder, but will dispose of it instantly, and we shall never be able to recover it. So my advice is: let's go! We've had good sport here. The Poles now know what the Cossacks are. We have avenged our faith as much as we could, and there's precious little gain to be had from a starving city. So my advice is: let's go!"

"Let's go! Let's go!" loud cries were raised in the different Cossack detachments.

Bulba did not relish these words and he lowered still more over his eyes his grizzled, beetling eyebrows, like bushes growing on the high crest of a mountain and thickly sprinkled with the sharp northern frost.

"No, General, your counsel is not right," he said. "You are wrong. You seem to have forgotten that we are leaving our men in the hands of the Poles. You would, it seems, have us dishonour the first sacred duty of comradeship and leave our comrades behind to be flayed alive or to be quartered and their dismembered bodies put up for show in every city and village, for that was what happened to the hetman and to the best soldiers in the Ukraine. Have they not done enough mischief? Have they not desecrated and dishonoured all that we hold sacred? What kind of people are we, I ask you. What kind of a Cossack is he who abandons his comrade in dire need, abandons him like a dog, to perish in an alien land? If it has come to this that there is not one among us who cares for Cossack honour any more, if it has come to this, that you don't mind if people spit in your faces and call you all manner of names, then I do and no one shall treat me like that. I will stay here alone."

Bulba's words made a deep impression on the assembled Cossacks, who visibly wavered.

"But have you forgotten, brave and gallant colonel," said the general, "that our comrades are prisoners in the hands of the Tartars also? That if we do not come to their rescue now they'll be sold into lifelong slavery among the heathens, which is much worse than the most cruel death? Have you forgotten that they have now all our treasure, won by Christian blood?"

The Cossacks pondered deep and did not know what to say. Not one of them was anxious to earn a bad name for himself. Then Kassyan Bovdyúg, the oldest man in the Cossack army, stepped forward. He was held in great honour by all the Cossacks. Twice he had been elected general, and he had also acquitted himself well on the battlefield, but for many years now he had been too old to take part in any campaign, or give advice to anybody. What the old soldier liked best was lying on his side in a Cossack ring and listening to the tales of adventure and Cossack campaigns. He never took part in their talk, but just listened, pressing down with his finger the ash in his short pipe which he hardly ever removed from his mouth. He would sit there for hours, his eyes screwed up a little, and the Cossacks found it hard to say whether he was asleep or still listening. He had stayed at home during all the recent campaigns, but this time the old man for some reason could not bear being left behind. With a wave of his hand, after the manner of the Cossacks, he had said. "Oh, well, I suppose I'd better be coming along, too. Who knows, maybe I shall be of some use to the Cossacks yet!"

All the Cossacks fell silent when he stepped forth before the assembly, for it was long since they had heard him speak. Every one wanted to know what Bovdyúg would say.

"It is now my turn to say a word to you, friends," he began. "Listen to an old man, children. Our general has spoken wisely, and, as the head of the Cossack army, he is in duty bound to look after it and to take care of the army treasury, and he could not therefore have spoken more wisely. Ay, that's the first thing I should like to say to you. And now listen to what I have to say next. What I have to say is that Colonal Taras (God grant him long years and may there be many more colonels like him in the Ukraine!) has also spoken the truth. The first duty and obligation of a Cossack is to observe the rules of comradeship. In all my long life I have never heard of a Cossack who has at any time or in any way deserted or betrayed a comrade. They are all our comrades, whether there are more or less of them with the Poles or the Tartars makes no difference. They are all our comrades and they are all dear to us. So this is what I'd like to say to you: those of you who have at heart the fate of our comrades taken prisoner by the Tartars, go after the Tartars, and those who have at heart the fate of the prisoners seized by the Poles, remain here. The general, as indeed is his duty, will go with half of the army in pursuit of the Tartars, while the other half will choose its commander here, and no man, if you do not mind taking the advice of an old man whose head has turned white, is more worthy of being in command of the remaining Cossack forces than Taras Bulba. There is no man among us who is his equal in valour."

So spoke Bovdyúg and fell silent; and all the Cossacks were glad that the old man had in this way showed them what they had to do. They threw their caps in the air and shouted, "Thank you, thank you, sir! For years you were silent, and now you have spoken at last. You said you would be useful to the Cossacks, and you were right!"

"Well, are you agreed to do this?" asked the general.

"Agreed! Agreed!" shouted the Cossacks.

"Is the assembly at an end then?"

"Yes, the assembly's at an end!"

"Then listen to my orders now, friends," said the general, stepping forward and putting on his cap, while all the Cossacks to a man took off their caps and stood bareheaded and with downcast eyes, as was the custom among the Cossacks whenever a commanding officer addressed them. "Now, friends, you must separate. Those who want to go, line up on the right, and those who want to remain, on the left; where the greater part of a detachment goes, there goes also their commander, and the men left over from a detachment will join other detachments."

And they all began crossing over, some to the right and some to the left. Whichever side the majority of a detachment joined, there its commander went also; and if only a small part of a detachment went over to one side or the other, it joined forces with another detachment; and the forces on either side were more or less equal in strength. Among those who decided to remain were almost the whole of the Nezamáykov detachment, the larger part of the Popóvich detachment, the entire Uman detachment, the entire Kanev detachment, the greater part of the Steblikív detachment, and the greater part of the Timoshev detachment. All the others volunteered to go in pursuit of the Tartars. There were many brave and stalwart Cossacks on both sides. Among those who decided to go after the Tartars was Chereváty, the good old Cossack Pokotípolye, Lemish, Khoma Prokopóvich; Demid Popóvich also joined them, for he was a Cossack of an incorrigible character who hated to stay too long in one place: he had already tried his strength with the Poles and now he wanted to try his strength with the Tartars. The detachment commanders of that force included Nostyugán, Pókrysha, Nevylýchky, and many other brave and renowned Cossacks wished to measure swords with the Tartars. There were not a few splendid fighters among the Cossacks who chose to remain: the detachment commanders Demitróvich, Kukúbenko, Vertýkhvist, Balabán and Ostap Bulba. There were many other famous and stalwart Cossacks, too: Vovtúzenko, Cherevichénko, Stepan Guska, Mikola Goostý, Zadorózhny, Metélitza, Ivan Zakrutýguba, Mossy Shilo, Degtyarénko, Sidorénko, Pisarénko, as well as Pisarénko the Second and Pisarénko the Third, and many other good Cossacks. All were men of great experience who had taken part in many campaigns. They had marched on the shores of Anatolia; on the salt marshes and the steppes of the Crimea; along the rivers, great and small, which fall into the Dnieper; along all the inlets, bays and islands of the Dnieper. They had been in Moldavia, Wallachia, and Turkey. They had sailed all over the Black Sea in their double-ruddered Cossack canoes; in fifty such canoes all in a row they had attacked the tallest and the richest ships. Many a Turkish galley had they sent to the bottom of the sea, and they had fired much powder in their day. Many a time had they torn up expensive brocades and rich velvets to wrap round their feet and legs. Many a time had they stuffed the purses fastened to a cord round their waists with sequins of the purest gold. And incalcuable is the wealth each of them has squandered on drink and revelry, as much as could have lasted another man a lifetime. They had spent it all in true Cossack fashion, treating everybody and hiring musicians that everybody in the world might be merry. Even now it was rare to come across any of them who had not some treasure buried somewhere: beakers, silver pitchers and bracelets, under the reeds on the Dnieper islands, that the Tartar might not find them, if by some lucky chance he should succeed in launching a surprise attack on the *Syech*. But the Tartar might have found it hard to discover it, anyway, for the owner himself was no longer sure where he had buried it. Such were the Cossacks who decided to remain and take vengeance on the Poles for their faithful comrades and the Christian faith! The old Cossack Bovdyúg also decided to remain. "I'm too old now to run after the Tartars," he said. "Long have I prayed to God that, when my time comes, I may end my life in a war for a holy and Christian cause. And so it has come to pass. There could be no more glorious end anywhere for an old Cossack."

When they had all separated and stood drawn up in two lines facing each other, the general passed between them and said:

"Well, dear friends, is one side satisfied with the other?"

"We're all satisfied, sir," replied the Cossacks.

"Well, then, embrace and take leave of one another, for God knows if we shall ever meet again in this life. Obey your commander and do what you know yourselves to be best: for you know very well what Cossack honour bids you."

And all the Cossacks, large as their numbers were, kissed one another. The first to bid farewell were the two commanders.

After stroking their grey moustaches, they kissed each other on each cheek, then, clasping hands and gripping them firmly, each wanted to ask the other, "Well, friend, shall we see one another again?" but they said nothing, they were silent, the two grey-haired soldiers sank into thought. All the Cossacks said a last farewell to one another, well knowing that there was much work in store for both forces. They decided not to separate until darkness hid from the enemy the reduction in the numbers of the besieging army. Then they went off to dinner in their separate detachments.

After dinner all those who had the journey before them lay down to rest, and they slept well and soundly, as though feeling that it might be the last time they would enjoy undisturbed sleep. They slept till sunset, and when the sun had gone down and dusk had fallen they began tarring their carts. Having got everything ready, they let their carts go on ahead and, after taking leave of their comrades once again, they set off quietly after their carts, the cavalry sedately, with never a shout or a whistle to the horses, tramping lightly after the foot-soldiers, and soon they disappeared in the darkness. All that could be heard was the hollow sounds of horses' hoofs and the creaking of some wheel which was not yet running smoothly or which had not been well tarred because of the darkness. The comrades they had left behind went on waving their hands to them for a long time from a distance, though nothing could be seen; and when they turned at last and went back to their places, when they saw by the light of the brightly twinkling stars that half of the carts were gone and that many, many comrades were no longer with them, sadness stole into the heart of every one of them, and they grew thoughtful and bowed down their reckless heads.

Taras saw how troubled the Cossack ranks had become and how despondency, so unseemly in a brave soldier, was slowly spreading among the Cossacks. But he kept silent, for he wanted to give them time to get used to everything, even to the dejection caused by the leave-taking. Meanwhile he was making preparations in silence to rouse them suddenly at one stroke by uttering the Cossack battle cry, and in this way to make sure that courage would come anew and with greater force than ever into the heart of every one of them—a transformation of which only the Slav race is capable; the great and mighty Slav race which compared with any other is as the ocean to a shallow stream: in a storm it roars and thunders, raising mountainous, foam-flecked billows as no impotent river can; but on a calm, windless day it spreads its boundless, mirror-like surface far and wide, clearer and serener than any river, a never-ending delight to the eye.

And Taras ordered his servants to unload one of his carts that stood apart. It was larger and stronger than any other cart in the Cossack camp; its mighty wheels were rimmed with double bands of iron; it was heavily laden, covered with horse-cloths and strong ox-hides, and bound with taut tarred ropes. In the cart were barrels and kegs of fine old wine, which had lain for many years in Bulba's cellars. He had brought it along with him, intending to keep it in reserve, so that if the great moment came when a decisive battle had to be fought, a battle worthy to be handed down to posterity, every single Cossack might taste of that precious wine and be filled with great courage in keeping with so great an occasion. Hearing the colonel's command, the servants rushed to the carts, cut the strong ropes with their broadswords, removed the stout ox-hides and horse-cloths and unloaded the kegs and barrels from the cart.

"Take all of you anything you can lay hands on," Bulba said to the Cossacks, "a jug or the bucket with which you water your horse, your gauntlet or your cap, and if you have nothing else just hold out your hands."

And all the Cossacks took whatever they could lay their hands on: one a jug, another the bucket with which he watered his horse, a third a gauntlet, a fourth a cap, and a fifth just held out his hands. Walking slowly along the ranks, Bulba's servants poured out from the barrels and kegs for all. But Taras bade them not to drink until he gave them a sign to drink together. It was plain that he wanted to say something to them. Taras knew that however strong good old wine was by itself, and however suitable to fortify the spirit of man, the wine's power and the man's spirit would be twice as strong if strengthened by the right kind of speech.

"I'm treating you, friends," said Bulba, "not in honour of your having made me your commander, great as such an honour is, and not to commemorate our leave-taking from our comrades: at another time either would have been seemly and proper, but now we are confronted with quite a different task. We are confronted with a task, friends, that will require the utmost exertion from all of us, a task that will put our great Cossack valour to the test. And so, friends, let us all drink, together; let us drink, first of all, to the holy orthodox faith, to the time when it will at last spread all over the world and everywhere will be only one holy faith, and all the Moslems on earth will become Christians! And, at the same time, let us drink to the *Syech,* that long may it stand to the utter undoing of the whole Moslem world, and that every year it should send out young warriors, each better than the last, each handsomer than the last. And let us also drink to our glory, so that our grandsons and the sons of our grandsons may tell that once there were men who never dishonoured their comradeship or betrayed their own people. So to our faith, dear friends, to our faith!"

"To our faith!" all who stood in the front ranks cried in deep voices. "To our faith!" those further away took up the cry—and all the Cossacks, old and young, drank to their faith.

"To the *Syech!*" said Taras, raising his hand high above his head.

"To the *Syech!*" boomed the deep voices in the front ranks. "To the *Syech!*" the old men repeated softly, twitching their grey moustaches, and with a flutter like young falcons the young Cossacks repeated the toast, "To the *Syech!*" And far, far away the plain heard how the Cossacks were honouring their *Syech.*

"Now the last drink, friends, to the glory of all the Christians in the world!"

And every single Cossack drank his last draught to the glory of all the Christians in the world. And for a long time the toast was repeated among the detachments: "To the glory of all Christians in the world!"

The pitchers were empty, but still the Cossacks stood with their hands raised; though the eyes of all, bright with wine, looked merry, they were wrapt in deep thought. They were not thinking of easy gain or the spoils of war; they were not wondering which of them would have the luck to collect great numbers of gold pieces, costly weapons, embroidered coats, and Circassian stallions. They were scanning the future like eagles perched on the summit of a rocky mountain, a high, precipitous mountain, from which the boundless sea, dotted with galleys like small birds, ships and all manner of vessels, can be seen stretching far into the distance; the sea, bounded on two sides with faintly visible thin lines of coast, with towns on the shore, like midges, and woods, drooping like fine grass. Like eagles they gazed all over the plain, as though trying to catch a glimpse of their darkly looming fate. Aye, the whole plain with its untilled fields and roads will all too soon be covered with their bleaching bones; soon, all too soon, will it be drenched in their Cossack blood and strewn with shattered carts and broken swords and splintered spears; their heads with tangles and gory tufts of hair and drooping moustaches will be scattered far and wide, and soon, all too soon, will the eagles swoop down and claw at and peck out their eyes. But from a death-bed so spacious and so wide great good will arise! Not one noble action will perish, and Cossack glory will not be lost like a tiny grain of powder from the barrel of a musket. The time will come when a bandore-player with a grey beard covering his chest, or perhaps a white-haired old man still full of vigor, a man prophetic in spirit, will utter a mighty and resounding word about them. And their glory will spread like a whirlwind all over the world, and generations still unborn will talk of them. For a mighty word is carried far and wide, being like the booming copper of a church-bell into which the bell-founder has blended much pure, precious silver that its lovely peal may ring out far over cities and villages, over hovels and palaces, summoning all alike to prayer.

🏴 I X

No one in the city knew that half of the Cossack army had gone in pursuit of the Tartars. From the tower of the town hall the sentries saw that some of the carts were moving out behind the wood, but it was thought that the Cossacks were preparing to lay an ambush, and the French engineer was of the same opinion. Meanwhile the general's words were coming true, and the city began to suffer from a shortage of food; as often happened in the old days the troops had underestimated the amount of food they would need. They tried to make a sortie, but one half of the bold men who took part in it were slain by the Cossacks on the spot and the other driven back into the city with nothing to show for their pains. The Jews, however, took advantage of the sortie to nose everything out: why and where the Cossacks had gone, and under which leaders, and what detachments and how many, and how many of them had been left, and what they were thinking of doing. In short, within a few minutes everything was known in the city. The two colonels plucked up courage and prepared to give battle. Taras saw what was happening from the commotion and the movement in the city, and he promptly took all the necessary measures, made the best dispositions of his troops, issued orders and instructions, divided his detachments into three camps, surrounding them with the carts by way of bulwarks, a battle formation in which the Cossacks were invincible. He ordered two detachments to lie in ambush, covered part of the plain with sharp stakes, broken weapons and fragments of spears, with the intention of driving the enemy cavalry there at the first favourable opportunity. And when everything had been done as well as could be, he addressed his troops, not because he wanted to encourage them or refresh their spirits (he knew very well that their spirits needed no refreshing), but simply to tell them all that was in his heart.

"I want to tell you, dear friends," he said, "what comradeship is. You have heard from your fathers and your grandfathers how greatly honoured our country was once by all men: she made her influence felt among the Greeks, she collected gold pieces as tribute from Constantinople, and her cities were wealthy cities, and her temples were rich temples, and her princes were princes of Russian descent and not Catholic infidels. All that was taken by the heathens; all was lost. We were left orphaned and defence-less. Just as a widow is left defenceless after the death of her strong husband, so were we, too, and so was our country. It was at such a time, friends, that we clasped each other's hands in brotherhood: this is what our comradeship is founded on! And there are no bonds more sacred than the bonds of comradeship. The father loves his child, the mother loves her child, and the child loves its father and mother; but, my friends, this is not the same: a wild beast, too, loves its young! But to become kindred in spirit, though not in blood, is what only man can do. There have been comrades in other lands, too, but such comrades as in Russia there have never been. More than one of you, I know, has had to live for many years in foreign lands: you could see that there are also men, God's creatures like you, and you talk with them just as you do with your own people; but when it comes to hearing a word uttered straight from the heart, then—no!—you feel at once that it isn't the same thing. They are clever people, but not the same; they are men like us, but not the same! No, my friends, to love as a Russian heart can love, to love not with your mind or with your heart, but with all that God has given you, with everything you have . . . ah!" Taras said, and with a wave of the hand, a twitch of the moustache and a shake of his grey head he added, "No, no one can love like that! I know that abominable infamy and shameful villainy have struck deep roots in our country. All the people seem to be concerned about is that their barns should be full of grain, that there should be plenty of hayricks in their fields, that they should have large droves of horses, and that their sealed casks of mead should be safe in their cellars; they ape the devil alone knows what heathen customs; they despise their own tongue; they do not care to talk to their own folk; they sell their own countrymen as people sell a soulless beast in the market. The favour of an alien king, and not of a king only, but the paltry favour of some Polish grandee who strikes them in the face with his yellow boot, is dearer to them than any brotherhood. But even the most villainous knave of them all, whatever he may be, even though he has been grovelling in dirt and bending the knee all his life, even such a man, my friends, has a grain of Russian feeling; and one day it will awaken and, poor wretch, he will smite his breast and tear his hair and curse in a loud voice this rotten life of his, ready to expiate by tortures his shameful acts. Let them therefore all know what comradeship means in Russia. If die we must, not one of them will ever die as we shall. No, not one, not one! They're too chicken-hearted for that!"

So spoke the commander, and when he finished his speech, he went on shaking his head, which had grown silvery in the service of the Cossack cause. All who had stood there listening to him were deeply moved by his speech, which went straight to their hearts. The eldest in the ranks stood motionless, their grey heads bowed, a tear quietly gathering in their old eyes, and slowly they wiped it away with their sleeves; and then, as though by common consent, they waved their hands at the same instant and shook their veteran heads. Without a doubt old Taras had recalled to their minds much of what is familiar and best in the heart of a man who has grown wise through sorrow, hard work, great bravery and all the vicissitudes of life, as well as in the heart of those who are too young to have gained such experience, but who have divined much with their pure, youthful souls to the abiding joy of the aged parents who begot them.

Meanwhile the enemy forces were already marching out of the city to the beating of drums and the blowing of trumpets, and the Polish nobles, arms akimbo, rode forth, surrounded by their innumerable servants. The stout colonel was issuing orders. And they began to advance in serried ranks against the Cossack encampments with flashing eyes and glittering copper trappings, uttering threats and taking aim with their harquebuses. As soon as the Cossacks saw that they had come within gunshot, they fired their long harquebuses all together, and they went on firing without ceasing. The loud reports resounded far and wide through the surrounding meadows and cornfields, mingling into one continuous roar. The whole plain was covered with smoke, but the Cossacks went on firing without a moment's pause. Those in the rear kept loading the guns and passing them across to those in front, causing consternation in the ranks of the enemy who could not understand how the Cossacks could fire without reloading their guns. By now nothing could be seen for the great smoke which hid the two contending armies; it was impossible to see who was hit and who was still on his feet, but the Poles felt that the bullets were flying thick and that things were getting a little too hot; and when they fell back to move out of the smoke and look about them, they saw that many were missing from their ranks, while among the Cossacks perhaps two or three were killed out of a hundred. And the Cossacks went on firing without ceasing. Even the foreign engineer was astonished, having never before seen such tactics, and he could not refrain from saying aloud before them all, "What brave fellows the Cossacks are! That's the way to fight! Everyone ought to take an example from them!" And he advised the Poles to turn their cannon at once upon the Cossack camp. Loud was the roar from the wide throats of the iron cannons; the earth shook and trembled a long way off as it re-echoed the sound of gunfire, and twice as much smoke rolled over the plain. Men smelt the gunpowder in the squares and streets of near and distant cities. But the Polish gunners aimed too high, and the red-hot cannon-balls described too high an arc: they flew through the air with a terrible whine, passed over the heads of all the Cossack forces, and plunged deep into the ground, throwing up the black earth high into the air. The French engineer tore his hair at such incompetence and began sighting the guns himself, paying no heed to the hail of bullets from the Cossacks.

Taras saw from a distance that the Nezamáykov and the Stevlikív detachments were in danger of being wiped out, and he shouted in a resounding voice, "Get out quick from behind the carts! Mount your horses! All mount your horses!" But the Cossacks could not have carried out either command if Ostap had not rushed into the very midst of the Polish artillery-men and struck the linstocks out of the hands of six gunners; he was driven off by the Poles before he had time to deal in the same way with the remaining four. Meanwhile the foreign captain himself took a linstock in his hand to fire off the biggest cannon the Cossacks had ever seen. Terribly it gaped with its huge throat, and a thousand deaths seemed to lurk there. And when it was fired, and after it the three others, making the earth shake four times as it re-echoed hollowly the thunder of the cannonade—great was the havoc they wrought! Many an old mother will weep bitter tears for her Cossack son, smiting her withered breasts with her bony hands; many a widow will be left in Glukhov, Nemirov, Chernigov and other cities. She will run out to the market every day, poor woman, stopping every passer-by, gazing into everybody's eyes to see whether the one dearer to her than all the world is not among. them; but hundreds of soldiers will pass through the city, and never will she find among them the one who is dearer to her than all the world.

Half of the Nezamáykov detachment had been wiped out: it seemed as though they had never existed. As a field, where every ear of corn glitters and is heavy with grain like a new, shining gold piece, is suddenly beaten down by hail, so were they beaten down and laid low.

Oh, how furious the Cossacks were! How they all attacked together! How Detachment Commander Kukúbenko boiled with rage when he saw that more than half of his men were gone! With his remaining Cossacks he made his way into the midst of the enemy forces. In his wrath he made mincemeat of the first Pole he came across, hurled many horsemen from their saddles, killing both horse and rider, fought his way to the gunners and captured one cannon. And he saw that the Uman detachment commander, too, was busy, and Stepa Gusska had captured the chief cannon. He left those Cossacks to carry on and led his men against another enemy throng: where the Nezamáykov Cossacks passed, they left a wide street, and where they turned, there was a lane. The ranks of the Poles could be seen dwindling and their dead were piling up in stacks. Vovtúzenko by the carts, Cherevíchenko in front, Degtyarénko by the furthest carts, and beyond Detachment Commander Vertýhvist. Degtyarénko had already raised two Poles upon his spear, but the third he attacked was not so easy to overcome. The Pole was an agile and a stalwart man, adorned with rich harness and surrounded by a retinue of no less than fifty servants. He pressed Degtyarénko hard, flung him to the ground and, swinging his sword over him, shouted to the Cossacks, "None of you, dogs, can hold his own against me!"

"Here's one who can!" said Mossy Shilo, stepping forward.

A mighty Cossack was Shilo. More than once had he been in command on sea, and many hardships had he suffered. The Turks had captured him and his men at Trebizond and placed them all aboard their galleys as slaves, putting iron chains on their hands and feet, giving them no millet for whole weeks together and only loathsome sea-water to drink. The poor prisoners suffered and endured all, and no torture could make them renounce their orthodox faith. But Mossy Shilo, their commander, gave in at last. He trampled underfoot the holy law, wound a vile turban round his wicked head, gained the confidence of the Pasha, became the steward on the Turkish ship and chief over-seer over all the galley-slaves. It was a grievous blow to the unhappy captives, for they knew that if any of their own people turned traitor to his faith and went over to their oppressors he would persecute them more mercilessly than any infidel; and so indeed it came to pass. Shilo put them all into new chains, three in a row, bound them with ropes that cut their flesh to the bone, and rained blows upon them with his fists. But when the Turks, glad to have procured such a servant, began feasting and, forgetting their own law, all got drunk, he produced the sixty-four keys and gave them to the galley-slaves that they might free themselves and cast their chains into the sea and take up sabres instead and cut down the Turks. The Cossacks took much booty and then re-turned to their country covered with glory, and long after the bandore-players glorified Mossy Shilo. They would have chosen him general, but he was a most eccentric Cossack. Sometimes he would perform some really amazing feat, such as would never have occurred to the wisest of them, but at other times he was guilty of the most foolish and irresponsible actions. He spent everything he had on drink and gay revelry, was in debt to every-one in the *Syech* and, in addition, was caught stealing like some petty thief. One night he abstracted the entire Cossack harness belonging to another detachment and pledged it with an innkeeper. For so shameful an act he was tied to the whipping post in the market-place and a cudgel was placed beside it that every Cossack might deal him a blow according to his strength; but not one man could be found among the Dnieper Cossacks who would lift the cudgel against him, for they all remembered his services in the past. Such was the Cossack Mossy Shilo.

"There are still men who can beat curs like you!" he said, advancing against the Polish nobleman.

Oh, how bravely they fought! The shoulder-pieces and breast-plates of both were dented by their mighty blows. The villainous Pole cut through Shilo's coat of mail, inflicting a wound on his body with his blade: the Cossack's coat of mail became red with blood, but Shilo paid no heed to it, and, swinging his sinewy arm (terribly strong was his stout arm!), hit him on the head with all his might and stunned him. The copper helmet was shivered and the Pole staggered and fell heavily upon the ground. Shilo began raining blows upon his stunned enemy, slashing him mercilessly with his sword. Cossack, take care! Do not dispatch your enemy! Turn around! But the Cossack did not turn round, and one of the servants of the slain nobleman stabbed him in the neck with a knife. Shilo turned and was about to lay his hand on the bold fellow, but he lost him in the smoke of the battle. From all sides came the cracking of matchlocks. Shilo staggered. He felt that his wound was mortal. As he fell to the ground, he put his hand upon it and said, turning to his comrades, "Farewell, dear friends. Long may the holy Russian land stand and may its glory never pass!" and he closed his weary eyes, and his Cossack soul flew out of his dour body.

By then Zadorózhny had ridden forth with his men, Detachment Commander Vertýhvist was harrying the Polish ranks, and Balabán was attacking them.

"Well, men," said Taras, calling to the commanders of detachments, "have you enough powder in your flasks? Is there strength left in the Cossack arm? Are the Cossacks standing fast?"

"Yes, sir, we have enough powder in our flasks! The Cossack arm is still strong! The Cossacks are standing fast!"

And the Cossacks pressed their foes hard, and the Polish ranks were thrown into utter confusion. The short colonel sounded a rally and ordered eight painted standards to be raised to gather his men who were scattered all over the plain. The Poles rushed to their standards, but they had hardly time to form into ranks again when Detachment Commander Kukúbenko launched another attack with his Nezamáykov men, hurling himself into their midst and riding full tilt against the big-bellied colonel. The colonel wilted under this sudden attack and, turning his horse round, fled at a gallop. Kukúbenko pursued him all across the plain, preventing him from joining his regiment.

Seeing this chase from a detachment on the flank, Stepan Gusska galloped to intercept the Polish colonel with a lasso in his hand, his head bent low over his horse's mane, and at the first opportunity cast the noose round the colonel's neck with one throw. The colonel's face turned purple, and he clutched at the rope with both hands, trying to tear it apart; but Gusska hurled his spear with terrific force, driving it straight through his belly, and there he was left, nailed to the ground. But now it was Gusska's turn. The Cossacks had scarcely time to look round when they saw Gusska raised on four spears! The poor fellow had just time to say, "May all our enemies perish and may Russia rejoice forever!" and then he gave up the ghost.

The Cossacks looked round, and there on the flank Metélitza was having good sport with the Poles, smiting them hip and thigh, while on the other flank Detachment Commander Nevelýchky was pressing the foe hard with his men; and at the carts Zakrutyguba was pitching into the Poles and putting them to flight, while at the distant carts Pisarénko the Third had driven off a whole horde of them; at the other carts hand-to-hand fighting was going on, the Cossacks and the Poles engaged in mortal combat on top of the carts.

And Taras rode out in front of all and called to the commanders, "Well, men, is there enough powder in your powder flask? Is there strength left in the Cossack arm? Are the Cossacks standing fast?"

"Yes, sir, we've still powder in our flasks! The Cossack arm is still strong! The Cossacks are still standing fast!"

But Bovdyúg had already fallen from the cart, struck by a bullet under the very heart. The old man rallied his last strength and said, "I'm not sorry to leave this world. May all men die like that! May Russia be glorious to the end of time!" And

Bovdyúg's soul flew straight into heaven to tell the old men long since dead how gallantly man can fight in Russia and, what is better still, how they can die for their holy faith.

Very soon after that, Detachment Commander Balabán was flung to the ground. He had received three mortal wounds from a spear, from a bullet, and from a heavy broadsword. One of the bravest of Cossacks, he had been in command of many sea expeditions, most famous of all being his raid on the coasts of Anatolia. They had collected many sequins at that time, rich Turkish possessions of all sorts, precious fabrics and all kinds of accoutrements. But on their way home disaster overtook them: the poor fellows came under Turkish fire. When the Turkish man-of-war fired a volley at them, it scored a direct hit and half the boats spun round and capsized and many a Cossack was drowned; but the reeds fastened to the sides of the boats prevented them from sinking. Balabán rowed away as fast as he could, steered his boat straight into the sun and so became invisible to the Turkish ship. They spent the whole of the following night baling out the water with their caps and pitchers and stopping up the holes. They cut up their wide Cossack breeches into sails, and so sailed away, making good their escape from the fastest Turkish ship. And not only did they arrive at the *Syech* without any further trouble, but they brought with them a gold embroidered chasuble for the bishop of the Mezhigorsk Monastery in Kiev and a setting for an icon of pure silver for the Church of the Intercession at the *Syech*. And the bandore-players went on glorifying the good luck of the Cossacks for many years. But now Balabán bowed his head, feeling the agonies of death upon him, and said quietly, "It seems to me, dear friends, I'm not dying such a bad death after all: I have cut down seven with my sword, I have slain nine with my spear, I have trampled many more under my horse, and I can't remember the number I have killed with my bullets. May Russia flourish for ever!" and his soul flew away.

Cossacks! Cossacks! Do not let down the flower of your army!

By now Kukúbenko was surrounded, seven men only remained of
the Nezamáykov detachment, and they were finding it hard work to
beat off the attacks of the enemy. Their commander's clothes were
already stained with blood. Taras himself, seeing the plight he was
in, hastened to his rescue. But the Cossacks were too late: before
the enemies who had encompassed him were driven off, a spear
had pierced his heart. Slowly he sank into the arms of the Cossacks,
who caught him as he fell, and his young blood gushed out of his
wound, like the precious wine brought by careless servants in a
glass vessel from the cellar: they slip, and the costly jar is smashed,
the wine is spilt on the ground and the master, who comes running
at the noise, tears his hair, for he has carefully kept the wine for
one of the happiest moments of his life when, if God so willed, he
should meet a friend of his youth in his old age that they might
together recall the good old days when men knew how to make
merry in a different and better fashion. Kukúbenko looked round
and said, "I thank God that I've had the good fortune to die before
your eyes, dear friends! May men have a happier life after us, and
may our country, dearly beloved of Christ, flourish for ever and
ever!" And the young soul flew out of the body and the angels
received it in their arms and carried it into heaven: it will be
well with him there. "Sit on my right hand, Kukúbenko," Christ
will say to him. "You haven't been false to your brotherhood;
you have been guilty of no dishonourable deed; you have never
deserted a man in trouble; you have always guarded and preserved
My Church."

Everyone was greatly grieved by Kukúbenko's death. The Cossack ranks were beginning to dwindle fast. Many, many a brave
man had fallen, but the Cossacks still stood fast.

"Well, men," Taras shouted to the remaining detachments,
"have you enough powder in your flasks? Are not your sabres
blunted? Is your strength giving out? Are the Cossacks still standing fast?"

"We've still enough powder, sir! Our sabres are sharp enough!

The Cossack arm is still strong! The Cossacks are still standing fast!"

And once more the Cossacks threw themselves into the fray, as though they had never suffered any losses. Only three detachment commanders were still alive; streams of blood ran red over the plain and across them the bridges made of the bodies of the Cossacks and the enemy rose higher and higher. Taras glanced at the sky and he saw a long string of gerfalcons flying across it. Well, someone at least was going to have a good time! Here Metelitza was lifted on a spear, there the head of Pisarénko the Second had been severed from the body and rolled on the ground, and yonder Okhrim Gusska staggered and crashed to the ground, cut into four pieces. "Now!" said Taras and waved his handkerchief. Ostap understood the signal and, dashing out of ambush, he bore down upon the enemy cavalry. The Poles could not hold out against his furious attack and turned tail, while he continued to pursue them, chasing them straight to the place where the stakes and broken spears were driven into the ground. The horses began to stumble and fall, and the Poles were flung headlong over their heads. At the same time the Cossacks of the Korsun detachment, seeing that the enemy was within range, opened up a murderous fire upon them with their matchlocks.

The Poles were overwhelmed and thrown into confusion, and the Cossacks recovered their spirits. "We've won! We've won!" shouts were raised on every side, and trumpets were sounded and a banner of victory was unfurled. The beaten Poles were running in all directions, looking for cover.

"No," said Taras, glancing at the gates of the city, "it's a bit too soon to shout victory!" And he spoke the truth.

The gates were opened and a regiment of hussars, the flower of all the Polish cavalry regiments, galloped out into the plain. All the riders were mounted on dun-coloured Caucasian stallions, and foremost rode a knight, bolder and handsomer than any of them all. His black hair streamed from under his copper helmet; a rich scarf embroidered by the hand of a peerless beauty was wound round his arm and waved in the wind. Taras was struck dumb when he recognized Andrey. Meanwhile, seized by the excitement and the heat of battle and eager to be worthy of the gift tied to his arm, Andrey raced along like a young wolfhound, the youngest, handsomest, swiftest in the pack. At the first halloo of the expert huntsman he races off, his legs flying in a straight line, his whole body sloping sideways, throwing up lumps of snow and ten times outstripping the hare in his headlong career. Old Taras stopped and watched his son scattering the Cossacks, clearing a path in their midst, and raining blows right and left. And Taras could not restrain himself any longer and shouted, "What? Your own people? Killing your own people, you damned villain?" But Andrey did not even see who was before him, whether friend or foe. He saw nothing. All he saw was curls, long, long curls, and a bosom like the breast of a swan on a stream, and a snow-white neck and shoulders, and all, all that is created for passionate kisses.

"Hey, there, lads! Get him into the wood! Entice him to the wood for me!" shouted Taras.

And at once thirty of the swiftest Cossacks volunteered to entice Andrey to the wood. Setting their caps firmly on their heads, they galloped right across the plain to intercept the hussars. They struck the front ranks on the flank and threw them into confusion, separated them from those behind, distributed a few presents here and there, while Golokopýtenko dealt Andrey a blow with the flat of his sword across the back, and straightway the Cossacks galloped away from them as fast as they could. Andrey was wild with fury. His young blood boiled with rage. Clapping his sharp spurs to his horse, he dashed off at a gallop after the Cossacks, without looking back, without seeing that only twenty of his men were following him. The Cossacks went on galloping at full speed and made straight for the wood. Andrey was close on their heels and in another minute he would have overtaken Golokopýtenko, when suddenly a strong arm grasped his horse's bridle. Andrey looked round: Taras was before him! He trembled all over and grew suddenly pale; so does a schoolboy who rashly picks a quarrel with one of his schoolfellows and receives a blow with a ruler on the forehead for his pains, blaze up like a flame and, jumping from the bench, run after his frightened friend, ready to tear him limb from limb, when suddenly he runs into the master as he is entering the classroom: in an instant his blind fury evaporates and his important rage melts away. So Andrey's anger was gone in an instant, as though it had never been. And he saw before him only his terrible father.

"Well, what shall we do now?" said Taras, looking him straight in the face.

But Andrey could say nothing in reply and he stood there without uttering a word, his eyes fixed on the ground.

"Well, son, have your Poles done you any good?"

Andrey was silent.

"So it's treachery, is it? Treachery! You'd betray your faith! Betray your own folk? Very well, get off your horse!"

Obediently, like a child, Andrey got off his horse and stood before Taras more dead than alive.

"Stand still and don't move! I begot you, and I will kill you!" said Taras and, stepping back, he took the gun from his shoulder.

Andrey was white as a sheet; only his lips moved faintly as he uttered someone's name. But it was not the name of his country, nor of his mother, nor of his brother that he uttered—it was the name of the beautiful Polish girl.

Taras fired.

Like a sheaf of corn cut by the sickle, like a lamb that feels the deadly steel at its heart, Andrey hung his head and fell upon the sward without uttering a word.

The murderer of his son stood still and gazed long at the lifeless body. Andrey was beautiful even in death. His manly face, so recently full of vigour and irresistible fascination to women, was still marvellously beautiful; his black eyebrows, like sombre velvet, set off his blood-drained features.

"What a fine Cossack he'd have made!" said Taras. "Tall and black-browed, and a face like the face of a nobleman, and his arm was mighty in battle—and now he has perished, perished ingloriously, like a vile dog!"

"What have you done, Father? Did you kill him?" asked Ostap, who had just at that moment ridden up.

Taras nodded.

Ostap looked intently into the dead man's eyes. He was sorry for his brother and said at once, "Let's give him an honourable burial, Father. Don't let us leave him here to be dishonoured by his enemies or to be torn to pieces by the birds of prey!"

"They'll bury him without us," said Taras. "He'll have many women weeping and mourning over him!"

And for a minute or two he still wondered whether to throw his son's body to the wolves or take pity on his knightly honour, which a gallant soldier was bound to respect in any man. But at that moment Golokopýtenko galloped up to him.

"Bad news, sir. The Poles have been reinforced. More fresh troops are coming to their aid!"

Before Golokopýtenko had finished speaking, Vovtúzenko galloped up.

"Bad news, sir. More fresh troops are coming to their aid!"

No sooner had Vovtúzenko spoken than Pisarénko came running on foot.

"Where are you, sir?" he cried. "The Cossacks are looking for you. Detachment Commander Nevylýchky is slain, Zadorózhny is slain, Chervichénko is slain, but the Cossacks are still standing fast. They don't want to die without a last look at you, sir. They want you to see them, too, before the hour of death."

"To horse, Ostap!" said Taras, and he hurried that he might see his Cossacks, that he might yet look upon them for the last time, and that they, too, might see their general before they died.

But before they had time to ride out of the wood, the enemy had already surrounded it on all sides, and riders appeared between the trees with drawn swords and spears.

"Ostap, Ostap, don't let them take you!" shouted Taras, drawing his sabre and striking at the enemy right and left.

Six men had suddenly fallen upon Ostap, but it seemed they had attacked him in an unlucky hour: for the head of the first flew off, the second slipped and turned head over heels, the third was hit in the ribs with a spear, the fourth, braver than the others, was just in time to miss a bullet in the head, but his horse was hit in the chest and, rearing, the frenzied animal fell to the ground and crushed his rider under him.

"Well done, son! Well done, Ostap!" shouted Taras. "Hold on! I'm coming!"

And all the time he was beating off the enemy who pressed upon him from every side. He fought and slashed away, handing out presents upon the head of many a Pole, and all the time he kept looking ahead of him at Ostap. Then he saw at least eight men attacking Ostap all at once.

"Ostap, Ostap, don't let them take you!"

But Ostap was already overpowered. One man had flung a noose round his head, and now they were binding him. . . . Ostap was captured.

"Oh, Ostap, Ostap!" cried Taras, forcing his way towards his son and cutting down mercilessly every one who stood between him and Ostap. "Oh, Ostap, Ostap!"

But just then Taras himself was hit on the head as though with a huge stone: everything spun round dizzily before his eyes. For a split second there flashed before him in a confused mass heads, spears, smoke, the gleam of a fire, branches covered with leaves that seemed to brush past his very eyes. Then he crashed to the ground like a felled oak, and a mist spread over his eyes.

🚩 X

"Must have been asleep a long time," said Taras, waking up as though from a heavy, drunken sleep and trying to recognise the objects around him.

A terrible weakness overpowered his limbs. He could make out only faintly the walls and corners of an unfamiliar room. At last he perceived Tovkatch sitting before him, apparently listening to every breath he took.

"Aye," said Tovkatch to himself, "you might have been asleep for ever!" but he said nothing, only shaking a finger at him and motioning him to be silent.

"But tell me where am I?" asked Taras again, racking his brains and trying to remember what had happened.

"Keep quiet," his comrade shouted sternly at him. "What more do you want to know? Can't you see that you've been badly cut to pieces? For the past fortnight we've been galloping without stopping, and you've been in a high fever all the time and talking wildly. This is the first time you've had a quiet sleep. Don't talk if you don't want to do yourself an injury."

But Taras kept on trying to collect his thoughts and to remember what had happened. "But wasn't I surrounded and almost captured by the Poles? I couldn't possibly have got away from that crowd, could I?"

"Keep quiet, will you?" shouted Tovkatch gruffly, like a nurse driven frantic by a naughty child. "What do you want to know how you got away for? Will it do you any good? Is it not enough that you did get away? There were men who would not leave you in the lurch: let that be enough for you! We've still many a night's ride before us. You don't think you could pass for a common Cossack, do you? No, sir. They have placed a price of two thousand gold pieces on your head!"

"And Ostap?" Taras cried suddenly, and he tried hard to rise, for all at once he remembered that Ostap had been seized and bound before his eyes and that he was now in the hands of the Poles. He was overwhelmed with grief. He tore off the bandages on his wounds and flung them away from him. He tried to say something in a loud voice, but instead he started rambling again. He relapsed into a delirium, and senseless, confused words poured from his lips. His loyal comrade stood before him, swearing and heaping countless harsh and reproachful words upon him. At last he seized him by the hands and feet, swaddled him like a baby, carefully replacing all his bandages, wrapped him in an oxhide, put him in splints, and, fastening him with cords to the saddle, set off again at a fast gallop.

"Dead or alive, but I'll bring you home! Never will I let the Poles dishonour your Cossack birth, tear your body to pieces and fling it into the water. If an eagle is to claw out your eyes, let it at least be one of our eagles of the steppe, and not one that comes flying from the land of the Poles. I'll bring you to the Ukraine, though I bring you there dead!"

So spoke his loyal comrade. He galloped without rest for many days and nights, and he brought him unconscious to the *Syech* below the Dnieper Falls. There he applied himself tirelessly to nursing him back to health with herbs and embrocations. He found a wise old Jewish woman who for a whole month gave him many different potions to drink, and at last Taras began showing signs of recovery. Whether it was the medicine or his own iron constitution that gained the day, it is hard to say, but within six weeks he was on his legs again; his wounds healed and only the scars left by the sabres showed how dangerously the old Cossack had been wounded. But he never recovered his high spirits: he looked sad and gloomy. Three deep lines furrowed his brow and never left it. He gazed about him: everything was new to him at the *Syech*. All his old comrades were dead. Not one was left of those who had stood up with him for the just cause, for faith and brotherhood. And those who had gone with the general in pursuit of the Tartars, even those had long passed away. All of them had laid down their lives; all of them had perished. Some had been killed honourably in battle; some had died of hunger and thirst amid the Crimean salt marshes; some had died in captivity, unable to endure the disgrace of slavery. And their former general himself had been dead a long time. Not one of his old comrades had been left alive; gone was the Cossack might, once irresistible, and grass had been growing over it a long, long time. All he had been able to gather was that there had been a great, noisy feast: all the drinking vessels had been smashed, not a drop of wine was left; the guests and the servants had carried off all the costly goblets and rich jars, and the master of the house stood bewildered, wondering if it had not been much better for the feast not to have taken place at all. In vain did they try to divert and to cheer Taras; in vain did the grey-headed, bearded bandore-players come in twos and threes and glorify his Cossack deeds! He looked upon the world with harsh indifference, and on his unmoved face unquenchable sorrow was graven deep, and with a bowed head he would murmur, "Ostap, my son, my son!"

The Dnieper Cossacks were making preparations for an expedition by sea. Two hundred boats were lowered into the Dnieper, and Asia Minor saw them with shaven heads and long tufts of hair, putting her flourishing coasts to fire and the sword; she saw the turbans of her Moslem inhabitants strewn on the earth like innumerable flowers, on her blood-drenched fields, and floating along her coasts; she saw hundreds of Dnieper Cossacks, their wide breeches smeared with tar and black whips in their hands. The Cossacks laid waste the vineyard and fed upon its grapes; they left heaps of dung in the mosques; they used costly Persian shawls to wind round their legs or gird round their soiled coats. Long afterwards their short pipes could be picked up in those parts. They sailed back in high spirits. A Turkish man-of-war with ten cannon pursued them and dispersed their flimsy canoes with one volley from all her guns. A third of their number found a grave in the depths of the sea, but the rest assembled again and reached the mouth of the Dnieper with twelve barrels full of sequins. But Taras remained unmoved by it all. He went off into the meadows and the steppes, as though to hunt; but the charge in his musket remained unfired, and, laying it down, he would sit on the seashore, full of gnawing grief. He would sit there like that for hours, with bowed head, murmuring, "Ostap, my son, my son!" Before him stretched the Black Sea, sparkling in the sun; in the distant reeds a seagull called; his white moustache gleamed like silver, and tears rolled down upon it one by one.

At last Taras could endure it no longer. "Whatever happens, I must go and find out whether he is still alive or in his grave, or whether there is anything left of him in the grave. I will find out, come what may!"

And a week later he was in the city of Uman, armed and on horseback, with spear and sabre, a travelling bag strapped to his saddle, a pot of porridge, a powder horn and bullets, a hobble for his horse, and other equipment. He rode straight up to a dirty, ill-kept little house, with small, grimy windows that could scarcely be seen, thick with dirt as they were; the chimney was stopped up with a rag and the roof was full of holes and covered with sparrows; a heap of refuse lay before the very door. A Jewish woman in a cap and with discoloured pearls looked out of the window.

"Is your husband at home?" said Bulba, dismounting from his horse and tying the reins to the iron hook near the door.

"Yes, sir, he's at home," said the woman, and she hurried out immediately with some wheat in a bucket for the horse and a beaker of beer for the rider.

"Where's your Jew?"

"He's in the other room, saying his prayers," said the woman, curtsying and wishing Bulba good health as he lifted the beaker to his lips.

"Stay here and see to my horse—he wants some fodder and

water—while I go and speak with him alone. I have business with him."

This Jew was our old friend Yankel. He had been there for some time, renting some land and keeping an inn, and gradually he had got all the nobles and squires in the neighbourhood into his hands, had gradually drained them of almost all their money and left a deep mark of his Jewish presence in that country. For a distance of three miles in every direction there was not a single cottage left in good repair: everything was tumbling down and falling into decay, everything was being spent on drink, nothing but poverty and rags remained; the whole countryside lay waste as after a fire or a pestilence. And if Yankel had stayed there another ten years he would most likely have laid waste the whole province.

Taras entered the room. The Jew was saying his prayers, covered with his rather dirty praying-shawl and, as was the custom of his faith, he turned to spit for the last time when he suddenly saw Bulba standing behind him. The first thought that flashed across the mind of the Jew was the reward of two thousand gold pieces placed on Bulba's head; but he was ashamed of his greed and did his best to suppress the everlasting thought of gold which twines like a worm round the soul of a Jew.

"Look here, Yankel," said Taras to the Jew, who first bowed to him and then locked the door carefully that they should not be seen. "I saved your life once. The Dnieper Cossacks would have torn you to pieces like a dog, if I had not stopped them. Now it's your turn to do me a service."

The Jew made a wry face. "What sort of service, sir? If it's some service I can do for you, I shall of course be glad to do it."

"Ask no questions. Take me to Warsaw!"

"To Warsaw? How do you mean, to Warsaw, sir?" said Yankel, his eyebrows and shoulders raised in astonishment.

"Don't ask any questions. Take me to Warsaw. Whatever happens, I must see him again, say just one word to him."

"To whom, sir?"

"To him. To Ostap, my son."

"But haven't you heard, sir, that . . ."

"I know, I know everything. They've offered two thousand gold pieces for my head. The fools! They know what it's worth, don't they? I'll give you five thousand, two thousand now (Bulba emptied two thousand gold pieces from his leather purse) and the rest when I come back."

The Jew immediately seized a towel and covered the money with it.

"Oh, what lovely money, what lovely money!" he said, turning a gold coin over in his hand and trying it with his teeth. "I expect the man you took these lovely pieces of gold from did not live another hour. Must have gone straight to the river and drowned himself. For who would like to lose such lovely gold coins, sir?"

"I wouldn't have asked you. I might perhaps have found the way to Warsaw myself, but I'm afraid those damned Poles may somehow recognise me and seize me. For to tell you the truth I'm not much good at clever tricks. It's just what you Jews have been created for. You can cheat the devil himself; you know all the tricks! That's why I've come to you. Besides, I couldn't have done much in Warsaw by myself. So get your cart out at once and take me there."

"So you think it's as simple as that, sir? Put your mare to your cart and gee-up Bess! Do you really think, sir, I could take you to Warsaw without taking good care to hide you first?"

"All right, hide me, if you must. Where will you hide me, though? Not in an empty barrel?"

"Oh dear, in an empty barrel indeed! Do you suppose, sir, you could be hidden in a barrel? Don't you realize, sir, that every man we meet on the road will at once jump to the conclusion that there must be vodka in the barrel?"

"Well, let him think there's vodka in it."

"Do you really mean it, sir? Let him think there's vodka in it?"

said the Jew, catching hold of his side-curls and then throwing up his hands in dismay.

"What are you so alarmed about?"

"But don't you know, sir, that God created vodka so that every man might taste it? In that country they're all fond of a good thing; they're all after vodka. A Polish gentleman will run five miles after a barrel, pierce a hole in it, and, finding nothing in it, he'll at once say to himself, 'A Jew will never carry an empty barrel. There's something wrong here. Seize the Jew! Take all the money away from the Jew! Throw the Jew into jail!' For the Jew, sir, is blamed for everything that goes wrong. It's all the Jew's fault! Everyone regards the Jew as a dog. Everyone thinks that if he's a Jew he's not a human being at all!"

"All right, put me in a cart with fish then."

"Oh dear, oh dear, that isn't possible, either, sir. All over Poland the people are now as hungry as dogs; they'll filch the fish and discover you under it."

"Well, carry me on the devil himself for all I care, only take me there!"

"Now listen to me, sir; listen to me!" said the Jew, tucking up the cuffs of his sleeves and approaching him with outstretched hands. "This is what we'll do. Fortresses and castles are being built all over Poland now, French engineers have arrived from Germany specially for that purpose, so lots of bricks and stones are being carted along the road. If you don't mind, sir, I'll put you at the bottom of the cart and cover you up with bricks. You look very strong and healthy, sir, and I don't suppose you'd mind it very much if it should feel a little heavy. I'll make a hole in the bottom of the cart, sir, and I shall feed you through that."

"All right, do as you like, only take me!"

And an hour later a cart-load of bricks left Uman, drawn by two mares. On one of them sat the tall Jew Yankel, and his long, curly side-locks fluttered in the wind from under his Jewish skull cap, and he jogged up and down on the horse, looking as thin as a rake and as long as a mile-post by the wayside.

🙰 XI

At the time when the events described here took place there were on the frontiers as yet neither customs officers nor customs guards, those veritable terrors of men of enterprise, and therefore anyone could take across the frontiers anything he liked. And even if a search or inspection was sometimes made, it was mostly done for the special delight of the official, particularly if the things in the cart exercised a powerful attraction on his eye and if his own arm was of sufficient weight and strength. But bricks aroused no interest and were allowed to be taken through the main gates of the city without interference. In his narrow cage Bulba could hear only the noises of the road and the shouts of the drivers. Yankel jogged up and down on his short-shanked, dusty trotter and, after going round in a circle a few times, turned into a dark, narrow street known as Dirty Street or Jewish Street, for in that street almost all the Jews of Warsaw were to be found. This street was very much like a back-yard turned inside out. The sun seemed never to peep into it at all. The completely blackened wooden houses with large numbers of clothes lines stretched from one side of the street to the other, greatly increased the general gloom. Only very rarely did one catch a glimpse of a red-brick wall between them, and even that had turned completely black in many places. Only here and there the stucco top of a wall caught the sunlight and gleamed with a whiteness that dazzled the eye. Here everything seemed made up of sharp contrasts: pipes, rags, shells of all sorts, broken pots, and discarded bins. Everyone flung into the street everything he had no further use for, giving the passers-by every opportunity of regaling every sense with all this rubbish. A man on horseback could easily reach with his hand the clothes lines on which were hung Jewish stockings, short breeches and a smoked goose. Sometimes the rather attractive face of a Jewish girl, adorned with begrimed beads, could be seen looking out of a dilapidated window. Scores of Jewish children, dirty and in rags, screamed and played about in the filth. A red-haired Jew, with freckles all over his face that made him look like a sparrow's egg, peeped out of a window and immediately addressed Yankel in his incomprehensible lingo, and Yankel at once drove into the yard. Another Jew came down the street, stopped, and also entered into conversation, and when at last Bulba scrambled out from under the load of bricks he was met by the sight of three Jews who were engaged in a very heated discussion.

Yankel turned to him and said that everything would be done, that his son Ostap was kept in the city dungeon, and that though it would be difficult to persuade the guards, he hoped to arrange a meeting.

Bulba then went with the three Jews into the house.

The Jews again began talking in their incomprehensible language. Taras looked at each of them and it seemed as though he were suddenly deeply moved by something: a consuming flame of hope, the hope which sometimes visits a man in the utmost depths of despair, suddenly lit up his harsh apathetic face. His old heart began beating violently, as though he were a young man.

"Listen, Jews," he said, and there was a note of exaltation in his voice, "you can do anything in the world, you can dig a thing up from the bottom of the sea, and there is an old saying that a Jew can even steal himself, if he wants to. Get my Ostap out of jail; give him a chance to escape from their diabolic hands! Here, I have promised this man twelve thousand gold pieces; I will add another twelve, I'll sell everything I possess, all costly goblets and the buried gold, my cottage, my last shirt, and will make a contract with you for the rest of my life to share whatever I obtain in war equally with you!"

"But I'm afraid it can't be done, sir! It can't be done!" said Yankel with a sigh.

"No, it can't be done," said another Jew.

All the three Jews exchanged glances.

"We might try," said the third Jew with a timid look at the other two. "With God's help we may carry it off!"

The three Jews began talking in German. But however much he strained his ears, Bulba could not make out anything; all he heard was the often repeated word "Mordecai," and that was all.

"Listen, sir," said Yankel, "we shall have to ask the advice of a man, the like of whom there has never been in this world. Oh, oh, oh! He's as wise as Solomon, and if he can do nothing, no one in the world can. Stay here, sir, lock the door and don't let anyone in."

The Jews went out into the street.

Taras locked the door and looked through the little window at the filthy Jewish thoroughfare. The three Jews had stopped in the middle of the street and had begun talking rather excitedly. They were soon joined by a fourth and finally by a fifth. He heard the same name repeated again: "Mordecai! Mordecai!" The Jews kept looking towards one side of the street; at last from behind some dingy house at the end of it there appeared a foot in a Jewish shoe and the fluttering skirts of a coat. "Ah! Mordecai! Mordecai!" the Jews all cried with one voice. A lean Jew, a little shorter than Yankel and far more wrinkled, with an enormous upper lip, drew near the impatient group; and all the Jews vied with each other in hurriedly telling him the story while Mordecai glanced several times at the small window, and Taras guessed that they were talking about him. Mordecai waved his arms about, listened, interrupted the conversation, often turned away to spit, lifting the skirts of his coat, thrust his hand into his pocket and took out some trinkets, incidentally displaying a pair of very shabby trousers. At length all the Jews raised such a clamour that another Jew who seemed to be standing on the look-out signalled to them to be silent. Taras was beginning to feel anxious about his own safety, but remembering that Jews cannot discuss anything except in the street and that Satan himself could not understand their language, he felt reassured.

A few minutes later the Jews came into his room all together. Mordecai went up to Taras, patted him on the shoulder, and said, "When God and we, sir, make up our minds to do a thing, everything will be all right."

Taras looked at this Solomon, the like of whom had never been seen in the world, and his hopes revived a little. And indeed his appearance could inspire a certain amount of confidence: his upper lip was really quite terrifying and its thickness had undoubtedly been increased by external circumstances. Solomon's beard had only fifteen hairs—and those on the left side; and his face bore so many marks of blows he had received for his pluck that he had doubtless lost count of them long ago and grown used to regarding them as birth-marks.

Mordecai went away with his companions, who were full of admiration for his wisdom. Bulba was left alone. He found himself in a strange and quite unusual situation: for the first time in his life he was conscious of anxiety. His mind was in a state of feverish excitement. He was no longer as he used to be: unbending, inflexible, steadfast as an oak. He was timid; he was weak. He started at the slightest noise, at the appearance of every fresh Jewish figure at the end of the street. In this condition he spent the whole day, without eating or drinking, and never for a moment did he take his eyes off the little window looking on to the street. At last, late in the evening, Mordecai and Yankel appeared. Taras Bulba's heart sank.

"Well, any luck?" he asked with the impatience of a wild horse.

But before the Jews had plucked up courage to reply, Taras noticed that one of Mordecai's side-locks which had hung down, rather untidily, in ringlets from under his skull-cap, was no longer there. He seemed to wish to say something, but what he did at last say made so little sense that Taras could make nothing of it. As for Yankel, he kept putting his hand to his mouth as though he were suffering from a cough.

"It's quite impossible, sir," said Yankel. "It's out of the question now. Upon my soul, it's impossible! Such vile people, sir, that nothing could be viler. Let Mordecai tell you, Mordecai did more than anyone in the world could have done, but it seems God did not want it to happen. Three thousand soldiers are guarding the prisoners, and tomorrow they are to be taken out to their execution."

Taras looked straight into the eyes of the Jews, but no longer with any impatience or anger.

"And if you want to see your son, sir, it must be done very early tomorrow morning, before sunrise. The sentries have agreed and their officer has promised his help. Oh, may they have no happiness in the next world! Oh, dear, what greedy people! I assure you, sir, you won't find such greedy people even among us: fifty gold pieces I gave to each of them, and to the officer. . . ."

"All right, take me to him!" said Taras firmly, recovering all his self-possession.

He agreed to Yankel's proposal to dress up as a foreign count who had arrived from Germany. The far-sighted Jew had already procured the clothes for the purpose. By now it was night. The master of the house, the red-haired, freckled Jew, pulled out a light mattress covered with some kind of matting and spread it on a bench for Taras. Yankel lay down on the floor on a similar mattress. The red-haired Jew helped himself to a glass of some liquid, threw off his coat, and, looking like a lean chicken in his socks and slippers, betook himself with his wife to a sort of cupboard. Two Jewish children lay down on the floor beside the cupboard like two little puppies. But Taras did not sleep; he sat motionless, drumming softly with his fingers on the table. He kept his pipe in his mouth and smoked, making the Jew sneeze in his sleep and pull the blanket over his face. As soon as a faint glimmer of light appeared in the sky, Taras poked Yankel with his foot.

"Get up, Jew," he said, "and let's have the count's dress!"

In a few minutes he was dressed. He blackened his moustache and eyebrows, put a little dark cap on the crown of his head, and not one among his closest friends could have recognised him. He did not look more than thirty-five. His cheeks glowed with health and the scars on his face helped to give him a commanding air. The gold-embroidered dress looked well on him.

The streets were still asleep. Not a single street merchant had yet appeared in the city with his basket on his arm. Bulba and Yankel came to a building which looked like a sitting heron. It was low, wide, huge and grimy, and on one side of it a long, slender tower rose like the neck of a stork, with a projecting piece of roof on top. This building was used for a number of different purposes: for barracks, a jail, and even a court of justice. Our visitors went in at the gate and found themselves in the middle of a spacious hall or covered courtyard. About a thousand men were asleep there. Directly opposite the entrance was a low door before which two sentries were sitting, playing a kind of game which consisted in one of them striking the other on the palm of the hand with two fingers. They took little notice of the newcomers and only turned their heads when Yankel said, "It's us! Do you hear, gentlemen, it's us!"

"Go in," said one of them, opening the door with one hand while he held out the other to his companion to receive his blows.

They went into a dark and narrow passage, which brought them again to a similar hall with small windows near the ceiling.

"Who goes there?" shouted several voices, and Taras saw quite a large number of soldiers, all fully armed. "Our orders are to admit no one!"

"But it's us!" Yankel cried. "It's us, gentlemen!"

But no one paid the slightest attention to him. Luckily there walked in at that moment a fat man who seemed to be their commanding officer, for he swore louder than any of them.

"It's us, sir. You know us, don't you? The count will be very obliged to you, sir."

"Let 'em go in, blast and damn you! And don't let anyone else in, and don't take your swords off, either, and don't make such a bloody mess on the floor. . . ."

The rest of his eloquent orders the visitors did not hear.

"It's us! It's me! It's your friends!" Yankel kept saying to everyone he met.

"Well, can we go in now?" he asked one of the guards, when they had at last reached the end of the corridor.

"I suppose so, but I don't know whether they'll admit you right into the jail; Yan isn't there now. There's another man on guard there," replied the sentry.

"Damn," said the Jew softly; "that's bad, sir."

"Let's go," said Taras stubbornly.

The Jew obeyed.

At the arched door leading to the dungeons stood a soldier with a three-tiered moustache: one tier turned backwards, the second straight forward, and the third downwards, which made him look uncommonly like a tom-cat.

The Jew sidled up to him cringingly. "Your excellency. . . . My lord. . . ."

"Are you speaking to me, Jew?"

"Yes, my lord, I'm speaking to you."

"Ha! I'm just a common soldier!" said the man with the three-tiered moustache, with a merry twinkle in his eyes.

"Dear, dear, and I thought you were the governor himself! Dear, dear, dear. . . ." Yankel wagged his head and spread out his fingers. "Oh, how splendid you look, sir! Just like a colonel, a regular colonel! Another finger's breadth and you would be a colonel. All you want, sir, is to be mounted on a horse, a real thoroughbred, sir, as swift as an arrow, and I'm sure you could drill a regiment!"

The soldier stroked the lower tier of his moustache and his eyes positively beamed.

"Oh, there's nothing in the world to beat a soldier!" the Jew went on. "Lord, what fine fellows! What splendid galloons! What love[...]y little decorations! How beautifully they gleam, just like the su[...]

self! And the ladies, sir. . . . Oh dear, oh dear. . . ." Yankel wagged his head again.

The soldier twirled the upper tier of his moustache and let out a sound that was not unlike the neighing of a horse.

"I'd like to ask you to do me a service, sir," said Yankel. "This prince here has come from abroad and he wants to have a look at the Cossacks. He has never seen a Cossack in his life."

The arrival of foreign counts and barons was a fairly common occurrence in Poland; they were often drawn there solely by curiosity to see this almost semi-Asiatic corner of Europe. They looked upon Muscovy and the Ukraine as parts of Asia. For this reason the soldier, making rather a low bow, thought fit to add a few words from himself.

"I don't know what you want to see them for, your excellency," he said. "They're dogs, not men, and their religion is such that everyone despises it."

"You lie, you damned rascal!" said Bulba. "You're a dog yourself! How dare you say that our religion is despised! It's your heretical faith that is despised!"

"Oho!" said the soldier. "I know who you are, my friend: you're one of the same lot I have in prison. Just a minute, I'll call our men here!"

Taras saw that he had made a bad slip, but his stubbornness and annoyance prevented him from thinking of something to mend matters. Luckily Yankel immediately came to his help.

"My lord, how is it possible that a count should be a Cossack? And if he really were a Cossack, how do you suppose he'd have come to be dressed like that? Why, doesn't he look a count?"

"Tell me another!" said the Polish soldier, about to open his big mouth and give a shout.

"Your royal highness, not a sound, please! For God's sake, not a sound!" cried Yankel. "If you quiet, we shall pay you as you've never been paid bef give you two gold pieces!"

"Two gold pieces d pieces is nothing to me! I pay

the barber that for shaving only half of my chin. A hundred gold pieces, Jew!" Here the soldier gave a twirl to the upper tier of his gigantic moustache. "And if you don't give me the hundred pieces, I'll raise the alarm at once!"

"Why so much?" the Jew murmured mournfully, turning pale and untying his leather purse.

But he was glad there was no more money in his purse and that the soldier could not count beyond a hundred.

"Come on, sir, let's go quickly! You see what a disgusting lot they are!" said Yankel, noticing that the soldier was fingering the money as though regretting he had not asked for more.

"What do you mean, you damned Pole," said Bulba. "You've taken the money and you don't intend to show them to me? You must show them to me. Now that you've got your money, you've no right to refuse."

"Go to the devil, both of you! Go on or I'll raise the alarm this very minute and then you'll. . . . Take yourselves off quick, I say!"

"Come on, sir, let's go!" cried poor Yankel. "To the devil with them! May they have such bad dreams that. . . ."

Slowly and with bowed head Bulba turned and retraced his steps, followed by reproaches from Yankel, whose heart bled at the thought of the wasted gold pieces.

"Why did you have to provoke him? Let the dog curse! Those fellows can't help cursing! O Lord, the luck of some people! A hundred gold pieces just for turning us out! And one of our people will have his side-locks pulled out and his face slapped so hard that you couldn't look at him without a shudder, but he won't be given a hundred gold pieces. Oh dear, no! O Lord, O merciful Lord!"

But their failure had a far greater effect on Bulba, which could be seen from the blazing fire in his eyes.

"Come on," he said suddenly, as though rousing himself, "let's go to the square. I want to see how they will torture him."

"But why go there, sir? We can't help him by going there, can we?"

"Come along!" Taras said obstinately, and the Jew trailed after him, sighing like a nurse.

It was not difficult to find the square where the executions were to take place: crowds of people were converging on it from all sides. In that savage age a public execution was one of the greatest attractions not only to the ignorant, but also to the upper classes. Numbers of old women of great piety, numbers of girls and young women who were so timid that all night afterwards they dreamed of bloodstained corpses and cried out in their sleep as loudly as a hussar, never missed a chance of satisfying their curiosity. "Oh, how horrible!" many of them cried hysterically, closing their eyes and turning away. "What dreadful tortures!" But they remained there all the same for quite a long time. One man stood gaping with his hands thrust forward, as though he meant to jump on the heads of the crowd to get a better view. A butcher poked his face out of the mass of narrow, small and ordinary heads, observing the whole proceedings with the air of a connoisseur and talking in monosyllables with a gunsmith whom he addressed familiarly because he had once been drinking with him in the same ale-house. Some engaged in heated discussions, others were even laying bets, but the majority belonged to the class of people who gape at everything that takes place in the world and go on picking their noses. In the front row, close to the city guards with their huge moustaches, a young gentleman, or at any rate one who looked like a gentleman, was standing. He was dressed in a military uniform and looked as if he had put on absolutely everything he had, leaving nothing in his lodging but a torn shirt and an old pair of boots. Round his neck he wore two chains, one on top of the other, with some kind of gold coins on them. He was standing with his sweetheart and kept glancing round all the time for fear someone should soil her silk dress. He explained everything to her, leaving nothing that could possibly be added. "All these crowds, my sweet," he told her, "all the people you can see here, have come to look at the execution of the criminals. And this man, darling, the one who's holding an axe and other instruments in his hand, is the executioner, and he will put them to death. And when be begins to break a criminal on the wheel and inflict other tortures on him, he will still be alive, but when his head is cut off, then, my sweet, he'll die at once. At first he'll scream and move, but directly his head is cut off he won't be able to scream, or eat, or drink, because he won't have any head, darling." And the girl heard it all with an expression of mingled horror and excitement on her face.

The roofs of the houses were black with people. Grotesque faces with moustaches and something that looked like women's nightcaps peered from dormer windows. The aristocracy sat on balconies under awnings. The pretty little hand of a laughing lady, gleaming white as sugar, lay on the railings. Illustrious noblemen, rather portly, looked on with an air of great dignity. A footman in a gorgeous livery with long, flowing sleeves was handing round various drinks and refreshments. Sometimes a playful young miss with a pair of sparkling black eyes would take a cake or some fruit in her lovely little hand and throw it to the crowd. A throng of hungry knights held out their caps to catch it, and a tall Polish gentleman in a faded red doublet with rows of tarnished golden cords, whose head towered above the crowd, was the first to catch it, thanks to his long arms, and he kissed the prize, pressed it to his heart and then put it in his mouth. A falcon, hanging in a gilt cage under the balcony, was also a spectator; with his beak on one side and one claw raised, he, too, gazed attentively at the people. But suddenly a hubbub arose in the crowd and voices were heard on all sides, "They're bringing them! They're bringing them! The Cossacks!"

They walked bareheaded, with long tufts of hair over their foreheads; their beards had been left to grow. They walked, looking neither afraid nor sullen, but with a kind of quiet dignity; their garments of costly cloth were threadbare and hung in rags about them. At the head of them all came Ostap.

What were old Taras Bulba's feelings when he saw his son Ostap? Oh, what he must have felt in his heart then! He looked at his son from the crowd and not one movement of his escaped him. Now the Cossacks drew near the scaffold. Ostap stopped. He was the first to drain that bitter cup. He looked at his comrades, raised his hand and said in a loud voice, "O God, grant that none of the heretics standing here may hear how a true Christian suffers and that none of us may utter a sound!" After this he went up to the scaffold.

"Well done, son! Well done!" Bulba murmured, and he bowed his grey head.

The hangman tore off Ostap's old rags; then they bound his arms and legs in specially made frames and . . . But we will not harrow the feelings of our readers with a description of the fiendish tortures, which would make their hair stand on end. They were the product of that coarse and savage age when man's whole life seemed to be steeped in violence and blood and his heart was so hardened that he felt no pity. In vain did some people, the few who were the exception in those days, oppose these dreadful acts. In vain did the king and many nobles, enlightened in mind and heart, argue that such cruel punishments could only inflame the vengeance of the Cossack nation. For the influence of the king and those who shared his enlightened views was of no avail beside the unbridled violence and arrogant spirit of the Polish grandees whose thoughtlessness, incredible lack of foresight, childish vanity and absurd pride turned the Seym into a travesty of government. Ostap bore the tortures and endured the agonies like a hero. Not a cry, not a moan was heard even when the bones of his arms and legs were being broken, when the awful cracking sound they made was heard amid the dead silence of the crowd, even by the remotest spectators, when the Polish ladies turned away their eyes—nothing resembling a moan escaped his lips, nor did his face falter. Taras stood in the crowd with a bowed head, but, at the same time, he murmured approvingly, raising his eyes proudly, "Well done, son! Well done!"

But when Ostap was subjected to his last mortal agonies, it seemed as though his strength was beginning to give way. He looked round. O Lord, there was not a single face he knew! Oh, if only one of his kindred were present at his death! He would not have cared to hear the sobs and lamentations of a weak mother or the frenzied cries of a wife, tearing her hair and smiting her white breasts; all he wished now was to see a resolute man who might have strengthened and comforted him with a wise word at his end. And his heart failed him and he cried out in the weakness of his spirit, "Father, where are you? Do you hear?"

"I hear!" a voice rang out amid the general silence, sending a shudder through the thousands of people who packed the square. A detachment of cavalry immediately forced their way through the crowd, carefully inspecting the people. Yankel turned pale as death, and when the mounted soldiers moved some distance away from him, he turned round fearfully to glance at Taras, but Taras was beside him no longer: he had disappeared.

🎵 X I I

Taras had reappeared. An army of one hundred and twenty thousand Cossacks mustered on the frontiers of the Ukraine. This was no small body of men or some detachment bent on plunder or out in pursuit of the Tartars. No, the whole nation had risen, for the patience of the people was at an end; they had risen to avenge the flouting of their rights, the humiliating disrespect shown to their customs, the insults heaped upon the faith of their forefathers and their sacred traditions, the desecration of their churches, the wild excesses of alien overlords, the oppression, the forced allegiance to the Pope, the shameful domination of the Jews in a Christian land, everything that had helped to store up and deepen for years and years the fierce hatred of the Cossack people. The young but intrepid hetman Ostranitza was in command of this vast Cossack army. At his side was Gunya, his aged and experienced counsellor and friend. Eight colonels led regiments of twelve thousand each. Two staff captains and one keeper of the badge of the hetman's office—a painted staff topped by a white horse-hair plume tied with red cords—rode after the hetman. The chief standard-bearer carried the principal banner; many more banners and standards fluttered in the distance; the assistants of the Keeper of the Hetman's Staff bore other badges of office. There were many other regimental ranks, officers in charge of transport and commissariat, regimental clerks and, with them, infantry and cavalry detachments; there were as many volunteers and partisans as there were regular army Cossacks. From all over the Ukraine the Cossacks had risen, from Chigirin, from Pereyaslav, from Baturin, from Glukhov, from the Lower Dnieper and from all the districts and islands of the Upper Dnieper. Horses without number and countless lines of carts trailed over the fields. And among all those Cossacks, among the eight regiments, one regiment was the best of all, and that crack regiment was under the command of Taras Bulba. Everything seemed to have combined to give him an advantage over the others: his age, his experience, his skill in manoeuvring his troops, and his hatred of the enemy, which was far more bitter than anyone's. His ruthless ferocity and cruelty seemed excessive even to the Cossacks. His grey head knew only one punishment: the fire and the gallows; and in the councils of war he had only one plan—total annihilation.

No need to describe all the battles in which the Cossacks had excelled themselves, nor the whole course of the campaign: all that is recorded in the pages of the Chronicles. Everybody knows what a war in defence of the faith is like in Russia: no force is stronger than faith. It is as firm and as terrible as the rock, unwrought by the hand of man, in the midst of the turbulent and ever-changeful sea. From the fathomless depths of the ocean it raises to the skies its indestructible walls, fashioned out of sheer rock. It can be seen from all sides and fearlessly does it challenge the waves as they dash themselves against it and roll past. And woe to the ship that is driven on it! Her weak masts and rigging are shivered, and everything aboard her is smashed and sinks beneath the wave; and the startled air is rent with the piteous cries of her doomed crew.

The pages of the Chronicles contain detailed descriptions of the flight of the Polish garrisons from the liberated cities; of the hanging of the unscrupulous Jewish contractors; of the weakness of the royal hetman Nicholas Potocki with his numerous army against the invincible Cossack force; of his defeat and pursuit and the loss of the best part of his troops in a small stream; of the siege by the relentless Cossack army of the little township of Polonnoye where he had fled with the remnants of his forces; and of his solemn oath, when finally driven into a corner, of full satisfaction on the part of the king and his government and the restoration of all their former rights and privileges. But the Cossacks were not so foolish as to be taken in by that: they knew very well what a Polish oath was worth. And Potocki would no longer have been prancing about on his six-thousand-rouble Caucasian stallion, the cynosure of the eyes of all the great ladies and the envy of the nobles, he would not have cut such a figure at the Diets, entertaining the Polish senators to sumptuous banquets, if he had not been saved by the Russian clergy of that little town. When all the priests came out to welcome the Cossacks in their bright gold chasubles, bearing icons and crosses, with their bishop at the head in his pastoral mitre and cross in hand, all the Cossacks bowed their heads and took off their caps. They would have shown no respect to anyone at that time, not even to the king himself; but they dared not do anything against their own Christian church and they showed respect to their own clergy. The hetman together with the colonels agreed to let Potocki go, taking from him a solemn oath to leave the Christian churches their full freedom, to forswear all ancient enmities, and to respect the honour of the Cossack army. Only one colonel would not consent to such a peace. That colonel was Taras. He tore a tuft of hair from his head and exclaimed:

"Hetman and colonels, do not act like old women! Don't trust the Poles; they'll betray you yet, the curs!"

When the regimental clerk presented the peace treaty for signing and the hetman put his authoritative hand to it, Taras took off his costly Turkish sabre of the finest steel, drew out the flashing blade and broke it, like a reed, in two, throwing the parts in different directions and saying, "Farewell, gentlemen! As the two parts of that sword can never be united and form one sword again, so shall we, comrades, never meet in this world! So remember my farewell words (as he said this, his voice swelled, rose higher, gathering unwonted strength—and all were abashed at his prophetic words): in the hour of your death you will think of me! You believe you've purchased peace and quiet, do you? You think every one of you is going to live like a lord, do you? You'll live like lords all right, only not the way you think: they'll tear the skin off your head, hetman, stuff it with chaff, and for years it will be seen at all the fairs! As for you, gentlemen, you won't keep your heads on your shoulders, either. In damp dungeons will you perish, immured within stone walls, if you are not boiled alive in cauldrons like sheep! And you, lads," he went on, turning to his followers, "which of you wants to die a soldier's death? Not by the stove or on comfortable beds, not drunk under the fence of an ale-house, like any other carrion, but an honourable Cossack death, all in one bed, like a bridegroom and his bride! Or do you prefer to go back to your homes, turn infidel and carry the Polish priests on your backs?"

"We go with you, Colonel! We go with you!" cried all who were in Bulba's regiment, and many others ran over to their side.

"Well, if it is with me you want to go, then follow me!" said Taras and, pushing his cap down on his head, he looked defiantly at all who stayed behind, straightened himself on his horse and shouted to his men, "Never fear; no man will reproach us or blame us! Away now, men! Let's pay a call on the Catholics!"

He whipped his horse, and one hundred carts with provisions and supplies moved off after him, and with them there were a great many Cossacks on horse and on foot, and, turning round, he again looked menacingly at those who stayed behind—and full of wrath was his look. No one dared to stop them. The regiment marched off in sight of the whole army, and Taras kept turning round and looking menacingly at them.

The hetman and the colonels were greatly disconcerted: they pondered deep and were silent for a long time as though oppressed by dark forebodings. Taras did not prophesy in vain: everything came true as he had predicted. A short time after the treacherous act at Kanev, the hetman's head was impaled on a stake, and the same fate was shared by many of the foremost men in the country.

And what did Taras do? He roamed at large all over Poland with his regiment, burnt eighteen small towns and about forty Catholic churches, and was already approaching Krakow. He had slain hundreds of Polish squires of all sorts, sacked some of the finest and richest castles; his Cossacks unsealed and spilt on the ground barrels of mead and wine hundreds of years old, carefully preserved in the cellars of Polish noblemen, cut to pieces and burnt costly cloths and garments, and smashed the vessels they found in cupboards and store-houses. "Spare nothing!" Taras kept repeating. Nor did the Cossacks spare the young, black-browed Polish ladies, white-bosomed and bright-eyed; even at the altars they could not save themselves: Taras burnt them together with their altars. Not many pairs of snow-white arms was raised from the flames to the skies, and the piteous cries would have made the damp earth itself tremble with pity and the tall steppe grass bend low. But the cruel Cossacks paid no heed to anything and, picking up the babes from the streets on their spears, they flung them into the flames, too. "That's for you in memory of Ostap!" was all Taras would say. And he celebrated Ostap's memory in this way in every town and village until the Polish Government realised that Taras Bulba's actions were something more than acts of brigandage, and the same Potocki was put at the head of five regiments and ordered to capture Taras without fail.

For six days the Cossacks retreated from their pursuers along country lanes. They fled so quickly that their horses could hardly stand the pace and just managed to save the Cossacks. But this time Potocki was equal to the task imposed upon him: he pursued them relentlessly and overtook them on the bank of the Dniester, where Bulba stopped for a rest in an abandoned, dilapidated fortress.

The fortress stood at the very edge of the precipitous bank of the river Dniester, with its shattered rampart and ruined remnants of walls. The top of the cliff was strewn with rubble and broken bricks and seemed about to topple over into the river. It was there that the royal Hetman Potocki surrounded Taras Bulba's forces on the two sides that looked out on the open plain. For four days the Cossacks fought hard against the Polish troops, using bricks and stones to keep the attackers at bay. But as their supplies had run out and their strength was exhausted, Taras decided to fight his way through the enemy ranks. The Cossacks would have fought their way through and their swift horses would perhaps have served them well once more, had not Taras suddenly stopped in full flight and shouted, "Halt! I've dropped my pipe and tobacco. I won't leave even my pipe to those damned Poles!" And the old Cossack commander bent down and began looking in 'the grass for his pipe with tobacco, which had been his inseparable companion by land and by sea, on the march and at home. Meanwhile a whole band of the enemy swooped down on him and seized him by his powerful shoulders. He strained every muscle in his body in an attempt to shake them off, but this time the Polish soldiers did not scatter on the ground as they did in the past. "Oh, old age, old age!" the stout old Cossack muttered and burst into tears. But old age was not to blame: superior force prevailed against force. Nearly thirty men were hanging on to his arms and legs.

"Caught you at last!" the Poles shouted. "Now all that remains to be done is to decide what honour to bestow on the dog!"

And with the hetman's permission, they decided to burn him alive in the sight of all.

A dead tree whose top had been struck by lightning stood only a few yards away from the place where they had captured him. They fastened him with iron chains to the trunk of the tree, nailed his hands to it, and having raised him up higher so that he could be seen from every side, they began to build a fire under the tree. But Taras did not look on the pile of wood, nor did he think of the fire in which they were going to burn him: the poor fellow gazed in the direction where the Cossacks were keeping up a steady fire against their pursuers. He could see everything plainly from his height. "Quick, men, occupy the hill!" he shouted. "The hill behind the wood! They can't get you there!" But the wind did not carry his words. "Oh, they're lost! They're lost!" he cried in despair and glanced below where the waters of the Dniester sparkled. A gleam of joy came into his eyes. He saw the sterns of four boats protruding from behind the scrub, and he shouted at the top of his voice, "To the river bank! To the river bank, lads! Take the cliff path on your left! There are boats on the bank! Bo-o-ats! Take 'em all! They won't be able to pursue you!"

This time the wind blew from the other direction, and the Cossacks heard every word he said. But for such advice he received a blow on the head with the back of an axe, and everything went black before his eyes.

The Cossacks rode full speed down the hill path with their pursuers hot on their trail. But the path twisted and turned too much, and, halting for an instant, they all said, "Come on, boys, we've nothing to lose! Down we go!" And they raised their whips and whistled. Their Tartar horses rose from the ground, flattened out in the air like snakes, leapt over the ravine and plunged straight into the Dniester. Only two of them did not jump far enough to fall into the river, and they hurtled down from the top of the cliff on to the rocks below and perished there with their horses without even uttering a cry. All the rest of the Cossacks were swimming in the river with their horses and unmooring the boats. The Poles stopped at the brink of the precipice, marvelling at the incredible feat of the Cossacks and wondering whether to jump or not.

One colonel, a hot-blooded, impetuous young man, the brother of the beautiful Polish girl who had bewitched poor Andrey, did not hesitate long, but leapt with his horse and crashed upon the sharp rocks. He was torn to pieces by the sharp stones and perished at the bottom of the precipice, his brains mingled with his blood, bespattering the shrubs which grew on the rugged walls of the chasm.

By the time Bulba recovered from the blow and looked at the Dniester, the Cossacks were in their boats and rowing away; bullets were showered upon them from above, but did not reach them. And the eyes of the old Cossack flashed with joy.

"Farewell, comrades!" he shouted to them from above. "Remember me and come here again next spring, and have a merry time! Well, who won, you damned villains? Do you think there's anything in the world a Cossack is afraid of? You wait, the time's coming when you'll learn what the orthodox Russian faith is! Already the nations of the world, far and near, are beginning to feel that a Czar will arise in Russia so mighty that there will be no power on earth that will not submit to him! . . ."

By now the fire was rising above the heap of dry wood, the flames were enveloping his legs, and in another minute they spread all over the tree. . . . But are there any fires or any tortures or indeed any force in the whole world that can prevail against Russian force?

The Dniester is no small river, and it has creeks, dense sedges, sandbanks and deep pools without number; the surface of the river, smooth as a mirror, sparkles and glitters, ringing with the loud call of swans, and the proud golden-eye skims swiftly over its waves, and there are many snipe, buff-breasted sandpipers and other wild fowl among its reeds and on its banks. The Cossacks rowed swiftly in the narrow, double-ruddered boats; they rowed as one man, carefully avoiding the sandbanks, rousing the birds, which took wing—and they talked of their commander.

PART II

*Viy**

As soon as the rather loud seminary bell, hanging at the gates of the Bratsky Monastery, rang out in the morning in Kiev, crowds of schoolboys and seminarists would come hurrying there from all over the town. Seminarists of the lower forms, known as grammarians and rhetoricians, and those of the higher forms, known as philosophers and theologians, trudged to their classrooms with their exercise books under their arms. The grammarians were still small boys and, as they walked along, they pushed each other and swore at one another in shrill treble voices; they almost all wore filthy, tattered clothes and their pockets were always full of all sorts of rubbish, such as knucklebones, whistles made out of feathers, a half-eaten pie, and sometimes even tiny sparrow chicks,

* Viy is a colossal creature of popular imagination. The Ukrainians give this name to the chief of the gnomes whose eyelids reach down to the ground. The whole story is a folk legend. I did not wish to change it and I tell it almost in the same simple way as I heard it.

one of whom suddenly chirruping in the dead silence of the class-room earned its patron sound blows with a ruler on both hands and, occasionally, a thrashing with cherry twigs. The rhetoricians walked more sedately: their clothes were quite often decent, but their faces almost invariably wore some adornment in the shape of a rhetorical trope: either one eye had disappeared right under the forehead, or there was a huge blister in place of a lip, or some other distinctive mark; these talked and swore among themselves in tenor voices. The philosophers went a whole octave lower; there was nothing in their pockets except strong tobacco made of the crushed roots of the plants. They kept nothing to eat later, but ate everything they came across there and then; they reeked of pipes and vodka so strongly that a passing workman would stop in his tracks and sniff the air for a long time like a setter dog.

The market, as a rule, was only begining to stir at that time, and the market-women with thick, ring-shaped rolls, ordinary rolls, water-melon seeds and poppy-cakes vied with each other in pulling at the skirts of those whose coats were of fine cloth or some cotton material.

"This way, young gentlemen, this way!" they would say from all sides. "Here are thick-rolls, poppy-cakes, twists, good white rolls! Good ones! Really good ones! Made with honey! I baked them my-self!"

Another market-woman, lifting something long made out of twisted dough, would yell: "Here's a bread-stick! Buy a bread-stick, young gentlemen!"

"Don't buy anything from her! See what a nasty woman she is— look at her ugly nose and dirty hands!!"

But they were afraid to accost the philosophers and theologians, for the philosophers and theologians always liked to taste things first and they usually helped themselves to handfuls.

On their arrival at the seminary, the crowd made their way to their low-pitched but fairly large classrooms with little windows, wide doors and dirty benches. The classroom was immediately

filled with all sorts of buzzing sounds: the "auditors," mostly students from the higher classes, heard their pupils repeat their lessons: the treble of the grammarian rang so loudly that it evoked
almost the same note from the window pane; in a corner a rhetorician, whose mouth and thick lips ought really to have belonged to
a philosopher, was droning in a bass voice and all that could be
heard at a distance was: "Boo, boo, boo. . . ." The auditor, while
hearing the lesson, would glance with one eye under the bench,
where a role or fruit dumpling or some melon seeds were peeping
out of the pocket of the seminarist placed under his supervision.

When this erudite crowd managed to arrive a little early and
when they knew that the professors would be later than usual, then
by general consent they got up a fight. In this fight everyone had to
take part, including the monitors whose duty it was to look after
the good behavior and the morals of all this learned profession.
The theologians usually made the arrangements for the battle:
whether each class had to defend itself separately or whether all
were to be divided into two parties: the bursars and the seminarists.
In any case, the grammarians were the first to start fighting, but as
soon as the rhetoricians entered into the fray, they ran away and
took up a position on top of the desks to watch the battle. Next the
philosophers, with long, black moustaches, joined in, and finally
the thick-necked theologians in their awe-inspiring wide trousers.
As a rule, it all ended by theology routing the rest, and philosophy,
rubbing its ribs, was forced back into its classroom and sat down
on the benches to rest. The professor, who had himself at one time
taken part in similar engagements could, on entering the class, see
in a flash from the red faces of his students that the fight had been
a good one, and while he was caning the rhetoricians on the fingers,
in another classroom another professor would be administering
punishment to philosophy's hands with a ruler. The theologians
were dealt with in quite a different way: they were each served,
to use the expression of a professor of theology, a measure of *large
peas* in the shape of short leather thongs.

On holidays and festive occasions the seminarists and the bursars went from house to house with their puppet shows. Sometimes they acted a play, in which case some theologian, almost as tall as the Kiev belfry, would distinguish himself in the part of Herodias or Potiphar's wife. As a reward they received a piece of linen or sack of millet or half a boiled goose, or something of that sort.

All that learned crowd, both the seminarists and the bursars, who conducted a sort of hereditary feud among themselves, were very hard up and could ill afford the bare necessities of life, and yet they were at the same time terrible gluttons; indeed, it was quite impossible to add up the number of dumplings each of them bolted during an evening meal and, therefore, the voluntary contributions of the well-to-do citizens could not be sufficient for them. It was then that the "senate" of philosophers and theologians sent the grammarians and rhetoricians, under the supervision of a philosopher, who sometimes joined them, with sacks on their shoulders to lay waste the kitchen-gardens—and pumpkin porridge made its appearance in the seminary. The "senators" gorged themselves on melons and water-melons, so that next day their "auditors" heard two lessons from them instead of one: one issuing from their lips and another growling from their stomachs. The bursars and the seminarists wore long garments resembling frock coats, reaching *to the present time,* a technical term, signifying below the heels.

The most solemn occasion for the seminary was the advent of the vacation, which began in June, when the students were usually sent back to their homes. Then the whole highroad was dotted with grammarians, philosophers and theologians. Those who had no homes of their own usually went to stay with one of their classmates. The philosophers and theologians usually got jobs as *temporary* tutors, that is to say, they undertook to teach children of well-to-do families so as to prepare them for the entrance examinations and received in payment a pair of new boots, and sometimes even a coat. The whole gang trailed along together like some gypsy encampment, cooked their porridge and slept in the open. Everyone carried a sack in which he had one shirt and a pair of leg-wrappers. The theologians were particularly thrifty and careful: anxious not to wear out their boots, they took them off, hung them on sticks and carried them on their shoulders, especially if it was muddy; rolling up their trousers above their knees, they then strode splashing through the puddles regardless of anything. The moment they caught sight of a hamlet in the distance they would turn off the highway and approaching a cottage which looked a little better kept than the rest, stood in a row in front of the windows and begin singing hymns at the top of their voices. The master of the house, some old Cossack villager, would listen to them for a long time, his head propped up on his hands, then he would weep bitterly and turn to his wife and say: "Wife, what the scholars are singing must be very wise: give them some bacon or anything else we have." And a whole bowl of dumplings were emptied into the sack, followed by a big lump of bacon, several white loaves, and sometimes even a trussed hen. Fortified with such a supply of food, the grammarians, rhetoricians, philosophers and theologians carried on with their journey. The further they went, however, the more their numbers dwindled. Most of them dispersed to their homes and only those remained whose parents lived further away.

Once, during such a journey, three bursars turned off the highway to replenish their supply of provisions at the first hamlet they came across, for their sacks had long been empty. They were the theologian Khalyava, the philosopher Khoma Brut and the rhetorician Tibery Gorobets.

The theologian was a tall, broad-shouldered fellow, and had an extremely odd habit: whatever lay within his reach, he was sure to steal, otherwise he was of an exceedingly gloomy disposition. When he got drunk he used to hide in the tall weeds, and it gave the seminary a great deal of trouble to find him there.

The philosopher Khoma Brut was of a merry disposition. He was fond of lying on his back and smoking a pipe. If ever he went on a drinking spree, he engaged musicians and danced the tropak. He often had a taste of the *large peas,* but he took it with perfect philosophical *insouciance,* saying that what had to be, had to be.

The rhetorician Tibery Gorobets had not yet qualified to wear a moustache, to drink vodka or to smoke a pipe. He only wore a long forelock on his shaven head and hence his character does not seem to have been sufficiently formed at that time, but to judge from the big bumps on his forehead with which he often appeared in class, one could safely assume that one day he would become a first-class warrior. The theologian Khalyava and the philosopher Khoma often pulled him by the forelock as a sign of their patronage and employed him as their errand boy.

It was evening when they turned off the highway. The sun had only just set and the warmth of the day still lingered in the air. The theologian and the philosopher walked along in silence smoking their pipes; the rhetorician Tibery Gorobets decapitated with his stick the thistles growing by the wayside. The road ran between scattered clumps of oak and nut-trees, growing in the meadow. Small, undulating hills, green and round like cupolas, sometimes intersected the plain. A cornfield with ripening wheat which ap-peared in two places showed that some village must be near. But it was more than an hour since they had passed the cornfield and still they had not come upon any dwelling. Dusk had fallen, the sky had grown completely dark, only in the west the faint scarlet glow of sunset was still visible.

"What the hell!" said the philosopher Khoma Brut. "I could have sworn we'd come across a hamlet any minute!"

The theologian said nothing, looked round at the surrounding countryside, then put the pipe back into his mouth, and they all continued on their way.

"Hell," said the philosopher, stopping again, "can't see a damn thing."

"Well, perhaps we shall come across some hamlet further on," said the theologian, without removing his pipe.

Meanwhile night had fallen, and a rather dark night too, it was. Small clouds increased the darkness and, as far as they could judge, they could expect neither stars nor moon. The seminarists noticed that they had lost their way and had for a long time been walking off the road.

The philosopher, after shuffling about with his feet in every direction, said at last abruptly: "But where is the road?"

The theologian said nothing and, after pondering for a while remarked: "Yes, it's a dark night all right."

The rhetorician walked off to one side and tried to feel for the road on all fours, but his hands only came upon foxes' holes. All round them was the steppe and it seemed that there was no one travelling across it just then. Our travellers made another attempt to carry on, but there was the same wilderness everywhere. The philosopher tried shouting, but his voice died away in the distance and met with no reply. A few moments later, though, they heard a faint moaning like that of a wolf.

"What the hell are we going to do?" said the philosopher.

"To do? Why, stay here and spend the night in the open," said the theologian, feeling in his pocket for the flint to light his pipe again.

But the philosopher would not agree to this. He had always been in the habit of tucking away for the night a thick slice of bread and four pounds of fat bacon and this time he had an insufferable feeling of loneliness in his stomach. Besides, in spite of his cheerful character, the philosopher was rather afraid of wolves.

"No, Khalyava," he said, "it's no good. How on earth can you expect anyone to stretch out and lie down on the bare ground like a dog without having first fortified himself properly. Let's try again. Maybe we'll come across some house and get at least a glass of vodka before turning in."

At the word "vodka" the theologian spat and said: "Why, of course. It's no use staying in the open."

The seminarists walked on and to their intense delight, they thought they could hear the sound of barking in the distance. Listening which direction it came from, they went ahead more boldly and after a little distance saw a light.

"A hamlet, damned if it's not a hamlet!" said the philosopher.

He was not wrong in his supposition: a few moments later they indeed caught sight of a little homestead, consisting of two cottages in one and the same courtyard. There was a light in the windows. A dozen plum-trees could be seen near the fence. Looking through the gates made of paling, they saw a yard filled with the ox-carts of traders who took grain to the Crimea and brought back dried fish and salt to the Ukraine. At that moment a few stars could be seen twinkling in the sky here and there.

"Now then, fellows, remember not to be put off. We must get a night's lodging at any cost!"

The three learned men knocked on the gates all together and shouted: "Open up!"

The door of one of the cottages creaked and a moment later the seminarists saw before them an old woman in an unlined sheepskin coat.

"Who's there?" she shouted with a hollow cough.

"Let's have a night's lodging, Granny. We've lost our way. A night in the open is as bad as an empty belly."

"What sort of people are you?"

"Why, we're humble fellows: Khalyava, a theologian. Brut, a philosopher, and Gorobets, a rhetorician."

"Sorry, I can't let you in," grumbled the old woman. "I've a lot of people in the house, every corner is full. Where am I to put you? And such big, hulking men too! Why, my cottage will fall to pieces if I put fellows like you in it. I know these philosophers and theologians! If I started taking in such drunkards, there'd soon be nothing left of my house and home. Be off with you! Be off! There's no place for you here."

"Take pity on us, granny. You wouldn't let Christian souls be lost for no reason at all, would you? Put us where you please. And if we do anything—anything at all—you understand—then may our arms be withered and may God punish us as He only knows how. Yes, ma'am!"

The old woman seemed a little mollified.

"All right," she said, as though considering what to do with them, "I'll let you in, only I'll put you all in different places. For if you're all together I shan't have a moment's peace of mind."

"You can do as you please," replied the seminarists. "We won't raise any objections."

The gates creaked and they went into the yard. "Look here granny, what about—er as they say—I mean, my stomach feels as though someone was driving a cart though it. Haven't had a bite since morning, you see. . . ."

"I see, so that's what you want," said the old woman. "Sorry, I've nothing, nothing at all to give you. Haven't even had my oven heated today."

"Why," said the philosopher, "we'd pay you for everything tomorrow morning in hard cash. Yes," he added in an undertone, "the devil a bit you'll get."

"Go in, go in, and be satisfied with what you're given. What fastidious young gentlemen the devil has brought us, to be sure!"

Khoma, the philosopher, was thrown into utter dejection by these words. But suddenly his nose perceived the smell of dried fish. He glanced at the wide trousers of the theologian who was walking beside him, and saw a huge fishtail sticking out of his pocket. The theologian had already succeeded in filching a whole carp from one of the oxcarts. And as he had done this from no motive of self interest, but simply from habit and forgetting his carp, was already looking for something else to filch, having no intention of missing even a broken wheel, Khoma, the philosopher, put his hand into the theologian's pocket, as if it were his own, and pulled out the carp.

The old woman put the seminarists in their several places: She found a place for the rhetorician in the cottage, she locked the theologian in an empty closet, and showed the philosopher to a sheep's pen, which was also empty.

Left by himself, the philosopher at once ate the carp, examined the wattled walls of the pen, kicked an inquisitive pig, which woke up, in the snout which it thrust in from the next pen, and turned over on the other side, intending to fall into a sound sleep. Suddenly the low door opened and the old woman, bending down stepped into the pen.

"Why, Granny, what do you want?" said the philosopher.

But the old woman was coming straight towards him with outstretched arms.

"Oho," thought the philosopher, "so that's it! No, my sweet, you're too old for that kind of lark!" and he moved away a little, but the old woman unceremoniously, came up to him again.

"Now, listen, Granny," said the philosopher, "it's a fast day today, and I'm not the sort of man who would do anything sinful on a fast day for a thousand gold pieces."

But, without uttering a word, the old woman was stretching out her arms in an attempt to catch him.

The philosopher got scared, especially when he noticed her eyes flash with a strange glitter.

"Granny, what's the matter with you? Go—go—in peace!" he shouted.

But the old woman uttered no word, but continued trying to catch him with her hands.

He jumped to his feet intending to run, but the old woman stood in the doorway, fixing her glittering eyes on him, and again began approaching him.

The philosopher wanted to push her away with his hands, but to his surprise he noticed that he could not lift his arms, that his legs would not move, and he perceived with horror that even his voice would not obey him: words stirred on his lips without a sound escaping them. All he heard was the pounding of his heart; he saw the old woman come up to him, she folded his arms, bent his head down, leapt with the alacrity of a cat upon his back, struck him with a besom on his side and, prancing like a saddle-horse, he carried her on his shoulders. All this happened so quickly that before he knew what he was doing, the philosopher clutched his knees with both hands, trying to stop his legs from moving; but, to his intense astonishment, they lifted against his will and leapt forward more swiftly than a Circassian racer. It was only when they had left the farm behind them and an open plain stretched before them with a forest, black as coal (on one side of it), that he said to himself: "Good Lord, she's a witch!"

The waning crescent of the moon was shining in the sky. The shy radiance of midnight lay, like a transparent veil, in a light haze over the earth. The woods, the meadows, the sky, the valleys— everything seemed to be slumbering with open eyes. Not a breeze fluttered anywhere even for a fleeting moment. There was something moistly warm in the freshness of the night. The shadows of the trees and bushes fell like comets in the pointed wedges of the sloping plain. Such was the night when Khoma Brut galloped along with the mysterious rider on his back. He felt a kind of exhausting, unpleasant and, at the same time, voluptuous sensation spreading to his heart. He lowered his head and saw the grass, which had been almost under his feet, growing far below him. Above it lay a sheet of water, as transparent as a mountain stream, and the grass seemed to be at the bottom of a lambent sea, limpid to its very depths—at least he saw himself and the old woman sitting on his back clearly reflected in it. It was a sun instead of a moon that he saw shining there. He heard the blue harebells ringing as they inclined their little heads. He saw a water nymph swimming out from behind the reeds. He caught a glimpse of her back and her leg— curved and supple, all made of brightness and shimmering. She turned towards him—there was her face, with its bright, sparkling, keen eyes. . . . She was singing and her song went straight to his heart. . . . Now her face was coming nearer and nearer, it was already on the surface, but, shaking with sparkling laughter, it moved further and further away. A moment later she turned on her back and her cloudlike breasts, matte like unglazed porcelain, gleamed in the sun round their white, supple, soft circumambience. The water in the shape of tiny bubbles covered them as with beads. She was all quivering and laughing in the water. . . .

Did he see it or did he not? Was it really happening or was he dreaming? But what was that? Wind or music? It was ringing and ringing and reverberating and coming nearer and nearer and piercing his heart with a kind of unendurable trill.

"What's all this?" thought the philosopher Khoma Brut, looking down as he galloped along at full speed. He was dripping with sweat. He was overcome by a fiendishly voluptuous sensation, by a kind of stabbing, a kind of exhaustingly thrilling pleasure. He often felt as though he had no heart at all any more and he clutched at it with terror. Worn out, confused, he tried to recall any prayer he knew. He called to mind all the exorcisms against evil spirits and, suddenly, he felt a little refreshed; he felt that his step was growing slower and that the witch's hold on his back was getting weaker. The thick grass touched him and he no longer saw anything in it. The bright crescent of the moon was shining in the sky.

"All right!" thought the philosopher Khoma to himself and began saying the exorcisms almost aloud. At last, quick as lightning, he sprang from under the old woman and in his turn leapt on her back. The old woman, with short, invisible steps, ran so fast that the rider could scarcely catch his breath. The ground seemed to flash by under him. He could see everything clearly in the moonlight, though the moon was not full. The valleys were smooth, but at that quick pace everything flashed by indistinctly and confusedly before his eyes. He snatched up a piece of wood that lay on the ground and began to rain blows on the old woman with all his might. She uttered wild cries; at first they were angry and menacing, then they grew fainter, sweeter, clearer, and then rang out softly like delicate silver bells, and went straight to his heart. Involuntarily the thought flashed through his mind: was it really an old woman?

"Oh, I can't any more!" she murmured, and collapsed exhausted on the ground.

He stood up and looked into her eyes: the sun was rising and in the distance the golden domes of the Kiev churches were gleaming. Before him lay a beautiful young girl, her lovely plait of hair undone and in disorder and her eyelashes as long as arrows. Her lean white arms were thrown back lifelessly and she kept moaning, her eyes staring upwards and full of tears.

Khoma trembled like a leaf on a tree: he was overcome by pity and a strange feeling of excitement and timidity he had never known before; he started running as fast as his legs would carry him. His heart throbbed uneasily as he ran and, try as he might, he could not explain to himself the new strange sensation that had taken possession of him. He no longer wanted to go begging at farms and hastened back to Kiev, thinking all the way about this incomprehensible adventure of his.

There were hardly any seminarists left in the town: they were dispersed about the farms, either taking jobs as tutors or simply wandering from one farm to another, for at the Ukrainian farms one could get dumplings, cheese, sour cream and curd or fruit puddings as big as a hat without paying a groat for them. The large, dilapidated house in which the bursars were lodged was quite empty and however much the philosopher rummaged in every corner and felt in all the holes, he could find neither a piece of bacon nor a stale white roll which were usually hidden away by the bursars.

However, our philosopher soon found a way of mending his affairs: he walked whistling three times through the market, winked at last at a young widow in a yellow bonnet, who was selling ribbons, shot and wheels—and was that very day fed on wheat dumplings, a chicken and—in short, it is quite impossible to enumerate the dishes on the table laid for him in the little mud house in the middle of a cherry orchard. The same evening our philosopher was seen in a tavern: he was lying on a bench, smoking, as was his habit, his pipe, and in the sight of all, flung the Jewish landlord half a gold ducat. A mug stood before him. He gazed at the people who came in and went out with cool, contented eyes and thought no longer about his extraordinary adventure.

Meanwhile rumours were circulating everywhere that the daughter of one of the richest Cossack captains, who lived about fifty miles from Kiev, had one day returned home from a walk beaten black and blue. She had hardly the strength to drag herself to her father's house and was lying at the point of death. But she had expressed the wish that one of the Kiev seminarists, Khoma Brut, should read the prayer for the dying over her and the psalms for three days after her death.

Our philosopher heard of it from the rector himself who had summoned him to his room and told him that he should set off on the journey without delay, for the distinguished Cossack captain had sent servants and a carriage to fetch him.

The philosopher shuddered from some unaccountable feeling which he could not explain to himself. A dark foreboding told him that something evil was in store for him. Without knowing himself why, he declared bluntly that he would not go.

"Listen, dominus Khoma," said the rector, who in certain contingencies talked very civilly to those under his authority, "I'm damned well not asking you whether you want to go or not. All I have to say to you is that if you go on showing off your cleverness and obstinacy, I'll have you so thoroughly flogged with green birch twigs all over your back and everywhere else that there will be no need for you to go to the bathhouse afterwards!"

The philosopher, scratching lightly behind his ear, went out without uttering a word, intending at the first favourable opportunity to put his trust in his heels. Sunk in thought, he went down the steep staircase leading into the yard, planted round with poplars, and stopped for a moment as he heard quite distinctly the voice of the rector giving orders to his butler and someone else, probably one of the servants sent to fetch him by the Cossack captain.

"Thank your master for the grain and the eggs," said the rector, "and tell him I will send him the books he writes about as soon as they are ready. I have already given them to a scribe to be copied. And don't forget, my dear fellow, to mention to your master that I know there are excellent fish on his farm, especially sturgeon, and I'd be glad if he'd send some when opportunity offers. Here in the market they are bad and dear. And you, Yavtukh, let the lads have a glass of vodka each, and tie up the philosopher or he'll run off."

"The dirty dog," the philosopher thought to himself. "Guessed it, the long-legged mountebank."

He went down and saw a covered waggon which he nearly mistook for a barn for drying crops on wheels. And indeed it was deep as a brick kiln. It was only an ordinary Cracow carriage in which about a score of Jews travel together with their wares to all the towns where their noses smell out a fair. Six healthy and stalwart Cossacks of early middle age were waiting for him. Their Ukranian tunics of fine cloth with tassels showed that they belonged to a rather important and wealthy master. Small scars on their faces bore evidence that at some time they had been in battle, not without glory.

"What's to be done?" thought the philosopher. "One cannot escape one's destiny!" And turning to the Cossacks, he said: "Good day to you, my friends."

"Good health to you, master philosopher," some of the Cossacks replied.

"So I shall be travelling with you?" he asked, clambering into the carriage. "A lovely carriage!" he went on. "You could hire some musicians and have a dance in it."

"Yes, sir, a regular chariot," said one of the Cossacks, seating himself on the box next to the driver, who had tied a rag over his head in place of the cap he had managed to leave behind in a pot-house. The other five and the philosopher got inside the waggon and settled themselves on sacks filled with the various purchases they had made in the town.

"It would be interesting to know," said the philosopher, "how many horses would be needed if this carriage were loaded with goods of some sort—say, salt or iron tires."

"Aye," said the Cossack on the box after a pause, "I expect it would need a fairish number of horses."

After such a satisfactory answer the Cossack considered that he was entitled not to utter another word for the rest of the journey.

The philosopher was very anxious to find out more about who the Cossack captain was, what kind of man he was, what was the latest news about his daughter who had returned home in so strange a way and was at the point of death and whose story was now connected with his own, how they all were and what was going on in their house. He plied them with questions, but the Cossacks, too, must have been philosophers, for they made no answer, but went on smoking their pipes as they lay on the sacks. Only one of them turned to the driver on the box with a brief order. "Mind, Overko, you old buzzard, when you get near the tavern on the Chukhraylovsky road, don't forget to stop and waken me and the other lads if any should happen to be asleep." After which he fell asleep, snoring loudly. However, these instructions were quite unnecessary, for as soon as this gigantic carriage drew near the tavern on the Chukhraylovsky road, they all cried in one voice: "Stop!" Besides, Overko's horses were already trained to stop at every tavern. In spite of the hot July day they all got out of the waggon and went into the dirty low-pitched room where the Jewish landlord rushed to welcome his old friends with every sign of delight. The Jew produced from under the skirts of his coat some ham and sausages and, after putting them on the table, at once turned away from this food forbidden by the Talmud. They all sat down round the table. Earthenware mugs appeared before each of the guests. The philosopher Khoma had to take part in the general merry-making and, as Ukrainians, when tipsy, invariably start kissing each other or crying, the whole cottage soon resounded with kisses. "Well, Spirid, let's kiss!" "Come here, Dorosh, I want to embrace you!"

A Cossack with a grey moustache, who was older than the rest, propped his head on his cheek and began sobbing bitterly because he had no father and no mother and was all alone in the world. Another, a great one for argument, kept consoling him, saying: "Don't cry, please, don't. I mean to say, God alone knows how it is and what it is all about. . . ." The one who was called Dorosh became very inquisitive and, addressing the philosopher Khoma, kept asking him: "What do they teach you at your seminary? Is it the same as what the deacon reads in the church or something else?"

"Don't ask," the moraliser drawled. "Let it be just as it is. God knows what is wanted. God knows everything."

"But I want to know," Dorosh said, "what's written in them books. Maybe it's quite different from the deacon's."

"Oh dear, oh dear," the worthy preceptor exclaimed, "Why go on like this. It's God's will. What He has decided cannot be altered."

"I want to know all that's written. I'll join the seminary, I will. You don't suppose I can't learn, do you? I'll learn everything, I will."

"Oh dear, oh dear," muttered the comforter as he dropped his head on the table, for he was quite incapable of supporting it on his shoulders any longer.

The other Cossacks were discussing their masters and then questioned why the moon was shining in the sky.

The philosopher Khoma, seeing the sort of state they were in, decided to take advantage of it and make his escape. He first addressed the greyheaded Cossack who was bemoaning the loss of his father and mother.

"What are you crying about, Uncle?" he said. "Look at me: I, too, am an orphan. Let me go, lads. What do you want with me?"

"Yes, let him go," several Cossacks agreed. "He's an orphan, isn't he? Let him go where he likes!"

"Oh Lord, oh Lord," said the comforter, raising his head. "Let him go. Let him go where he likes!"

And the Cossacks were indeed about to lead him outside to let him go, but the one who had been so inquisitive stopped them.

"Don't touch him," he said. "I want to talk to him about the seminary. I'm going to join it myself . . . !"

The escape could hardly have taken place in any case, for when the philosopher made up his mind to get up from the table, his legs felt as if they were made of wood and he began to see such a multitude of doors in the room that it is doubtful if he could have discovered the real one.

Not before evening did the entire company wake up to the fact that it was time to resume their journey. Hoisting themselves up into the waggon, they drove slowly along the road, urging on the horses and singing a song, the words and the meaning of which no one could have made out. After driving aimlessly all over the countryside for most of the night, losing their way again and again, though they knew every inch of the road, they drove at last down a steep hill into a valley, and the philosopher noticed a palisade or wattle fence running alongside it with low trees and roofs peeping out behind them. This was the big village belonging to the Cossack captain. It was long past midnight; the sky was dark and there were little stars twinkling here and there. No light was to be seen in a single cottage. They drove into the yard to the accompaniment of the barking of dogs. Thatched barns and little cottages could be seen on both sides. One of them, standing exactly in the middle opposite the gates was larger than the others and was apparently the residence of the Cossack landowner. The carriage pulled up before a small shed that seemed to serve for a barn and our travellers went off to bed. The philosopher, however, wished to have a closer look at the outside of the manor house, but hard as he stared, he could make out nothing distinctly: instead of a house he fancied a bear, and the chimney turned into the rector. The philosopher gave up his idea of making his escape and went to bed.

When the philosopher woke up the whole house was in an uproar: the daughter of the Cossack captain had died in the night. Servants were running to and fro; some old women were crying; a crowd of peasants were peering through the fence at the house as though they might see something there.

The philosopher began inspecting at his leisure the things he had not been able to make out at night. The manor house was a small low-pitched building such as were usually erected in the Ukraine in the old days. The roof was thatched. A small, high, pointed pediment with a little window, looking like an eye turned upwards, was all painted in blue and yellow flowers and red crescents. It rested on small oak pillars, round above and hexagonal below, with a fanciful carving at the top. Under this pediment was a little porch with benches on each side. At either side of the house were awnings resting on similar pillars with spiral carvings on some of them. A tall pear-tree with a pyramidal top and trembling green leaves grew in front of the house. Two rows of grain barns in the middle of the yard formed a sort of wide street leading to the house. Behind the barns and next to the gate two triangular storehouses stood facing each other; they, too, were thatched. Each triangular wall had a little door and all sorts of pictures painted on it. On one of them was painted a Cossack sitting on a barrel and holding a mug over his head with this inscription: "I'll drink it all." On another was painted a bottle, a number of flagons, and at the sides as a special ornament a horse upside down, a pipe, a tambourine, with the inscription: "Vodka is the Cossack's delight." Through the huge window of the loft of one of the barns could be seen a drum and brass trumpets. Two cannons stood at the gates. Everything pointed to the fact that the

master of the house was fond of merrymaking and that the courtyard often resounded with the cries of revellers. There were two
windmills outside the gate. Behind the house were orchards and
all that could be glimpsed through the tops of the trees were the
dark caps of the chimneys of the cottages which were hidden in
a green thicket. The whole village lay in the broad and level ter-
race of a hill. From the north everything was screened by the
steep side of the hill. The courtyard lay at its very foot. Looked at
from below, the hill seemed even steeper, and here and there on
its tall top irregular stalks of gaunt weeds stood out black against
the clear sky. The sight of its bare loamy surface was, somehow,
depressing; it was all gashed with gullies and ravines scooped out
by the rains. In two places on its steep slope stood two cottages; a
spreading apple-tree, banked up with earth and supported with
short stakes near the roots, extended its branches over one of them.
Knocked off by the wind, the apples rolled down right into the
yard of the manor house. The road, meandering down the hill
from its very top, ran past the courtyard to the village. When the
philosopher surveyed its terrible steepness and recalled their journey of the previous night, he came to the conclusion that either
the master had very clever horses or the Cossacks had very strong
heads to have known even while in an alcoholic daze how to avoid
crashing down head over heels with the enormous waggon and
the goods in it. The philosopher was standing on the highest point
in the yard; when he turned and looked in the opposite direction,
the view that met his eyes was quite different. The village and the
remaining slope of the hill abutted upon a plain. Boundless meadows stretched as far as the eye could see, their brilliant verdure
growing darker the further away they were; whole rows of villages
could be clearly seen in the blue distance, though they must have
been at least fifteen miles away. On the right side of the meadows
was a range of hills and far, far away the Dnieper gleamed inter-
mittently—a barely perceptible streak of light and darkness.

"Oh, what a glorious spot!" said the philosopher. "How I

wish I could live here, fishing in the Dnieper and the ponds, catching birds with nets or shooting little bustards or king-snipe. There must be lots of great bustard, too, in those meadows, I shouldn't wonder. One could also dry lots of fruit and sell it in the town, or, better still, make vodka of it, for vodka distilled out of fruit is incomparably superior to any grain vodka. Still, I might as well consider how to slip away from here."

He noticed a little path behind the fence completely hidden by tall weeds. He set his foot on it mechanically, intending first to go for a walk, make his way quietly between the cottages, and then dash into the open country, when he suddenly felt a rather heavy hand on his shoulder. Behind him stood the old Cossack who on the previous evening had so bitterly bewailed the death of his father and mother and his own loneliness.

"You're not thinking, Mr. Philosopher, of giving us the slip, are you?" he said. "This is not the sort of place you can run away from, and the roads too are bad for one on foot. You'd better come with me to the master: he's been expecting you for some time in the parlour."

"Let's go by all means," said the philosopher. "I don't mind I'm sure," and he followed the Cossack.

The cavalry captain, an elderly man with a grey moustache and an expression of gloomy sadness, was sitting at a table in the parlour, his head propped up on his hands. He was about fifty, but the deep despondency on his face and a kind of gaunt pallor showed that his soul had been crushed and shattered all at once, in one moment, and all his old gaiety and noisy life had vanished forever. When Khoma and the old Cossack came in, he removed one hand and nodded slightly in response to their bow.

Khoma and the old Cossack stopped respectfully at the door.

"Who are you, where do you come from, and what is your calling, my good man?" said the captain neither affably nor sternly.

"I'm a bursar, sir. Philosopher Khoma Brut."

"Who was your father?"

"I don't know sir."

"And your mother?"

"I don't know my mother, either. It is reasonable to suppose, of course, that I had a mother. But who she was, where she came from and when she lived, that, sir, I simply don't know."

The captain was silent and for a minute seemed to ponder.

"How did you get to know my daughter?"

"I didn't know her, sir. On my word of honor, I didn't. I have never had anything to do with young ladies, sir. Never in my life. Never went near them, sir. Beshrew them, saving your presence, sir."

"Why, then, did she want you and no one else to read the psalms over her?"

The philosopher shrugged his shoulders. "Goodness only knows. I can't explain it. It's a well-known thing, sir, that the gentry sometimes get something into their heads that the most learned men could not explain. As the proverb says, sir: The devil skips as the master bids."

"You're not telling me lies, philosopher, are you?"

"May I be struck by lightning on this very spot, sir, if I'm lying."

"If only she had lived one minute longer," the captain said sadly, "I'd have found out everything. Don't let anyone read over me, Daddy" she said to me, "but send at once to the Kiev seminary and fetch the bursar Khoma Brut. Let him pray three nights for my sinful soul. He knows . . . But what he knows I did not hear. That's all she, poor darling, could say before she died. I expect you must be known for your holy life and your pious works and she may have heard of you."

"Me?" said the philosopher, stepping back in amazement. "Holy life?" he ejaculated, staring straight in the captain's face. "Good Lord, sir, what are you saying? Why, though it's hardly decent to mention it, I paid a visit to the baker's wife last Maundy Thursday."

"Well . . . I suppose there must be some good reason for it. You will begin your duties from this very day."

"If you don't mind, sir, I'd rather—er—I mean to say, sir, every man versed in holy scripture may—er—as far as—er—it's in his power, of course—but, you see, sir, in this case a deacon or at least a sacristan would—er—be much more fitted for it. They have had plenty of experience of this sort of thing and they know what to do, while I . . . You see, sir, I haven't got the right voice for it and, besides, I'm just no damn good myself—I mean, I haven't got the proper figure for it, have I?"

"I don't know about that, but I shall carry out my darling's last wish without regard for anything. If for three nights from today you say the prayers over her in the way that is customary, I will reward you. If not, well, I shouldn't advise the devil himself to anger me."

The last words were uttered with such vigour that the philosopher fully grasped their meaning.

"Follow me," said the captain.

They went out into the entrance hall. The captain opened the door into another room, opposite the first. The philosopher paused for a minute in the hall to blow his nose and crossed the threshold in inexpressible panic. The whole floor was covered with red cotton material. On a high table in the corner under the icons lay the body of the dead girl on a coverlet of blue velvet adorned with a gold fringe and tassels. Tall wax candles, entwined with sprigs of guelder rose, stood at her feet and head, shedding their dim light, lost in the daylight. The dead girl's face was hidden from him by the disconsolate father, who sat facing her with his back to the door. The philosopher was struck by the words he heard.

"What grieves me so much, my dearly beloved daughter, is not that, to my great sorrow and affliction, you have left this earth in the flower of your age, without living the rest of your allotted days, but that, my darling, I don't know the man—my mortal enemy—who was the cause of your death. For if I knew the man who as much as thought of hurting you or of even saying anything offensive to you, I swear to God he should not see his children again, were he as old as I, nor his father and mother, were he still in the prime of life, and his body would have been thrown out to be devoured by birds and beasts of the steppe. But what's so awful, my wild little marigold, my sweet little quail, my poor darling, is that I shall spend the rest of my days without joy, wiping away with the skirt of my coat the tears flowing out of my old eyes, while my enemy will be making merry and secretly laughing at a feeble old man. . . ."

He stopped short, for his unendurable grief dissolved in a flood of tears.

The philosopher was touched by such inconsolable sorrow. He coughed and uttered a hollow groan in an effort to clear his throat.

The captain turned round and motioned him to a place at the head of the dead girl, in front of a small lectern with books on it.

"I'll do it for three nights somehow or other," thought the philosopher, "for I'm sure the old fellow will stuff my pockets with gold pieces for it."

He drew near and, clearing his throat again, began reading, paying no attention to anything and not daring to glance at the face of the dead girl.

A profound silence reigned in the room. He noticed that the captain had gone out. Slowly he turned his head to glance at the dead girl and . . .

A shudder ran through his veins; before him lay a girl so beautiful that there was no one like her in the world. It seemed that never could a face have been formed of such striking and yet harmonious beauty. She lay as though she were alive. Her forehead, fair and delicate as snow, as silver, seemed to be deep in thought; her eyebrows were like a night amid a sunny day, fine and even, raised proudly over the closed eyes, and her eyelashes, falling like arrows on her cheeks, glowed with the warmth of secret desires; her lips were like rubies, ready to break into a smile . . . But in them, in those very same features, he saw something terribly poignant. He felt his heart beginning to ache painfully, just as though in the midst of a whirl of gaiety and dancing crowds someone had struck up a song about an oppressed people. The rubies of her lips seemed to brim over with blood from her very heart. Suddenly something horribly familiar appeared on her face.

"The witch!" he cried in a frenzied voice. He looked away, turned deathly pale and began reading his prayers.

It was the witch he had killed.

When the sun was setting, they carried the dead girl to the church. The philosopher supported the coffin, covered with a black cloth of mourning, and he felt something cold as ice on his shoulder. The dead girl's father walked in front, supporting on his arm the right side of her narrow coffin.

The wooden church, grown black and adorned with green lichen, with its three cone-shaped cupolas, stood dismally near the end of the village. It was quite obvious that no service had been held in it for a long time. Candles had been lighted before almost every icon. The coffin was placed in the centre opposite the altar. The old Cossack captain kissed the dead girl once more, prostrated himself and went out together with the coffin-bearers, giving orders that the philosopher should have a good meal and be taken to the church after supper. Back in the kitchen the men who had carried the coffin began touching the stove with their hands, something the Ukrainians usually do after seeing a dead body.

The hunger which the philosopher began to feel at that moment made him for a few moments forget all about the dead girl. Soon all the house-serfs began gradually to assemble in the kitchen. In the captain's house the kitchen was something of a club, where all the inhabitants of the yard gathered together, including even the dogs who, wagging their tails, came to the door for bones and slops. Wherever anyone was sent and on whatever business, he first of all went to the kitchen to have a rest on the bench even for no more than a few minutes, and smoke a pipe. All the unmarried men in their smart Cossack tunics lay there almost all day long on the bench. Under the bench, on the stove—anywhere, in short, where a comfortable place could be found to lie on. Besides, every-one invariably left behind in the kitchen his cap, or a whip for stray dogs, or something of the kind. But the largest company gathered there at supper-time, including the coachman, who had driven the horses into their paddock, and the herdsman who had taken the cows to be milked and everyone else who was not to be seen during the day. At supper the most taciturn tongues wagged happily. Everything was usually discussed there: who had got himself new breeches, what was to be found in the interior of the earth, and who had seen a wolf. There were lots of witty fellows there, of whom there is no lack among Ukrainians.

The philosopher found a place among them in the large circle in the open air in front of the kitchen door. Soon a woman in a red bonnet appeared at the door holding in both hands a steaming pot of dumplings and she set it down in the midst of those who came to have their supper. Each pulled a wooden spoon out of his pocket, or for want of a spoon, a wooden stick. As soon as their jaws began to move slowly and the wolfish appetite of the assem-bled crowd was somewhat assuraged, many of them started talking. The conversation naturally turned on the dead girl.

"Is it true," said a young shepherd, who had put so many buttons and brass discs on the strap on which his pipe hung that he looked like a small village shop, "is it true that any young lady—may the Lord forgive me for saying it about her, was familiar with the evil one?"

"Who? our young lady?" said Dorosh, whom our philosopher already knew. "Why, she was a regular witch! I'll take my oath she was a witch!"

"Really, really, Dorosh," said the man, who had shown a great readiness to console everybody on the journey, "it's no business of ours. Let it be. No good talking about it."

But Dorosh was not disposed to hold his tongue. He had a little earlier gone to the storehouse with the butler on some urgent business and, having once or twice bent over two or three barrels, had come out exceedingly merry and talked without stopping.

"What do you want me to do? Hold my tongue?" he said. "Why, she had a ride on me herself. She had, I tell you."

"I say, Uncle," said the young shepherd with the buttons, "can you tell a witch by some signs?"

"No, you can't," replied Dorosh. "Quite impossible to tell. Even if you read through all the psalter you wouldn't be able to tell."

"You can tell, Dorosh, you can," said the former comforter. "Don't say that. It's not for nothing that God has given every living creature its own special habit. Scholars say that a witch has a little tail."

"When a woman's old, she's a witch," a grey-headed Cossack said coolly.

"You're a fine lot too, I must say," put in the woman who was at that moment pouring fresh dumplings into the empty pot. "Regular fat hogs."

A smile of satisfaction appeared on the lips of the old Cossack, whose name was Yavtukh and nickname Kovtun, when he observed the effect his words had had on the peasant woman, while the cow-man guffawed so loudly that it sounded like the bellowing of two bulls as they stood facing each other.

The conversation had aroused the philosopher's curiosity. He felt an irresistible desire to find out more particulars about the dead girl. Wishing to bring the conversation back to that subject, he addressed his neighbour as follows: "I'd very much like to know why this whole company sitting at supper here thinks that the young mistress was a witch? Did she cause any mischief to anyone or was she the undoing of anyone?"

"There were all sorts of things," replied one of the company, whose face was so flat that it resembled a spade.

"Why, there was that huntsman Mikita and. . . ."

"Wait, let me tell about the huntsman Mikita," said Dorosh.

"No, let me," said Spirid.

"Let Spirid tell it! Let Spirid tell it!" the crowd shouted.

"You, Mr. Philosopher Khoma," Spirid began, "did not know Mikita. Oh, he was a man in a thousand, he was. He knew every dog as if it was his own father. The huntsman we have now, Mikola, that fellow next to me but one, isn't fit to hold a candle to him. Mind you, he knows his job all right, but compared to the other he's nothing but trash, nothing but slops."

"Aye," said Dorosh, nodding his head approvingly, "you're telling the story well enough."

"He'd see a hare quicker than you'd wipe the snuff from your nose," Spirid went on. "He'd only to whistle: 'Come on, Roby! Come on, Speedy!' while he himself was off like lightning on his horse, and it was impossible to say who'd outstrip the other: he the dogs or the dogs him. Why, he'd knock back a pint of vodka without winking. A fine huntsman he was! Now, some little time back he began staring at the young mistress a little too much. Whether he'd fallen head over ears in love with her, or whether she'd bewitched him—whatever it was, the poor lad was done for, grown soft, turned into goodness only knows what—oh, it's too disgusting to talk about."

"Aye," said Dorosh.

"As soon as the young mistress looked at him, he dropped the bridle out of his hand, couldn't remember the name of his dogs, stumbled and didn't know what he was doing. One day the young mistress came into the stables when he was rubbing down a horse. 'Would you mind, Mikita,' she said, 'if I put my foot on you?' And the damned fool looked as pleased as Punch: 'Not only your foot,' said he, 'you can sit on me, if you like.' The young mistress raised her foot, and as soon as he saw her bare, plump white leg, her witchery knocked him completely silly, so Mikita said. He bent his back, the damn fool, and clasping her bare legs in his hands, went galloping like a horse over the countryside. He could not for the life of him say where they had been, but he came back more dead than alive and since that day he withered like a chip of wood, and one morning when they went into the stable, all they could find was a heap of ashes and an empty pail: he had burnt up, burnt up by himself. And what a fine huntsman he was! You couldn't find another like him anywhere in the world."

When Spirid had finished his story, all sorts of opinions about the fine qualities of the late huntsman were expressed on all sides.

"You haven't heard of Sheptun's wife, have you?" Dorosh said, addressing Khoma.

"No."

"Good Lord, they don't teach you a great deal at the seminary, do they? Well, then, listen. There's a Cossack called Sheptun in our village. A good Cossack, he sometimes tells lies without rhyme or reason, and he sometimes likes to pinch something, but he's a good Cossack! His cottage is not far from here. Just about the time we sat down to have our supper, Sheptun and his wife, having had theirs, went to bed, and as the weather was fine, his wife lay down in the yard and Sheptun on the bench in the cottage—no, no! I'm sorry, it was his wife who lay on the bench in the cottage and Sheptun in the yard. . . ."

"Not on the bench, she lay down on the floor," the peasant woman, standing in the doorway with her cheek propped up on her hand, corrected him.

Dorosh looked at her, looked down, then again looked at her.

"When I strip you of your petticoat before everybody," he said after a short pause, "you won't like it."

This warning had its effect. The old woman fell silent and did not interrupt again.

"And in the cradle hanging in the middle of the cottage," Dorosh went on, "lay their one-year-old child—boy or girl, I don't know which. As Sheptun's wife lay there, she suddenly heard a dog scratching at the door and howling fit to make you run out of the cottage. She got frightened, for women are so silly that if you put out your tongue at one in the evening from behind a door, her heart's in her mouth. 'However,' she thought, 'I'd better give that damned dog a good whack on the nose and perhaps he'll stop howling,' and picking up the poker, she went to open the door. She had scarcely time to open it properly when the dog rushed in between her legs and headed straight for the baby's cradle. At that moment Sheptun's wife saw that it was not really a dog, but the young mistress. Now, if it had been the young mistress as she knew her, it would not have been so bad. The extraordinary thing is that she was all blue and that her eyes glowed like coal. She snatched up the baby, bit its throat and began sucking its blood. All poor Mrs. Sheptun could do was to scream, 'Oh, a werewolf!' and she rushed out of the room. But the front door in the passage was locked, so she ran up to the loft. There she sat shaking with terror, the silly woman. After a little while she saw the young mistress coming up to the loft to her; a moment later she pounced on the silly woman and began biting her. It was not till the morning that Sheptun dragged his wife down from the loft, bitten black and blue all over. The next day the silly woman died. So that's the sort of monstrous and passing strange things that happen in this world! You see, she may be a highborn young lady, but once a witch, always a witch!"

After such a story Dorosh looked round self-complacently and thrust a finger into his pipe in preparation for filling it. The subject of the witch seemed inexhaustible. Everyone hastened to tell some story about her in turn. One of them had seen the witch come right up to the door of his cottage in the shape of a haystack; another had had his cap or pipe stolen by her; many village girls had had their plaits cut off by her; others had had several pints of blood sucked from them by her.

At last the whole company came to their senses and realised that they had been chattering too long because it was quite dark in the yard. They all began dispersing to the places they usually went to sleep in at night, such as the kitchen or the barns or the courtyard.

"Well, sir," said the greyheaded Cossack, addressing Khoma the philosopher, "it's time we too went to our deceased mistress."

The four of them, including Spirid and Dorosh, set off for the church, lashing out with their whips at the great multitude of dogs in the street, which gnawed their sticks furiously.

Though he had fortified himself with a good glassful of vodka, the philosopher secretly felt more and more frightened the nearer they got to the lighted church. The stories and strange occurrences he had heard helped to work on his imagination. The darkness under the paling and the trees grew less dense; the place was getting more open. At last they entered the small churchyard behind its ramshackle fence, beyond which not a tree was to be seen, nothing but open country and meadows swallowed up in the darkness and night. The three Cossacks walked up the steep steps to the porch and entered the church. There they left the philosopher after wishing him to carry out his duties satisfactorily and, at the request of their master, locked the door after them.

The philosopher was left alone. At first he yawned, then he stretched himself, then blew into both his hands, and at last looked round. In the middle of the church stood the black coffin. The candles glimmered before the dark icons; the light from them lit up only the icon-case and faintly the middle of the church. The distant corners of the nave were wrapped in darkness. The tall, ancient icon-case already showed signs of falling into decay; its open fretwork, once gilt, only glittered here and there. In one place the gilt had peeled off, in another it had grown altogether black; the faces of the saints completely darkened, gazed somewhat dismally from their frames. The philosopher cast another look around him.

"Well," he said, "what is there to be afraid of? No living man can come in here and as for the dead and apparitions from the other world I have such prayers for them that I have only to read them and they won't lay a finger on me. I don't care," he said, dismissing the subject, "let's read!"

As he went up to the lectern, he noticed several bundles of candles.

"That's good," thought the philosopher "I'd better light up the whole church so that everything will be visible as in daytime. What a pity one can't smoke a pipe in God's temple!"

And he proceeded to stick wax candles to all cornices, lecterns and icons, without regard to expense, and soon the whole church was filled with light. Only overhead the darkness seemed to have grown more intense and the sombre icons looked even more sullenly out of their ancient carved frames, which glittered here and there with specks of gilt. He went up to the coffin, looked timidly at the face of the dead girl and could not help screwing up his eyes with a faint shudder: such terrible, brilliant beauty!

He turned away, intending to move off, but urged on by strange curiosity, by a strange self-contradictory feeling that does not leave a man especially in a moment of panic, he could not resist casting another look at her as he was going away and then, feeling another cold shiver running down his spine, he looked at her again. The striking beauty of the dead girl certainly seemed terrible. Perhaps she would not have instilled such panic fear in him if she had been a little less beautiful. But there was nothing dull, torpid, lifeless in her features; that face was alive, and the philosopher could not help feeling that she was looking at him with closed eyes. He even imagined that a tear rolled down from under her right eyelid, and when it rested on her cheek, he saw distinctly that it was a drop of blood.

He walked away hastily to the lectern, opened the book and, to cheer up his spirits, began reading in a very loud voice. His voice resounded from the wooden church walls, so long deaf and silent, forlornly and without an echo in the absolute dead stillness that it struck him as a little queer.

"What's there to be afraid of?" he was thinking meanwhile to himself. "She won't get out of her coffin, for she will hear the word of God. Let her lie there! And what sort of Cossack am I to be afraid? Well, I've had a drop too much and that's why it seems so terrifying. Let's have a pinch of snuff! Lovely snuff, good snuff!"

However, as he turned over the pages, he kept throwing a side-long glance at the coffin, and an involuntary feeling seemed whispering to him: "She's going to get up! There! She's going to rise! She's going to look out from the coffin! Any minute now! There! There!"

But the silence was deathlike. The coffin stood motionless. The candles shed a perfect flood of light. What could be more terrifying than a church lit up at night with a dead body in it and not a living soul anywhere near!

Raising his voice, he began singing in different keys in an attempt to drown his still lurking fears. But every minute he turned his eyes to the coffin, as though asking himself involuntarily. "What if she should rise? What if she should get up?"

But the coffin did not stir. If only there'd be some sound, some living creature—a cricket chirping in a corner! All he could hear was the faint sputter of a candle from some distant corner of the church, and the light, slightly reverberating, sound of a drop of wax falling on the floor.

"What if she should get up? . . ."

She raised her head.

He gave her a wild look and rubbed his eyes. But she was indeed not lying down any more, but sitting up in the coffin. He turned away his eyes and then once more turned them with horror on the coffin. She got up. . . . She was walking about the church with closed eyes, continually stretching out her arms, as if trying to catch someone.

She was coming straight towards him. In a panic he drew a circle

round him and began reading the prayers with an effort and pro-
nouncing exorcisms he had been taught by a monk who had seen
witches and evil spirits all his life.

She stood almost on the very line, but it was evident that she
had not the power to step over it, and she turned livid all over
like one who had been dead for several days. Khoma had not the
courage to look at her. She was terrifying. She gnashed her teeth
and opened her dead eyes. But unable to see anything she turned
with fury—this was apparent from her twitching face—in another
direction, stretching out her arms, clasping every pillar and corner
with them, trying to catch hold of Khoma. At last she stopped dead
and, after shaking a finger at him, lay down in her coffin. The
philosopher could not recover his senses and he kept gazing with
horror at the narrow habitation of the witch. At last the coffin
suddenly broke loose from its place and began flying with a whistling sound all over the church, criss-crossing the air in all directions. The philosopher saw it almost over his head, but at the same
time noticed that it could not cross the circle he had drawn, and
he went on with his exorcisms with redoubled strength. The coffin
came down with a crash in the middle of the church and remained
there motionless. The corpse again rose from it, livid and green.
But at that moment the crowing of the cock was heard in the
distance. The corpse dropped back into the coffin slamming the
lid.

The philosopher's heart was pounding and he was dripping wet
with sweat. But, heartened by the cock's crowing, he read more
rapidly the pages he should have read before. At the first break of
dawn the sacristan and greyheaded Yavtukh, at that time perform-
ing the duties of a beadle, came to relieve him.

On reaching his distant lodging-place, the philosopher could not
fall asleep for a long time, but his fatigue got the better of him and
he slept on till dinner-time. When he woke up, the events of the
previous night seemed to him to have happened in a dream. To
keep up his strength he was given a pint of vodka at dinner, during

which he felt more at ease, joining in the conversation once or twice and eating a rather aged sucking pig almost by himself. However, for some inexplicable feeling, he could not bring himself to say anything about what had happened to him in the church and to the questions of the inquisitive he replied: "Yes, there were sorts of wonders!" The philosopher was one of those people who, if they are well fed, display quite an extraordinary degree of philanthropy. Lying down with his pipe between his teeth, he gazed at all of them with honied eyes and kept spitting to one side.

After dinner the philosopher was in excellent spirits. He managed to go round the whole village and make the acquaintance of almost everyone. He was even thrown out of two cottages, one good-looking young woman catching him a painful blow on the back with a spade when he took it into his head to feel her chemise and skirt to find out the material they were made of. But at the approach of evening the philosopher grew more pensive. An hour before supper almost all the house-serfs gathered to play a game of skittles in which long sticks are used instead of balls and the winner has the right to have a ride on the loser's back. This game became highly entertaining for the onlookers, for often the coachman, who was as broad as a pancake, was mounted on the swineherd, a feeble little man, who was all wrinkles. Another time the coachman had to bend his back and, leaping on it, Dorosh always said: "What a strong bull!" Those who were more stolid sat at the door of the kitchen. They looked on very gravely, smoking their pipes, even when the young people laughed heartily at some witty remark by the coachman or Spirid. Khoma tried in vain to take an interest in this game: some kind of sombre thought stuck in his head like a nail. However much he tried to cheer himself up at supper, panic spread in him with the growing darkness over the sky.

"Now then, seminarist, it's time we went!" said the greyheaded Cossack he had got to know so well, getting up from the table together with Dorosh.

Khoma was taken to the church again in the same way; he was again left there alone and the door was locked behind him. As soon as he was alone, apprehension once more began stealing into his breast. Again he saw the dark icons, the flashing frames and the familiar black coffin, standing motionless in the middle of the church, in the menacing stillness.

"Well," he said to himself, "now there's nothing surprising in this uncanny business. It's only terrifying the first time. Yes, it's just a little terrifying the first time, but now it's no longer terrifying. Why, it's not terrifying at all!"

He took his stand at the lectern hastily, drew a circle round him, uttered a few conjurations and began reading aloud, deciding not to raise his eyes from the book and to pay no attention to anything. He had been reading for about an hour and was beginning to feel a little tired and to cough. He took his horn out of his pocket and, before putting the snuff to his nose, stole a timid glance at the coffin. His heart turned cold.

The corpse was already standing before him on the line he had drawn and stared at him with her dead, greenish eyes. The seminarist shuddered and a cold shiver ran down his limbs. Dropping his eyes on the book, he began reading his prayers and exorcisms more loudly and heard the corpse gritting her teeth and waving her arms in an attempt to catch him. But he noticed out of the corner of his eye that the corpse was trying to catch him where he was not standing and that she evidently could not see him. She began muttering hollowly and uttering terrible words with her dead lips; they blubbered hoarsely like the bubbling of boiling pitch. He could not tell what they meant, but there was something terrifying in them. The philosopher realised with horror that she was uttering incantations.

A wind blew through the church at her words and he heard the noise of a multitude of flying wings. He heard the beating of wings on the panes of the church windows and on the iron window frames, and the whining and the scratching of claws upon the iron, and countless numbers of evil spirits trying to smash the door and break into the church. His heart was pounding violently all this time, but, half closing his eyes, he went on reading prayers and exorcisms. At last a shrill sound was suddenly heard in the distance: it was a distant cock crowing. The philosopher, utterly exhausted, stopped and breathed freely again.

The people who came to relieve the philosopher found him more dead than alive. He was leaning with his back against the wall and stared motionless at the Cossacks who were trying to push him out of the church. He was almost carried out of it and he had to be supported all the way back. On arriving at the courtyard, he shook himself and demanded to be given a pint of vodka. When he had drunk it, he smoothed down the hair on his head and said:

"There's a lot of trash of every kind in this world. As for the different kinds of terror—well! . . ." The philosopher dismissed it all with a wave of a hand.

The group of people who gathered round him bowed their heads when they heard it. Even the small boy whom all the servants felt entitled to depute in their place when it came to mucking out the stable or fetching water, even that poor boy gaped at the philosopher.

At that moment a good-looking and still quite young woman, the old cook's assistant, happened to pass by in a tightly fitting hempen dress, which showed off her round, firm figure, a terrible flirt, who always found something to pin to her cap, a bit of a ribbon, a carnation, or even a piece of paper, if she could find nothing better.

"Good morning, Khoma," she said, seeing the philosopher. "Good heavens, what's the matter with you?" she cried, clasping her hands.

"Why, what is it, you silly woman?"

"Why, you've gone all grey!"

"Dear me," said Spirid, staring attentively at the philosopher, "she's right! You *have* gone grey, as grey as our old Yavtukh."

Hearing this, the philosopher rushed headlong into the kitchen, where he had noticed a flyblown triangular bit of a looking-glass glued to the wall before which were stuck forget-me-nots, periwinkles and even a wreath of marigold, showing that it was used for her toilet by the flirtatious assistant cook who was fond of showing off her fineries. He was horrified to see the truth of their words: half of his hair had indeed gone white.

Khoma Brut hung his head and sunk into thought.

"I'll go to the master," he said at last, "tell him everything and explain that I can't carry on with the reading. Let him send me back to Kiev at once."

With these thoughts in his mind he turned to go up the front steps of the manor-house.

The Cossack captain sat almost motionless in his parlor. The hopeless grief the philosopher had seen in his face was still there, except that his cheeks were more sunken than before. It was obvious that he did not eat sufficiently or, indeed, did not touch any food at all. His extraordinary pallor gave him a look of almost stony immobility.

"Good morning, old fellow," he said on seeing Khoma standing cap in hand at the door. "How are things with you? Everything satisfactory?"

"It's satisfactory, I suppose, sir, except that there are such devilish things going on that the best you can do is pick up your cap and run as fast as your legs will carry you."

"Oh?"

"Well, you see, sir, it's that daughter of yours. I mean, if you look at it sensibly she's, of course, a well-born girl. No one can deny that. But I hope you don't mind my saying so, sir, your daughter, may she rest in peace. . . ."

"Well, what about my daughter?"

"Your daughter, sir, is in league with Satan. She is the cause of such horrors that reading of Scripture is of no avail at all."

"Keep on reading! It was not for nothing she sent for you. She was worried, poor darling, about her soul and was anxious to drive away with prayers all evil thoughts."

"It's for you to say, of course, sir, but I tell you I simply can't go on with it."

"Read, read!" the Cossack captain went on in the same admonishing voice. "You've only one night left. You'll do a Christian deed and I'll reward you."

"It's not a question of reward. You can do as you please, sir," Khoma declared firmly, "I will not read."

"Now, listen to me, philosopher," said the Cossack captain and his voice grew firm and menacing, "I don't like these tricks. You can do it in your seminary but not with me: if I give you a flogging, it will not at all be the same thing as when your rector gives you one. Do you know what good leather thongs are like?"

"Of course, I do, sir," said the philosopher, lowering his voice. "Everyone knows what leather thongs are like: in a large dose, it's quite unendurable."

"Aye, only what you don't know is how my lads can thrash," said the Cossack captain sternly, rising to his feet, and his face assumed an imperious and fierce expression, revealing the unbridled violence of his character, restrained only for a time by his grief. "Here they first give you a thrashing, then sprinkle you with vodka, and then begin all over again. Run along, run along, and get on with your task. If you don't, you won't get up again: if you do—a thousand gold pieces."

"Oh-ho! Why, he's a fire-eater!" thought the philosopher as he went out. "He's not to be trifled with. But, wait, wait, my friend, I'll show you such a clean pair of heels that you and your hounds will never catch me."

And Khoma made up his mind definitely to run away. He was only waiting for the servants to get under the hay in the barns, which they usually did after dinner, and then break into such snores and whistling that the courtyard of the manor-house sounded more like a factory. The time at last arrived, even Yavtukh closed his eyes as he lay stretched out in the sun. The philosopher made his way with fear and trembling into the captain's garden from where he thought he could escape into the open country more easily and without being observed. This garden, as usual, was terribly neglected and was therefore extremely useful for any secret undertaking. With the exception of only one path, trodden by the servants for their pressing needs, everything else was hidden by overgrown cherry trees, elders and burdock, which pushed up to the very top its tall stalks with their clinging pink burrs. Wild hops covered as with a net this motley assemblage of trees and bushes, forming a roof over them, got on to the fence and, falling from it, mingled in coiling snakes with the bluebells. Beyond the fence, which formed the boundary of the garden came a perfect forest of tall weeds, which apparently no one was interested enough to look into, and indeed a scythe would have been smashed into smithereens if it attempted to touch with its blade their thick, stout stalks.

When the philosopher tried to step over the fence, his teeth chattered and his heart beat so violently that he was frightened. The skirts of his long loose garment seemed to cling to the ground as though someone had nailed them down. As he was climbing over the fence a voice seemed to shout in his ears with a deafening hiss: "Where? Where?" The philosopher darted into the weeds and took to his heels, constantly stumbling over old roots and trampling on moles. He saw that on emerging from the weeds, he had only to run across a field, beyond which lay a thicket of blackthorn, in which he thought himself safe. For on getting through the thicket, he should, according to his calculation, come upon the Kiev highway. He crossed the field at a run and found himself in the blackthorn thicket. He crawled through the blackthorn bushes, leaving by way of a toll bits of his coat on every thorn, and came out into a small hollow. The spreading branches of a willow tree bent down here and there almost to the ground. A little stream sparkled, pure as silver. The first thing the philosopher did was to lie down and drink, for he was terribly thirsty.

"Lovely water!" he said, wiping his lips. "I'd better rest here."

"No, sir, we'd better run on or they'll be after you."

These words resounded above his ears. He looked up: before him stood Yavtukh.

"Damn Yavtukh," thought the philosopher angrily to himself. "I've a good mind to take you by the feet and . . . I'd like to bash in your ugly face, too, and the rest of you with an oaken log."

"You shouldn't have gone such a long way round," went on Yavtukh. "You ought to have taken the road I took: straight by the stable. Besides, it's such a pity about your coat. It's good cloth. How much was it a yard? But we've had a good walk: it's time to go home."

The philosopher scratched himself and trudged after Yavtukh. "The damned witch will give it to me good and proper now," he thought. "Though what the hell am I so worried about? What am I afraid of? Am I not a Cossack? Why, I've been reading for two nights and with God's help I'll do it for the third night too. I suppose that damned witch committed a good number of sins for the evil powers to stand up for her so much."

Such were the reflections that occupied him as he stepped into the courtyard of the manor-house. Having reassured himself by these remarks, he asked Dorosh, who through the patronage of the butler sometimes had access to his master's storehouses, to get out a keg of raw brandy, and the two friends sat down by the barn and drank no less than half a pailful, so that the philosopher, getting up, shouted: "Musicians! Let's have musicians!" Without waiting for the musicians, he was off dancing a tropak in a clear space in the middle of the yard. He danced till it was time for the twelve o'clock meal, and the servants who stood round him in a circle, as is the custom on such occasions, got bored at last and walked away, saying: "Fancy a man dancing such a long time!" At last the philosopher lay down and fell asleep on the spot and it took a pail of cold water to wake him up for supper. At supper he talked about what a Cossack was and how he should not be afraid of anything in the world.

"Come on," said Yavtukh, "it's time to go."

"A splinter through your tongue, you damned boar!" thought the philosopher and, getting up, said: "Let's go!"

On the way to the church the philosopher kept looking from side to side and tried to engage his companions in conversation. But Yavtukh was silent and Dorosh was not very talkative, either. It was a hellish night. Whole packs of wolves could be heard howling in the distance. Even the barking of the dogs, somehow, sounded dreadful.

"It seems as if something else is howling," said Dorosh. "That's not a wolf."

Yavtukh said nothing; the philosopher could not think of anything to say, either.

They came to the church and entered under its decaying wooden vaults which showed how little the owner of the estate cared for God and his own soul. Yavtukh and Dorosh withdrew as before and the philosopher was left alone. Everything was the same. Everything had the same familiar and menacing aspect. He stood still for a minute. The coffin of the horrifying witch was still standing motionless in the middle of the church. "I won't be afraid, I swear I won't be afraid!" he said, and, drawing a circle around him as before, he began calling to mind all his exorcisms. The silence was awful; the candles flickered and flooded the whole church with light. The philosopher turned over one page, then another and noticed that he was not reading what was written in the book. In a panic, he crossed himself and began chanting. This put some heart into him; the reading progressed and page followed page with lightning rapidity. Suddenly—amid the stillness —the iron lid of the coffin burst open with a crash and the corpse rose up. It was more terrible than the first time. Its teeth knocked horribly against each other, its lips twitched convulsively and, screeching wildly, incantations poured from its mouth. A whirlwind swept through the church, the icons fell to the ground, broken glass came flying down from the windows. The doors broke loose from their hinges and a countless multitude of monsters flew into the church of God. The whole church was filled with the terrible noise of wings and scratching claws. All flew and rushed about looking for the philosopher.

The last traces of intoxication disappeared from Khoma's head. He kept crossing himself and repeating any prayers he could remember. At the same time he heard the evil spirits rushing round him, almost touching him with the tips of their wings and their repulsive nails. He had not the courage to take a look at them; all he saw was that a kind of enormous monster filled the whole width of the wall in its tangle of hair as in a forest; two eyes glared horribly through the meshes of hair, their eyebrows raised a little. Above it something in the shape of a huge bubble was hanging in the air and a thousand claws and scorpion stings extended from its centre. Black earth hung from them in clods. They were all gazing at him, looking for him, but, surrounded by his magic circle, could not see him.

"Bring Viy! Go and fetch Viy!" resounded the words of the corpse.

And suddenly a stillness fell upon the church; the howling of wolves was heard in the distance and soon heavy footsteps resounded throughout the church; glancing out of the corner of his eye, the philosopher saw that they were bringing in a huge, squat, bandylegged creature. He was covered all over with black earth. His arms and legs were sprinkled with earth and protruded like strong sinewy roots. He trod heavily, stumbling at every step. His long eyelids hung down to the very ground. Khoma noticed with horror that he had an iron face. Supported under the arms, he was led straight to where Khoma was standing.

"Raise my eyelids; I can't see!" said Viy in a subterranean voice.

And the whole crowd of devils rushed to lift his eyelids.

"Don't look," an inner voice whispered to the philosopher. But he could not contain himself and looked.

"There he is!" cried Viy and pointed an iron finger at him. And all of them rushed upon the philosopher. Breathless he fell to the ground and right there his soul flew from his body with terror.

There was a sound of a cock crowing. It was the second cock crow; the gnomes had missed the first one. The frightened spirits rushed helter-skelter to the windows and doors, but it was too late, and there they remained, stuck in the doors and windows. When the priest arrived he stopped dead at the sight of such a desecration of God's holy place. And so the church was left forever, with monsters stuck fast in the doors and windows, and it was overgrown with trees, roots, tall weeds, and blackthorn bushes; and no one can now find the way to it.

When the rumours of this reached Kiev and the theologian Khalyava heard at last of the fate of the philosopher Khoma, he spent an hour in meditation. Great changes had befallen him during that time. Fortune had smiled on him; at the conclusion of his course of studies, he was appointed bellringer of the highest belfry in Kiev and he almost always walked about with a bruised nose because the wooden staircase to the belfry had been extremely carelessly made.

"Have you heard what happened to Khoma?" Tibery Gorobets, who had by now become a philosopher and sported a newly grown moustache, asked, coming up to him.

"It's God's will," said Khalyava the bellringer. "Let's go to a tavern and drink to his memory."

The young philosopher who was beginning to make use of his privileges with the ardour of an enthusiast, so that his wide trousers, his coat, and even his cap reeked of spirits and cheap tobacco, at once gave his consent.

"A jolly good fellow Khoma," said the bellringer as the lame landlord put down the third mug before him. "An excellent fellow And came to a bad end for nothing!"

"I know why he came to a bad end. It was because he was afraid. Had he not been afraid, the witch could not have done anything to him. All you have to do is to cross yourself and spit on her tail. Then nothing will happen. I know all about it. You see, all the market women in Kiev are witches, all of them."

To this the bellringer nodded in token of agreement. But noticing that his tongue was incapable of uttering a single word, he carefully rose from the table and, reeling from side to side, went to hide himself away in the remotest spot in the tall weeds. From force of habit, however, he did not forget to carry off the sole of an old boot that was lying about on the bench.

🏴 The Story of How Ivan Ivanovich Quarrelled with Ivan Nikiforovich

CHAPTER I

Ivan Ivanovich and Ivan Nikiforovich

What a glorious coat Ivan Ivanovich has! A most splendid coat! And the astrakhan! Hang it all, such astrakhan! Dove-grey with a touch of frost. I bet you anything you please you won't find anyone who has astrakhan like that. Just have a look at it—do have a look at it, especially when he stops to talk to someone: what a wonderful sight! Impossible to describe it: velvet! silver! fire! Dear Lord, St. Nicholas the miracle worker, God's saint, why haven't I got such a coat? He had it made a long time ago before Agafya had gone to Kiev. You know Agafya Fedoseyevna, don't you? I mean the lady who bit the assessor's ear, of course.

Ivan Ivanovich is such a wonderful man! What a house he has in Mirgorod! It is surrounded on all sides by an awning supported on oak pillars, and everywhere under the awning there are seats. When it gets very hot Ivan Ivanovich flings off his coat and under garments, keeping only his shirt on, and takes a rest under the awning, watching what is going on in the yard and in the street. What marvellous apple and pear trees he has under his very windows! Open the window and the branches burst into the room. Now, all this is in front of the house. You have only to see what he has in his garden! What hasn't he got there? Plums, morello cherries, black cherries, all sorts of vegetables, sunflowers, cucumbers, melons, beans and peas, even a threshing floor and a smithy. Ivan Ivanovich is such a wonderful man! He is very fond of melons. It's his most favourite dish. As soon as he has his dinner and comes out under the awning in nothing but his shirt, he orders Gapka to bring him two melons. He cuts them himself, collects the seeds in a special piece of paper and starts eating them. Then he tells Gapka to fetch an inkwell, and himself, with his own hands, writes an inscription on the paper containing the seeds: "These melons have been consumed on such and such a date!" If he had a visitor at the time, he would add: "So and so took part."

The late Mirgorod judge always looked at Ivan Ivanovich's house with admiration. Yes, to be sure, it is not at all a bad house. What I like about it is that all sorts of large and small outhouses are built round it, so that if you look at it from a distance all you see is roofs one on top of the other, which reminds one of a plateful of pancakes, or, better still, of fungi growing on a tree. All the roofs are thatched with reeds, though; a willow, an oak and two apple trees lean their spreading branches on them. Between the trees you can catch a glimpse of little windows with carved, whitewashed shutters which seem to run out even into the street.

Ivan Ivanovich is such a wonderful man! The Poltava government commissioner knows him too. Everytime Dorosh Tarasovich Pukhivochka comes from Khorol he always stops at his house. And Father Peter, the chief priest who lives in Koliberda, when he has half a dozen visitors, always declares that he knows no one who carries out his duties as a Christian and knows how to live as Ivan Ivanovich does.

Heavens, how time flies! Even then he had been a widower for more than ten years. He never had any children. Gapka has children who run about in the yard and Ivan Ivanovich always gives each of them a roll baked in the shape of a ring, or a small piece of melon or a pear. Gapka carries the keys of his cupboards and storehouses, though the keys of the middle cupboard and the large trunk in his bedroom Ivan Ivanovich keeps himself and no one is allowed to go to there. Gapka is a healthy looking wench and she always wears a homespun woolen piece of material instead of a skirt, and has fine calves and fresh cheeks.

And what a pious man Ivan Ivanovich is! Every Sunday he puts on his fine coat and goes to church. Once there, he exchanges greetings with everybody and then usually takes his place in the choir and joins in the singing in his nice bass voice. After the service Ivan Ivanovich can never restrain himself from making the round of the beggars. He would not perhaps have wasted his time on so boring an occupation, had he not been impelled to do so by his innate goodness.

"Good morning, my dear," he usually said, having sought out the most crippled beggar-woman in a tattered dress, made up of all sorts of patches. "Where are you from, poor woman?"

"I've come from the country, good sir. Haven't had a bite or a drop to drink for the last three days, sir. My own children have driven me out of house and home."

"Oh, you poor thing! What have you come here for?"

"Why, sir, I've come here to ask for alms to see if anyone would give me something to buy bread with."

"Oh, well, do you really want bread?" Ivan Ivanovich usually asked.

"Why, of course, I do, sir. I'm as hungry as a dog."

"H'm," Ivan Ivanovich usually said. "I suppose you'd like some meat too, wouldn't you?"

"Why, anything you'd be good enough to give me, kind sir."

"H'm . . . is meat then better than bread?"

"Beggars can't be choosers, sir. Anything kindly given to a starving creature will be welcome, sir."

At this point the old woman usually held out her hand.

"Well, go in peace," Ivan Ivanovich said. "What are you standing here for? I'm not beating you, am I?" and after putting the same questions to a second and a third, he went home at last or went round to have a glass of vodka with his neighbour Ivan Nikiforovich or the judge or the mayor.

Ivan Ivanovich likes very much to receive a present from anyone. He likes that very much.

Ivan Nikiforovich, too, is a very good man. His yard is next door to Ivan Ivanovich's. They are close friends such as the world has never seen. Anton Prokofyevich Popuz, who still goes about in his brown coat with light blue sleeves and dines on Sundays at the judge's, used to say that the devil himself had tied Ivan Nikiforovich and Ivan Ivanovich together with a rope. Where one went, the other one was sure to follow.

Ivan Nikiforovich has never been married. Though people did say that he had been married, it was a barefaced lie. I know Ivan Nikiforovich very well and I can state that he has never had any intention of getting married. Where do all these scandalous stories originate I'd like to know. There was even a rumour that Ivan Nikiforovich was born with a tail. But this story is so ridiculous and indecent and infamous as well that I do not think it even necessary to deny it to my enlightened readers who, I have no doubt, are aware that among witches even only a few have tails, and those, of course, belong to the female rather than the male sex.

In spite of their close friendship, these rare friends were not altogether alike. Their characters can be best understood by comparing them. Ivan Ivanovich possessed the unusual gift of talking very pleasantly. Dear me, how he talked! This sensation can only be compared with the sensation you experience when someone is scratching your head or gently passing a finger over your heel. You listen and listen and you hang your head. It's pleasant! Extremely pleasant. Like a nap after a bath. Ivan Nikiforovich, on the other hand, is mostly silent, but if he does say something, it is so much to the point that you had better look out: it's sharper than a razor. Ivan Ivanovich is tall and lean. Ivan Nikiforovich is a little shorter, but makes up for it in corpulence. Ivan Ivanovich's head is like a horse-radish, tail downwards; Ivan Nikiforovich's head is like a radish, tail upwards. Ivan Ivanovich lies in his shirt, under the awning; only after dinner. In the evening he puts on his astrakhan coat and goes off somewhere—to the town shop which he supplies with flour or to the country to catch quails. Ivan Nikiforovich lies all day long in the porch—usually with his back to the sun if it is not too hot—and has no wish to go anywhere. If he feels like it, he will go round the yard in the morning, see to things in the house and the garden, and back to rest again. In the old days he would occasionally pay a visit to Ivan Ivanovich. Ivan Ivanovich is a man of quite extraordinary delicacy. He will never utter an improper word in decent company and he will take offense at once if he hears one. Ivan Nikiforovich sometimes finds it difficult to control his tongue; then Ivan Ivanovich gets up from his seat and says: "That'll do, Ivan Nikiforovich, I'd rather have a walk in the sun than listen to such ungodly words." Ivan Ivanovich is very cross if a fly happens to get into his beetroot soup: he loses his temper—pushes away his plate and gives his host a piece of his mind. Ivan Nikiforovich is extremely fond of bathing and when he is sitting up to his neck in water, he orders a table and a *samovar* to be put in the water too, and he is very fond of drinking tea in such pleasant coolness. Ivan Ivanovich shaves twice a week; Ivan Nikiforovich only once. Ivan Ivanovich is extremely inquisitive. Heaven help you if you start telling him something and do not finish the story! If he is dissatisfied with anything, he lets you know at once. To look at him it is very difficult to say whether Ivan Nikiforovich is pleased or angry; even if he is overjoyed at something, he will not show it. Ivan Ivanovich is of a somewhat timid disposition. Ivan Nikiforovich, on the other hand, wears trousers with such wide folds, that were you to blow them up, you could get his whole yard with the barns and outhouses into them. Ivan Ivanovich has large expressive snuff coloured eyes and a mouth that is a little like the letter V; Ivan Nikiforovich has small, brownish eyes, which disappear completely between his thick eyebrows and chubby cheeks, and a nose that looks like a ripe plum. If Ivan Ivanovich offers you a pinch of snuff, he first of all licks the lid of the snuff-box, then flicks it with a finger, and, as he offers it to you, says if he happens to know you, "May I make so bold as to ask you to help yourself, sir?" and if he does not know you, he says, "May I make so bold as to ask you to help yourself, sir, though I have not the honour of knowing your name or your patronymic or your rank in the service?" Ivan Nikiforovich, on the other hand, just thrusts his horn straight into your hands, simply adding, "Help yourself, sir." Both Ivan Ivanovich and Ivan Nikiforovich greatly dislike fleas; that is why neither Ivan Ivanovich nor Ivan Nikiforovich ever let a Jew trader pass without buying from him all sorts of little jars of an elixir against those insects, first giving him a thorough scolding for professing the Jewish faith.

Still, in spite of certain dissimilarities, both Ivan Ivanovich and Ivan Nikiforovich are excellent fellows.

🕱 CHAPTER II

From which you can learn what it was that Ivan Ivanovich desired to have, what the conversation between Ivan Ivanovich and Ivan Nikiforovich was about and how it ended.

One morning—it was in the month of July—Ivan Ivanovich was lying under the awning. The day was hot, the air was dry and vibrating. Ivan Ivanovich had already managed to go and see the haymakers and the farm and question the peasants and the women where they had come from, where they were going and why; he felt very tired and he lay down to rest. While lying down, he had a good look at the storehouse, the yard, the barns, and the hens running about in the yard, and he thought to himself, "Now, what a good farmer I am! What have I not got? Fowls, outhouses, barns, everything I fancy, distilled vodka and fruit and herb brandies, pears and plums in the orchard, poppies, cabbages, peas in the kitchen garden . . . what is there I have not got? I'd like to know what there is I haven't got. . . ."

Having put so profound a question to himself, Ivan Ivanovich sank into thought; meanwhile his eyes were finding new things, and stepping over the fence into Ivan Nikiforovich's yard, were involuntarily caught by a curious spectacle. A lean peasant woman was carrying out of the house clothes that had been put away for a long time and hanging them out piece by piece on a line to air. Soon an old army uniform with threadbare cuffs stretched out its sleeves in the air and embraced a brocaded blouse, after it a nobleman's uniform with crests on the buttons and a motheaten collar came into view behind it; white cashmere trousers covered with stains which had once upon a time been drawn over the legs of Ivan Nikiforovich and which now would hardly be drawn over his fingers. Then another pair of trousers in the shape of an elongated letter L were hung up, then a dark blue Cossack quilted jacket which Ivan Nikiforovich had had made twenty years before when he had been meaning to join the militia and was already growing a moustache. At last, one by one, a sword appeared, looking like a spire sticking up in the air, then the skirts of something resembling a peasant's overcoat, grass-green in colour, with copper buttons as big as a five-copeck piece, fluttered in the breeze. From behind the skirts peeped out a waistcoat, trimmed with gold braid and cut very low in front. The waistcoat was soon covered by an old cotton petticoat of a deceased grandmother with pockets in each one of which a watermelon could have been placed. All this blended together, made up a highly entertaining spectacle for

Ivan Ivanovich, while the sunbeams, catching here and there a green or blue sleeve, a red cuff or a bit of gold brocade, or playing on the sword-spire, transformed it all into something extraordinary, like the puppet-shows which strolling vagrants bring to the villages. Especially when a crowd of people, closely packed, gape at King Herod in a golden crown or at Anton leading a goat; behind the puppet-stage a fiddle squeaks, a gipsy bangs his hands on his hips by way of a drum, while the sun setting and the great coolness of the southern night imperceptibly presses closer and closer to the fresh shoulders and breasts of the plump village-girls.

Soon the old woman came out of the storehouse, groaning and dragging along an old saddle with broken stirrups, with worn leather pistol-holders and a shabrack which had been crimson once, and embroidered in gold and with copper discs.

"What a stupid old woman!" thought Ivan Ivanovich. "I shouldn't be surprised if she dragged out Ivan Nikiforovich to air next!"

And, to be sure, Ivan Ivanovich was not altogether wrong in his surmise. Five minutes later the nankeen breeches of Ivan Nikiforovich rose up in the air and took up almost half the yard. After that she brought out his cap and his gun.

"What on earth can it mean?" thought Ivan Ivanovich. "I have never seen a gun at Ivan Nikiforovich's. What is he up to? Doesn't go out shooting, but keeps a gun! What does he want it for? A lovely gun, though! I've been wanting to get a gun like that for a long time. Yes, indeed, I'd like to have his gun very much. I like to have some fun with a gun. I say," Ivan Ivanovich shouted, beckoning to the old woman.

The old woman went up to the fence.

"What have you get there, granny?"

"You can see for yourself, sir—a gun."

"What kind of a gun?"

"How do I know what kind of a gun it is, sir? If it was mine, I might have known what it's made of. But it's the master's, sir."

Ivan Ivanovich got up and began examining the gun closely,

quite forgetting to tell off the woman for hanging it up with the sword to air.

"I suppose," the old woman continued, "it's made of iron."

"H'm," Ivan Ivanovich said to himself, "iron. Why iron? How long has your master had it?"

"A long time, I should think, sir."

"A lovely thing!" Ivan Ivanovich went on. "I'll ask him for it. What does he want it for? Or I'll swap it for something. Is your master at home, granny?"

"Aye, he is, sir."

"What's he doing? Lying down?"

"Yes, sir."

"All right. I'll come and see him."

Ivan Ivanovich dressed, took his gnarled stick to ward off the dogs with, for there are many more dogs in the streets of Mirgorod than there are men, and went out.

Though Ivan Nikiforovich's yard was next to Ivan Ivanovich's and one could climb over the fence from one to the other, Ivan Ivanovich preferred to go by the street. From the street he had to pass into a lane which was so narrow that if two one-horse carts happened to meet in it, they could not pass each other but had to stay in that position until they were each dragged by the back wheels in opposite directions into the street. A pedestrian walking through it would be adorned with burdocks, growing on either side of it, as with flowers. Ivan Ivanovich's stable looked out into this lane on one side and Ivan Nikiforovich's barn, gates and dove-cote on the other.

Ivan Ivanovich went up to the gates and rattled the latch. There was a barking of dogs from within, but the pack of multicoloured dogs soon ran off at recognizing a familiar face. Ivan Ivanovich crossed the yard in which variegated Indian pigeons, (fed by Ivan Nikiforovich with his own hand) water-melon and melon rinds, greenery in one place and in another a broken wheel or a hoop off a barrel or a boy wallowing in the dirt in a muddy shirt—made up a picture painters love so much! The shadow cast by the clothes on the line covered almost the whole yard and gave it some coolness. The woman met him with a bow and stood still gaping. Before the house, the front steps were adorned with a roof on two oak pillars —an unreliable shelter from the sun, which is no joke at that season of the year in the Ukraine and covers a pedestrian from head to foot with a hot sweat. This shows how strong was Ivan Ivanovich's desire to acquire something he wanted so badly, for he had brought himself to go out at that time of the day contrary to his invariable rule of going for a walk only in the evenings

The room which Ivan Ivanovich entered was quite dark because the shutters were closed and the sunbeam, on passing through the hole in the shutter, assumed the colours of a rainbow and, striking the wall opposite, painted on it a gay landscape of thatched roofs, trees and clothes hanging in the yard, but all upside down. This plunged the whole room into a kind of wondrous twilight.

"The Lord's blessing!" said Ivan Ivanovich.

"Ah, good morning, Ivan Ivanovich," a voice replied from a corner of the room. It was only then that Ivan Ivanovich noticed Ivan Nikiforovich lying on a rug spread out on the floor. "I'm sorry I'm in a state of nature."

Ivan Nikiforovich was lying without anything on, not even his shirt.

"Don't mind me. Have you slept well today, Ivan Nikiforovich?"

"I have. Have you, Ivan Ivanovich?"

"I have too."

"So you've got up now, have you?"

"Got up now? Good Lord, Ivan Nikiforovich, how could one sleep till now? I've just come from the village. Wonderful cornfields along the highroad, sir! Marvellous! And the hay, too, is so tall, so soft, and so lush!"

"Gorpina," shouted Ivan Nikiforovich, "fetch some vodka and some pies with sour cream for Ivan Ivanovich."

"It's a lovely day."

"Don't praise it, Ivan Ivanovich. The devil take it. No place to go to from the heat."

"Why mention the devil, Ivan Nikiforovich. Mark my words, you'll catch it in the next world for such ungodly language!"

"What have I done to offend you, Ivan Ivanovich? I haven't said anything derogatory about your father and mother, have I? I don't know how I've offended you."

"Forget it, sir, forget it!"

"I never thought of offending you, Ivan Ivanovich, I assure you."

"It's strange the quail doesn't yet come out at the bird-call. Don't you think so, sir?"

"Think what you like, but I, sir, have done nothing to offend you."

"Can't imagine why they don't come," said Ivan Ivanovich, as though not listening to Ivan Nikiforovich. "Isn't the season right for it yet? But then the weather certainly seems to be just right."

"Did you say the cornfields were good?"

"Marvellous, simply marvellous!"

This was followed by a pause.

"Why are you hanging out your clothes, Ivan Nikiforovich?" said Ivan Ivanovich at last.

"Well, you see, that damned old woman has ruined my practically new clothes. I'm having them aired now. Excellent, firm cloth. All they need is turning, then they can be worn again."

"I liked one thing there, Ivan Nikiforovich."

"Which one?"

"Tell me please what do you want for the gun that has been hung out to air with the clothes?" Here Ivan Ivanovich held out his snuffbox. "May I be so bold, sir, as to ask you to help yourself?"

"Thank you, help yourself. I'll take a pinch of my own," said Ivan Nikiforovich, feeling about him and getting hold of his horn.

"What a damn stupid woman! Hung out the gun, too, has she? Excellent snuff the Jew makes in Sorochintsy. I don't know what he puts in it, but it's so fragrant! Reminds me a little of balsam. Here take some, taste a little on your tongue. It is like balsam, isn't it? Take some. Help yourself."

"Tell me, Ivan Nikiforovich, that gun of yours, I mean, what are you going to do with it? You don't really want it, do you?"

"Not want it? And what if I should want to go out shooting?"

"Dear me, Ivan Nikiforovich, when will you be going out shooting? At the Second Coming perhaps? So far as I know, and others will bear me out, you haven't killed a single duck and, besides, God hasn't endowed you with a nature for shooting. You have such a dignified carriage and figure. How could you go trailing about the swamps when even now a garment of yours, which it is not nice to mention in polite society, is hung out to air. What would it be like then? No, sir. What you want is rest, repose." (Ivan Ivanovich, as was mentioned earlier, had an extraordinarily picturesque way of talking whenever he found it necessary to persuade somebody. How he talked! Heavens, how he talked!) "Yes, sir, you ought to do everything with decorum. Look here, let me have it."

"I can't let you have it. It's an expensive gun. You can't find a gun like that anywhere today. I bought it from a Turk when I was going to join the militia. And now you want me to give it away! Out of the question! It's indispensable!"

"Indispensable? What for?"

"What for? And what if robbers should attack my house? I should think it is indispensable. Now, thank God, my mind is at rest and I'm not afraid of anybody. Why not? Because I know I have a gun in my cupboard!"

"Some gun! Why, my dear sir, its lock doesn't work."

"Well, what about it? It can be repaired. All you have to do is to put a drop of hemp oil on it to prevent its rusting."

"I'm sorry, Ivan Nikiforovich, but from what you say I can see that you have no friendly feeling towards me. You don't do anything for me to show your goodwill."

"What do you mean, sir? I am showing you my goodwill! Aren't you ashamed? Your oxen graze on my land and I have never once impounded them. When you go to Poltava you always ask me for my trap and I have never refused you, have I? Your children climb over the fence into my yard and play with my dogs and I have never said a word about it; let them play so long as they don't touch anything. Let them play!"

"Well, if you won't make me a present of it, let's exchange it for something."

"Why, what will you give me for it?" asked Ivan Nikiforovich, leaning on his elbow and looking steadily at Ivan Ivanovich.

"I'll give you the brown sow for it, the one I've been feeding up in the sty. An excellent sow. You'll see if she won't give you a litter of piglets next year."

"I don't know how you can bring yourself to say a thing like that, my dear sir. What do I want your sow for? To hold a wake for the devil?"

"Again! You simply have to bring in the devil, haven't you? It's a sin, sin, a sin!"

"But really my dear sir, how could you offer me for the gun the devil knows what—a sow!"

"Why is a sow the devil knows what, Ivan Nikiforovich?"

"Why? Don't you know it? This is a gun, something everyone knows about, and that—why, that's the devil knows what—a sow! If it had not been you who said it, I might have taken it as a personal insult."

"What have you noticed about a sow that's so bad?"

"Who do you take me for, sir? That I should exchange a sow. . . !"

"Sit down, sit down! I won't—I won't . . . Keep your gun. Let it rot and rust standing in the corner of the cupboard. I don't want to speak of it again."

A pause followed.

"They say," began Ivan Ivanovich, "that three kings have declared war on our Tsar."

"Yes, Pyotr Fyodorovich told me about it. What's the war about? What kind of war?"

"Impossible to say for certain what it is about, Ivan Nikiforovich. I suppose the kings want us to accept the Turkish faith."

"Good Lord, the fools, what a thing to want!" said Ivan Nikiforovich, raising his head.

"Well, you see, that's why our Tsar declared war on them. No, says he, you'd better accept the Christian faith!"

"What do you think, Ivan Ivanovich? Our fellows will beat them, won't they?"

"Of course, they will. So you won't exchange the gun, Ivan Nikiforovich?"

"I'm surprised at you, Ivan Ivanovich. You are, I believe, a man well known for his learning, and you talk like an ignoramus. Do you think I'm such a fool as to. . . ."

"Sit down, sit down. Never mind that gun. Let it go to rack and ruin. I won't speak of it again."

At that moment the drinks and snacks were brought in.

Ivan Ivanovich drank a glass of vodka and ate a pie with sour cream.

"Look here, Ivan Nikiforovich. I'll give you two sacks of oats in addition to the sow. You haven't sown any oats, have you? You'll have to buy oats this year, anyway."

"Good Lord, Ivan Ivanovich, one can only talk to you with a bellyful of peas." (This is nothing, Ivan Nikiforovich lets off phrases much worse than that.) "Who ever heard of swapping a gun for two sacks of oats? I don't suppose you'll throw your astrakhan coat, will you?"

"But you seem to forget, sir, that I'm giving you the sow too."

"What! two sacks of oats and a sow for a gun?"

"Why, isn't it enough?"

"For the gun?"

"Of course, for the gun."

"Two sacks for the gun?"

"Not two empty sacks, but full of oats. And have you forgotten the sow?"

"You can go and kiss your sow, and the devil, too, sir, if you prefer him to the sow."

"Oh, you are touchy, aren't you? You wait, they'll lard your tongue with red-hot needles in the next world for such ungodly words. One has to wash one's hands and face and fumigate oneself after talking to you."

"I'm sorry, Ivan Ivanovich, but a gun is a gentlemanly thing, a most engaging pastime, apart from being a very agreeable ornament in a room."

"You, sir, carry on about your gun like a *foolish child about a new toy,*" said Ivan Ivanovich with vexation, for he was beginning to be angry in good earnest.

"And you, sir, are a regular gander!"

If Ivan Nikiforovich had not uttered that word, they would still have quarrelled, but, as usual, parted friends. But now something quite different happened. Ivan Ivanovich flushed crimson.

"What did you say, Ivan Nikiforovich?" he asked, raising his voice.

"I said that you were like a gander, Ivan Ivanovich."

"How dare you, sir, forget decorum and respect for a man's rank and family to dishonour him by such an offensive name?"

"What's offensive about it? And what are you waving your hands about like that for, Ivan Ivanovich?"

"I repeat: how dare you, contrary to all the rules of decorum, call me a gander, sir?"

"Oh, to hell with you, Ivan Ivanovich! What are you kicking up such a fuss for?"

Ivan Ivanovich could no longer contain himself: his lips were quivering, his mouth changed its usual resemblance to the letter V and assumed the shape of the letter O; he kept blinking so much that it was becoming quite alarming. That happened very rarely with Ivan Ivanovich. He had to be greatly insensed to behave like that.

"Then let me tell you, sir," said Ivan Ivanovich, "that I do not want to know you."

"A lot I care! I assure you, my dear sir, this won't make me shed tears," answered Ivan Nikiforovich.

He was lying, he was lying, I am certain of that! He was greatly upset by it.

"I will never set my foot in your house again."

"Oho—ho!" said Ivan Nikiforovich, hardly knowing what to do from vexation and, contrary to his habit, rising to his feet. "Hey there, woman, boy!" At his call the same lean old woman appeared in the doorway, followed by a small boy, swathed in a long and ample coat. "Take Ivan Ivanovich by the arms and show him to the door!"

"What? A nobleman?" Ivan Ivanovich cried indignantly with a feeling of injured dignity: "Don't you dare! Come one step nearer and I'll annihilate you together with your stupid master! The crows won't find your carcasses!" (Ivan Ivanovich used to express himself very forcefully when his soul was greatly shaken.)

The whole group presented a most striking picture: Ivan Nikiforovich, standing in the middle of the room in his full and completely unadorned beauty! The old maid, with gaping mouth and a completely senseless and terror-stricken expression on her face. Ivan Ivanovich, with an arm raised as the Roman tribunes used to be depicted! It was an extraordinary moment, a magnificent spectacle! And yet there was only one spectator: the boy in his immense frock-coat, who stood very calmly picking his nose.

At last Ivan Ivanovich picked up his cap.

"You're behaving wonderfully well, Ivan Nikiforovich, sir! Excellently! I won't let you forget it!"

"Get out, sir, get out! And mind you don't cross my path again. If you do, I'll batter your ugly mug for you!"

"That's how much I'm afraid of you!" answered Ivan Ivanovich, cocking a snook at him and slamming the door, which sprang open again with a raucous creak.

Ivan Nikiforovich appeared in the doorway and tried to add something, but Ivan Ivanovich was rushing out of the yard without looking back.

🍃 CHAPTER III

What happened after the quarrel of Ivan Ivanovich and Ivan Nikiforovich.

Aznd so two men of high repute, honoured, and ornaments of Mirgorod, had quarrelled! And over what? Over some nonsense, over a gander. They refused to see each other, they broke off all relations, though before they had been known as inseparable friends. Every day Ivan Ivanovich and Ivan Nikiforovich used to send to inquire after one another's health. They used often to talk to one another from their balconies and say such agreeable things that the heart rejoiced to listen to them. On Sundays Ivan Ivanovich in his thick woollen coat and Ivan Nikiforovich in his yellowish-brown nankeen Cossack tunic used to set off to church almost arm in arm. And if Ivan Ivanovich, who had extremely sharp eyes, first noticed a puddle or some filth in the middle of the street, a thing which sometimes happens in Mirgorod, he would invariably say to Ivan Nikiforovich: "Mind, look where you step, for it's not nice here." For his part, Ivan Nikiforovich displayed the most touching signs of friendship, and however far he happened to stand, he always stretched out his hand with his horn of snuff and said: "Help yourself!" And what excellent farms both of them had! And these two staunch friends . . . I was simply thunderstruck when I heard of it. For a long time I refused to believe it. Good Lord! Ivan Ivanovich has quarrelled with Ivan Nikiforovich!

Such esteemable men! Is there anything durable in this world?

When Ivan Ivanovich got home he was for a long time in a state of violent agitation. Whenever he came home before he would go first of all to the stable to see whether the mare was eating her oats (Ivan Ivanovich had a roan mare with a black tail and mane and a white patch on her forehead, a very good little horse); then he would feed the turkeys and piglets with his own hands, and only after that go indoors, where he either made wooden dishes (he used to make all sorts of things out of wood, as good as a turner), or he would read a book, published by Lubya, Gary and Popov (Ivan Ivanovich did not remember its title, because the maid servant had long ago torn off the upper part of the title-page in trying to amuse a child), or would rest under the awning. But now he did not take up any of his usual occupations. Instead, on meeting Gapka, he began scolding her for loafing about and doing nothing, while actually she was dragging buckwheat into the kitchen; he threw a stick at the cock who came up to the front steps for his usual reward; and when a grubby little boy in a tattered shirt ran up to him, shouting, "Daddy, daddy, give me a cake!" he shook his fist at him and stamped his foot so terrifyingly that the frightened boy fled and hid himself where no one could find him.

At last, however, he calmed down and began to engage in his ordinary pursuits. He had a late dinner and it was almost evening when he lay down to rest under the awning. The good beetroot soup with pigeons Gapka had cooked completely ousted the incident of the morning. Ivan Ivanovich once more began to gaze at his garden and orchard with pleasure. At last his eyes rested on his neighbor's yard and he said to himself: "I haven't been to see Ivan Nikiforovich today: I'll go and see him now." Having said this, Ivan Ivanovich picked up his stick and his cap and went out into the street; but the moment he walked out of the gate he remembered his quarrel, spat and turned back. Almost the same sort of thing took place in Ivan Nikiforovich's yard. Ivan

Ivanovich saw the maidservant put her foot on the fence with the intention of climbing over into his yard, when he suddenly heard Ivan Nikiforovich's voice shouting, "Come back! Come back! I've changed my mind." Ivan Ivanovich, though, felt exceedingly bored. It is quite possible that these worthy men would have become reconciled next day, were it not for a particular occurrence in Ivan Nikiforovich's house which completely destroyed every hope of reconciliation and indeed poured oil on the fire of their hostility which was on the point of going out.

On the evening of the same day Agafya Fedoseyevna arrived on one of her regular visits to Ivan Nikiforovich. Agafya Fedoseyevna was not a relation, nor a sister-in-law, nor indeed any close friend of Ivan Nikiforovich's. One would have thought she had no reason at all to visit him, and he himself was not particularly pleased to see her, but she did visit him all the same and stayed with him for whole weeks at a time, and sometimes even longer. On those occasions she took charge of the keys and took the whole housekeeping into her own hands. Ivan Nikiforovich did not like it at all, but, to everybody's surprise, he obeyed her like a child, and though he did sometimes try to argue with her, Agafya Fedoseyevna always had the best of the argument.

And, I confess, I do not understand why it has been so arranged that women should grab us by the nose as smartly as they take hold of the handle of a teapot. Either their hands are so created or our noses are not fit for anything else. For though Ivan Nikiforovich's nose was rather like a plum, she grabbed him by that nose and made him follow her like a lapdog. During her visits he even changed, involuntarily, his ordinary daily routine: he did not lie so long in the sun, and when he did lie there, it was not in the nude, but he always put on his shirt and his wide trousers, though Agafya Fedoseyevna did not demand it at all. She was not one to stand on ceremony and when Ivan Nikiforovich had a feverish cold she used to rub him down from head to foot with turpentine and vinegar. Agafya Fedoseyevna wore a cap on her head, three warts on her nose, and a coffee-coloured dressing-gown with yellow flowers on it. Her whole figure was like a tub and that was why it was as hard to find her waist as to see one's nose without a looking-glass. Her legs were very short and formed like two cushions. She liked to gossip and eat boiled beetroots in the morning, and she was a great master at invective, and yet all through these various occupations her face never for one moment changed its expression, a talent that women alone seem, as a rule, to be endowed with.

As soon as she arrived everything was turned topsy-turvey.

"Don't you, Ivan Nikiforovich, be reconciled with him, and don't apologise to him, either. He wants to ruin you. That's the sort of man he is, you don't know him!"

The damned woman kept whispering and whispering till she made it quite sure that Ivan Nikiforovich would not even hear Ivan Ivanovich's name mentioned.

Everything was different now: if their neighbour's dog found its way into the yard, it was thrashed with anything at hand: the little boys who climbed over the fence, came back howling with their shirts held up and marks from birching on their backs. Even the maidservant, when Ivan Ivanovich was about to ask her something, committed an act of such indecency that Ivan Ivanovich, a man of exquisite refinement, spat and could only say, "What a nasty woman! Worse than her master!"

Finally, as a finishing touch to all his insults, that odious neighbour of his, put up directly opposite his house, at the spot where one usually climbed over the fence, a goose-pen, as though with the special intention of emphasising the insult. This goose-pen, which Ivan Ivanovich found so utterly obnoxious, was built with diabolical rapidity in a single night.

This made Ivan Ivanovich wild with rage and aroused a desire for revenge in him. He did not, however, show any outward signs of vexation in spite of the fact that the goose-pen had encroached on some of his land, but his heart pounded so violently that he found it extremely hard to preserve this outward calm.

So he spent the day. Night came. . . . Oh, if I were a painter, I would have depicted the charm of that night wondrously well! I would have depicted the whole of Mirgorod alseep; how the countless stars were looking steadily down upon the sleeping town; how the palpable stillness was broken by the everlasting barking of dogs; how the love-sick sacristan streaked past them and climbed over a fence with chivalrous intrepidity; how the white walls of the houses, bathed in moonlight, looked whiter, the trees that over-hang them darker, the shadows cast by them blacker, the flowers and the grass that had grown silent more fragrant, while the crickets, the indefatigable minstrels of the night, started their ringing songs in unison from every corner. I would depict how in one of these low clay houses a black-browed town girl, tossing on her solitary bed, dreamed with heaving breasts of a hussar's moustache and spurs, while the moonlight laughed on her cheeks. I would depict the black shadow of a bat across the white road flitting as it settled on the white chimneys of the houses. . . . But I could hardly have depicted Ivan Ivanovich as he went out that night with a saw in his hand. Oh, how many different emotions were written on his face! Quietly, quietly he stole up to the goose-pen and crept under it. Ivan Nikiforovich's dogs knew nothing as yet of the quarrel between them and therefore allowed him, as an old friend, to approach the pen, supported entirely on four oak posts. Creeping up to the nearest post, he put the saw to it and began sawing. The noise of the saw made him look round every minute, but the thought of the insult he had suffered restored his courage. The first post was sawn through; Ivan Ivanovich set to work on the second. His eyes were burning and he could see nothing for fear. Suddenly Ivan Ivanovich uttered a cry and was stupefied with terror: he thought he saw a corpse; but he soon recovered, for he realised that it was only a goose craning its neck at him. Ivan Ivanovich spat with indignation and carried on with his work. The second post, too, was sawn through: the goose-pen leaned on its side. Ivan Ivanovich's heart began to throb so violently when he started on the third post that several times he had to stop; more than half of the post was sawn through when all of a sudden the tottering goose-pen rocked violently. . . . Ivan Ivanovich just managed to leap aside when it came down with a crash. Snatching up the saw, he ran back home in a terrible panic and threw himself on the bed, feeling too dispirited to look out of the window at the results of his terrible deed. He fancied that the entire household of Ivan Nikiforovich had assembled: the old maidservant, Ivan Nikiforovich himself, the boy in the immense frock-coat—all of them armed with cudgels and led by Agafya Fedoseyevna were marching to sack and demolish his house.

The whole of the following day Ivan Ivanovich spent in a kind of a fever. He kept imagining that in revenge his hateful neighbour would set fire to his barn at least. He consequently gave orders to Agapka to keep watch round the house continuously to make sure that no dry straw had been put down anywhere. At last, to anticipate Ivan Nikiforovich, he decided to forestall him and start an action against him in the Mirgorod district court. What the action was about may be learnt in the next chapter.

🎵 CHAPTER IV

Of What Took Place in the Mirgorod District Court

Mirgorod is a wonderful city! What a great variety of buildings it has! Some thatched with straw and some with reeds, some even with wooden roofs; a street to the right, a street to the left, an excellent fence everywhere; over it twines the hop, on it hang pots, behind it the sunflower displays its sun-like head, poppies blush and fat pumpkins gleam. . . . Sheer magnificence! The fence is always adorned with objects which make it still more picturesque: a striped thick woollen petticoat stretched out on it or a chemise or a pair of wide trousers. There is no thieving nor swindling in Mirgorod and therefore everyone hangs anything he likes on his fence. If you approach the city square, you will most certainly stop for a moment to admire the view. There is a puddle in it—a wonderful puddle, a puddle the like of which you have never seen in your life. It occupies almost the whole square. A splendid puddle! The big and small houses, which might be taken in the distance for haystacks, stand round admiring its beauty.

But I am of the opinion that there is no better house than the district court. Whether it is built of oak or birchwood is of no account to me; but, gentlemen, it has eight windows! Eight windows in a row, looking straight onto the square and the stretch of water I have mentioned which the city mayor calls a lake! His is the only one to be painted the colour of granite; the other houses in Mirgorod are simply whitewashed. Its roof is all made of wood, and it would have been painted red, if the oil prepared for the purpose had not been seasoned with onions and eaten by the office clerks, for, as luck would have it, it was Lent and so the roof stayed unpainted. The front steps project on the square, and the hens often run up and down them, because there are always grains or anything else edible scattered on the steps, which is not done on purpose, however, but is due solely to the carelessness of the plaintiffs. The court is divided into two sections. One is the court proper and the other is the jail. The court consists of two clean, whitewashed rooms: one, a waiting room for petitioners, and the other has a table adorned with inkstains; on it stands the triangular prism with Peter the Great's edicts glued to its facets, the symbol of office. Four oak chairs with high backs; along the walls iron-bound chests, in which files of documents relating to the slander suits of the district are preserved. On one of the chests a boot polished with blacking was standing at the moment. The court had been sitting since early morning. The judge, a rather stout man, though a little thinner than Ivan Nikiforovich, with a kindly face and in a greasy coat, was talking to his clerk over a pipe and a cup of tea. The judge's lips were under his very nose and that is why his nose could sniff his upper lip as much as it pleased. This upper lip served him instead of a snuffbox, for the snuff on its way to the nose was almost always deposited on it. And so the judge was talking to his clerk. A barefoot girl was holding a tray full of cups at one side.

At the end of the table the secretary was reading the verdict of the court in such a monotonous and dejected tone of voice that the plaintiff himself would have fallen asleep listening to him. The judge would without a doubt have been the first to do so if he had not been engaged in an interesting conversation.

"I made a point of finding out," said the judge, sipping his tea from a cup that had gone cold, "o how they contrived to make them sing so well. Two years ago I had an excellent blackbird, and what do you think? It suddenly aged—started singing goodness only knows what. The longer it went on, the worse it became. Began burring and wheezing. I was almost tempted to throw it out. And yet it was just a trifle. What happens, you see, is that a small tumour, no bigger than a pea, grows under her throat. This little tumour has to be pricked with a needle. Zakhar Prokofyevich showed me how to do it and, if you like, I can tell you exactly how it happened. One day I went to see him. . . ."

"Shall I read the next one, Demyan Demyanovich?" interrupted the secretary who had finished reading some minutes before.

"Oh, have you finished already? You are quick. I haven't heard a word of it. Where is it? Give it to me. I'll sign it. What else have you got?"

"The case of Cossack Bokitka's stolen cow."

"All right, read. Well, so I arrived at his place. I can even tell you in detail how he entertained me. A sturgeon was served with the vodka—the only one of its kind! No, sir, nothing like the sturgeons. . . ." At this point the judge clicked his tongue while his nose sniffed his ever present snuffbox. ". . . which our Mirgorod grocery shops serve us. I did not have any herring because, as you know, it gives me heartburn. But I did taste the caviare—wonderful caviare!—it was first-class. Then I had a glass of peach brandy distilled with centaury. There was a saffron brandy, too, and it's very good, at least I'm told it whets your appetite, but then it also puts the finishing touch to it. Well, well, see who's here!" the judge cried suddenly as he caught sight of Ivan Ivanovich walking in.

"Good morning, how are you?" said Ivan Ivanovich, bowing in all directions with the agreeableness peculiar to him alone. Dear me, how he could bewitch us all with his fine manners! I have never seen such refinement anywhere. He was very well aware of his own worth and therefore regarded the universal respect in which he was held as his due. The judge himself offered a chair to Ivan Ivanovich, his nose drew in all the snuff from his upper lip, which was always a sign of great satisfaction with him.

"What will you have, Ivan Ivanovich?" asked the judge. "A cup of tea?"

"No, thank you kindly," replied Ivan Ivanovich, and he bowed and sat down.

"Please, just a cup," repeated the judge.

"No, thank you," said Ivan Ivanovich. "I greatly appreciate your hospitality." He bowed and sat down again.

"One cup," repeated the judge.

"No, please, do not trouble, Demyan Demyanovich."

Ivan Ivanovich once more bowed and sat down.

"Just a little cup?"

"Well, so be it. Perhaps one little cup!" said Ivan Ivanovich and put out his hand to the tray.

Heavens above, the infinite refinement of the man! It is impossible to put into words the pleasing impression such manners produce.

"You won't have another cup, will you?"

"No, thank you," replied Ivan Ivanovich, putting the cup, which he had turned upside down on the tray and bowing.

"Please, Ivan Ivanovich!"

"I'm sorry, I cannot. Thank you very much." And, saying this, Ivan Ivanovich bowed and sat down.

"Ivan Ivanovich, do me a favour, sir, just one more cup!"

"No, thank you, I greatly appreciate your kindness."

Having said this, Ivan Ivanovich bowed and sat down.

"Only a little cup! Just one little cup!"

Ivan Ivanovich put out his hand to the tray and took a cup.

Damn it all! The way the man knows how to keep up his dignity! How does he do it, I wonder.

"I, Demyan Demyanovich," said Ivan Ivanovich after drinking the last drop, "I—er—have some urgent business with you. I—I want to bring an action, sir." With this Ivan Ivanovich put down his cup and took out of his pocket a sheet of stamped paper covered with writing. "An action against an enemy of mine, sir. A mortal enemy."

"Against whom is that?"

"Against Ivan Nikiforovich Dovgochkhun."

At these words the judge almost fell off his chair.

"What are you saying?" he cried, clasping his hands. "Ivan Ivanovich, is this you?"

"You can see it is me."

"The Lord have mercy on us and all the holy saints! Why have you, Ivan Ivanovich, become the enemy of Ivan Nikiforovich? Was it your lips that uttered those words? Say it again. Are you sure that there's no one hiding behind your back and speaking instead of you?"

"What is there so improbable about it? I can't bear the sight of him: he had done me a deadly injury. He has insulted my honour."

"Holy Trinity! How shall I make my mother believe this? She, poor old dear, says every day when my sister and I quarrel: 'You, children, live like cats and dogs. Why don't you take an example from Ivan Ivanovich and Ivan Nikiforovich? They are real friends, they are. They are truly worthy men.' Some friends! Real friends, forsooth! Tell us what's it all about! What happened?"

"This is a matter of great delicacy, Demyan Demyanovich. It cannot be told. You'd better ask your secretary to read my petition. Here, take it from this side. It would be much nicer here."

"Read it, Taras Tikhonovich," said the judge, turning to his secretary.

Taras Tikhonovich took the petition and, blowing his nose as all secretaries in district court blow their noses, that is, with the help of two fingers, began to read:

"From Ivan, son of Ivan, Pererepenko, nobleman and landowner of the Mirgorod district, petition; wherefor the following points make clear: 1) The nobleman Ivan, son of Nikifor, Dovgochkhun, known to all the world for his impious, legally criminal acts, exceeding all limits and arousing disgust, on the seventh day of July of this year of our Lord 1870 perpetrated a deadly insult upon me, both personally affecting my honour and equally leading to the degradation and confusion of my rank and family. The aforesaid nobleman, who is, moreover of an odious appearance, has a quarrelsome character, and abounds with blasphemous and abusive words of every description. . . ."

At this point the reader stopped to blow his nose again, while the judge folded his arms with an expression of veneration and just said to himself: "What a glib pen! Lord, how the man does write!"

Ivan Ivanovich asked the secretary to carry on with his reading and Taras Tikhonovich continued:

"The aforementioned nobleman, Ivan, son of Nikifor Dovogochkhun, when I came to him with friendly propositions, called me publicly by an insulting name derogatory to my honour, to wit, 'gander,' while it is well known to the whole Mirgorod district that I have never borne the name of that odious animal and do not intend to bear such a name in future. The proof of my noble origin will be found in the parish register of the church of the Three Bishops, in which is recorded both the day of my birth and the name given me in baptism. A 'gander,' as everyone knows who is in anyway versed in learning, cannot be inscribed in a birth certificate, for a 'gander' is a bird and not a man, which everyone knows for a fact even without having been to a seminary. But the abovementioned malignant nobleman, though fully aware of this fact, called me by that odious name for the sole purpose of inflicting a deadly injury upon my rank and station.

"The same shameless and ungentlemanly nobleman encroached upon my private property, inherited by me from my father, a gentleman in holy orders, Ivan of blessed memory, son of Onisim, Pererepenko, inasmuch as in contravention of every law he moved a goose-pen exactly opposite the front steps of my house, which was done with no other purpose than to aggravate the injury done me, for the aforementioned goose-pen had till then been standing in its proper place and was reasonably strong. But the odious purpose of the aforesaid nobleman was solely to make me witness unseemly incidents: for it is a well known fact that no man goes into a pen, and particularly a goose-pen, for any seemly business. In perpetrating this illegal action, the two foremost posts have trespassed upon my private property, which was left to me during the lifetime of my father, Ivan of blessed memory, son of Onisim, Pererepenko, starting from the barn and running in a straight line to the place where the women wash their pots.

"The above-described nobleman, whose very Christian name and surname inspire disgust, cherished in his heart the wicked intention of setting fire to me in my own house, whereof the unmistakable signs become clear from the following: first, the above-mentioned pernicious nobleman has begun coming out frequently from his house, which he never did in the past on account of his laziness and the repulsive obesity of his body; secondly, in the servant's quarters adjoining the very fence which forms the boundary of my land, inherited by me from my late father, Ivan of blessed memory, son of Onisim, Pererepenko, there is a light burning every day and for quite an unusual length of time, which is positive proof of it, for hitherto because of his miserly parsimoniousness not only the tallow candle, but also the oil-lamp was always extinguished there.

"And, therefore, I repeat that the above-mentioned nobleman, Ivan, son of Nikifor, Dovgochkhun, being guilty of arson, of insulting my rank, name and family, and of predatorily misappropriating my property, but, above all, of the despicable and reprehensible coupling with my surname the appellation of 'gander,' be sentenced to a fine together with the payment of all costs and damages, and himself, as a lawbreaker, be put in irons and sent to the prison of the town, and that, in accordance with this my petitions, an appropriate decision should be taken promptly and immediately. Written and composed by Ivan, son of Ivan, Pererepenko, nobleman and landowner."

When the petition had been read, the judge went up to Ivan Ivanovich, buttonholed him and began addressing him as follows:

"What are you doing, Ivan Ivanovich? Have you no fear of God? Drop the petition, to hell with it! (let it dream of Satan!) Much better shake hands with Ivan Nikiforovich, embrace and kiss, and get a bottle of Santurin or Nikopol wine or simply make some punch and invite me. We'll have a good drink together and forget it all."

"No, Demyan Demyanovich, this is not that sort of business," said Ivan Ivanovich with the air of importance that always suited him so well. "It is not the sort of business that can be settled amicably by arriving at some satisfactory arrangement. Good-bye sir. Good-bye to you, too, gentlemen!" he went on with the same air of importance, turning to them all. "I hope my petition will be dealt with in the appropriate manner!" And he went out, leaving everybody present in amazement.

The judge sat without uttering a word; the secretary took a pinch of snuff; the clerks upset the bit of broken bottle which served them for an inkstand, and the judge himself absentmindedly kept spreading the ink on the table with his finger.

"What do you say to this, Dorofey Trofimovich?" said the judge, turning to the clerk of the court after a short pause.

"I'm saying nothing," replied the clerk of the court.

"The things people do!" continued the judge.

But he had hardly uttered the words when the door creaked and the front part of Ivan Nikiforovich squeezed through into the courtroom, the other part still remaining in the hall. The appearance of Ivan Nikiforovich in a courtroom of all places seemed so extraordinary that the judge uttered a cry of astonishment and the secretary interrupted his reading. One clerk, in a frieze semblance of a frockcoat, put the pen in his lips, another swallowed a fly. Even the veteran who discharged the duties of messenger and caretaker and who had been standing at the door scratching himself under his dirty shirt with a stripe on the shoulder—even he gaped and stepped on somebody's foot.

"Fancy seeing you here! What brought you here? How are you, Ivan Nikiforovich?"

But Ivan Nikiforovich was more dead than alive, for he had stuck in the doorway and could not take a step forwards or backwards. In vain did the judge shout to anyone who might be in the waiting room to push Ivan Nikiforovich from behind into the court. There was only an old woman petitioner in the waiting room and she could do nothing with her bony hands in spite of all her efforts. Then one of the clerks, a fellow with broad shoulders, thick lips, a thick nose, a pair of squinting, drunken eyes, and tattered elbows, approached the front half of Ivan Nikiforovich, folded his arms across his chest, as if he were a baby, and winked to the veteran who, resting his knee on Ivan Nikiforovich's belly, began to shove till, in spite of Ivan Nikiforovich's piteous moans, he was squeezed out into the waiting room. Then they moved back the bolts and opened the second half of the door. While this was being done, the united efforts of the clerk and his assistant the caretaker, and their heavy breathing spread such a powerful smell that for a time the courtroom seemed transformed into a pot-house.

"You are not hurt, Ivan Nikiforovich, are you? I'll ask my mother to send you a lotion and all you have to do is to rub your back and loins and it will pass off."

But Ivan Nikiforovich sank into a chair and except for prolonged groans could say nothing. At last he brought out in a faint voice which was hardly audible from exhaustion:

"Please. . . ." and taking his horn out of his pocket, added: "Take some, help yourself!"

"Very glad to see you," said the judge. "But I'm afraid I still can't imagine what has made you take all this trouble and give us such an agreeable surprise by your visit."

"I've come—er—with a petition. . . ." was all Ivan Nikiforovich could enunciate.

"With a petition? What sort of a petition?"

"With a complaint—er," here his breathlessness led to a prolonged pause. "Oh dear, with—er—a complaint against the scoundrel—er—Ivan Ivanovich Pererepenko."

"Good Lord, you too! Such rare friends! A complaint against such a pious man!"

"He's Satan himself!" Ivan Nikiforovich pronounced abruptly.

The judge crossed himself.

"Take my petition and read it."

"It can't be helped," said the judge. "Read it, Taras Tikhonovich."

He turned to the secretary with an expression of displeasure on his face, his nose involuntarily sniffing his upper lip, something it did before only when greatly gratified. Such an instance of self-assertiveness on the part of his nose caused the judge even more

vexation. He took out his handkerchief and flicked off all the snuff
from his upper lip to punish its insolence.

The secretary, after sounding his usual tocsin, which he invariably did before beginning to read, that is, blowing his nose without
the help of a handkerchief, began in his ordinary voice, as follows:

"The petition of Ivan, son of Nikifor, Dovgochkhun, nobleman
of the Mirgorod district, whereof the points are as follows:

"(1). Incited by spiteful hatred and undisguised ill-will, Ivan,
son of Ivan, Pererepenko, who calls himself a nobleman, is committing all sorts of mischievous, injurious, malicious and dreadful
actions against me, and last night like a robber and a thief, broke
with axes, saws, chisels and all sorts of carpenter's tools into my
yard and into my own pen situated therein, and with his own
hands hacked it to pieces in a most disgraceful way, to which on
my part I had given no cause whatever for so lawless and piratic
an action.

"(2). The aforesaid nobleman Pererepenko has designs upon
my very life and on the seventh of last month, concealing the said
design, he came to me and began in a friendly and cunning fashion
wheedling out of me a gun, which I keep in my room, and with his
characteristic meanness, offered me for it many useless things,
such as a brown sow and two measures of oats. But guessing his
criminal intent at the time, I did my best to dissuade him from it;
but the said knave and scoundrel, Ivan, son of Ivan, Pererepenko,
swore at me like a peasant and since then has cherished an irreconcilable hostility towards me. Besides, the aforesaid and frequently
mentioned ferocious nobleman and brigand, Ivan, son of Ivan,
Pererepenko, is of a very ignoble birth: his sister was known to
the world as a strumpet and went off with a company of chasseurs
stationed five years ago at Mirgorod, and registered her husband
as a peasant. His father and mother were also exceedingly lawless
people and both were quite inconceivable drunkards. But the
afore-mentioned nobleman and brigand Pererepenko has sur-
passed all his relatives by his brutish and reprehensible actions,

and under a show of piety commits the most heinous offences: he does not keep the fast, for on the Christmas Eve fast this apostate bought a ram and next day ordered his mistress Gapka to slaughter it on the pretext that he was then in need of tallow for candles and oil-lamps.

"Wherefore I petition that the aforesaid nobleman be put in irons as a brigand, blasphemer, and scoundrel, and sent to prison or the state jail and, at the discretion of the authorities, be deprived of his ranks and nobility, beaten soundly with thorns and be sent to penal servitude in Siberia for as long a term as needed, and be ordered to pay costs and damages, and that sentence be passed in accordance with this my petition. To this petition Ivan, son of Nikifor, Dovgochkhun, nobleman, has put his hand."

As soon as the secretary had finished reading, Ivan Nikiforovich picked up his cap and bowed with the intention of leaving.

"Where are you off to, Ivan Nikiforovich?" the judge called after him. "Stay a little longer. Have some tea. Oryshko, what are you standing there for, silly girl, winking at the clerks? Go bring some tea."

But Ivan Nikiforovich, fearful of having come away so far from home and of having endured so perilous a quarantine, had managed to squeeze through the door. "Don't trouble yourself, I—er—with pleasure. . . ." he murmured, closing the door behind him and leaving all the court in amazement.

There was nothing to be done about it. Both petitions had been received and the affair was about to take a rather interesting turn when an unforeseen circumstance gave it an even more exciting character. When the judge had left the court-room accompanied by the secretary and the clerk of the court, and while the other officials were putting away into a sack the chickens, eggs, loaves, pies, cakes and all sorts of other trifles brought by the petitioners, a brown sow ran into the room and, to the surprise of all present, seized not a pie nor a crust of bread, but Ivan Nikiforovich's petition, which was lying at the end of the table with its pages hanging down over the edge. Having seized the petition, the brown snorter ran off so quickly that no one of the court officials could catch her in spite of the rulers and ink-pots thrown after her.

This extraordinary incident caused a terrible commotion because no copy of the petition had been taken. The judge, or rather his secretary and clerk, spent a long time discussing this unprecedented occurrence; at last it was decided to write a report on it to the mayor, for it was really a matter for investigation by the civil police. The report, No. 389, was dispatched to the mayor the same day, and as a result a rather interesting conversation took place, of which the reader may learn in the next chapter.

❧ CHAPTER V

In which is described a consultation between two worthy personages of Mirgorod.

No sooner had Ivan Ivanovich seen to the affairs of his farm and gone out, as was his custom, to lie down under the awning, than, to his immense astonishment, he caught sight of something red at the garden gate. It was the red cuff of the mayor, which, like his collar, had acquired a gloss and at the edges was transformed into patent leather. Ivan Ivanovich thought to himself: "I'm glad Pyotr Fyodorovich has come to have a talk with me." But he was very surprised to see the mayor walking very fast and brandishing his arms, which, as a rule, happened very rarely with him. The mayor's uniform sported eight buttons, the ninth had been torn off during a procession at the consecration of the church two years before and the police constable had not yet been able to find it, although in the daily reports to the superintendents he constantly inquired whether the button had been found. The eight buttons had been sewn on as peasant women sow beans: one to the right and the other to the left. His left leg had been shot through in his last campaign and that was why, as he limped along, he flung it so far to one side that he practically brought to naught the whole labour of his right leg. The faster the mayor put his infantry into action, the slower it moved forward. This was why, while the mayor was approaching the awning, Ivan Ivanovich had ample time to rack his brains about what led the mayor to brandish his arms at such a speed. It interested him all the more as he could not help feeling that the mayor's visit must be of the utmost importance, since he was actually wearing a new sword.

"Good morning, Pyotr Fyodorovich," cried Ivan Ivanovich, who, as has been mentioned before, was extremely inquisitive and could not restrain his impatience at the sight of the mayor trying to take the front steps by storm without raising his eyes and at odds with his infantry which seemed quite unable to take one step in one swing.

"A very good day to my dear friend and benefactor, Ivan Ivanovich," answered the mayor.

"Pray be seated. I can see you are tired, for your wounded leg impedes. . . ."

"My leg, sir!" cried the mayor, casting at Ivan Ivanovich a glance a giant casts on a pigmy or a learned pedant on a dancing master. As he said it, he stretched out his foot and stamped on the floor with it. This act of valour, however, cost him dearly, for his whole body lurched forward and his nose hit the railing. But to conceal his discomfiture the sage guardian of law and order at once recovered his equilibrium and put his hand into his pocket as though to take out his snuffbox. "Let me tell you, my dear friend and benefactor, Ivan Ivanovich, that I've made much worse marches in my time. Yes, seriously, I have. For instance, during the campaign of 1807. . . . Oh, I could tell you how I climbed over a fence to visit a pretty German girl. . . ." The mayor screwed up one eye and gave a devilishly roguish smile.

"Where have you been today?" asked Ivan Ivanovich in an attempt to cut the mayor short and elicit from him the cause of his visit. He would very much have liked to ask what it was the mayor intended to tell him. But his refined knowledge of the world made him realise the whole impropriety of such a question, and Ivan Ivanovich had to control himself and wait for the solution of the mystery, though his heart was pounding against his ribs with unusual violence.

"Very well," said the mayor, "I'll tell you where I've been. First of all, though, I must point out the lovely weather we've been having today. . . ."

At his last words Ivan Ivanovich almost died with suspense.

"But, I don't mind telling you," continued the mayor, "that I've come to you today on a very important matter." Here the mayor's face and deportment assumed the same worried expression as when he was trying to storm the front steps.

Ivan Ivanovich revived and shook as though in a fever, without omitting, as was his habit, to ask a question:

"What sort of important matter? Are you sure it is important?"

"Well, see for yourself. First of all, my dear friend and benefactor, Ivan Ivanovich, let me observe that you—er—mind you, so far as I'm concerned I don't care a rap, but the policy of the government, you see, the policy of the government demands it. You see, my dear fellow, you've committed a breach of public order."

"What are you saying, Pyotr Fyodorovich? I don't understand anything."

"Now, really, Ivan Ivanovich, how can you say you don't understand anything. Your own beast has carried off an important official document and after that you say you don't understand anything!"

"What beast?"

"If you don't mind my saying so, your own brown sow."

"And what have I got to do with it? Why does the court caretaker leave the doors open?"

"But, Ivan Ivanovich, the beast is your property, so you are to blame."

"Thank you very much for putting me on the same level as a sow."

"I never said anything of the kind, sir. Never. Now, please consider it in all honesty yourself. You, no doubt, are aware that, in accordance with the policy of the government, unclean animals are forbidden to walk about in the town, and especially in the main thoroughfares of the town. You must admit that that is forbidden."

"Good heavens, what are you talking about? What does it matter if a sow does go out into the street?"

"Let me tell you, Ivan Ivanovich, let me tell you, sir, that it's utterly impossible. But what are we to do? The authorities decree what is to be and we have to obey. I admit that sometimes hens and geese do run out into the street and even into squares, but, my dear sir, observe: hens and geese! But already last year I issued an order that pigs and goats were not to be allowed in public places. I gave instructions that this order should be read out aloud to the entire population of this town."

"No, Pyotr Fyodorovich, I can't see anything in all of this except that you're trying your utmost to insult me."

"That, my dear friend and benefactor, you can't say, you can't say that I'm trying to insult you. Now, be fair: I didn't say a word to you last year when you put up a roof a whole yard higher than the prescribed height, did I? On the contrary, I pretended I hadn't noticed it at all. Believe me, my dear friend, that now, too, I am absolutely—I mean—er—but my duty, in a word, my duty demands that I should look after public cleanliness. I mean, consider yourself when all at once in the main street. . . ."

"Your main street, forsooth! Every peasant woman goes there to throw out anything she doesn't want."

"Let me point out to you, sir that it's you who are insulting me now. It is true it sometimes does happen, but mostly under a fence or behind barns or sheds. But that a sow in farrow should be allowed to make her way to the main street or square, I mean, it's something that. . . ."

"Really, Pyotr Fyodorovich, isn't a sow God's creature?"

"Agreed! All the world knows that you are a man of learning, that you are versed in the sciences and all manner of subjects. Now, I have never studied any sciences. I began to learn to write when I was thirty. As you know, I rose from the ranks."

"H'm," said Ivan Ivanovich.

"Yes, sir," continued the mayor. "In 1801 I was in the 42nd regiment of chasseurs, a lieutenant in the fourth company. Our company C.O. was, I must tell you, Captain Yeremeyev."

The mayor paused and put a finger into the snuffbox which Ivan Ivanovich held open, crushing the snuff between finger and thumb.

Ivan Ivanovich murmured:

"H'm."

"But my duty, sir," continued the mayor, "is to obey the orders of the government. Do you know, Ivan Ivanovich, that anyone who steals an official document from a court of law is liable to be put on trial for a criminal offence like any other malefactor?"

"I know that and, if you like, I can tell you something. All this applies to human beings, for instance, if you were to steal a document the same would apply to you."

"But a sow is an animal, God's creature."

"That's all very well, but all the law says is: 'one guilty of stealing. . . .' Kindly listen attentively: 'one guilty.' There is nothing here about the species, sex, or rank of the culprit, therefore, an animal, too, may be guilty. I'm sorry, but, before a sentence is passed on it, the animal must be taken to the police station as guilty of a breach of law and order."

"No, sir," Ivan Ivanovich said cooly, "this will not be."

"As you like, but I am bound to follow the regulations as laid down by the government."

"Are you trying to frighten me? You're not going to send the one-armed soldier for her, are you? I'll tell my serf-girl to kick him out with the oven-fork. She'll break his remaining arm for him."

"I don't want to argue with you. In that case, if you refuse to take her to the police station, you can do as you like with her: slaughter her for Christmas, make hams out of her, or eat her as pork. Only if you will be making sausages I'd be glad if you'd send me a couple of those your Gapka makes so cleverly out of blood and lard. My Agrafena Trofimovna is very fond of them."

"Why, of course, I'll be delighted to send you a couple of sausages."

"I'll be very grateful to you, my dear friend and benefactor. Now let me say one thing more to you: I have been asked by the judge and, indeed, by all our friends to—so to speak—to reconcile you with your old friend, Ivan Nikiforovich."

"With that boor? You want me to be reconciled with that coarse and impertinent fellow? Never! I'm not going to. Never!" Ivan Ivanovich was in an extremely firm state of mind.

"Just as you like," said the mayor, regaling his nostrils with snuff. "I will not venture to advise you, but let me tell you this: now you are at odds with one another, but when you've made up your quarrel. . . ."

But Ivan Ivanovich began talking about the best way of catching quail, which usually happened when he wished to change the subject.

And the mayor had to go about his business without having achieved any success whatever.

🐦 C H A P T E R   V I

From which the reader may easily learn all that is contained in it.

However much they tried to conceal the affair, the next day the whole of Mirgorod knew that Ivan Ivanovich's sow had carried off Ivan Nikiforovich's petition. The mayor himself, in a moment of forgetfulness, let the cat out of the bag. When Ivan Nikiforovich was told about it, he made no comment, but only asked: "Was it the brown one?"

But Agafya Fedoseyevna, who was present at the time, again began worrying him.

"Aren't you going to do anything about it, Ivan Nikiforovich? Why, they'll all be laughing at you for being such a fool as to let him get away with murder and what sort of nobleman will you be after that? You'll be worse than the peasant woman who sells the sweets you are so fond of."

And the wicked busybody of a woman made him change his mind. She unearthed from somewhere a little middle-aged man with a swarthy and blotchy face, wearing a dark blue coat with patches on the elbows—a perfect departmental inkpot! He smeared his topboots with tar, carried three quills behind his ears and a small bottle tied to a button instead of an inkpot; he would devour nine pies at a meal and put the tenth into his pocket and fill a whole sheet of stamped paper with so many pieces of legal chicanery that no clerk was able to read it all out aloud without interrupting his reading again and again with coughing and sneezing. This little semblance of a man rummaged about, plodded away and at last concocted the following document:

"To the Mirgorod District Court from Ivan, son of Nikifor, nobleman.

"Concerning the aforesaid petition of mine that was handed in by me, Ivan, son of Nikifor, Dovgochkhun, nobleman, at the same time as the one from Ivan, son of Ivan, Pererepenko, nobleman, to which the Mirgorod District Court itself manifested its connivance and the aforesaid insolent self-assumption of power by the brown sow, which was kept a secret and reached our ears from persons unconnected with this case. Inasmuch as the aforesaid admission and connivance, being of evil intent, is strictly a matter for the court, for the aforesaid sow, being a foolish creature, is thereby more capable of stealing official documents. Wherefore it is manifestly obvious that the sow frequently aforementioned could not but have been incited to the same by the plaintiff himself, who calls himself Ivan, son of Ivan, Pererepenko, nobleman, and who has already been shown up as guilty of robbery, attempted murder and sacrilege. But inasmuch as the aforesaid Mirgorod Court with its characteristic partiality has evinced its tacit connivance; for without which connivance the aforesaid brown sow would never have been admitted to the stealing of the document: for the Mirgorod District Court is well provided with service, to prove which it is enough to name a soldier who is all the time present in the waiting room and who, though blind in one eye and possessing only one arm, has all the necessary faculties for driving out a sow and striking her with a cudgel. Wherefrom the connivance of the aforesaid Mirgorod Court is amply proven and the division of the ill-gotten gains therefrom to the mutual advantage of both parties is abundantly manifest. The aforesaid and aforementioned brigand and nobleman Ivan, son of Ivan, Pererepenko, is without a doubt the criminal accomplice therein. Wherefore I, Ivan, son of Nikifor, Dovgochkhun, nobleman, do herewith inform the District Court in the right and proper manner that if the abovementioned petition is not recovered from the aforesaid brown sow or her accomplice, the nobleman Pererepenko, and a fair decision in my favour not taken, then I, Ivan, son of Nikifor, Dovgochkhun, nobleman, will lodge a complaint with the higher court concerning such illegal connivance of the aforesaid district court, transferring the case thereto in accordance with the proper legal procedure.

"Ivan, son of Nikifor, Dovgochkhun, nobleman of Mirgorod District."

This petition produced its effect: for the judge, like all kind-hearted people, was a man of a cowardly disposition. He asked the advice of the secretary. But the secretary let out a deep "H'm" through his lips, while his face assumed an indifferent and diabolically ambiguous expression which only appears on the face of Satan when he sees the victim who has run to him for help at his feet. There was only one thing they could do: to reconcile the two friends. But how were they to set about it when all their attempts had so far ended in failure? However, they decided to try again; but Ivan Ivanovich declared bluntly that he refused to have anything to do with it, and even worked himself into a passion about it. Ivan Nikiforovich turned his back instead of answering and never uttered a word. Then the lawsuit went forward with the tremendous speed for which courts of justice are so famous. The document was registered, entered into a book, numbered, sewn in, signed—all in one and the same day, and then the case was put away in a cupboard, where it lay and lay and lay—a year, two years, three years. Hundreds of young girls had got married; a new street was laid down in Mirgorod; the judge lost one molar tooth and the side teeth; more children were running about Ivan Ivanovich's yard, and God alone knows where they sprang from; Ivan Nikiforovich, to spite Ivan Ivanovich, built a new goose-pen, though a little further away than the first and built so many outhouses alongside Ivan Ivanovich's fence that these two worthy men hardly even saw each other's faces—and still the case lay, in perfect order, in the cupboard, which the inkstains had marbled.

Meanwhile an event occurred of the utmost importance to everyone in Mirgorod.

The mayor was giving a ball! Where can I find the brushes and colours to paint the variety of the assembly and the magnificence of the entertainment? Take a watch, open it, and see what is going on there. A veritable hotchpotch, isn't it? Well, just imagine that as many, if not more, wheels were standing in the mayor's courtyard. What town and country carriages were not there! One with a wide back and a narrow front; another with a narrow back and a wide front. One was a town and country carriage all in one; another neither barouche nor chaise; one was like a huge haystack or a fat merchant's wife; another was like a dishevelled Jew or a skeleton that had not quite dispensed with its skin; one looked in profile exactly like a pipe with a long mouthpiece, another looked like nothing on earth, an extraordinary contraption, utterly horrible and extremely fantastic. From among this chaos of wheels and box-seats there arose the semblance of a carriage with a window like that of a room, intersected by a thick transom. Drivers in grey Cossack coats, tunics and grey jerkins, in sheepskin hats and caps of different shapes and sizes, with pipes in their hands, led the unharnessed horses through the courtyard. What a splendid ball the mayor gave! Give me leave to name everyone who was there: Taras Tarasovich, Yevpl Akinfovich, Yevtikhy Yevtikheyevich, Ivan Ivanovich—not our Ivan Ivanovich, but the other, Savva Gavrilovich, our Ivan Ivanovich, Yelevfery Yelevferiyevich, Makar Nazaryevich, Foma Grigoryevich . . . I can't go on. It is too much for me. My hand is tired with writing. And how many ladies were there! Dark and fair, long and short, stout as Ivan Nikiforovich, and so thin that it seemed that each of them could be hidden in the scabbard of the mayor's sword. How many bonnets! How many dresses! Red, yellow, coffee-coloured and green, blue, new, turned, remade; fichus, ribbons, reticules! Farewell, poor eyes! You are no good for anything after that spectacle. And what a long table was pulled out! And how they all talked; what an uproar they all raised! A mill with all the grindstones, wheels, pinions and mortars is nothing to it! I cannot tell you for certain what they talked about, but I expect it must have been about all sorts of pleasant and useful things, such as the weather, dogs, wheat, bonnets, ponies. At last Ivan Ivanovich—not *the* Ivan Ivanovich, but the other, who was blind in one eye, said: "How strange my right eye" (the one-eyed Ivan Ivanovich always spoke ironically of himself) "does not see Ivan Nikiforovich."

"Refused to come," said the mayor.

"How's that?"

"Well, it's two years, thank God, since they quarrelled, I mean, Ivan Ivanovich and Ivan Nikiforovich, and where one goes, the other will not go on any account."

"You don't say!" At this the one-eyed Ivan Ivanovich raised his eyes upwards and clasped his hands together. "Well, now, if people with good eyes don't live in peace, how can I be expected to live in concord with my one blind eye?"

At these words they all laughed heartily. Everyone was very fond of one-eyed Ivan Ivanovich because he used to crack jokes which were absolutely in modern taste. Even the tall, lean man in thick woolen coat with a plaster on his nose, who had been sitting in a corner and never once changed the expression of his face, even when a fly flew up his nose—even this gentleman got up and moved nearer to the crowd surrounding the one-eyed Ivan Ivanovich.

"Listen," said the one-eyed Ivan Ivanovich when he saw that a large company was standing around him, "instead of gazing at my blind eye, as you are doing now, let's reconcile our two friends. While Ivan Ivanovich is talking to the women and the young girls— let's send for Ivan Nikiforovich in secret and let's push them together from behind."

All unanimously accepted Ivan Ivanovich's proposal and decided to send at once to Ivan Nikiforovich's house and beg him most particularly to come to the mayor's dinner party. But the important question to whom to entrust this important mission confounded everybody. They argued at length about who was most capable and most skilful in the diplomatic line and at last came to the unanimous conclusion to entrust Anton Prokofyevich Golopuz with this task.

But first we must make the reader a little acquainted with this remarkable person. Anton Prokofyevich was a perfectly virtuous man in the full meaning of the word: if any of the worthy citizens of Mirgorod gave him a neck-tie or some underwear, he thanked them; if anyone gave him a slight fillip on the nose, he thanked them even then. If he was asked: "Why is your coat brown but your sleeves blue?" he invariably answered: "You wouldn't have such a one, would you? Wait a bit, it will soon be shabby and then it will all be the same." And, to be sure, the blue cloth began, from the effect of the sun, to turn brown and now it harmonises perfectly with the colour of the coat. But what's strange is that Anton Prokofyevich usually wears cotton clothes in the summer and nankeen in the winter. Anton Prokofyevich has no house of his own. He had one before on the outskirts of the town, but he sold it and with the proceeds bought three bay horses and a small chaise, in which he used to ride about visiting the neighbouring landowners. But as the horses gave him a great deal of trouble and as, besides, he needed money to buy them oats, Anton Prokofyevich exchanged them for a fiddle and a serf-girl, receiving on top of it a twenty-five-rouble note. Then Anton Prokofyevich sold the fiddle and swopped the girl for a Morocco purse set with gold. And now he has a purse the like of which no one in the town can boast of. The enjoyment of this unique treasure, however, makes it impossible for him to visit the estates of his friends and he has to stay in town and to spend his nights at different houses, especially of those noblemen who take a delight in flicking him on the nose. Anton Prokofyevich is fond of good food, and plays tolerably well at "Fools" and "Millers."

Obedience was natural to him and that is why, picking up his cap and stick, he set off at once. But on the way he began wondering how to induce Ivan Nikiforovich to go to the banquet. The somewhat stern temper of that otherwise worthy man made his task almost an impossible one. And how indeed could he be expected to make up his mind to go when even to get out of bed gave him a great deal of trouble. But supposing he did get up how could he be expected to go where—as he undoubtedly knew—his irreconcilable enemy was to be found. The more Anton Prokofyevich thought of it, the more obstacles he found. The day was sultry; the sun was scorching; he was dripping with sweat. Anton Prokofyevich, though he was flicked on the nose, was rather a cunning man in many ways. It was only in the matter of exchange that he was not so lucky. He knew very well when it was necessary to pretend to be a fool, and sometimes he knew what was best to do in situations of which a clever man would find it difficult to get out with credit.

While his inventive mind was considering the best means of persuading Ivan Nikiforovich and was valiantly determined to deal with any eventuality, an unexpected circumstance somewhat disconcerted him. In this connection it may not be amiss to inform the reader that Anton Prokofyevich had a pair of trousers so fantastically odd that whenever he put them on the dogs invariably bit his calves. As ill-luck would have it, he had put on those trousers that day. He had therefore barely had time to give himself up to his reflections when a terrible barking from every direction smote his ears. Anton Prokofyevich raised such a clamour—no one could shout louder than he—that not only Ivan Nikiforovich's maidservant and the inmate of the immeasurable frock-coat ran out to meet him, but even the little dogs from Ivan Ivanovich's yard came running out to him, and though the dogs only managed to bite one leg, this greatly reduced his courage and he walked up to the front steps feeling more than a little timid.

☙ CHAPTER VII

And Last

Ah, good afternoon! What are you teasing my dogs for?" said Ivan Nikiforovich, on seeing Anton Prokofyevich, for no one ever spoke to Anton Prokofyevich except jestingly.

"Me teasing them? A plague on them all!" answered Anton Prokofyevich.

"You don't mean it!"

"I most certainly do! Pyotr Fyodorovich asks you to dinner."

"H'm."

"He does. In fact, he insists on your coming. Absolutely bent on it. 'Why,' he says, 'is Ivan Nikiforovich avoiding me as if I was his enemy. He never comes for a chat or to sit down for a while.' "

Ivan Nikiforovich stroked his chin.

" 'If,' he says, 'Ivan Nikiforovich will not come now, I shan't know what to think. I hope he is not plotting something against me. Do me a favour, Anton Prokofyevich, persuade him to come.' Well, what about it, Ivan Nikiforovich? Let's go. There's an excellent company assembled there."

Ivan Nikiforovich began to scrutinise a cockerel, who was standing on the front steps and crowing with all his might.

"If only you knew, Ivan Nikiforovich," the zealous delegate continued, "what sturgeon and fresh caviare have been sent to Pyotr Fyodorovich's!"

At this Ivan Nikiforovich turned his head and began to listen attentively.

This encouraged the delegate.

"Let's make haste and go, Foma Grigoryevich is there too. What's the matter?" he added, seeing that Ivan Nikiforovich was still lying in the same position. "Well, are we going or not?"

"I don't want to."

This "I don't want to" struck Anton Prokofyevich as ominous. He had already imagined that his persuasive pleading had completely won over this in every respect worthy man, instead of which he heard a firm "I don't want to."

"Why don't you want to?" he asked almost with vexation, which he showed extremely rarely, even when people put a burning piece of paper on his head, an amusement the judge and the mayor were particularly fond of.

Ivan Nikiforovich took a pinch of snuff.

"You can do as you like, of course, Ivan Nikiforovich, but I really don't know what's preventing you."

"Why, should I go?" Ivan Nikiforovich said at last. "The brigand will be there." That was what he usually called Ivan Ivanovich.

Merciful heavens! And not so long ago . . .

"I swear he won't be there. As God is holy, he won't. May I be struck dead by lightning on this very spot!" declared Anton Prokofyevich, who was ready to take his oath a dozen times an hour. "Let's go, Ivan Nikiforovich!"

"But are you sure you're not lying, Anton Prokofyevich? He is there, isn't he?"

"Indeed, he's not! may I never leave this place if he is! And, really, why should I tell you lies? May my arms and legs be withered! Don't you believe me even now? May I drop dead in front of you! May my father, my mother, and myself never see the kingdom of heaven! Do you still not believe me?"

Ivan Nikiforovich was completely reassured by these asseverations and told his valet in the immeasurable frock-coat to bring his white trousers and his nankeen Cossack coat.

I consider it quite superfluous to describe how Ivan Nikiforovich put on his trousers, how his cravat was tied, and how, finally, he was helped on with his Cossack coat which split under the left sleeve. It suffices to say that during that time he preserved a decorous composure and did not answer one word to Anton Prokofyevich's proposal to exchange something for his Turkish purse.

Meanwhile the assembled guests were waiting with impatience for the decisive moment when Ivan Nikiforovich should make his appearance and when, at last, the universal desire that these two worthy men should be reconciled might be gratified. Many were almost certain that Ivan Nikiforovich would not come. The mayor even offered to bet one-eyed Ivan Ivanovich that he would not come, and only desisted because one-eyed Ivan Ivanovich demanded that the mayor should wager his wounded leg against his blind eye, a proposal that greatly offended the mayor, while the company laughed surreptitiously. No one had yet sat down to table, though it was long past one o'clock—a time when people in Mirgorod have been dining for some time, even on grand occasions.

No sooner had Anton Prokofyevich appeared at the door than

he was surrounded by all the assembled guests. In answer to all questions he shouted in a firm voice, "He's not coming!" He had scarcely uttered those words and before a shower of reproaches and abuse and perhaps even Philippics descended on his head for the failure of his mission, the door opened and—in came Ivan Nikiforovich.

If Satan himself or a corpse had suddenly appeared, he would not have produced such general amazement as that into which Ivan Nikiforovich's entrance plunged the whole company, while Anton Prokofyevich split his sides with glee that he had played so wonderful a joke on them.

Be that as it may, it seemed almost incredible to everyone that Ivan Nikiforovich should have managed to dress as befits a gentleman in so short a time. Ivan Ivanovich was not in the room at that particular moment; he had gone out for something. Recovering from their amazement, the entire company showed their concern for Ivan Nikiforovich's health and expressed their delight that he had grown so much fatter. Ivan Nikiforovich exchanged kisses with everyone and said, "Much obliged!"

Meanwhile the smell of beet-root soup drifted through the room, agreeably tickling the nostrils of the starving guests.

All streamed into the dining room. A string of ladies, both talkative and taciturn, lean and fat, filed in ahead and the long table sparkled with all the colours of the rainbow. I am not going to describe all the dishes on the table. I will not mention the cheesecakes, the sour cream, the sweetbread served with the beet-root soup, the turkey stuffed with plums and raisins, the dish that bore a striking resemblance to a boot soaked in *kvas,* nor the sauce which was the *pièce de résistance* of the old cook—the sauce served in flaming spirits to the great agitation as well as the terror of the ladies. I am not going to talk about these dishes because I would rather eat them than expatiate upon them in conversation.

Ivan Ivanovich very much enjoyed the fish prepared with horse-radish sauce. He gave his special attention to this useful and nourishing exercise. Picking out the smallest and thinnest fishbones, he laid them on the plate and by sheer chance happened to glance across the table. Good Lord, by some strange coincidence Ivan Nikiforovich was sitting opposite him!

At that very moment Ivan Nikiforovich also looked up. No! I cannot! . . . Give me another pen. My pen is too limp, too dead, with too thin a nib for this picture! Their faces, frozen with amazement, seemed to have turned to stone. Each saw a long familiar face, someone whom, one would have thought, he would involuntarily approach as an old friend and offer his snuffbox to with the words, "Help yourself" or "May I be so bold as to ask you to help yourself," but at that moment that face was terrible as some evil portent. Beads of perspiration rolled down the faces of Ivan Ivanovich and Ivan Nikiforovich.

All who were sitting at the table were struck dumb as they stared at the two old friends, unable to take their eyes off them. The ladies, who till then had been engaged in a rather interesting conversation about the best way of preparing capons, suddenly interrupted it. A hush fell upon the room. It was a picture worthy of the brush of a great artist.

At last Ivan Ivanovich took out his hankerchief and began blowing his nose; Ivan Nikiforovich looked round and fixed his eyes on the open door. The mayor immediately noticed this movement and ordered the door to be shut securely. Then each of the friends began eating and did not once look up at each other again.

As soon as dinner was over, the two former friends rose from their seats, and began looking for their caps with the intention of slipping away. Then the mayor gave a wink and Ivan Ivanovich— not *the* Ivan Ivanovich, but the one-eyed one—took up a position behind Ivan Nikiforovich's back, while the mayor took up a position behind Ivan Ivanovich's back, and both began shoving them from behind so as to push them towards each other, intending not to let them go till they had shaken hands. Ivan Ivanovich, the one-eyed one, pushed Ivan Nikiforovich, a little askew it is true, but still successfully, to the place where Ivan Ivanovich was standing; but the mayor took a line too much to one side, for he could not control his headstrong infantry, which this time refused to listen to any command and, as though to spite him, swung a long way off in quite the opposite direction (which quite possibly may have been due to the great number of various liqueurs on the table), so that Ivan Ivanovich fell back on a lady in a red dress, who out of curiosity had thrust herself into their very midst. Such a portent boded no good. However, the judge, anxious to mend matters, took the place of the mayor and, sniffing up all the snuff from his upper lip, pushed Ivan Ivanovich in the other direction. This is the usual method of bringing about a reconciliation in Mirgorod. It is not unlike a game of ball. As soon as the judge gave Ivan Ivanovich a push, the one-eyed Ivan Ivanovich pressed his hands against the back of Ivan Nikiforovich, from whom the sweat was pouring like rainwater from a roof, and gave him a mighty shove. Though both friends stoutly refused to move an inch, they were yet pushed together, because both sides received considerable reinforcements from the other guests.

Then they were surrounded on all sides and were not allowed to go until they agreed to shake hands.

"Good gracious, Ivan Ivanovich and Ivan Nikiforovich, what did you quarrel about? Tell us honestly. Wasn't it about something of no importance? Aren't you ashamed before men and before God?"

"I don't know," said Ivan Nikiforovich, panting with exhaustion (it was noticeable that he was not at all opposed to a reconciliation), "I don't know what I have done to Ivan Ivanovich. Why did he cut down my goose-pen and plot to ruin me?"

"I am not guilty of any evil design," said Ivan Ivanovich, without looking at Ivan Nikiforovich. "I swear before God and before you, honorable gentlemen, I have done nothing to my enemy. Why, then, does he defame me and cast aspersions on my rank and social position?"

"What kind of aspersions have I cast on you?" said Ivan Niki-forovich.

Another moment of explanation and the long standing feud was about to be wiped out. Ivan Nikiforovich was already about to put his hand in his pocket to take out his horn and say "Help yourself."

"Was it not an aspersion," said Ivan Ivanovich, without raising his eyes, "when you, sir, insulted my rank and name with a word which it would be unseemly to repeat here?"

"Let me tell you as a friend, Ivan Ivanovich," said Ivan Nikiforo-vich, putting a finger on Ivan Ivanovich's button, "you took offence over the devil knows what, over me calling you a *gander.* . . ."

Ivan Nikiforovich realised at once that he had committed an indescretion in uttering that word; but it was too late; the word had been uttered.

All was lost.

Since Ivan Ivanovich had been beside himself and had got into a rage such as God grant one may never see at the utterance of that word without any witnesses, then, gentle reader, what was it now when this deadly word was uttered in a large company among whom there were a great many ladies, in whose society Ivan Ivano-vich liked to appear particularly punctilious. Had Ivan Nikiforo-vich acted differently, had he said *bird* and not *gander,* it might still have been possible to save the situation.

But—all was over!

He cast a glance at Ivan Nikiforovich—and what a glance! If that glance had been endowed with executive powers, it would have reduced Ivan Nikiforovich to ashes. The guests grasped the meaning of that glance and hastened of their own accord to sepa-rate them. And this man, this model of gentleness, who did not let one beggar woman pass without questioning her, rushed out in a terrible rage. So violent are the storms that passions arouse!

For a whole month nothing was heard of Ivan Ivanovich. He shut himself up in his house. The treasure chest was opened, from the chest were taken—what? Silver roubles! Old, ancestral silver roubles! And these silver roubles passed into the dirty hands of pettifogging lawyers. The case was transferred to a higher court. And it was only when Ivan Ivanovich received the glad tidings that it would be settled the next day that he showed interest in the world at large and decided to go out. Alas, for the next ten years the higher court kept announcing every day that the case would be settled the next day.

Five years ago I was passing through the town of Mirgorod. It was a bad time for travelling. It was autumn with its damp and dreary weather, mud and fog. A sort of unnatural verdure—the work of wearisome, incessant rains—covered in a thin network the fields and meadows, which was as little becoming to them as fun and games to an old man or roses to an old woman. In those days the weather affected me greatly; I felt depressed when it was dreary. In spite of this, however, my heart began beating violently as I got nearer to Mirgorod. Dear me, how many memories! I had not seen Mirgorod for twelve years. At that time two unique men, two unique friends lived here in touching amity. And how many distinguished men had died! The judge, Demyan Demyanovich, was dead by then and so was Ivan Ivanovich, the one with only one eye. I drove into the main street; there were poles everywhere with whisps of straw tied to them; a kind of new town planning scheme was in the process of being carried out. Several cottages had been pulled down. The remnants of wooden and wattle fences were left standing disconsolately.

It was a holiday. I ordered my matting-covered carriage to stop in front of the church and I went in so quietly that no one turned round. It is true there was hardly anyone there to do so. The church was deserted. It was clear that even the most devout were afraid of the mud. The candles on this overcast or rather sickly day seemed somewhat strangely unpleasant; the dark front part of the church was gloomy, the long windows with their round panes were streaming with tears of rain. I walked to the front of the church and addressed a venerable old man with grizzled hair.

"Tell me, is Ivan Nikiforovich living?"

At that moment the lamp in front of an icon flared up and the light fell full on the old man's face. Imagine my surprise when, looking closely, I recognised familiar features. It was Ivan Nikiforovich himself. But how he had changed!

"Are you quite well, Ivan Nikiforovich? You look so much older."

"Yes, I do. I've come today from Poltava," replied Ivan Nikiforovich.

"Really? You went to Poltava in this dreadful weather?"

"What else could I do my lawsuit. . . ."

I could not help fetching a sigh. Ivan Nikiforovich noticed it.

"Don't worry," he said. "I am reliably informed that the case will be decided next week, and in my favour."

I shrugged my shoulders and went to find out something about Ivan Ivanovich.

"Ivan Ivanovich is here," someone told me. "In the choir."

It was then that I caught sight of his gaunt figure. His face was covered in wrinkles, his hair was completely white; but his astrakhan coat was still the same. After the first greetings, Ivan Ivanovich, turning to me with his cheerful smile which suited so well his funnel-shaped face, said:

"Shall I tell you a good piece of news?"

"What news?" I asked.

"Tomorrow my case will be most definitely settled. They told me so for certain in the high court."

I fetched a deeper sigh and, after saying good-bye hastily, for I was travelling on very important business, got into my carriage. The lean horses, known in Mirgorod by the name of express horses, set off, making an unpleasant sound as their hoofs sank into the grey mass of mud. The rain poured in torrents on the Jewish coachman, sitting on the box and covered with matting.

The damp went through and through me. The dismal toll-gate with a sentry box, in which an old soldier was cleaning his grey accoutrements, slowly passed by. Again the same fields, furrowed and black in some places and green with sprouting winter crops in others, the wet crows and jackdaws, the monotonous rain, the tearful sky without a glimmer of light.

It's a tedious world, gentlemen!